This novel is dedicated to Aleix Dorca
from
Andorra la Vella Andorra
in recognition of the many positive comments
he has made regarding the Crossman novels.

———————

Author's Note

With the place names in this novel I chose to keep
to modern spellings. However, even modern spellings vary,
so choices had to be made. I apologize in advance if a choice
annoys a reader, but one had to be made.

Acknowledgements

Thanks must go to David Greenwood for his continued interest in
and advice on Crossman's adventures. Also to my editor
Krystyna Green and the whole team at Constable & Robinson
for their unfailing support of this series of historical war novels.
Colin Murray too, has been a great prop over the last few books:
he has an eagle's eye for fine detail and lurking error.
Finally, thanks for ever and aye go to Maggie Noach and Jill Hughes:
two stalwart champions of their band of writers.

Readers may wish to visit my website www.garry-kilworth.com
for books new and old, or for more information on the author.

BROTHERS OF
THE BLADE

BROTHERS OF THE BLADE

Lieutenant Fancy Jack Crossman in India

Garry Douglas Kilworth

CONSTABLE • LONDON

Constable & Robinson Ltd
3 The Lanchesters
162 Fulham Palace Road
London W6 9ER
www.constablerobinson.com

First published by Constable,
an imprint of Constable & Robinson Ltd 2004

A copy of the British Library Cataloguing in
Publication Data is available from the British Library.

ISBN 1-84119-821-8

Printed and bound in the EU

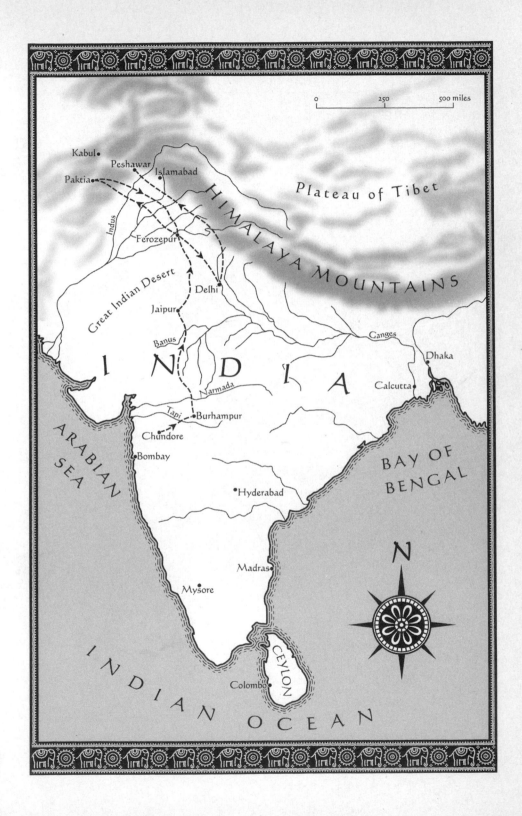

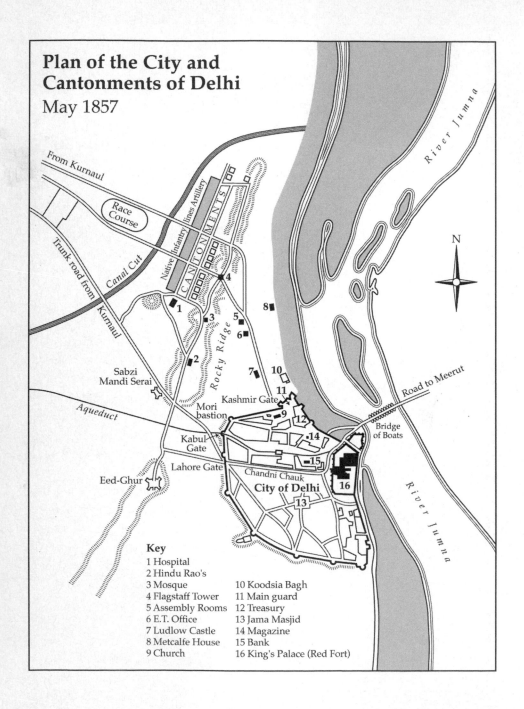

Plan of the City and Cantonments of Delhi
May 1857

River Jumna

From Kurnaul

Race Course

Trunk road from Kurnaul

Canal Cut

Native Infantry lines Artillery

CANTONMENTS

Rocky Ridge

N

1

4

8

5
3
6

2

7   10

11

Sabzi
Mandi Serai

Kashmir Gate

Aqueduct

Mori
bastion

9
12

.14

Road to Meerut

Bridge
of Boats

Kabul
Gate

15

Lahore Gate

Chandni Chauk

Eed-Ghur

City of Delhi

16

13

River Jumna

Key
1 Hospital
2 Hindu Rao's
3 Mosque
4 Flagstaff Tower   10 Koodsia Bagh
5 Assembly Rooms   11 Main guard
6 E.T. Office   12 Treasury
7 Ludlow Castle   13 Jama Masjid
8 Metcalfe House   14 Magazine
9 Church   15 Bank
                      16 King's Palace (Red Fort)

1

The market in Chundore was a mass of dark bodies sprinkled with white: grains of salt amongst the pepper. Crossman had never seen anything to match it. He would have liked to think there was a great deal of work going on, that the activity had some purpose, but it seemed to him that the figures, mostly attired in a dhoti, were simply struggling for air space. There was a religious festival in progress – the anniversery of the birth of Sri Ramakrishna – and the air was heavy with incense smoke. Knots of devotees gathered in various places, along with those who were purchasing goods. A native infantry battalion was garrisoned within the town, the sepoys adding to the mass of humans and animals crammed in the square.

'The sooner we get out of here, the better,' Crossman muttered to King and Gwilliams. 'Too many people by half.'

In the colourful jam they found it easier to lead their horses. They elbowed their way between packed bodies. There was one mounted man in the market, but he was at the far end, where the crowd was thinner. The rider was a British officer. He was having difficulty, the noise of clashing cymbals, beating drums and blaring horns making his horse skittish. Crossman guessed it was taking all the man's skill and energy to prevent his charger bolting, as sudden shrill cries went up from the festival crowds.

The wind lifted: saris and stall covers billowed like sails. A cloud of ochre-red spice wafted from somewhere. Dust and powder got in Jack's eyes and nose: he began sneezing. A foul odour came from a huge black vat which bubbled nearby: someone was boiling up ancient cooking fat. All three men shied away from this stink, seeking cleaner air space. Corporal Gwilliams cleared his throat and spat as well as any local, to rid himself of the taste of hair grease, unavoidable as heads bumped his mouth.

'Are we getting anywhere?' asked Sergeant King, threading his way through asses and bullocks. 'I'm getting crushed here and the mare doesn't like it one bit. I'm sick of people breathing garlic in my face. Can't we get out between that mosque and that stable?'

Suddenly, something like a wave went through the mass, and on the far side of the packed-earth square came a shout of alarm. Crossman frowned as his gelding jerked on the reins. He tried to see what the problem was, over the heads of the people. There were soldiers at the far end: musket muzzles stood proud above the heads of the crowd. What was going on? Commotion. Bustle and con-fusion. The officer on the horse had drawn his sword and he was holding it aloft. His mount danced this way and that, as if they were in a gymkhana.

'What's happening?' asked King, who was shorter than Crossman and unable to get the same viewpoint. 'Who's causing a fuss?'

The ripples in the crowd came and went, initiated at some distant point. Clearly something was wrong, people could sense it, even the newly arrived lieutenant and his NCOs. Those taking part in the festival continued with their noisy music and chanting, which added to the confusion, while stall owners were trying to stand on stools to see what was causing the ruckus.

As the trio forced their way closer to the officer, an infantry major, they could see he was involved in the disturbance. He was yelling down at someone, possibly one of his sepoys, his face red and his voice hoarse with fury. He was hewing the air with his sword in an angry manner.

Jack heard a shot. The major's head jerked backwards. His sword flew from his hand and landed point-first in his horse's neck. Then the officer seemed to lean forward. A moment later he slid to the ground. His mount whinnied, shook itself free of the blade, ran a few paces, then stopped and stamped. Blood seeped from the wound in its neck.

'What the hell?' cried Gwilliams. 'Did you see that, sir?'

Sergeant King, still not at a vantage point, said, 'Was that a musket? Who's firing?'

Crossman stood there, numbed by what he had witnessed. He could not see who had fired the weapon, but he knew the sound of a Brown Bess when he heard it. Someone had shot the British officer, had knocked him clean out of his saddle.

The immediate area miraculously cleared and people found space where there was none before, as they always do when danger threatens, no matter how thick the crowds.

Now there was an open avenue between Crossman and the body.

The riderless horse bolted, charging with wild eyes down the path which had been cleared, hitting Gwilliams on its way past, spinning him off his feet.

In the open space stood a sweating sepoy. His Kilmarnock cap was lying in the dust. The front of his coatee was unbuttoned from the waist of his dhoti to his neck. Crossman could see streaks of damp dust on his bare chest as he calmly reloaded his musket. There were other sepoys standing nearby, about thirty in number, but they were simply staring at their comrade who it seemed had just murdered a British major. Looking down the now wide gap, through the crowd, the sepoy saw Crossman, King and Gwilliams. He turned to his watching comrades and yelled at them.

'Come and help me, you cowards! Here's some more sister-violators. Was it all talk in the barracks? Am I the only one to protect our religion from the British? They will make us into Christians. They will make us eat pork fat. Come on, use your weapons. Kill these men too.'

The sepoy then raised his musket and aimed at the three white men and fired his weapon again.

Crossman heard the ball hum by his left ear. Somewhere behind him a local man shrieked and fell to the ground. The struck man began writhing in the dust. Ahead, the havildar in charge stepped from the ranks. He made a tentative move towards the renegade sepoy but then hesitated. There was a reluctance there to issue any orders or take care of matters himself. Instead of disarming the criminal he glanced back at his men.

'What are you waiting for?' Crossman called to the native NCO. 'Arrest him. Why are you all just standing there?'

'He is crazy on substance, sir. What can I do?'

The sepoy began to load for the third time, efficiently enough, but with wild eyes and quick breath. Crossman, King and Gwilliams all had the same idea and started to run towards him. Seeing them coming, the sepoy abandoned his attempt to reload and quickly snapped on his bayonet. Holding his musket at the ready he charged towards them, screaming at the top of his lungs. Crossman stopped in his tracks, drew his revolver and shot the oncoming sepoy in the chest. The first round failed to check the man's run but the second stopped him dead in his rush. His musket flew from his hands and he dropped almost at the feet of Sergeant King.

A ripple of sound went through the ranks of the dead man's regiment. For a moment it seemed the sepoy might have stronger sympathizers than first appeared. Even the havildar was staring angrily at the prone body of the soldier on the ground. Gwilliams took a carbine from its holster and began loading it. King, who had taken to wearing a sword in India, drew the blade. The three *firinghi* stood there, waiting to see if the sepoys were going to avenge their comrade-in-arms.

Suddenly the tension was broken by the arrival of a thin-faced young lieutenant, leading a much larger contingent of soldiers. The rebellious sepoys shuffled back into their ranks. Their havildar stepped forward and saluted the British officer very smartly.

'Clear the market place,' the lieutenant ordered. 'You there! Havildar! What's happened here? Is that the major? Oh my good God! Who's responsible for this? I say, you. Lieutenant? Who are you? Where did you come from? Did you see what occurred here?'

The square was cleared. The injured local man was taken away for treatment but it looked to Crossman as if his wound was fatal. Sepoys removed their fallen comrade, one on each corner of the corpse. The major's horse was recovered and his limp body was draped over it, to be taken back to the barracks. Jack explained the events as they had unfolded to him.

The young lieutenant whose name was Fowler was clearly quite shocked. His face was grey and he shook his head as he said, 'I don't know how his wife will take this. The havildar did nothing you say? Are you sure they weren't just stunned by it all. I don't know the murderer. Hardly know any of 'em. You know how it is. Don't understand why he did this. There's been some grumbling about the new Enfields, but they're not even using them. I don't understand it, I really don't.'

Crossman said, 'Could this just be a case of running amuck? I've heard of such things happening.'

4

'But when someone does that, they kill randomly. They don't pick out white faces to attack. They simply go in wildly, slashing at anyone in their way. This is different . . .'

Crossman told Fowler who he was and that he was on his way to the North-West Frontier. 'I'll write a report for you to give to your commanding officer,' he offered. I realize there's got to be a full enquiry over this, but I can't stay. Special duties.'

'Appreciate it,' said the snaggle-toothed Fowler. 'I just don't understand it at all.'

Jack then explained that Chundore was their first stop after leaving Bombay and that they were going to recruit coolies in the town as bearers for their journey.

'My sergeant is a mapmaker and I fancy he'll want one or two men to help him with that task. Any ideas, Lieutenant?'

'You'll need to go that way,' said Fowler, pointing to a street which led to the west of the town. 'There's an area out on the periphery, near the camel market, where the labour is to be found. Just follow your nose. You can smell a camel market from a hundred miles. Some elephants too, but you want men you say, not beasts? From there, you can see the barracks. You'll want to stay with us, I suppose, for a few days? I'll be in the mess this evening, around six. Have a drink with me.'

'Come on King, Gwilliams. Let's gather ourselves together,' called Crossman to the pair. King was leading Jack's horse by the reins, as well as his own. 'We're to go this way. The sooner we get this done, the better. I don't want to be around this town for too long.'

King and Gwilliams spent the next hour discussing the incident in the marketplace, turning every moment over and over, examining each one, giving their opinions as to the cause and outcome.

In the labour market were some British officers in full regimental dress, sweating profusely, moving amongst a sea of coolies and lascars. News of the murder had not yet reached their ears and they strode around with great confidence and more than a touch of arrogance. Here and there were batches of sepoys from the Bombay army in colourful uniforms, many of them similar to the Queen's army. Crossman found himself approached time and time again by civilians who wished to either sell him something, take him somewhere or provide him with information. One man, a Sikh, Crossman was told, came up and saluted him with military smartness and asked if he could be Crossman's guide in the city and perhaps beyond.

'I have been in the army, sahib,' said the man. 'I was naik in a famous regiment.'

Although he wanted guides, this one when questioned could not recall the name or number of this regiment, how many years he had served in it, and where it was presently located. Crossman decided to do without his services. The procession of local people – and foreigners from other provinces – who wished to help the three white newcomers was endless.

Crossman was suddenly overcome with weariness. He had not completely shed the lethargic habits of the voyage: almost three months at sea. The clipper had been exciting at first: it was the fastest vessel Crossman had ever been on. But after a while, especially following the storm in the Atlantic, the business of sailing palled. When he was not ill he was missing his wife. A kind of lethargy set in and he did nothing but wander the deck, when it was permitted, or sleep in his cot. His legs, now that he had hit solid ground again, felt wobbly and weak. The land seemed to tilt and rock in the way that the deck of the ship had done.

'Once we find our men,' Jack told the other two, 'we need to set out for Ferozepur as soon as possible.'

Sergeant King asked to be allowed to do the recruiting and the fatigued Crossman let him get on with it. The lieutenant and Corporal Gwilliams went to the barracks to find accommodation. Later, King arrived in front of Crossman's quarters and told him how many men he had employed. The lieutenant, now relaxed and enjoying a fruit drink on his veranda, was mildly shocked by the figure.

'What are you talking about, man?' he said to King. 'We can't travel swiftly with a caravan that size.'

'Sir,' said the sergeant, firmly, 'I need porters, flagmen, chain-men and, as they are called here, perambulator-wallahs – men to push the measuring wheel. We have to have coolies to carry the tents and supplies, so why not get my team of helpers together here and take them with us?'

'Damn it, you aren't going to map the whole journey?'

'No, of course not, sir, that would take many, many years. In any event, much of it has already been done on this side of India. But

6

where I see a hole in the present maps, I should like to fill it where time permits. If we're pushed, then I shan't, but if we're making good progress I see no reason why I can't do some mapping. Route maps are always welcomed by the army. Roads are features that constantly change, fall into disrepair, or improve. I must have my team of Indians, sir, if you please.'

Crossman fired his line of cannons.

'And who's to pay for them?'

King's jaw dropped. All the fizz went out of him immediately: his firmness and enthusiasm dropped to zero. Clearly this question had not occurred to the sergeant, much less the answer. It was the sort of thing an army sergeant rarely thought about or needed to think about. He paid for much of his own kit, but outside of that someone else paid for the rest: guns, horses, limber, transport, tents.

'Well, the *army*,' King said, grasping at the obvious.

The lieutenant gave him amused look. 'The army. Who in the army? The Commissariate? I can assure you they will not. Which army? Ours? How about the Indian army? No, I don't think John Company will fund our little expedition, do you? Who have we got left? Central government? Think again, soldier. That leaves the commanding officer, which is me. Commanding officers, and regiments as a whole, do pay for a lot of equipment and men. Lord Cardigan's Light Brigade would not have had cherry bums otherwise. So, Sergeant, here I am. Persuade me.'

King looked so utterly dejected that Crossman burst out laughing, which he knew was patronizing, but he couldn't help it.

'All right, Sergeant,' he said, 'I'll make it easy for you. I'll stump up the rupees for your chain-men and perambulator-wallahs.'

'Oh, no sir, you – you couldn't do that. Could you?'

'Well, I'm not a rich man in my own right, I must admit, but I do have a rich father-in-law who's generous to a fault. The *family* coffers are reasonably full and I have carte blanche to draw on them. I don't suppose your men will break the bank, King, so yes, you may have them. What you say about helpers is no doubt true. We'll probably lose a few of them on the way for various reasons. Let's see how we go along.'

'Thank you,' cried the sergeant, his enthusiasm returning. 'I'm most grateful. May I shake your hand, sir?'

'No, you may not. It's against regulations, or damn well should be.' A flying beetle the size of a sparrow was battering at the lamp glass, threatening to break it with its ceramic-hard wings. The distracted Crossman smacked it with his cap, sending it like a bullet out into a night full of the sounds of crickets and other rhythmic creatures. 'I hope you've recruited wisely. We don't want any badmashes. I hope they're good honest Indians, who won't rob us and run off, once we bed down for the night. Understood?'

'I've done my best, sir, but who can tell character at a glance? There're one or two of them I believe to be trustworthy. The rest have to be vouched for by those one or two.'

'All right, Sergeant.'

In fact, King was no fool and had found a cotton exporter from Aberdeen who lived close to the barracks in a large private house. The expatriate Scot had soon fixed him up with a team of Indians, some of whom had already assisted on surveying expeditions.

'All Hindus. Not that ye often get too much trouble between Hindus and Muslims, but it helps if your whole team have their festivals on the same days, otherwise they'll all take advantage of both sets of holidays and ye'll find yourself idling your days away waiting for them to finish one ceremony or the other. There's one Jain amongst 'em, to handle pay and money matters. The Jains are very good with money and they won't cheat ye. Ye won't get the better of them in a bargain, but they're more likely to be honest.'

Their numbers even included an older man, a Hindu who had been a flagman with Andrew Waugh and his artificer, Saiyid Mir Mohsin. Waugh was known to Sergeant King from his studies: a mapmaker who had taken over from Colonel George Everest, the man who had extended the Great Indian Arc of the Meridian up the whole length of the Indian subcontinent to the foothills of the Himalayas in the thirties and forties.

'You are the compass-wallah, sir?' enquired the man. 'I am called Ibhanan.'

King, much to the astonishment of the furniture maker from Aberdeen, had shaken the Indian's hand. 'Compass-wallah,' mused King, 'I like the sound of that. Is that what they call surveyors here?'

'Some do, sahib,' replied Ibhanan, smiling.

'Well then, that's what I am, the compass-wallah.'

Ibhanan then told him how he had assisted Waugh until that man became Surveyor-General. He had even worked with the great

8

Everest who had taught him the use of the heliotrope, a round mirror some eight or nine inches in diameter fixed to the top of a pole. It had been Ibhanan's job to set the heliotrope on to a mountaintop or high point so that it could be used as a marker by Everest's surveyors located at various different compass points.

'But sahib Everest, he would shout at everyone,' said Ibhanan, with a wry smile. 'He was very bad-tempered man.'

The Scot intervened here. 'Ye be careful ye don't malign people.'

'Oh, I not malign him, sahib. Everyone says it.'

King and Ibhanan liked each other straight away, seeing something of the brass and glass in each other's soul. King made Ibhanan his head man. Anyone who had touched the iron hem of Everest's Great Theodolite, that monstrous metal beast which had been dragged by oxcart the length and breadth of the Indian subcontinent, was akin to a disciple of the Lord so far as the sergeant was concerned. Ibhanan was one of the apostles and he, Sergeant King, had come immediately after. He wanted to hear stories, of traversing jungles, of crossing droog country, of temple towers crowned with night lights, of gullys and gorges choked with vegetation. Here was a man who helped build the holy grid-iron of the triangulation tree which grew from the south of India to the north, spreading its webbed branches from coast to coast as it grew, flourishing only on sweat and death.

Once he had his team together, King set out to purchase a pair of camel carts to carry the men and his equipment. He knew Crossman, his new commanding officer, wished to get to the North-West Frontier as soon as possible. Personally, King could not see what the almighty hurry was, but then he granted that Crossman had more knowledge of the situation in India than he did himself. He just wished that Crossman was not such a man of excitable character. The lieutenant seemed to him to be a rash of enthusiasms, few of which he appeared to have explored in any great depth. King could not comprehend why Crossman was interested in so many things, from auxometers to zambombas, yet failed to fix that interest. He was one of those gentlemen – a class which King held in mild contempt – who collected everything they could lay their hands on and displayed them in glass cases for the admiration of their visitors. Seashells, dried monkey brains, antipodean flutes, Polynesian war bonnets, volcanic-lava jewellery.

All right, King conceded, he had not actually seen one of those cases in Crossman's house, but he would not put it past the officer to have a display room into which he showed only his own circle.

King, on the other hand, had one great passion, mapmaking, and he would sacrifice everything – even at the risk of his life – to go into a region which was uncharted. He knew all the names of the famous pioneers of mapmaking in India – James Rennell, the naval officer who had begun the great affaire; Francis Wilford, of the Bengal Engineers, an ex-clerk who had become bored with life in England just as King had done; the initiator, William Lambton, of course, whose shoulder had been behind the Great Trigonometrical Survey; and finally, George Everest himself. Those men, and the multitude of Indian surveyors whose names were not yet known to King, had drawn the sergeant to his present post. He felt it was his destiny to map an unknown region, a place where the length, breadth and height of the topography was still merely guesswork. He wanted to put exactitudes down on a chart, show the actual course of a river, tell the real height of a mountain, track a vague road through wild country so that strangers might follow it without fear of becoming lost or of taking a false trail.

The closer he came to the forbidden region of Tibet the better he liked it, for he would take any chance to enter the fastness of that territory. There were no accurate charts of Tibet. The man who mapped it, measured its mountains, traced its rivers, would be famous. He had made the mistake of mentioning this to Lieutenant Crossman, who spoke very firmly to him, telling him that any attempt by Sergeant Farrier King or any of his disciples to cross the border into Chinese Tartary would be met with severe disciplinary action. King had nodded gravely, saying it had never entered his mind that *he* should be the one, while at the same time he nursed the dreadful desire, the longing, the determination, to be the first mapmaker in those mountains.

He reported back to his commanding officer who seemed pleased with his efficiency.

'Camel carts, eh? Well done. We shall have our horses, of course, but we won't be able to work them too hard in this heat. We'll start the journey north early tomorrow.'

'Yes, sir.'

King went back to the barracks, contented with himself.

10

Crossman, whose limbs and back ached, went for a hot bath in a tub out in the yard. While he was in the tub, to his great astonishment an Indian slipped under the curtain which screened a man's bathing from prying eyes. The man, a sleek gentleman wearing dark clothes, stared at him with a smile on his face, until Jack became exasperated.

'Who sent you? I need no one to scrub my back. I'm quite capable of doing that myself with the loofah.'

The man's palms came together and he bowed his head.

'No, sahib – I am no washing-man. I am an assassin by trade. Do you need someone killed? I will kill anyone you wish – anyone at all. If you need promotion, I will kill the next higher officer, to make a space for you. You owe money? I will kill your creditor. Is there some family business left unattended? A sister violated? I will kill her lover. Ah, I see you have lost your hand. I could kill the man who took it from you, in his bed, so that when they come in the morning they will think he has passed on in his sleep. A sword through a mattress from underneath. Anyone. Anyone at all. My fees are very reasonable, sir. If it must look like an accident, then it is of course more expensive. I am an expert with a knife. A thin blade through a door or mud wall, as a man leans against it to light his pipe. Simple. I can strangle a victim with a knotted cord and he will make no sound. Poisons? I know them all. A kerchief soaked in a potion and a man will blow his nose and die convulsing. Please, if you require my services, tell me now.'

Crossman's astonishment did not leave him.

'What's your name?'

'My name, sahib?' the man in black smiled. 'I am not shy, like some of my profession. My name is Arihant. It means *one who kills his enemies*. But I do not only kill my enemies, I kill anyone.'

'So you said. No, I can't think of anybody I wish to get rid of at this time. Sorry.'

Arihant bowed again. 'Not to worry, sir. If you do, before you leave this place, come to the coffee shop in the main square. This is where I sit every day. Peace be with you.'

'And with you.'

Arihant slipped out, leaving Jack wondering if he should keep his revolver with him at all times. What if he had been the victim? Was it so easy to hire a murderer here in India? His bathwater could be

11

red with blood by now and it would be goodbye Fancy Jack Crossman.

Once he had soaked out the weariness and had dressed again, he was visited by the subaltern, Fowler, of the Balooch Battalion.

'Shall we tiff?' asked Fowler. He looked around as if expecting to see a shadow standing near. 'Where's your boy?'

'I beg your pardon?'

'Can you get your boy to fetch us luncheon?'

'Oh. Actually, I don't have an Indian man-servant – not yet anyway.'

'You won't be able to do without one here, you know old chap. No one can. Well, I can eat later. This stifling heat destroys the appetite anyway. Now, what were we talking about? Oh, yes. The Dum-Dum rumours. I heard today that there's been a mutiny at Berhampur. There's quite a bit of disquiet in India at the moment. I put it down to soft handling. Wouldn't happen in *my* battalion. We treat them with firmness. Besides, my men love their colonel. You often hear them saying so. They would lay down their life for him.'

'What do you call that incident in the market?'

Fowler frowned and seemed annoyed. 'That? Just an isolated case of a sepoy being intoxicated by some drug or other.'

'Really? Nothing to do with a rebellion?'

'Why would it be? We've been in India for so long,' argued Fowler. 'Our government of them is just. We do so much to improve their lot. They were served far worse under the Mughals.'

'Still, it must be expected, especially from disgruntled individuals.'

'Changing the subject, how many men have you got?'

'What men? You mean coolies?'

Fowler was aghast. 'No, I don't. I mean armed men. You're surely taking a troop of sowars with you? Yes please, another chotapeg would fortify the spirit for the walk back to my own bungalow.'

Crossman gave him his second dram of brandy.

'We're travelling as light as possible,' admitted Crossman. 'Just myself, my corporal and a sergeant who makes maps. We're all the military men on the expedition. Sergeant King has a number of his own Indians to assist him with his mapmaking, but apart from them . . .'

'But there are all sorts out there, man. Fierce tribesmen, bad-mashes, dacoits, thugs, tigers – the list is long. I suppose,' granted Fowler, 'as a small party you might slip along virtually unnoticed.

12

There is that to your advantage. Personally, I would never ride such a distance. It's nearly a thousand miles to the Punjab. It'd take me a year to be carried there.' Fowler laughed. 'Anyway, old chap, beware of blue turbans . . .' He went on to explain what he meant by that and Crossman listened intently.

Crossman poured himself a glass of water. He found himself forever thirsty in this land of heat and dust. He was also getting bored with Lieutenant Fowler. At first he had been grateful that a brother officer had taken the time to visit him: for the most part he had been ignored by the Bombay army. It was true he had been to tea at a colonel's house, where the colonel's wife had cornered him for two hours and had twittered in his ear about all the terrible things she had to bear, which included her servants, in 'this dreadful country which I hate beyond anything'. He had met a major who was so enthusiastic about India and the Indians you would have thought he had died and gone to heaven. And he had spoken briefly with the colonel himself, who seemed preoccupied with the current relationships between the maharajahs, nawabs and the Company.

But whatever Crossman had to say was of little concern to any of these people. In fact, they talked over the top of his replies to their questions, interrupting him without listening to what he had to say. They were Company men, not Queen's army, and they really were not interested in him.

But Fowler's attitudes and idiosyncrasies were playing on Crossman's nerves.

He said, hardly paying attention now, 'You said earlier you wouldn't travel if you weren't carried. What did you mean by that?'

'Why, in a palanquin of course. No one walks, old chap. Hardly anyone rides. Then you don't even have to find your own way. You just say to your head man "I wish to be in Bunpoor for the hunt on Tuesday" and leave it to them. Well, I can see you're tired. Good luck, old boy.' Fowler threw back his dram and held out his hand. As Crossman shook it, the Indian army man added cheerfully. 'Don't suppose we'll ever see each other again. India is a big place and if you look at the statistics you'll find that a lot of us die before our time, mostly of some ailment or other.'

Fowler left with Crossman staring thoughtfully after him. The departing lieutenant, he decided, was not a bad sort, underneath. It seemed that something happened to people when they came to the subcontinent. They became careless of themselves and, yes, life. When one saw dead bodies laying unattended in the street it turned one's spirit. There was great poverty in Britain of course – and one only had to go to Ireland to understand the horrible effects of starvation – but, if life was as precarious there, death was certainly a cause for sorrow and attention. It was the indifference which was hard to bear here: the fact that no one seemed to care.

It was really far too early to make a judgement and Lord knew Crossman had met so very few people yet, but it did seem to him they worried about trivialities, like what sort of china was on the table, and who was carrying on with whose wife. They had not enough to occupy their minds. The army officers seemed to live for the next meal which they grumbled about when it came to the table, attended the odd parade here and there, but rarely showed their faces to their men. It appeared to Crossman that the whole place was in the doldrums. A kind of purgatory which one served out in order to get pensioned and retire to England.

He sat down and wrote a letter to Jane, telling her briefly about the voyage and giving her his first impressions of India. They were not altogether truthful impressions: he kept his descriptions and anecdotes positive. There was little of his disillusionment in there. This was pure selfishness. He hoped that one day she would be able to join him in India and didn't want to set her against this vast and strange land about which he yet knew very little. Time enough later to tell her how he felt about it and whether it would suit her or not.

2

'Get out of the road, you idiot!'

Preoccupied with his recent meeting, Crossman, in full dress uniform, hurriedly stepped aside as a coach and four swept past him, the nearside wheels narrowly missing the toes of his boots. He heard the word 'Peacock!' which was the coach driver delivering a final rebuke at the army man who had presumed to cross the street in front of his precious horses. Soldiers were meant to be unseen as well as not heard in their own land. They should be overseas somewhere, fighting for the empire, not littering the roads.

'Your servant, sir,' called Jack Crossman at the thundering vehicle, knowing his sarcasm was wasted. 'And be damned.'

His new rank still felt clean and fresh on Lieutenant Jack Crossman. He was in London, staying at one of the houses his father had kept for his own use there, in Knightsbridge. His older brother James had suggested he and Jane use it while they were in the city, James now having power of attorney over their father, whose mind had gone. James was now managing the family estates in Scotland, while Jack remained in the army, a man on special duties for the Crown. It was simply age that had addled their father's mind. Along with his wife, the baronet was looked after by a devoted servant: a man that his two sons disliked intensely but retained for his loyalty.

Crossman's bride Jane had now gone back to Derbyshire, to stay with her father. The officer was not only newly promoted, but newly married. He was not quite sure which felt the most awkward. He loved his wife, of course, with a great passion. He enjoyed his new

15

status after spending several years in the rank and file. But these two newcomers were still strangers to him and one is always awkward with a stranger.

Jane and he had spent almost a month in London, but when it was rumoured Jack might go to the Punjab they realized that it would be impractice for Jane to follow for the moment. The North-West Frontier was no place for woman at this time, even should her husband's duties keep him there. In fact it was most likely that Crossman would be here, there and everywhere, and rarely in one spot for more than a few days. In any case, Jane's father had fallen ill not long after the wedding and continually asked for her. It was not a good way to start a marriage, they both admitted to the other, but there were many who had it worse. In time, when her father no longer needed her and the Punjab was not such a turbulent region, or indeed if Jack were to be based somewhere less volatile, she would go to India.

A dray being pulled by a slow, plodding horse took an age to get out of his way as the lieutenant tried to recross the road. He went behind the waggon, avoiding stepping in a steaming pile of dung. A soldier in infantry corporal's uniform was signalling him from the corner of the street and he made his way to him.

'Gwilliams? I thought I said I'd see you at the inn.'

'Yeah I know, sir,' said the corporal in an accent he had brought with him from North America, 'but I couldn't wait to hear.'

'We're leaving on the twelfth of January,' Crossman told him. 'Does that satisfy your curiosity? We have passage on a clipper ship.' Jack frowned as he remembered another detail from his meeting with Mr Cadwaller, a director of the Honourable East India Company whom he had met at their offices in Leadenhall Street. 'There's another man coming with us, a Sergeant King. Queen's army, of course. He's on his way into London now.'

'What? I thought we was on our own on this one?'

Gwillams glanced down at his arm, at the chevrons there. Crossman knew what he was thinking. Gwilliams had only recently joined the British army and had been made a corporal immediately at the insistence of Colonel Hawke as well as Crossman. Gwilliams had been one of Crossman's band of spies and saboteurs in the Crimea and had earned his stripes. But now the new corporal was thinking that here was some jumped-up sergeant coming into the new clique,

16

without a by-your-leave. Had it been a private it would not have troubled either man, but a sergeant meant Gwilliams was being pushed further down the pecking order and Crossman was having to deal with an NCO whom he knew nothing about.

'Well, he's a mapmaker, apparently. His main duty will be to draw maps of some of the places we pass through. It seems he has a talent for it. God knows why they aren't already mapped – or perhaps they are but for some reason not too accurately. I wasn't told. But the fact remains, we will gather information while mapping the topography. We may even go into Chinese Tibet, though that's not official. It's something I had from Major Lovelace, earlier.'

'I'm not looking after this King fellah too!' insisted Gwilliams. 'I don't mind watching your back for you, sir, you being my commanding officer, but this Sergeant King can look after hisself.'

'It's not expected, Gwilliams. Not in the British army.'

'Nor in the American, neither, so that's flat. Did you need a massage, sir? You look a bit achy to me.'

Gwilliams had learned the art of massage from a tribe of Huron he had lived with in Canada. Crossman did indeed feel somewhat weary to the core of his bones, and Gwilliams had the hands to put that right. But as a reserved British gentleman he was uncomfortable enough as it was having the corporal put his hands, and sometimes his feet, on his body. He was certainly not going to take Corporal Gwilliams home with him to do it there in front of his housekeeper and her husband.

'It can wait,' he said. 'There'll be plenty of time on the ship.'

Gwilliams shrugged. 'Suit yerself, sir.'

Now that Gwilliams had been appraised of the situation he took his leave of Crossman. The corporal made his way to the Cock Inn, where he had a room, and the officer to his family house. There he was met at the door by Betty, the housekeeper, whose husband Tom Hodges took care of the garden and the maintenance. It was not a large house and two people could manage it well enough, especially as it was rarely used these days.

Betty told him there was a meal 'on the go' and she would serve it in the dining room in half-an-hour if it pleased him.

'I'll have it in the kitchen, Betty – if you don't mind.'

The middle-aged woman looked shocked. 'In the kitchen, sir?'

'It's warmer there. The dining room is freezing, even with that fire

17

going. I much prefer the kitchen. Oh, don't look at me like that, Betty, I had a thousand times worse than your kitchen when I was in the Crimea . . .'

'If I hear those words *when I was in the Crimea* one more time, Master Alexander,' she said, using his old name, 'I swear I'll take a ladle to your backside.'

He laughed. 'You can't do that any more, Betty. Not that you ever did anyway. You're all puff. You used to threaten, but your threats were empty. However, I grant there's nothing worse than a soldier back from a campaign who keeps repeating *when I was in* wherever. It must grate on the nerves. I promise I won't say it again. Not in front of you, anyway. Now Tom enjoys hearing about my exploits in the Crimea. So if you hear me saying it to him you'll just have to block your ears.'

As she took his shako and sword from him the scabbard of his weapon knocked against his left hand with a wooden sound. Betty stared at him. He shrugged and smiled.

'No pitying looks, Betty,' he warned. 'We talked about that, remember?'

She nodded, then sailed away with his shako and sword at arm's length, as if they carried some sort of plague. With his one good hand Crossman undid his coatee with its 88th Connaught Rangers' yellow facings on the collar and cuffs, struggled out of it and went upstairs to change into something more comfortable. Later he went down dressed in a civilian suit and sat on one of the high stools at the old oak table. The iron kitchen range was glowing red hot. Obviously Betty had taken him seriously, when he said he was cold, and was in no way going to be responsible for any chills in her kitchen.

He ate the soup with more appearance of relish than he actually felt because he knew it took Betty several days to make a consommé, since it had to be strained and left to settle several times. The meat stew afterwards was more to his liking, though he still had to be careful he did not overeat. The many months in the Crimea, without adequate or proper food, had done something to his digestion which was taking time to mend. It was as if his stomach had shrunk and it certainly rejected rich offerings. Little food and often seemed to be the best for him, though it had hurt both Jane and Betty to see him push away his plate and announce he was satisfied after what appeared to them to be enough only to feed a mouse.

'Thank you, Betty,' he said, afterwards. 'Where's Tom?'

'He's gone visiting his brother Edward, just for an hour, if it doesn't matter, sir.'

'No, no. It doesn't matter to me. I'm sure he works hard enough to earn an hour or two off when he can take it. I just wondered if he would give me a hand tomorrow morning in my workshop? There's one or two things he could help me with.'

'I'm sure he'll be happy, sir.'

'Thank you. And one more thing. I've been curious ever since arriving. The first room on the landing appears to be locked. I wonder, do you have the key? I just want to check there are no rotting corpses in there, or mad relations chained to the wall. You read of such things these days in novels and it does make you wonder. Not that I read novels, you understand, Betty. It's simply that I can't bear dark secrets.'

Again, Betty rewarded his frivolity with a shocked look.

'That was your father's room, sir. He called it his *studio,* whatever that means. It's where he did his painting. There are no dead bodies in there, sir, nor no one else to my knowledge.'

'Oh? Well, may I see it sometime?'

'You can see it now, sir, if you wish. I'll just get the key . . .'

3

The next day, very early, the party set out for Burhanpur which sat in the pass to the west of the distant Gawilgarh Hills. Sergeant King was feeling disgruntled. There were two more Indians with the lieutenant when he had joined the party that morning. On enquiry King had found out that they were guides.

'What do we need guides for?' he had said. 'I have very adequate maps, sir. I can find the way.'

'This is a not a game, Sergeant,' was the reply. 'I need to get to the North-West Frontier as quickly as possible. These men know the country and its foibles. We have no need to turn this into a scouting expedition. It is almost a thousand miles to the Punjab.'

'Ordinary miles, sir? Or geographical miles?'

The lieutenant's eyes narrowed and he reacted as King had expected he would.

'There's a difference? What the devil are geographical miles?'

'The same as nautical miles only they're on dry land, not on water.' He could see Crossman losing patience with him, so he had added very quickly, 'A geographical mile is one minute of latitude measured along the equator.'

'That means about as much to me as the consistency of a bowl of maize porridge.'

'Well, sir, a British mile is 5,280 feet, whereas a geographical mile is 6,082.66 feet.'

'We'll pace it out, shall we, as we go along? Then we'll discover what scale of measurement we ought to have used.'

King laughed at the ludicrous image this brought to mind. So did Crossman. For a minute or two their spirits met in humour. Then Crossman walked off to mount his horse. King did the same. A short while afterwards they were on their way, weaving through a market where a handful of beans displayed on a blanket was often the sum total of a seller's stock.

So King was not going to be permitted to show his officer how excellent were the maps of his colleagues. He had hoped to prove something to Lieutenant Crossman but was not going to be allowed to do it. He spoke to Gwilliams about it.

'Corporal, you've been with the lieutenant for a while now.'

'Less than a year,' replied Gwilliams, 'including Thanksgiving and weekends.'

Gwilliams was a little too facetious about most things, which irritated King a little, but he persisted with his questioning.

'What kind of man would you say he was?'

'Well, he's a Christian soul, even though he don't go to church.'

'Is he a Quaker then?'

Gwilliams shook his head. 'Why would you say that, Sergeant?'

'Well, you said he was Christian yet did not attend church. I assumed you meant he attended some other establishment. Quakers go to Meeting Houses. Is that what you meant?'

'Nope. I mean he holds to the Christian ideals but he don't worship much. I mean if you want someone you can trust when you're in a tight hole, he's a good man to have by your side. What is he really like?' Gwilliams sighed. 'I guess he's loyal and mostly courteous to his men and hell with the ladies – or was, until he got wed. It'll be interestin' to see how he is here amongst these lovely ladies with their big brown eyes and nekkid middles. I never seen such flesh myself, King. How about you?'

King did not want to talk about women, he wanted to know about his commander.

'Did the lieutenant see much action in the Crimea?'

'More than enough to last any man a lifetime.'

'I know he lost his hand there – but someone told me that it was an accident – that a ladder fell on it.'

'The lieutenant, or sergeant as he was then, was shot, stabbed and pummelled more times than you've put your butt on a horse. That ladder was a siege ladder, which took ten to twelve men to carry.

21

Moreover, the air was thicker'n a hailstorm with bullets, shells and balls flying this way an' that, and a forest of bayonets was waitin' for those in front. It was hell, fire and damnation in the thick of that battle, and he walked out of it, so don't you go belittlin' Fancy Jack's war for him. I seen it happen.'

King snatched at one word. 'He was a sergeant?'

'Promoted due to his courage under fire – and some other stuff which I ain't supposed to talk about.'

This was news to Farrier King. From the accent, from the demeanour of his commanding officer, from what he had heard of his family background which admittedly had come only from Gwilliams, he had expected that Lieutenant Crossman had purchased his commission. What was the story here, then? A man of a good family, a noble family, who had been a sergeant in the ranks? No doubt the family was very poor, shabby genteel as they said, and could not afford to buy commissions. King mentioned this to Gwilliams.

'You couldn't be more wrong, sergeant,' replied the corporal. 'His pa was a major and his brother an officer too, in the 93rd. Both bought into the regiment. Rich Scotch family. And the pa of that new wife of his is drownin' in money. It was a choice. The lieutenant joined as a common soldier and worked his way through to his present status. He's as stubborn as a jackass, that man, and don't like the easy routes to the top.'

'Thank you, Gwilliams. I see him in a new light.'

King said this, but felt that Gwilliams had probably missed some family skeletons in the cupboard. It had to be more than just someone out to build themselves up from nothing. There was more to it than that. And the 'Fancy Jack' nickname. Where had that come from? From being *hell* with the ladies?

Now, however, he needed to turn his attention to his camel carts. They were moving very slowly and the lieutenant, far ahead, kept looking back with a frown on his face. If they did not keep in touch with the commanding officer, King would be getting a tongue lashing about time-keeping. However, to King's surprise, the camels could be encouraged to increase their pace, and did so, responding to their driver's urgent shouts. He had imagined they had one speed and worked to this internal pace rigidly.

Once he got them to move faster, King was able to study the hills through which they were passing. Brown hills, with scattered green trees, bushes and patches of grass amongst them. He looked for the spots where he would have set up his heliograph for triangulation. There, or perhaps there. The haze was a factor of course. It would distort vision through a telescope. Having studied the charts he was carrying, King would have liked to do some elevation measuring in these hills. He knew the current figures were based on barometric levelling, a method which was quick and easy in rugged territory but not very accurate. Differential levelling, with a telescopic spirit level and a levelling rod would give better readings. But he knew it would be hopeless to ask Crossman to allow him such a leisure so soon after their journey had begun. It was more prudent to bide his time until they came across an area which was crying out for accurate readings.

He trotted his mare alongside the first camel wagon. Ibhanan looked up at him and smiled. King was experiencing the beginnings of a friendship with the older man. They seemed to have an affinity with one another which of course had to come out of their mutual love of surveying.

'Ibhanan,' said King. 'Do names mean anything, here in India? I expect they must, since they do in most places.'

'Yes, sahib – Hindu names do.'

'And what does your name, Ibhanan, mean?'

His features were expressionless when the Indian explained that it meant *elephant face*.

'Elephant face,' murmured King, savouring the words.

Ibhanan said, 'You do not laugh, sahib. Mostly Englishmen laugh when they hear what my name means.'

'Well, I imagine your parents did not name you in order for others to ridicule you, so I supposed it was not meant to be amusing.'

'No, sahib, it is not. Ganesha is the elephant-headed god of wisdom and success and it is he who I have been named for. But one corporal tell me I should be named *horse bum*.'

'Then he was an ignorant man. Do you know what my name means? Farrier King?'

Ibhanan's face wrinkled again. 'I know what is a king – a maharajah.'

'Yes, and a farrier is a man who makes horseshoes and nails them to the horses.'

'Kings and horses – the most noble of both races.'

King did not correct Ibhanan's error. Instead he looked keenly at the man. 'Ibhanan, would you teach me Hindi?' he asked. 'My lieutenant has studied Hindi and some Afghan tongue. I, on the other hand, speak nothing but my native English. I should like to learn another language.'

'Most decidedly, sahib. If you will teach me how to draw maps.'

'But you were with George Everest!'

'Yes, but I was only a young man. My interest was in other things and I was a simple porter, though I could do some things with the instruments. But I would like to know *all*.'

'You wish to become a surveyor?'

'Yes, sahib, if it possible.'

'Agreed,' King shook hands with him. 'You shall teach me Hindi and I shall teach you to make maps.'

4

The trek to Burhanpur was reasonably easy. They kept clear of villages since Crossman preferred to camp in the wilderness. He, King and Gwilliams travelled more or less in uniform, though they often shed their coatees and rolled up their shirt sleeves. Local dignitaries, seeing redcoats in the area, occasionally invited them to share hospitality, but Crossman usually refused. He preferred to be in the open where he and his men were not so much at risk. He actually enjoyed the outdoor life, a night under a sky encrusted with stars, or inside a tope grove – a mango orchard – this new and unusual fruit to hand. It was pleasant being woken in the morning by a softly spoken, 'Chai, sahib,' and finding the cup of steaming hot tea by his straw pillow. He was *beginning* to enjoy the food, especially the different breads and roasted goat meat, but even that was better outside, cooked on an open fire, the smoke filtered by a canopy.

One thing troubled Crossman deeply. He could not shake off the feeling that they were being followed. Once or twice he had looked back along the trail to see a dark figure in the distance. But the shape was distorted by the natural haze created by the heat and dust. Sometimes Jack stood watching intently, hoping the figure would only come a little closer so that he might be able to see this mysterious hanger-on, but whoever it was managed to move only within the warping heat waves. Then at other times Jack thought that perhaps his imagination was running away with him, in this land where the real and unreal mingled under the sun.

In this initial stage of their journey north they met no savage tribes, nor robber bands of dacoits, nor tigers. One evening a lone wolf wandered through their camp but no one was mauled and the beast was permitted to go on his way without being molested. On a clear morning in some foothills Crossman, Gwilliams and King were under a tamarind tree tracking a herd of gazelle. They had breech-loading hunting rifles with them. On sighting the wild creatures Crossman gave King the first shot.

'Get the small mottled one,' he murmured, as King took aim, 'the one with the broken horn.'

King took an inordinate time to aim, which tried the patience of Gwilliams, who finally whispered, 'Hell man, shoot!'

King fired. The ball zinged off a rock three yards to the left of the gazelle. The herd stirred, looked about them, but didn't scent the hunters who were downwind then. The animals continued to graze on the side of the hill. Crossman, thinking that King had been put off his aim by something, quickly handed him his own rifle. King realized he had to shoot again, took aim, fired. This time the shot went even wider of its mark. The herd started to run. Gwilliams quickly took a bead on one of the fleeing herd. He squeezed the trigger. A young gazelle spun into the air, its racing momentum carrying it up into a somersault, and it landed in the dust. The rest of its companions were soon gone, into a line of bushes.

'Damn, Sergeant,' said Gwilliams, 'you can't hit a barn.'

King handed Crossman's rifle back to him.

'The sight was out,' he said. 'It's not an accurate weapon.'

Crossman stared at his sergeant. 'You missed with *both* sporting guns. These are excellent hunting weapons. I purchased them myself and they haven't been out of their chamois-leather holsters until now. There is nothing the matter with either of them. I can't believe how inept you are.'

'Well – the wind is wrong,' replied King, desperately. 'It's blowing too hard in the wrong direction.'

'The *wrong* direction, hell,' spluttered Gwilliams. 'You just can't shoot for nothin', can you? I seen men like you before. When you was aimin', that damn muzzle was waving around fit to draw circles in the air. Can't you hold it still, man?'

'It just sort of does that,' replied King, miserably, giving up on his pretence. 'I can't help it. It's always been the same.'

Gwilliams nodded, his eyes narrowing. 'I tell you, sir, I heared about this fellah. He was in the 28th Foot and they threw him out.'

'Is that true, Sergeant King?' asked Crossman. 'Were you in the infantry?'

'Yes I was, sir.'

'And they let you go?'

'I couldn't shoot straight. It's something I can't do. Never have been able to do.'

Crossman took off his forage cap and threw it down into the dust to register his disgust.

'Damnation. They give me a cross-eyed sergeant no one wants. Why can't you shoot?' he cried. 'We're down to two men now, if we get attacked.' Something occurred to the lieutenant. 'How can you survey land if you can't see straight? You have to look through telescopes and things – what do you call it – your theodolite? It doesn't make sense. What if we were to get you some spectacles?'

'It's not my vision, sir. I have perfect eyesight. I don't know why I can't shoot. I just can't, that's all. Something goes wrong between my brain and my hands. The rifle just won't line up for me at the right time, at the right moment to fire. Not everyone can fire a weapon well.'

'Everybody *I* know can,' stated Gwilliams. 'What's so hard? You point the thing, you line up the sights with the target and you squeeze on the trigger. There ain't nothin' to it.'

King stiffened and attempted to retrieve some of his dignity.

'Well it doesn't work in my case.'

At that moment they were distracted by the sight of a leopard dragging their kill away to its own feasting ground. Already it had got about twenty yards with it, a tell-tale snaking mark in the dust. Crossman yelled 'Hi!' and went running up the slope towards the scavenger. The leopard stood its ground, snarled and spat, then crouched ready to leap on the approaching man. Gwilliams took out a revolver and fired at the leopard, the shot hitting the dust near the beast's forepaws. It growled once more, then slunk away behind some boulders, leaving Crossman standing over the prey with his sword drawn, ready to battle for his breakfast.

'There you are, Corporal, you've just missed yourself!' cried King, triumphantly, pointing at the smoking revolver in Gwilliam's hand. 'You failed to hit your target.'

27

Gwilliams curled his top lip. 'I weren't tryin' to hit it. If I'd have shot the beast with this peashooter, it would've only made it mad and the lieutenant would be peeling leopard off his chest by now.'

'Oh.'

Back at the camp, the word soon got around the Indians that their 'sergeant sahib' who knew all about maps was no good with his matchlock and if they had expected protection from him to expect it no more. Ibhanan was annoyed with his companions. What did it matter that the sergeant sahib could not fire a musket? He was a mapmaker, not a killer of men.

Crossman calmed down, once back in the camp, and called King to his tent.

'I'm sorry I berated you so hard out there. It was a surprise.'

'They should have told you. I should have told you.'

'Well, we shall manage as best we can. Are you any good with a sword, if we get to close quarters? I need to know.'

'I can use most blades efficiently.'

'It's not the killing, then?'

The sergeant shook his head. 'I'm not *fond* of killing, but I will do it if I am called to.'

'Good. Good. What is it that you're chewing?' asked Crossman. 'Is that dried beef?'

King looked at what was in his hand and then said, 'Oh, no – it's something Ibhanan showed me. Tamarind. You chew on the seed case. It's very sweet . Here, try some.' He broke Crossman a piece off the hard reddish-brown shell which contained some dry beans.

'You sure you don't eat the seeds themselves?' asked Crossman, staring suspiciously at the sliver which looked like a piece of old bark left in the sun too long. 'It seems strange to eat the shell and not the nuts themselves.'

'No, I am assured by Ibhanan. Didn't your mam give you the bark of a willow to chew, when you had a headache as a youngster? Mine did. What's so different about chewing the seed case?'

Crossman nibbled at the seed case and found it tasted delightfully sweet.

'I haven't got a headache, for a start.' Jack did not add that it was his nurse and then his governess who used natural cures on him, not his mother. 'You're sure it's not poisonous?'

'Yes I am – but I wouldn't eat too much of it. I'm told the Indians eat it once a month to "clean out their insides" whatever that means. I suspect the stuff scours the guts, or something like. I am also informed that it will clean military brasses to parade inspection brilliance.'

Crossman said, 'A purgative, eh? That's the *last* thing I need at the moment. Something to hold it in would be better received by my intestines. I don't know about you, King, but everything I eat at the moment seems to turn to liquid once it reaches my belly. I did think it was a return of Crimean dysentery, but it's not quite as bad as that. Just bad enough to keep me on the hop.'

King's square face broke into a grin. 'Me too, sir.'

The two men parted on better terms, having shared their problems with bowel movements.

Gwilliams' skills as a barber were only matched by his talents as a masseur. The Huron in Canada had taught him 'bone and muscles manipulation' which he practised on Jack. The lieutenant was plagued with aching limbs and he found that a session with Gwilliams pulling him this way and that, pummelling his upper arms, thighs, calves and other muscled parts of the body, gave him relief from pain for some days to come. However, the lieutenant was quite embarrassed at having the rough corporal lay hands on his aristocratic form, so this was done in private in the officer's tent, leaving Jack with the uncomfortable feeling of having a sordid secret. He felt he was participating in something not quite the thing among gentlemen.

When they eventually reached Burhanpur they went through the town and beyond. Supplies and provisions were purchased as they passed by the various stores. Crossman then finally gave way and accepted the offer from a local rajah to stay at the rajah's hunting lodge. The rajah's last name was Singh and this confused Crossman.

'I'm told the rajah is a Hindu, but I thought if one was named Singh one was a Sikh.'

Ibhanan answered him, 'All Sikhs are Singhs, but not all Singhs are Sikhs.'

'Ah, I see – the lion surname is general, not exclusive.'

The hunting lodge was a sprawling one-storey building covering a wide section of ground on the edge of a small dusty plain. Not particularly impressive on the outside, the interior was magnificent, with marbled tiled floor and walls, the marble inlaid with semi-precious stones such as jasper, agate, malachite, onyx, lapis-lazuli, garnet, and others. There were tigers' heads decorating many passageways and in the dining room, fountains in the gardens and halls and even in some of the bedrooms, latticed windows that let the cool breezes blow through. In the gardens outside were oleanders, jasmine and hibiscus, which added their fragrance to the subtle scent of burning incense.

In Crossman's sleeping quarters there was a huge four-poster bed with fine muslin curtains hanging all round to keep out the mosquitoes and flies. A punkah-wallah – an enslaved orphan without family to protect him from powerful rajahs – sat like a shadow-puppet on a rush mat in the corner of the room and pulled on the string connected to a flapping ceiling fan. When no one was in the room, the young boy dozed softly where he sat. His meals were brought to him by one of his fellow servants. Crossman wondered whether the boy ever saw the light of day. Certainly his skin was much paler than that of most untouchables. When he tried his Hindi out on the boy, he got a lazy response. Crossman asked the boy what was making the noise he could hear which seemed to be coming from a tree in the courtyard.

'Owls, sahib,' said the boy, brightening. 'May I show you?'

He took Crossman outside and pointed up, into the branches of an oak-like tree. There were three spotted owls up in the crook of two boughs. They stared down at Crossman with round wondering eyes. Crossman was not very knowledgeable on wild life, but the punkah-wallah, whose name was Sajan, began to point out other birds and give Crossman their Indian names. When Crossman went to move the branches of a particular tree, though, Sajan stopped him, telling him it was a tree sacred to Hindus.

'What is it called?'

'It is a peepul tree, sahib.'

'People?' repeated Crossman. 'How strange.'

'Not to us, sahib. It is not strange to Hindus at all.'

Crossman laughed at the boy's earnestness.

'You're a very bright young man,' said Crossman. 'How old are you?'

'I think eight years.'

'Well, you're a very intelligent for your age.' He gave the boy four annas. 'Spend this wisely Sajan.'

'I shall, sahib.'

30

5

There is always a village which springs up near any rajah's palace or hunting lodge. The villagers are on hand to provide vegetables, meat and services required by the rajah at a moment's notice. A living is to be had by simply being available to rich and powerful men and their retinues. A rajah must be able to simply snap his fingers for his desires to be met.

Sergeant King knew where this village was located and, once he was off duty, walked to it alone. There he began asking questions of the local people, who were naturally suspicious of him. They answered him guardedly, saying they did not know such a one, that there was nobody in the district who went by that family name. King did not believe them, of course, for he knew that a family with that surname had lived in the area, not so many years ago, when King had been billeted there with his regiment.

Although Crossman did not know it, Sergeant King had been to India before, when he first had joined the army at sixteen. He was seventeen when he had been standing in this very square, in the centre of the village, marvelling at all he saw and heard. Major Lovelace knew the sergeant had been in India. So did Colonel Hawke. Neither had thought to inform Lieutenant Crossman, though there was nothing sinister in that omission. It was simply a matter of forgetting, since it was not greatly important. King had been a private in those days, his emotions swamped by his first visit to the orient, and his experiences in the subcontinent had overwhelmed his spirit. He loved it with all his being – and now he had returned with stripes on his arm, to conquer the land which had conquered him.

There had been a girl, of course. No memory of a new land is overwhelming unless love is involved, especially the first taste of love in an innocent youth during first blossom. India had awakened King's soul and love had opened his heart wide enough to take in the Himalayas. His spirit had expanded, his mind had realized what riches there were to be had, and he had thrilled to the whole world. His ambitions, his inner joy, his love of knowledge had soared to heights of which he had not previously dreamed.

There had been a dashing down, before everything became balanced again, but hope had never left him stranded.

Yet, now, in the village, those hopes were being crushed. No one could tell him where the girl was. They swore they had never heard of her or her family. He dragged his feet back to the hunting lodge, disappointment like a lump of lead in his breast. Would he ever pass this way again? And if he did, would they still deny him? He guessed what it was. The girl was probably married now, to one of her own kind. Some handsome local boy had stolen her heart and they were even now sitting down to a meal of chapattis and curried potatoes, laughing with each other. He would have to bear it, that was all. He would have to carry his cross.

6

That evening all three soldiers were invited to dine with the rajah.

'Today is a religious day – the festival of Rama Navami,' said the servant bearing the message, 'and my master would be pleased to entertain you on such an auspicious occasion.'

His master's name was Rajah Jaswant Singh. This rajah was a young man, not more than twenty years of age, with a flawless complexion and very white teeth. Gwilliams was suspicious of him because he used make-up around his eyes, but King told the corporal that was probably quite usual for young Indians with some wealth. Certainly it would seem from the trophies that decorated the walls he was no wilting flower. Crossman asked the rajah if he had shot all the tigers, blackbucks and gaurs himself.

'No, Lieutenant, my father shot some of them. But I am responsible for at least half of the beasts.'

'What do you use? Your hunting weapon?'

'I have some English guns – Purdeys.'

'Ah, I have a good friend, a major in the British army, who swears by Purdeys.'

The rajah drew deeply on a hookah, before replying, 'I too am very persuaded by them. Would you like to come hunting with me tomorrow morning? I should be pleased to let you try them.'

'Forgive me, sir, but I am unable to delay my journey. I thank you kindly for your offer and sincerely regret having to excuse myself. Perhaps, if I pass this way again . . .?'

'I understand, Lieutenant. There is a wind of unrest in the land. You should be where you are most needed.'

The rajah did not expand upon this and Crossman did not feel he could question him further. However, after a little thought, Jack decided it would not hurt to lose a morning. He might learn more if he accepted the rajah's offer.

'Your Highness,' he said, 'could I make a change of mind? On reflection I believe my schedule is not so tight as to prevent me from one morning's pleasure.'

'By all means,' cried the delighted rajah. 'Tomorrow it is then!'

The was another European guest of the rajah at their table. He was a big bluff bearded man with a North England accent. His box coat and trousers were made of heavy black cloth and there was a black broad-brimmed hat on the floor beside his seat. Beneath his coat he wore a grey shirt with a black-ribbon tie that hung loosely down inside his collar. There was a thick black leather belt around his waist and black boots on his feet. He looked a truly formidable man, in a depressing way.

John Stillwell, as he gave his name, told the soldiers he was a Methodist minister, though he quickly assured the rajah it was not his intention to convert the local people to his religion.

'I am what is known as a Primitive Methodist and am on my way to Delhi to offer my services to the Europeans who live in that city. May I ask what is thy persuasion, Lieutenant?'

Crossman divined correctly that the minister wanted to know what was his religious denomination. He replied that he was a Presbyterian when at home in Scotland. Sergeant King was not asked but offered the information that he was 'just ordinary church, myself'. Gwilliams, true to his wandering nature, had been every-thing from a 'Ebionite Baptist' to a 'Pharisee Pentecostalist' but at the moment was between 'denominations and sects of any kind'.

'Every man should have a Church,' admonished Stillwell, 'so I suggest you find one very soon, Corporal.'

At one point, King, who was sitting next to John Stillwell, leaned over and in a low voice asked what it was the rajah was smoking.

'I believe it is bhang, sir,' boomed the minister, in a very loud voice. He sniffed the air, drawing it in noisily through his nostrils as though he wished to suck the dust of ages from the room. 'Yes, that is what it is — bhang. It enlivens the mind for a short while, before the smoker becomes befuddled and over-placid. Would thee like some? I could ask our host to provide thee with another hubble-bubble. I'm sure he would oblige.'

34

'No, no,' mumbled an embarrassed Sergeant King, shrinking down into his cushions, 'please do not trouble.'

'I wouldn't mind trying it though,' the lieutenant said, surprising both the sergeant and the minister. 'Do you think the rajah has a second pipe?'

The rajah was delighted to have the officer join him.

After the meal, the rajah announced that he wished to provide his guests with some entertainment. He himself made his excuses and said he had to be elsewhere, but he adjured his guests to remain and enjoy 'the wonderful magicians'. Crossman felt enlivened and content, though he could see King was weary almost to the point of exhaustion. However, it would have been ill-mannered to leave early, so he did not give King permission to go. Instead, he lay back on the silk cushions still smoking the bhang, his mind full of fantastical scenes. A little later, through heavily hooded eyes, he saw the entertainers enter the room.

To the delight of Gwilliams the first act was a woman stripped to the waist. She straightened her neck and to the accompaniment of musicians on sitars and drums, eased a sword down her throat up to the hilt. Then she paraded around the room, while the minister explained that her lack of modesty was to show there was no deception with the blade.

'My grandpappy used to do a trick,' Gwilliams told the other two. 'Used to eat a whole eel in one go, cooked o' course – just tilted his head back and fed the eel down his throat. Then he'd straighten up, close his mouth, look you right in the eye, and draw the eel's backbone down through one of his nostrils.'

'That's disgusting,' said King. 'That's not even a trick.'

'Ain't it, though? You try it.'

A painted man, decorated with pictures of bulls, elephants, tigers and cobras, and hung with many-coloured ribbons, whirled like a dervish and took honey from a finely honed sword blade with his tongue as he did so. He did this trick several times, without once cutting himself.

Finally, a woman swallowed a piece of red cloth the size of a handkerchief and then slit her own side with a knife, before drawing the handkerchief from the open wound.

Once the magicians had finished, Gwilliams left for the quarters he and King shared. King suggested that it was time they all went to bed. The sergeant looked completely fatigued, his physical tiredness probably not helped by the heavy meal and the drink he had imbibed that evening. But there was a stubbornness about him. He was not happy at leaving Crossman smoking the bhang.

'You go,' said Crossman, pleasantly. 'I'll stay for a while.'

King said, sternly, 'That stuff isn't good for you.'

Crossman ignored him.

'Major Lovelace told me you were once addicted to laudanum.'

Crossman's eyes opened wide, despite the pleasantness of the bhang smoke, and he felt a rising irritation.

'Major Lovelace has no right to tell you such things.'

'He said to watch out for it, if there was no one senior to do so.'

'Did he now?' The irritation was flaring into anger. 'Well, I tell you what, Sergeant, you mind your own business, how's that?'

'You are my business, sir, when you're like this.'

'Like what, sir? Like what? You are an impertinent sergeant. An insubordinate NCO. I shall . . .' He suddenly lost the thread of his sentence and all interest in where it was leading.

'Sir?' King pleaded.

Crossman lifted heavily hooded eyes and stared into the middle distance as if he could see some vision there.

'Have you ever had a woman, King? Lovely creatures, women.'

The sergeant hesitated, then said, 'I fell for a church girl, once.'

'Is she waiting for you?'

'No, not her.'

Crossman sucked on his pipe, drawing the bhang smoke into his lungs gratefully.

'Was she *beautiful*?'

'When she smiled, she filled you with sunshine – she was a most beautiful woman, when she smiled.'

'So?'

'Well then, she so rarely smiled.'

'You did right not to ask her to wait, Sergeant. There's nothing so terrible as living with a dough-faced woman. They make your life . . .'

Jack tailed his sentence away as a huge wave of lethargy overcame him. Suddenly he could no longer keep his eyes open and King had to help him to his feet. The sergeant supported his officer back to his quarters, rolled him on to his bed, and then left. The lieutenant slept for about three hours, before waking with a start, and finding he could not back to sleep again for love nor money. Tangled with the muslin curtains of the four-poster, he still had his boots on. He also had a foul taste on his tongue which could only have come from the bhang.

He sighed and murmured to himself, 'How difficult it is not to indulge in these corrosive pleasures.'

Sajan was lying on his rush mat in the corner of the room, snoring softly, his hand still clutching the cord to the punkah.

Jack watched the boy's chest rising and falling for a long time, before he too finally dropped off to asleep again.

He was wakened about two hours later by a large dark figure who loomed over him and shook him. It was the methodist minister, who seemed inclined to talk. The man sat on the edge of his bed, while Crossman removed his boots and got himself a drink of water. He asked the minister to keep his voice down as there was a child asleep in the corner. John Stillwell raised his eyebrows but made an attempt to keep his tone low.

'I wonder, Lieutenant, if I could prevail upon thee to allow me to accompany thee northwards, as far as Jaipur? It is dangerous to travel alone in these times. Yesterday I was insulted by a crowd as I passed through a village. Several people spat at my feet. They were cowed when I roared at them, but still there is a little tension in the air.'

'To what do you attribute this tension?' asked Crossman, remembering the rajah's words about *a wind of unrest*.

'To my mind there are several causes,' said the minister, thoughtfully. 'The recent annexation of Oudh has not helped matters and there have long been complaints about interference in Indian rituals, such as *suttee*, which are naturally distasteful to civilized men such as you and I.'

'Ah, the burning of the dead man's widow.'

'Burning or live burial of the widow, yes. But I do not believe this is the time for aggressive evangelizing. Some of the customs here are not to our taste – in fact they are a direct affront to God – but we must wait our time. These rites have been several thousand years in the making and we attempt to obliterate them in a day. Too much Christian zeal at this moment will only enflame the natives and give them fuel for the fires of rebellion.'

Crossman did not really want the older man to join his party, which was a military mission, not a wandering tribe gathering lost souls on the way, but it would have been difficult to refuse him. If indeed anything happened – should John Stillwell be murdered by bandits or attacked by some wild beast and torn apart – some blame might be laid at the lieutenant's door. An Englishman was asking for protection on the road: what could he do but agree to the request and allow the minister to accompany them.

'We leave at noon,' warned Crossman, 'in the heat of the day.'

'Ah, yes – the Hot. It is our burden in this land. You have no sepoys with you?'

'No, what you have seen is all there is of us.'

The minister left Crossman in peace and the lieutenant once more climbed into his bed, this time he did it properly, after removing his uniform and other accoutrements.

Crossman passed the next day's tiger hunt in what he later realized was a kind of dazed stupor. The previous evening's debauch, lack of sleep, stomach upsets and a general malaise all served to send him inside himself. There were also the other agents of an Indian day: the hot sun, the stench of defecating elephants and camels, and the less obnoxious smell of horses. They were bothering him. Thus the activities going on around him were of less interest to him than his own lack of well-being.

The array of personnel required to corral and shoot a tiger was dazzling. Scores of matchlock men surrounded the rajah, presumably to protect him against attacks by big cats, assassinations and other royal hazards. Household soldiery, more handsomely armed and garbed than the matchlock men, stood in watchful groups nearby. There were several richly adorned elephants whose howdahs contained female admirers of the prince. These bristled with weaponry. Servants in magnificent livery, all the colours of the earth, carried tables laden with fruits, bread, sweetmeats, drink and other hunters' necessities. Several dozen coolies went back and forth, bearing all manner of equipment, including a small chased-brass cannon and a cauldron of fire swinging between two carrying poles.

The hunt assembles outside the local inn. Scarlet coats dazzle the peasantry who have shambled out to watch. The well-bred mounts of the huntsmen and huntswomen fret and chafe, ready to fly at the nearest gate or wall. A goblet of wine is passed from mouth to mouth: red liquid for those who prepare to shed red fluid. Then the Master of the Hunt leads off, over the ploughed fields, the hounds calling from afar.

It was all brilliant sunlight and deep shadow. A golden creature with black stripes needed nothing more than the light and shade in which to hide. In the distance, an army of beaters began to move their line into the forest. Gongs, cymbals, drums, trumpets, yells and bells: wildlife for miles around suddenly panicked and ran headlong through the trees and out towards the long elephant-high grasses fringing their world. The matchlock men shot these, randomly it seemed, allowing some to escape and blasting others. Several kinds of deer leapt past the guns, two large boars, many birds with magnificent plumage, strange agile cats, canines, a huge flowing river of smaller mammals, some with short bodies, others with long.

The horn sounded clear and cold as the bark of a fox in the sharp early morning. Huntsmen charged down the hedges and fences. A ploughboy at his duty was knocked aside by the mount of a careless rider, left to nurse a bruised shoulder in a shower of divots from flying hooves. 'Halloo! Halloo!' Elated riders thundered over the turf of a following meadow, franking the frosty ground with horseshoe prints.

At one point all the matchlock men formed an imperfect line and went down on one knee. They fired a single volley into the high grasses. One of them was too close and the flame that leapt from his musket's muzzle started a flashfire. This was quickly quenched by the water carriers with their jars. In the meantime the beaters came nearer and nearer. Despite his torpitude Crossman's heart began to pump faster. His eyes flicked back and forth along the forest pale. There was a great deal of noise now, not only from the beaters but also from the rajah's retinue. The excited prince took aim and fired one of his Purdeys into the wavering grass in front.

A rider took a fence too sharply. His horse broke at the knees on the far side and sent him hurtling through the air. He landed on his back knocking all the wind from his lungs. Other huntsmen were close behind, the hooves of their horses swinging dangerously close to his head. He remained there, the rest of the hunt dashing away into the bright clarity of the day, leaving him to stare up into the great vault of the sky.

The yell that followed the rajah's shot was human. One of the beaters staggered out of the grasses with a bleeding shoulder. He fell, ignored by everyone, at the feet of an elephant. Then a ripple went all along the the front of the spear-tipped fronds. Sunlight and shadow. The matchlock men let loose another volley, ragged this time. Several of them turned and ran away, fleeing an unseen

39

monster. The rajah fired his second Purdey, clearing a whole avenue through the foliage in his sights.

A flash of rufous fur, dancing between the trees. Hounds swarmed after it, skipping around roots, leaping small shrubs, their excitement bubbling forth. Blood was hot, blood was high, blood was coursing swiftly through the veins. The brassy note of the horn sounded again.

'There!' cried a voice amongst the hullabaloo. 'In those thorn bushes!'

'The rajah, dressed in an English shooting jacket and trousers, Italian boots and an Austrian hat with a cockade, stepped forward. Brilliance and shade. Crossman squinted, peering into the under-growth, into the dappled shadowy world below the thorn trees. Did something move? He was not sure. A horrible scream. A few minutes later a coolie was dragged by his heels from the vegetation, his body covered in blood. Mauled? Had claws raked those marks on his back? Were they teeth marks on his arm? More shouting at the far end of the line. The rajah fired long again, seemingly reluctant to vacate his present spot. Let the tiger come to *him*. A horse bolted, crashing through a tent-pavilion in the rear, scattering crockery and other utensils. Then that ripple again, along the front of the grasses. Sporadic fire from several weapons, but no signs of a tiger.

Down the hole went the fox, brush just escaping the jaws of the leading hound. The dogs gathered, yelping, some frantically digging with their paws. Gone to earth. Gone to earth. The huntsmen and huntswomen arrived, disappointed, staring at the bolt hole. Gone to earth, the bloody bugger. Couldn't stand and face the foe. Sodding coward. Reynard, deep down below, panting, heart almost bursting in his chest, wondering whether they would dig him out or go on for that vixen over the next hill.

It seemed it was all over. The tiger had fled, the bloody bugger, the cowardly sod. Bored elephants were turned by the mahouts to carry their human cargo back to the hunting lodge. Matchlock men began to move away. The rajah came over to Jack, stood at his side.

'Did you see her, Lieutenant?'

'I saw – no, no, I only saw movement under the trees – I think – but no tiger.'

'What a great pity!' A white-toothed smile. 'Perhaps next time? You have not even used one of my sporting guns.'

Crossman's own weapon, an Enfield, was still loaded ready to fire.

'We have already presumed too much on your generosity and hospitality, Your Highness.'

'Such a great pity. Never mind.' He stared towards the forest. 'I know her now. I shall have her, never fear.'

'I wish you good luck.'

'Thank you, Lieutenant.'

Crossman asked, 'How are the men who were hurt? There were two, I think. Are they all right?'

The rajah looked surprised, as if it had not occurred to him to wonder.

'Oh, all right, I expect.'

'Good.'

Late afternoon the party set off northwards again, heading vaguely towards Kota and the Chambal river. The going was indeed hot and dusty, the track not straight nor the surface good. The temperatures were growing daily, creeping steadily into the hundreds. Crossman ordered a halt at three and said they would rest in the shade of some thorn trees. There was a muddy waterhole nearby where the animals could drink, while the humans made do with their goatskin carriers.

Shortly after the halt, while Crossman was shaving, Ibhanan brought the boy to him.

'He was hiding under a blanket, sahib,' said Ibhanan. 'Shall I send him back?'

It was Sajan the punkah-wallah, who had stowed away in one of the camel carts.

'I won't go back,' came the defiant reply. 'I shall follow you for ever.'

Crossman shook his head at the boy. 'What am I to do with you? I must send you back to the rajah. You're his servant.'

'I don't wish to go back to the rajah,' replied the boy with a defiant curl to his lip. 'I wish to be a chain-man, like these others.'

Crossman wiped the soap from his chin with his good hand and looked at Ibhanan.

'How did the boy get into the cart?'

Ibhanan seemed to hesitate, then he obviously decided that Crossman was a man who preferred the truth at all times.

'He gave one of my men two annas to hide him.'

Crossman shook his head, wearily. 'He can't stay, of course.'

'Sahib, the rajah purchased this boy and is therefore his property. If you keep the boy you will be stealing from the rajah.' The older man paused before continuing. 'But, then again, the rajah has many

41

boys like this and will surely not miss one of them. And also, more importantly, it is not likely we shall be travelling this way again, and therefore will not have to face the rajah and answer his questions.'

John Stillwell, who understood Hindi, had been listening to this exchange. He now intervened.

'I think the child should go back to where he belongs. What if his father comes for him? Thou art bound for the borders of Chinese Tartary, where the child will never again see his family.'

'We are certainly *not* bound for China,' protested Crossman. Then he saw Sergeant King, hovering nearby. 'Have you been telling this man we are going to Tibet?'

King said quickly, 'We should keep the boy. Look at his skin! He has European blood in his veins.'

'An Anglo-Indian?' Stillwell said. 'I wouldn't have thought so. His pallor could be the result of a lack of sun.'

'Yes, yes, he must be,' insisted King. 'We can't send him back, sir, to that tyrant. We must keep him.'

Crossman said, 'There's no *must* about it, sergeant.'

The boy stemmed any further argument between the officer and his senior NCO by crying, 'My mother is dead. I am told my father was in the army of a nawab. I never saw him. I was raised by a woman who is married to a charcoal-maker, but she has five children already. She will have five more before too long and does not want me. I do not want to spend the rest of my life pulling on string, sahib. Please take me with you? I shall work until my hands fall from my arms. I shall work until my eyes drop out.'

Crossman studied the boy's troubled eyes. His concern was that the expedition was turning into a circus. Seeing the child's desperation, he wanted to dismiss the minister's fears and let Sajan stay with them. But what if all the boy said were not true? Perhaps he was a valuable hostage from a warring neighbour? All his practical instincts told him to send the boy back with one of the men. All his emotions reacted strongly against such a decision. What would Jane have done?

He sighed, knowing *exactly* what she would have done. Yet, she was a woman, governed by such things as kindness to strangers. He was an officer in the army and as such was expected to make hard brittle decisions.

Yet, as Ibhanan had said, they would probably never pass this way again, and if they did he could always protest that the boy was not

42

found until they were two days out. Deception, deception. But he could not bring himself to consign Sajan to a listless and apathetic life of pulling on a length of string. He could not save all the punkah-wallahs in India of course, but this one had touched his life.

When John Stillwell got the gist of what was happening he threw his hands up in horror.

'This is abduction, sir. We shall be held to account for it. The rajah or the boy's father will force a court martial.'

'Mine will be the sole responsibility, Minister. I am the officer commanding this expedition.'

'We shall all be tarred with the same brush.'

'The boy stays. That is my decision.'

John Stillwell seemed to gather in size and formidability, like a great black bear fluffing its fur coat.

'This is a very dangerous decision, Lieutenant.'

'You, sir,' said Crossman, 'are a guest of my expedition and have no voice here. If you wish to travel with us you may do so. Otherwise you may go it alone. But I will not have my authority questioned by civilian camp followers.'

'Dost thou mean to insult me, Lieutenant?' cried the minister. 'I have powerful friends.'

'Not as powerful as mine, sir. Now, no insult was intended. I simply tell you how it is. If you don't mind, I will finish my shaving. Gwilliams, my stump's hurting. Do you have another pot of that soothing balm?'

The corporal nodded. 'One pot of soothing balm, coming up, sir.'

'Thank you. Sergeant, you're dismissed. Ibhanan, get those two annas back and return them to the boy. The rest of you, be about your duties.'

They all wandered away, the minister looking very aggrieved.

Sajan's face was a picture which Crossman would never forget, even though inside he was mentally kicking himself. This was India, a place quite new to him. He should be erring on the side of caution all the time, getting the feel of the place before asserting himself. But no, he was rushing in like a fool, following his heart instead of using his head. The boy might not even turn out to be grateful in the end. In another week he might be homesick for the rajah's hunting lodge and be whining to be returned! It was all of a piece. Yet, he could feel Jane's smile on him, warming him like a pleasant English sun in

43

springtime. Let it be the only stupid decision he would make in India and he would settle for that.

'Here's the balm, sir,' said Gwilliams, coming up behind him as he stared at his half-shaved face in the mirror attached to the tent pole. 'Shall I rub it in for you? Why are you shaving yourself?'

The last sentence was delivered in an aggrieved tone.

Crossman glanced down at the raw stump where his hand used to be.

'No, it's very sore. I'll do it. Thank you, Corporal. And I'm just making sure I can still look after myself, even with one hand. I keep forgetting I've had one wing clipped. I was at the opera on one of my last nights in London and tried to applaud.'

Gwilliams peered at him through narrowed eyes. 'Is that a joke?'

'Not at all. It's true.'

'You're welcome, then. Damned if you ain't. Next time, I'll do the shavin' around here.'

Crossman was probably the most manicured officer on the road, travelling as he did with his own personal barber.

The road north continued to be difficult. They travelled during the cool hours, when they could. Sergeant King and Ibhanan spent some of the rest stops practising the dark arts of mapping the terrain. In spite of himself, Crossman became interested in their machinations. He admitted to himself that he was envious of their skill.

At the end of one day they were out on a windless plain disturbed only by dust swirls. After they had passed a hovel made of camel dung, its outer walls decorated with patterns much in the same way as an English cottage might be covered with pargeting, Crossman gave the order to make camp. Evening was coming on, but the light was still good. Sergeant King and Ibhanan had got their instruments out as usual. Swallowing his ignorance, the lieutenant approached the two men and requested a demonstration on triangulation.

'It's based on simple geometry,' explained King, the enthusiasm in his voice almost childlike. 'If you know the length of one side of a triangle, and two of the angles, you can discover the rest of the properties belonging to that triangle. See the peak of that hill over there? We make sightings on that from two ends of a line measured with our chains. We know the length of the base line, which is in this case is a thousand yards. Separate lines, drawn from the end, sighting points using the theodolite, will give us the angles. The intersection of the two lines on that peak ahead will close the triangle, revealing the third angle. Thus we can calculate the distance to that hilltop without ever going there,' he finished, triumphantly.

'That's it? You know the distance? That's all?'

'You sound a little disappointed, sir,' said King, sounding equally upset by his commanding officer's reaction. 'But consider this, once you have done this exercise you know the lengths of the other two sides of the triangle, even though you haven't physically measured them, and they can be used as base lines for further triangles. Isn't that a marvel? Thus only one base line need be physically measured for a whole region! Of course there are other measurements to be made – the determining of angular elevations of the stars and planets to establish latitude. We might do that with an octant or a sextant . . .' King paused. It was obvious that his lieutenant still remained unimpressed. He drew a deep breath and delivered his *coup de grâce*. 'Did you know, sir, that I could work out the exact distance from Earth to the moon, if I used two distant points on this planet as a base line?'

Crossman reacted at last. This was quite startling news: that a sergeant in the Engineers could make such calculations.

'Really?'

'It has been done, sir. Not by me, but I could do it, given the resources. I could reach up and touch, as it were, a heavenly body all the way out there in the blackness of the ether.'

Lieutenant Crossman stared out at the distant hill for a few moments, then said to King, 'May I use your theodolite?'

'Certainly,' said the sergeant, his enthusiasm rising again. 'Here is the telescopic sighting tube, these are the horizontal and vertical scales . . .' But Crossman had bent down and was looking through the telescope at the distant hills.

'What do you see, sir? Do you see the peak of which I spoke?'

'No,' replied Crossman, in measured tones, 'I see a band of marauders. Call the men to arms. We are about to be attacked.'

King looked bemused for a moment, then took the instrument and looked for himself. He focused on a dust cloud in the distance.

'Horsemen, waving swords!' he exclaimed.

'Just what I said, Sergeant. Rouse the camp, quickly.'

Within a few minutes they were ready to repel the oncoming bandits, which numbered around a dozen. Crossman had made his

45

men practise their defence against just such an attack, their last drill being only a day earlier. The two wagons were placed at the flanks, while Crossman, Gwilliams and King lay in the gap between them, a rise in the ground protecting their front. There was a single perambulator-wallah with them. He had been a sepoy in the Bombay army. This ex-soldier had his own Brown Bess.

Gwilliams and King were armed with Enfields. Crossman had his Tranter revolver. One or two of Ibhanan's chain-men had their own matchlocks. The others had been armed with tulwars which Crossman had purchased in Bombay. The chain-men remained behind the line of rifles, looking nervous and afraid. Sajan was further back, out of the line of fire, looking after the camels. John Stillwell, the minister, was standing with his bible just behind one of the wagons, reading verses aloud. In his left fist he held the black book. In his right, a long-barrelled pistol.

'*He arose,*' roared Stillwell, '*and smote the Philistines until his hand was weary, and his hand clave unto the sword: and the Lord wrought a great victory that day . . .*'

The attackers wore white cottons and blue turbans. They rode small but sturdy horses that hammered the hard earth with their hooves. Crossman had been warned about the 'blue turbans' by Lieutenant Fowler in Bombay. They were a robber band, originally a single family but now inflated with badmashes and dacoits which they had gathered on the way. They had begun their career in a part of Northern India known as Ali Moorads Territory: a long narrow rectangle of land that cut into Scinde. Clearly this was but a fragment of the band of raiders, there being not above twelve riders. Out there on the hot plains they made a hazy target.

Crossman glanced back to check that his own horses were hitched to the wheels behind the wagons. He was satisfied that they were secure. He then turned his attention to the oncoming attackers.

'You will not shoot until I give the order,' said Crossman in a firm and steady voice. 'Then you will fire at will. And before you make any comment, King, I have heard the joke above a dozen times.'

'I wasn't going to say anything,' protested the sergeant.

The horsemen came on, through the heat haze that rippled the air, making them a difficult target. Behind them was a huge molten sun, furnace red, resting gently on the edge of the Earth. At that moment a pack of wild dogs trotted across the ground between the two bands

46

of men, some glancing at men on horseback, some at men lying in wait. It was a surreal moment, touched with fire, in a seemingly tranquil evening. Then the dhole were gone, having slipped down into a dry riverbed, leaving the world to violence.

Crossman waited until the enemy were 300 yards away. There was no doubt they were being attacked. Swords were out and one or two wild shots had been fired from horseback, which fell in the dust yards ahead.

'Now!' he roared.

Three rifles blazed out. The matchlock men on the flanks also opened fire. One horse buckled at the knees in front, sending its rider hurtling through the air. A rider also fell sideways from his saddle, trailing his tulwar in the dirt.

'Shit!' growled Gwilliams, glaring at Sergeant King, 'can you at least load? You load and I'll damn well shoot.'

By that, Crossman guessed King had missed his target, while Gwilliams had hit his. Thus began a very efficient load-and-fire team, as King took the advice. As the riders got closer, Crossman began to use his revolver. He hit one man in the thigh and saw him veer away. Then the matchlock man to his left took a bandit out of the saddle. The marauders began to realize they were up against formidable fire power. Three of them split from the oncoming force and rode in a wide arc to get round behind the wagons. The rest of them leapt from their horses and lay down on the ground, firing their muskets. A chain-man was hit low in the face. He jumped up with a gargled yell and ran away, heading back towards where Sajan stood with the camels. A musket ball struck his upper arm and took it clean off at the shoulder joint. He rolled away, into the dust.

'Horses, Sergeant!' snapped Crossman.

The two men ran to their horses and mounted.

Crossman rammed his revolver in his belt and drew his sword.

King had left his Enfield with Gwilliams.

They rode out to meet the three riders who were charging the camp from the rear.

Crossman and King had line infantry officers' swords, not sabres, so they leaned forward into the charge. Their right arms were straight as fire pokers, their swords level with the ground. They let out yells to encourage each other. Three tribesmen came sweeping in, slashing the air with their tulwars, screaming oaths and insults. Crossman

47

took one man full in the breast, ducking to avoid the slash of the tulwar. His sword went right through the man's chest. The weight of the tribesman's body caused it to slide off the blade and drop down to the earth. The riderless horse charged on.

The point of King's sword went in a little higher, taking his man under the chin, spitting his neck.

The third bandit, this man left-handed, came up on Crossman's unarmed side. His sword-stroke threatened to split the lieutenant's head like a melon: would have done if Crossman had not parried the blow with his false hand. The tulwar struck oak, hacking away two wooden fingers from the palm. King had rallied himself by this time and rode up to run the man through the side, sending him to join the other in the dust. The first man King had struck was still in the saddle, but riding off into that red sun, holding his throat with one hand and his reins with the other.

Lieutenant and sergeant then turned their horses and galloped back to the camp. On seeing them, the remainder of the bandits remounted and rode off whence they had come. Indians and Europeans let rip with a cheer. Stillwell was kneeling by the wounded chain-man. When Crossman approached him Stillwell lifted his head and shook it.

'Dead,' he murmured. 'Gone where the heathen goes.'

7

Crossman had expected the boy Sajan to be a problem. He knew he had acted unwisely in allowing the child to stay with the expedition. Still the thing was done now. If he tried to send the rajah's young slave back, with one of the chain-men, there would be a riot in the camp. The child had ingratiated himself with most of the adults there. Chief amongst those who doted on the boy was Sergeant King. King seemed so taken with him, and, he had him by his side most of the day, teaching him all sorts of things, not the least of which was surveying. His affection for the child was so obvious Jack suspected the sergeant of ulterior motives. It came to the point where he had to speak to his senior NCO.

King was visibly shocked on being confronted. 'You accuse me of such a terrible crime?'

'I don't accuse you, I'm asking you outright – is that your interest in the child?'

'I – I don't know what to say, sir. This is – that is, I have no such intent. I *abhor* men who take boys to their beds.' A shudder went through the man, who seemed in a highly emotional state. 'You – you don't know everything, sir. In fact you know very little about men like me. I am *rightly* fond of the boy. Why should I not be? He's a bright child, full of interest and enthusiasm for surveying. I could teach him all I know.'

'Sergeant, if you're not telling me the truth, I shall certainly have you flogged, perhaps even worse.'

King blanched. 'I'm not concerned about a flogging, but I am

49

concerned that you think me so low a creature, sir. We've not known each other long, but I would have thought – well, there it is.' He sighed. 'All I can do is *assure* you that my intentions are not ignoble. Sajan is a good boy and I would personally kill any man who tried to corrupt him. I would tear them apart with my bare hands. You have no need to fear anything of that sort from me. Such men are worthless, black-hearted scum.'

King was dismissed and the sergeant left Crossman with more questions than answers. He believed the sergeant when he said he had no interest in boys in general, but there was something about his relationship with this one which was unusual. He decided to keep a close eye on matters. The child was in his care now that he had decided to keep him with the caravan. Sajan was his responsibility, under his protection. He would remain so until they came across a trustworthy third party, a group of nuns or some orphanage which had room for him.

Sajan was a problem, but not so great a problem as was the minister.

The methodist preacher insisted on rising at every dawn and bellowing out hymns while standing under the nearest tree. Sleep was impossible after the first light, but no amount of threatening or persuasion would deter the Reverend John Stillwell from this unhallowed practice. He stood like a rock in a pair of dirty long grey underpants and thundered on regardless, about all things bright and beautiful and creatures great and small. Everyone argued, *pleaded* with him, including some of the most obsequious of King's workers, but he would not budge. The Lord needed praising. The Almighty must be lauded. It was a minister's daily duty.

'It wouldn't be so bad,' complained King, 'if he had some kind of musical tone and could hold a note.'

'It's an affront to the human voice,' agreed Crossman. 'It grates on the nerves and makes the head jangle.'

'I could shoot him,' Gwilliams offered. 'I wouldn't mind doing that.'

But the lieutenant reluctantly drew the line at murder. It was a difficult decision to make, but Gwilliams was not given his wish. They had to put up with the minister and his foibles. If one of the chain-men or perambulator-wallahs took a knife to him Crossman told himself he would feel only partly responsible. The minister was trying the patience of everyone in the camp.

Crossman attempted to repair his wooden hand, but was left with an appendage that appeared to be making an obscene gesture. Gwilliams couldn't help laughing, every time he saw it. King kept his amusement more private.

'Damn it,' said the lieutenant, holding his fist up to the light, 'why couldn't he have severed the whole hand? It would've been easier to put back together again.'

'Sir, I suggest you call yourself fortunate,' replied King. 'It could have been your neck.'

Jack Crossman acknowledged this and decided to try fitting his iron hand, the invention that he and Tom had worked on.

8

Tom Hodges met Jack in the garden summerhouse which had been converted into a workshop. Here Crossman had been indulging his passion with inventions by making himself a mechanical hand to replace the one he had lost in the attack on the Redan. The strange claw-like contraption was held by a bench vice while Crossman made some adjustments to the 'fingers'. Tom came in with snow on his coat and Crossman looked through a window to see flakes falling.

'Maybe the snow will help to warm it up,' he said. 'What do you think, Tom?'

'It often seems to,' replied Tom, 'though I'm thinking it'll be more in the mind than in the fact of it.'

The formalities of the British weather out of the way, they began to discuss the grotesque iron claw in the vice. Crossman told Tom, not without some pride, that he had had to make his own nuts and bolts.

'There were none this small manufactured.'

But they needed more hands than one to tighten them.

'If you could just grip the bolt heads with this spanner, Tom, while I turn the nuts, I would appreciate the assistance.'

'Maybe, sir, it would be better round the other way. You take the bolt heads, while I tighten the nuts, me having the stronger arm.'

'Oh, and what makes you think that?'

'What, that I'm the stronger, sir? Oh, well, I've only been at manual work for all my life, that's all. Now you're going to say to me *when I was in the Crimea . . .*'

'No I'm not, Tom. I promised Betty I would henceforth keep my silence on that phrase.'

'Well, some-at like it, at any rate. Fact is, sir, I'm the labouring man here, and you're the army officer. I'm the one who turns nuts and if there's nobody else in the region, you're the one who holds the bolt heads. That's how the world works, an't it? Or have I missed my station, sir?'

'Tom, if you worked for anyone else you'd be given notice for impertinence.'

Tom smiled the rugged smile of an older man who felt he was dealing with a pubescent youth trying to assert himself.

'That's as maybe, sir, but then I work for the Kirks, and they've always been somewhat more lenient, as they say. Even your father, hard man though he was, could take more than your average gentleman by way of advice, when it came to matters of expert.'

'Yes, but that was before I made these nuts and bolts. I am no longer an apprentice, Tom. I have served my term.'

Tom raised his eyebrows so that they almost touched the rim of his cap.

'Ah,' said Crossman, 'you think that is for you to decide, being the man of trade, so to speak.'

The eyebrows came down to form part of a smile.

'I shall hold the bolt heads, then, and you shall turn the nuts,' Crossman finally agreed.

Later, they fitted the invention to the stump. The fingers were worked by a series of levers fitted to thin metal pipes. The pipes themselves went up to a unit which nestled in Crossman's armpit. This underarm device was a hollow rubber ball which, when pressure was applied by Crossman's upper arm against his chest, forced air down the tubes. The air pressure was converted to mechanical movement at a point near the elbow, forcing levers to open the metal fingers, or close them into a locked position.

If the fingers were in the locked position Crossman had to slip a catch on the back of the mechanical grab with his good right hand, but that was the only time assistance was required from anything else but the hollow rubber ball. It was a crude tool, this metal hand, but it seemed to work. Crossman gripped a sickle in that fist and wielded

53

it like a sword, easily severing the tops from several winter cabbages. Once it had locked it was the devil to get it unlocked however, if his real fingers were frozen cold.

'Just don't shake hands with this thing,' muttered Tom, making some minor adjustments, 'or you'll start a man's eyes from his head.'

'Thank you, Tom. I shall have to remember not to grip articles which might give under the pressure. Thin wine glasses, ladies' hats, small dogs, that sort of thing.'

'Especially small dogs.'

'Quite.'

Tom's genius came to the fore in fitting the device. It was Tom who invented the complex web of straps – the 'harness' as he called it – which enabled the metal appendage not only to be attached to the lieutenant's body, but to remain comfortable for many hours. Crossman had anticipated sores and sweat bands, but these did not arrive. There were of course marks, but nothing exceptional, nothing too serious. Crossman was really pleased with the hand. He told himself he might even get rid of the nickname 'Fancy Jack' now that he had this machine fitted to his wrist.

'Iron-hand, that's what I shall be know as in future,' he muttered. 'Iron-hand, or Iron-fist. More fitting for a married man than Fancy Jack, which smacks of the *beau monde*.'

That evening Crossman was burning the midnight oil. He was studying the languages of Hindi and Pashto, with a little Urdu 'for dessert'. It was something that came to him easily, learning foreign tongues. Not many things did. He found it strange that he enjoyed such study, because he was not particularly proficient in the structure and grammar of the English language and had no desire to write any kind of book, or even read one unless it be instructive in some way. Figures were closer to his heart than letters: mathematical problems came easier than essays. Yet he had this power to unravel and retain the puzzles and complexities of an alien language. This was a mystery to him. He could only deduce that learning languages was akin to calculating. That seemed to him the only answer.

The following morning a letter arrived for him from Jane. She told him first how much she missed him and that she had to see him one more time before he left for India, if that was possible. Then she went on to tell him the family news. Her father's condition remained stable but his general health was still a cause for much concern.

Although he was appreciative of her presence it seemed it was *expected* of her to be there, at his side, even though she now had responsibilities elsewhere. Fathers like Jane's did not let go of their daughters easily. While Mulinder liked his son-in-law, Jack was a newcomer to the family and could not possibly have precedence over someone like a father, who had been the main male figure in Jane's life from as far back as the cradle. That was Mr Mulinder's opinion for the present and it would remain so for a long time to come.

9

It is difficult to do things in private when men are thrown together in a camp. There are eyes everywhere. There is always *someone* at your elbow, no matter how much space is available. A few men do not mind it at all, most find it at some time an irksome aspect of army life. To escape the myriad body sounds, from fart to belch; the stink of armpits, bad breath, fetid socks; the inane incessant moaning of the complainer; these and all the other aspects of army life: this is a forlorn dream in a camp. Jack Crossman would have liked a very private room to fit his equipment, but in fact he had to do it out in the open, to avoid catching the canvas of his tent and damaging it with the metal parts of his aparatus.

Thus he stood in his undershirt, struggling to get the thing over his shoulder, with its wires and metal strips, padding and more chunky metal parts, while others pretended not to watch at first. Yet as the operation progressed and their leader got into more and more difficulties, Asian and European alike stopped what they were doing to turn and stare. The Indians were wide-eyed with curiosity at this machine the British officer was trying to strap to himself. They shook their heads at each other and whispered, asking if their neighbour knew what was going on. Is it a weapon? they asked one another. Is it some form of self-punishment? What is it?

Finally Crossman yelled, 'Well *help* me Gwilliams! And what the hell are you lot gawking at? Get back to your duties. Have you nothing better to do than watch a man dress himself? Away with you.'

The watchers scuttled this way and that, looking for something on which to place their idle hands, but not failing to continue to stare from beneath an arm or from around the edge of a tent.

'Stand still, dammit sir, I'm doing my best here.'

Gwilliams finally got his officer into the harness and tightened the straps. Crossman tested his machine. It clacked and clicked in the correct places, like a mechanical lobster on the end of his arm. The Asians were bug-eyed now. The camp dog, startled by the demonstration, ran away and hid under a blanket. The lieutenant thanked his aide and now felt more than a little pleased with himself. But his pleasure was short-lived. The sun heated the metal claw until it burned into his stump. There had been no thought of the heat and cold when it was being made. The temperature had not been taken into account. Now, if he accidentally touched the artificial hand on some unprotected part of his body, it seared the flesh. He decided, in the end, to go without either wood or metal, and to hell with the ungentlemanly image. He pinned the bottom of his sleeve to itself and left it at that.

My Dearest Darling, he wrote that night, *I am a comedy act for my men, who think me quite the biggest fool they have met in many a year . . .*

The caravan continued its northward trek, into the heart of Rajputana. They went through valleys littered with babul trees, covered in long wicked thorns and wound about by tumbo creepers. The game in these valleys was wide and varied. Sambar deer let out high, trumpet-sounding calls when approached. Herds of chinkara were flushed into the clear on hearing them coming and chital deer, sleek and handsome, shot out into open meadows. Gwilliams found a rock python with a yet undigested mammal in its gut, sunning itself in its bloated condition, not a care in the world except man. Once, they glimpsed a female panther with two cubs, wandering out of the long grass to claw at the trunk of a tree, her interest in humans nil.

The minister, John Stillwell, continued to be a nuisance.

Stillwell was inclined to burst in on Crossman in his tent without announcing himself first and without waiting to be asked to enter. On one occasion Jack was having his spine walked by his bone manipulator, Gwilliams. The officer was lying stripped to the waist, face down, on the hard floor of his tent, trying to ignore the ants which trotted happily over his sweaty torso, while the corporal stepped up and down his back, using hard horny feet to massage the

57

lieutenant's spine, when Stillwell suddenly threw back the flap and entered the space within.

'Lieutenant,' began the minister, 'I wonder . . .' The intruder stopped in mid-sentence and stared. Then he said, 'I do beg thy pardon,' and left very quickly, probably convinced he had just interrupted one of those pagan rites which should never be witnessed by a man of God.

Gwilliams roared with laughter and would have jumped in the air in glee if he had not still been standing on his commanding officer's back.

Following this incident Stillwell showed he was capable of exhibiting his own eccentricities, unbecoming of a Victorian gentleman.

One evening Jack was enjoying the last shades of day, sitting on a knoll and viewing a glorious sunset such as had never touched a British sky. It was so vast, and of such colours – red, black, turquoise, blue, yellow, pink, mauve, purple – that it filled his heart with unfathomable yearnings. Such beauty, such magnificence, was only possible in tropical skies.

While Jack was sitting there, he became aware of a presence. Stillwell had joined him, sitting down next to him. Yet Crossman saw that the minister was completely naked except for his shoes and hat. Crossman was no prude but he was concerned about the Asians, who were prim about showing genitalia. They did not even take off their loincloths to wash. They would surely be upset by the sight of this hippopotamus walking around nude.

'Sir, you have no clothes on. You look ridiculous.'

'The human form is divine, Lieutenant,' grunted Stillwell, engrossed in the sunset. 'God made it in his own image and I'm sure thee do not mean to insult the Lord. I find it very cooling to shed my attire in the early evening. I say, look at that cloud! Does it not remind thee of an elephant?' The minister pointed. 'And how mellow are those hues. God's hand sir, has been liberal with the paintbrush this evening. The Almighty has dipped into the palette of heaven and produced a masterpiece.'

'And you smell,' said Crossman. 'Quite offensively.'

'My embrocation, Lieutenant. It's quite innocuous, I assure thee. It has buffalo wax in it, which is probably the odour you refer to. I need to smear myself once every three days, or my skin produces a rash between my legs and under my arms, not to mention between my fingers and toes. The creases of the body, sir, need to be attended. A Chinese gentleman in Bombay sold me the grease, which works very well. If ever thee need some, thee only have to ask. I shall be happy to let thee dip into the jar.' Stillwell then stood up and said with some dignity. 'However, I can see my presence disturbs thee, Lieutenant. I shall take my body elsewhere.'

The minister began to step out, walking into the darkness that was sweeping in rapidly. Crossman was suddenly concerned that Stillwell would get lost, or be bitten by something dangerous. He warned the minister to stay close to the camp and advised him to take a weapon.

Stillwell held up his right hand, in which he grasped a black book.

'I have my weapon, sir, and God help those against whom it is used. They will have to face the Thunder of the Captains, and the Shouting. The able Job will assist me in smiting my enemies. Good evening, sir.'

With that, the minister strode out. Much to Crossman's surprise, he returned later, unharmed but complaining of insect bites.

'The balm attracts them,' he explained to Gwilliams as he stood gesturing, his white body stark in the firelight, 'and I have no answer to them. I now have more spots than a stippled trout. More insect marks than the freckles on the sergeant's face. May they be damned, Corporal, for their unwanted attentions. They are the devil's creatures, sir, not the Lord's. They have been manufactured in hell and released to give us but a taste of its eternal tortures. They are demons in miniature. I abhor them.'

When Crossman neared Jaipur he sent an Indian runner ahead to request permission to enter the city. Later, he received word back from the Chandra Mahal, the Moon Palace where Maharajah Ram Singh II was in residence. He was welcome and was to present himself to the maharajah on arrival in the city. This was a daunting prospect. The ruler was a powerful man: the monarch of a great state. If Crossman did or said anything at which offence might be taken he would be in serious trouble. Ibhanan had said that Rajputana had never been conquered – not by the Mughals nor any who followed – and the Rajputs were a proud warrior race. Crossman was still not totally au fait with the customs and manners of the country and it would be easy to make a blunder.

'Sergeant King will accompany me,' he told Gwilliams, 'while you remain with Ibhanan and the other men.'

'Oh, I savvy. I'm not good enough to meet this maharajah fellah, bein' as I'm a rough man from the Americas.'

Crossman sighed. 'That's not it at all. I need someone back here I can trust. The sergeant won't meet the ruler either. He'll go as far the palace gates with me as my escort. I'm the only one who's going to be presented to the maharajah. Now, Corporal, will you help me with my uniform? I must go in all my gold braid with my best sword. Is the white lace still white, we ask? What about the shako badge? Are the gilt and silver stars still gleaming? If they aren't, we must set to and polish them up a little, so they shine like real stars. And we must brush that red coat till it looks like new . . .'

'Don't panic,' muttered Gwilliams, beginning to unpack the precious uniform, 'you'll look fine and dandy for the maharajah. Now, you'll need to take a gift. They expect it, these people. What about the jewelled dagger we found on that bandito we kilt, back there on the trail? The one Ibhanan calls a tiger dagger, with the handle shaped like a haitch, which you grip by the crossbar.'

'I was hoping to take that home.'

'Ain't nothin' else here worth a damn.'

'You're right, there isn't. Now, will I fit into this thing any better now? It was a little tight for me last time I tried it on, after several Christmas plum puddings and roast beef lunches . . .'

Indeed, he found he fitted into the uniform with ease, having lost some considerable weight since arriving in India.

The middle-aged maharajah was a good English speaker. He turned out to be almost ordinary and while Crossman drank tea and ate sweetmeats with him, the ruler professed to be very fond of 'English jokes'. He asked Crossman to tell him some. There is nothing so difficult as having to tell jokes on demand: even natural comics have been known to dry up at such a request. The lieutenant had to dredge his mind for humorous tales heard in the mess in Bombay. His delivery was not good, his punch lines faltered, but still he managed to amuse the great ruler with his stories. The maharajah then asked him what was the symbol on his cap badge. Was it the many-stringed bow of an English warrior, who could fire as many arrows as the number of strings at one release?

Crossman told him gravely that it was an Irish harp and then

60

suddenly realized that the 'warrior's bow' had been a maharajah's English joke, and rather too late the lieutenant roared with false mirth.

The subject then switched quickly to mapmaking. Ram Singh was curious about Crossman's hand. Where did he lose it and how did it affect his mapmaking work? He told the maharajah that his hand still resided on the Crimean peninsula and that he managed as best he could without it. His Highness's questions then became more searching, requiring a depth of knowledge the lieutenant did not have. Crossman now had a flutter of panic and wished he had paid more attention to his sergeant's chattering, for he was being asked questions that he should know, if he were a surveyor.

'Do you prefer the octant or the sextant, Lieutenant? Which is the most accurate for your purposes of producing maps?'

'Er, the sextant, Your Highness.'

'This is the better instrument of the two?'

'Oh, oh yes, by far. But of course we look mostly to the theodolite for our calculations, with its spyglass, compass and spirit level.' Crossman felt pleased with himself. He had been looking at just that instrument not four hours previously. 'That's the device we rely on most when producing our maps.'

'But the theodolite, my dear Lieutenant, is used for non-astronomical angle measurements, while the sextant and octant – and of course the old quadrant, quite an ancient device now . . .' he laughed and Crossman laughed hollowly along with him '. . . are for determining the angular elevations of heavenly bodies.'

Crossman took immediate refuge in flattering generalizations.

'Your knowledge, Your Highness, is boundless.'

'Not *boundless*, Lieutenant, but I not an ignorant man on this subject. My ancestors were astronomers. Have you seen our observatory?'

Crossman said he had not, but he would try to find the opportunity, and immediately put the idea out of his mind. He had visions of the observatory as a sort of inflated gazebo with astrological designs all over its facade. There were many, many beautiful buildings in India, some of which took the breath away, but he had not time to see them all. He hoped his lack of interest had not shown on his face and strove to recover ground.

They continued drinking tea and eating cakes, during which the maharajah probed Crossman on his journey. The lieutenant did not mention the attack by the blue-turbaned tribesmen, but told the ruler more or less everything else that had happened. Ram Singh sighed and said it must be nice to be an 'ordinary man' for when he himself travelled it could not be without a great deal of elephants, all weighed down by howdahs and decorated with jewelled blankets and other trappings. The ruler also had the misfortune to have to take with him 'almost an army', including infantry, cavalry and baggage train.

'Unlike you, Lieutenant, who can ride with the wind, just yourself and a small contingent of happy men – more cake, sir? There is plenty.'

'Thank you,' murmured Crossman, finding the cake rather dense and overfull of fruit and nuts. 'It is delicious.'

The maharajah looked at his guest masticating stolidly on the rich confectionery.

'This cake is like the British army, is it not?' said the ruler with a twinkle in his eyes. 'Too many kernels.'

Here Crossman let out a genuine bellow of laughter, which delighted Ram Singh, who felt he had scored well with his English joke.

They talked further, the maharajah asking politely how the lieutenant had lost his hand. Was it in an heroic action? Of course, it must have been. Did it impede his duties much? There had been several British heroes with missing limbs, of course. Admirals such as Horatio Nelson. Generals such as Lord Raglan. The lieutenant was in good company.

Crossman, for his part, probed as well as he could without appearing to, gathering as much information as possible while avoiding alarming or insulting his host. His time in the Crimea, his visits amongst the enemy in Sebastopol, had given him practice at gathering tidbits of information without appearing to be searching. Certainly the maharajah did not seem to suspect anything untoward and he must have found Crossman amusing, or interesting, or even both. The local ruler was quite taken with his gift of the tiger dagger, because he later paraded some twenty tall Rajput warriors before Crossman and told him to choose one as his bodyguard and companion for the length of his time in India.

'While you are here mapping in this vast land, there will be many who will try to kill you, Lieutenant. There are savage tribes to the north. There are raiders and assassins to the west. You will need a good man to protect your back. These are my personal guard. I call them "the Immortals". All of them speak reasonable English, apart from one or two of our own languages. I insist upon it. One of them also speaks French. Please choose one man as your own personal protector and guardian . . .'

Crossman felt he should politely reject this offer, but when he hinted such the maharajah's face hardened. Could he believe his ears? The British officer was about to refuse to accept his gift? Crossman quickly retracted his remark, asked to be forgiven if it was misinterpreted, and proclaimed his gratitude and thanks for the maharajah's generosity.

Crossman walked along the line, studying the guards. They were all dressed in the maharajah's livery, with red turbans, loose shirts overworn by waistcoats with embroidered gold centripetals, and pantaloons. Each man wore a sword at his hip. The men inside the clothes came in many shapes and sizes. He stopped at a barrel-chested fellow who looked as if he could mince a bear with his hands. But the man's eyes were too close to his nose and altogether rather too vacant. Then there was the small fierce-looking fellow with the tight mouth. He too was studied intently, but eventually rejected for his height.

Finally, Crossman stopped at a tall lean young man who looked as if he could be the maharajah's son. The Rajput flicked his head once or twice, ever so slightly. Crossman completely missed the implications of this gesture, thinking the young man had some sort of twitch. Crossman peered into the man's eyes, finding intelligence there. He was not over-muscled, but in the lieutenant's view this was to his advantage, for large men were often slow and inclined to clumsiness. The Rajput appeared to have suppleness about him: better the cobra than the buffalo, in his opinion.

'This one,' he said. 'He looks a very fine fighter.'

The expression on the warrior's face became one of dull resignation.

'This man? Ishwar Raktambar. He is one of my best soldiers,' confirmed the maharajah. 'He is a killer of men, destroyer of armies, annihilator of barbarous hordes. I give him to you with infinite sadness and regret, he being the best of my soldiers. He will be a courageous, loyal, devoted servant of yourself. He will root out treachery and meet frontal attack without fear or concern for his own life. Henceforth this man will be your shadow and strive to keep you from harm.'

Once out of earshot of the maharajah, however, Ishwar Raktambar seemed a very reluctant bodyguard.

'Why did you choose me?' he grumbled. 'I do not wish to be your protector. Choose someone else. You think I will be like the big Pathan that is John Nicholson's faithful servant? I will not. I will be no good servant to you. Leave me here, take someone else with you.'

'All right, I'll send a message to the maharajah, telling him you don't wish to accompany me.'

The young man's eyes widened and revealed fear.

'No – no. We must say nothing to the maharajah.'

'Then I haven't any choice but to take you with me.'

'I shall be very miserable. I was about to take a wife. You have stolen my bride from me. I can never forgive you for this.'

Crossman was exasperated. 'Look, I had no idea you were to be married, I certainly did not ask the maharajah to offer you as a bodyguard and as for my back, I can watch it myself, thank you very much.'

The lieutenant himself would have been only too pleased to reject the tall Rajput. The obvious had occurred to him: that the maharajah was suspicious of his seemingly innocuous questions. These people, Crossman reminded himself, were past-masters at intrigue. They had had centuries of plotting and conspiring against each other and against their enemies. It was entirely possible that this Ishwar Raktambar was the maharajah's spy, put into Crossman's camp for the sole purpose of reporting back to the ruler. Jack did not think for a minute that he had fooled the prince when he had been questioned about mapping. No, Raktambar had been planted in the enemy camp to keep an eye on this travelling gatherer.

Both men, fuming within themselves, left the palace and made their way to the lodgings where Crossman had left his men. This was a wayhouse on the edge of Jaipur, near to Amber. The old fort could be seen from one of the windows, its strength and grandeur undiminished by time. When they arrived at the house, Crossman introduced the Rajput to Ibhanan, King and Gwilliams, but Raktambar simply threw up his arms and removed himself from their sight, his head high in the air.

'What's with him?' asked Gwilliams. 'Got a spider up his nose?'

'No,' explained Crossman, 'the maharajah's ordered him to be my bodyguard. He doesn't like it. In fact he says he's due to be married and now his plans have been shattered by this order.'

Gwilliams snorted. 'He'll thank us later, for saving his life.'

'I might remind you, Corporal, that I'm happily married myself.'

'Only just.'

'What's that supposed to mean?'

'It means, sir, that it ain't been given enough time to be otherwise but happy. It ain't been given but a few months to settle into what's real. Give it five years. Give it ten. If it's still good after ten years, then I'll grant you happy. So soon after you've been wed, it don't mean a damn.'

Crossman decided to ignore this cynical philosophy, but when alone in the room he began to project. What would marriage be like in ten years' time? He would have plenty of time to reflect on this curiosity over the next few months, perhaps – a horrible thought – the next few years. When would he see Jane again? Certainly he couldn't send for her while he was trundling over a subcontinent with a parcel of Asians and Europeans. She wouldn't have minded it. She might even revel in it. But her presence would interfere with his work. He couldn't watch over a wife and spy.

A terrible thought came to him. It was farfetched, but not entirely beyond the realms of possibility that it would be ten years before he would see her next. What? No, that was ridiculous. He would see her within the year, he hoped. Settle her somewhere in some safe haven where the Queen's army was strong and visit her whenever possible. Yes, that was what would happen, provided nothing untoward happened to stop it.

He missed her more than he imagined he would. He missed her laughter, her insights, the way she looked at things differently from him and found the words to change his own views. He missed her warm body next to his own at night and he *craved* their lovemaking still, though he hoped the feeling would dull over time. It surely could not remain at such an intensity or he would go mad? In quiet moments he sat and tried to imagine her face, the way it lit up with a smile, and the way her eyes flashed anger when she was upset, and it put him out of sorts when he could not hold those pictures of her in his mind. How frail was his imagination! Were all minds like his, with imperfect recall? The essence of Jane was there, but the pictures warped and faded, leaving him feeling bereft and guilty. Surely a man

65

in love, so soon after his wedding, should have a better grasp on his own brain? Was the mind so faithless? Were the thoughts so ephemeral? Her fleeting images made him enraged with himself, for their inconstancy.

Sergeant King, however, was not interested in Rajputs nor the solemn statehood of marriage. While Crossman had been visiting and having tea with the local monarch he had heard from Ibhanan that here, in this very city, was an astronomer's park, a place of giant instruments to tell the time, to track the stars, and to gauge direction by the use of heavenly bodies. At his insistence Ibhanan had taken him there, where he had met the royal astronomer from the court of Ram Singh. Having seen this miracle of science, he came rushing into Crossman's room, uninvited, to blurt out his news.

'There are instruments to determine celestial latitude and longitude to a precise accuracy,' said King, excitedly. 'Others reveal the zenith and altitude of the sun. There's a sundial with a gnomon ninety feet tall! I took my chronometer with me and the comparison's astonishing. The Samrat Yantra as it's called can keep time to within two seconds of my timepiece. *Two seconds*! These are the kings of astronomical instruments. I've just returned from the park. You should see it. Giant astrolabes with maps of the night heavens etched into their metal faces. They're said to be made of seven alloys so they remain unaffected by changes in temperature. You must come with me now, sir, and visit it before it gets dark. You might not get another chance.'

Crossman smiled. 'I can see you're enthralled, Sergeant, but does it really call for such enthusiasm?'

'It's a marvellous wonder,' said King. 'This park will make your mouth water. We've nothing like it in England. I don't suppose there's another to rival it anywhere. These instruments are magnificent. They soar! There're some eighteen superb devices. Will you come?'

10

Outside in the London street, the snow was thick upon the cobble-stones. Crossman was reading a letter from Jane, with mixed emotions washing through him, when Betty came to tell him that there was a soldier at the door.

'Not an officer and gentleman, sir, but a common soldier.'

Gwilliams? thought Crossman.

'Show him in, Betty. I'll see him in the parlour.'

'Very good, sir.'

Crossman finished his chocolate drink then went to see what Gwilliams could possibly want at this time of the day. In the hallway he was surprised to see a large, long crate made of wood. It was sturdily made and it looked heavy. Crossman passed the crate with a puzzled frown and entered the parlour.

A sergeant, forage cap in hand, stood on the rug near the fire. He immediately put his cap on, came to attention and saluted.

'That's all right, Sergeant,' said Crossman. 'You may remove the headgear. Mrs Hodges does not like hats worn in the house.'

'Thank you, sir.'

The voice had deep timbre. In fact everything about the man looked sturdy. He was square-faced with a solid-looking jaw, his shoulders were broad, his chest deep and his limbs stocky. A strong-looking man, if a good deal shorter than Crossman. The hair was a reddish-chestnut colour and the eyes a muddy brown, the bridge of the nose and cheeks sprayed with a constellation of freckles. Fingers that gripped the cap were short and square-ended. He stood at his full height, straight as an iron poker, and returned Crossman's stare without a blink. Here was a confident man, thought Crossman, if a little impertinent in his stance before an officer.

'Is that your crate in the hallway, Sergeant?'

'Yes sir, it is.'

'Name?'

'Sergeant Farrier King, sir, of the Engineers.'

So this was the mapmaker he had been led to expect.

'Farrier? That's an unusual Christian name.'

'It's my father's trade, sir. He never wanted for me to be a smithy like him, but he wished for me to remember my origins.'

'I see. Well, Sergeant, I'm at a bit of a loss. I know we sail together soon, but why are you here, at my house?'

'It's the box, sir.'

'And just what is that thing doing in my hallway?'

'I'm sorry for that, but it contains valuable instruments. It would hurt the army's purse for it to be stolen, so I couldn't leave it on the steps. I was wondering, sir, if you would keep it here until we leave for Southampton? I shall no doubt find myself lodgings, but I would rather have it safe with someone I believe I can trust.'

'Oh, you believe you can trust me, do you?'

'Sorry for how it sounds, sir, but the contents of the case are very valuable.'

'So you said.'

They stood there, the two of them, still taking one another in. Crossman felt the sergeant had an enormous cheek, but then he saw the man's dilemma. If the 'valuable instruments' were lost it might delay their departure and Crossman wanted none of that. Such a crate would be a temptation to bootboys and scullery maids at inns. They would not necessarily break into it themselves but they were often loose-tongued, for a fee, and there were always rapscallions in alehouses who would steal its contents without a second thought. Crossman made a sudden decision, one that surprised him as much as it did his visitor.

'I think you should stay here too, Sergeant, until we leave.' Unfortunately he couldn't resist tacking on one of those patronizing comments which often came out of the mouths of gentlemen when they were dealing with the lower classes. 'You can hold a candlelight vigil over your valuable instruments to make sure nothing goes missing.'

'I'd rather not stay, sir.'

Crossman was taken aback.

'Why not? Is the house not to your liking?'

There was a firm and stubborn look to the jaw.

'It's in the way you offer, if you don't mind me saying so.' There was no *sir* on the end of this sentence. He was gripping his forage cap with all ten digits. 'I'm an educated man. Just Church School in the first instance, but trained later in surveying. I don't like to be spoke down to and since we're here in a private way, if you don't mind, I'd like to get it straight. It seems I must serve under you for some time to come, in close company. It won't do either of us any good if I make out I'm willing to be trod on. I am the NCO and you the commissioned officer, and as such I must respect and obey you, but I won't be laughed at as a silly man.'

God, thought Crossman, the fool was too sensitive by half.

'I did not call you silly, Sergeant.'

'There was an implication, sir.'

'Well, I'm sorry for it.' He now remembered that he had been a sergeant himself not so very long ago and how he had hated those lisping lieutenants who mocked him with the same sort of condescending remarks. 'You're right, Sergeant,' he admitted, 'I was being supercilious. That's not very commendable. Now, I shall ask you again, would you prefer to stay here or find lodgings? It would give us an opportunity to get to know each before we ship out.'

The sergeant was quiet for a while and then he said, 'If it's all the same to you, sir, I shall find lodgings.'

Crossman found himself irritated. 'Very well. You might try the Cock Inn. I'll give you the address. You'll find Corporal Gwilliams there. He's my corporal and will be travelling with us. He seems to find the place comfortable enough.'

'Thank you, sir, and my instruments can stay here?'

'Yes. Look, Sergeant, I haven't offered you any refreshment. Would you like a drink of some kind? You must be weary from travelling. I don't have any ale in the house . . .'

'I don't drink beer, sir, but a cup of coffee would quench the thirst.'

'I shall ask my housekeeper to make you one. In the meantime, please sit down.'

Crossman left the room, still annoyed by the sergeant's refusal of his offer to stay at the house. Was the man going to be on his high horse the whole time? What more could Crossman do but apologize for the remark. All right, he was trying to be clever at another man's expense, but surely it was a forgivable offence? King was acting as if he had just suffered the grossest of indignities.

They sat down a little later and drank coffee at the kitchen table together. King was again being rather starchy with him and Crossman had to guess why.

'I rather like a kitchen, don't you, King?' he said, looking round. 'I always say it's the warmest room in the house, don't I, Betty?' His housekeeper turned and dutifully nodded. 'That's why I eat most of my meals out here, though Mrs Hodges disapproves.'

'I do indeed, sir. It's not a fit place for a gentleman.'

Sergeant Farrier King did indeed seem to relax after this disclosure and Crossman felt he was right in thinking that King was disgruntled with being consigned to the kitchen. The sergeant no doubt thought he was there because his commanding officer wanted to keep him from soiling the dining room. Many officers might have acted that way.

'So what *is* in that crate of yours, or is it a surveyor's secret?'

King took a sip of his coffee before answering.

'No secret, sir. A theodolite, sextant, boning device, chronometers, a chain measure made by Ramsden. That sort of thing.'

Some of those names were gobbledegook to Crossman, but he wasn't going to say so.

'Chronometers? In the plural? I mean, why several.'

'Only two. In case one gets damaged. It's always good to have a spare. Would you like to have a look?'

Jack said he would and they went into the hallway. There King opened the lid of the crate and began naming the instruments. Crossman took all this in, but pointed to one device in particular and asked what it was.

'That black monster there, the thing that looks like a tangled iron grate?'

'That's the theodolite, sir, made by Troughton and Simms. It's for measuring vertical and horizontal angles.'

'But the size of it! Must weigh a ton.'

'Three hundred and twenty-nine pounds. Hardly a ton, sir. It is, as you say, constructed mostly from iron.' King placed a fond proprietorial hand on the large cumbersome-looking instrument. 'This is only a twelve-inch theodolite and not as accurate as one of the larger ones. The thirty-six-inch theodolite Mr Everest used is called the Great Theodolite and weighs almost half-a-ton. He carried it on an ox-cart thousand of miles around India.'

They were both quiet with one another for a few minutes. Then they went back into the kitchen. Mrs Hodges poured another coffee into King's cup without him asking, after which she went to the stove and began peeling potatoes. Crossman broke the ensuing silence.

'A sextant, eh?'

'For my astronomical observations, sir.'

'You need the stars to draw a map of the Earth? Is this a celestial map, or a mundane one?'

King smiled indulgently and was almost in danger of being patronizing himself.

'You have to pinpoint your position on the ground. The map would not be accurate without you do that. In order to do it you need to take an angular altitude of stars to determine latitude, while timing the observations with a chronometer. Accuracy is the key word, sir. One also needs to know the elevation above sea level, and the . . .'

'Whoa!' said Crossman, holding up his hand. 'A little at a time, if you please, Sergeant. That's enough for one evening. I would like to hear more sometime though. When we have time enough to wile away. You and I have something in common. A shared enthusiasm, by your tone. You might not know, indeed you don't, but my pastime interest is inventions. I have a close relationship with machines.'

The lieutenant leaned his chair back.

'Best of all I like devices such as those you mention. Glass and brass instruments. Clocks and watches, and locks. Those precision-made delicate machines are my forte. Secret levers, wheels within wheels, ratchets, levers, escapements. Brass cogs with teeth that fit neatly together, sometimes a dozen in a row, all of different diameters. Trembling hairsprings. Lenses, polished spyglasses, metal arcs.'

King nodded. 'After listening to you, sir, I see there is a difference between us though – a difference in our particular interest.'

71

'And what is that?'

'You enjoy these contrivances for how they are made and what they are. I am only interested in them for what they can do.'

Crossman thought about that and decided King was right.

The lieutenant was not so much concerned with actually *using* a clock. Rather what fascinated him were the workings themselves. So it told the time? All well and good. But *how* did it mark the time? What wonderful whispering machinations were going on beneath its face to enable it to calculate the seconds, minutes and hours? And how marvellous were those workings! More stirring than a Vivaldi concerto. More beautiful than a painting by Raphael. More profound than a sonnet by Shakespeare.

It appeared that the sergeant could not care less how his chronometer or theodolite did its work, so long as it told him to the second what was the time or calculated a curve according to the shape of the Earth. He needed to stun the moment on the head in order to get his own sums correct. What was it to him how the device got to the answer, so long as it had reckoned it with supreme accuracy? If a pebble could have given him the same reading, with a true scale, Sergeant King would have just as much interest in that smooth stone as he did that dark-iron theodolite.

'Yes, it would appear so, Sergeant.'

King stood up, draining the last of his coffee.

'Thank you kindly for the refreshment Mrs Hodges.' Having no hat on he touched his forelock. 'It was much appreciated.'

'You're very welcome, Sergeant,' she replied.

'Now I must go and find my quarters.'

Crossman rose to see him to the door. On the way Crossman happened to say, 'I think our scheme will be very successful, Sergeant. There are survey teams all over India at the present time. Our disguise will serve very well.'

King stopped and flexed his broad shoulders. 'Disguise, sir?'

Crossman wondered what was wrong. 'Yes, our pretence at being interested in mapmaking, while all the time we are gathering information.'

'Spying,' said the sergeant, calling a spade by its correct name.

'Right.'

King had started to put on his forage cap, but now took it off again.

'My understanding,' he said, after clearing his throat, 'is that the surveying *is* our primary task. I was told the officer and his man would be observing other things while we did it, but the main work would be the mapping of the regions to which we are sent or through which we pass.'

'No, no, no. We are to be an intelligence-gathering team.'

King's mouth was firm. 'That's are not what I was told, sir. I have my instructions. I was told for definite that the unit will survey the territories and, as a side issue, do a bit of spying on the locals.'

Crossman's voice rose a pitch. 'I'm the damned commanding officer of this *unit*, Sergeant. Don't you think I know my own orders?'

In the excitement of getting his point across, the lieutenant accidentally knocked his wooden hand against the sergeant's elbow. King stared at the hand, then after a second or two, said, 'No one told me about that. Is it just the hand, sir, or the whole arm?'

'If it's any of your damn business, it's just the hand. I lost it in the Crimea.'

The spleen was lost on the sergeant, who continued to speak in the same calm tones he had used since arriving in the house.

'My father,' he said, looking candidly into Crossman's eyes, 'has got a set of Napoleon teeth. He lost his own to the butt of a musket when it was used like a club on his face. Some Frenchy did it.'

'Napoleon teeth?' repeated Crossman, faintly.

'Yes, you know. After Waterloo the surgeons pulled the teeth out of the mouths of the dead lying on the battlefield. They sent them home to England in sacks. The surgeons over here matched them up as best they could and set them in false gums, and gave them to the veterans of the war. Those that needed 'em. My pa now uses a set of dead men's teeth to chew his meat with.'

'What's all this got to do with my hand?'

King smiled and shook his head. 'Nothing really, sir. It's just that seeing you with that false hand reminded me of my pa's false teeth. Well, now we've got it all straight, I'll bid you good night.' He gave his precious crate of instruments one last possessive glance. 'Thank you, sir.'

Within a moment Sergeant King had opened the door and was gone, out into the dusk. Crossman stood there, staring after him. How was he going to bear this man? Of all the sergeants to send him! He tried to think what kind of man he had expected. Someone

73

compliant to his will, that much was certain. He was now a lieutenant and he expected that subordinate ranks would treat him with
enough respect to fall into line. Was he wrong to expect that? He was
the commanding officer of the expedition, he had said as much, and
as such it was he who would decide what were the aims and goals of
that expedition. Officers led and rankers followed. Wasn't that how
it was supposed to be? Otherwise, why have ranks at all, if no one was
going to take any notice of them? A little deference, that's all he
wanted. Hadn't he earned it over the last few years?

Of course there were many kinds of sergeant. He had been one
himself and he was neither unintelligent nor obsequious. Wynter,
who had served under him in the Crimea had been obstructive,
belligerent and sullen. He was also now a sergeant. Crossman
shuddered when he thought they might have given him someone like
Wynter. At least King was not the worst that could have ended up
in his team.

'Yet this King has an obstinate streak which might turn to
stubbornness if not watched closely. And he thinks a lot of himself,
simply because he has been given a little education,' Crossman
muttered to himself, more than a little put out by the sergeant's
general demeanour and attitude.

The lieutenant went back to the kitchen, to thank Mrs Hodges for
her show of hospitality.

'What a nice soldier he was,' said Betty, wiping the kitchen table
top with a damp rag. 'Such a polite young man, with good manners.'

'I'm glad you think so,' said Crossman, through gritted teeth. 'I'll
bid you good night, Betty. I'm off to White's for the evening. Don't
wait up for me, nor even listen for the key in the lock. I'm quite
capable of putting myself to bed.'

'Yes, sir. What time shall I wake you in the morning?'

'Seven o'clock, if you please.'

11

So Crossman went along with King, drawn more by his sergeant's excitement than his descriptions. The lieutenant was however as breathtaken by the sight of the observatory as any man who had entered the park. It was truly a wondrous experience for someone who held scientific instruments in awe. The evening sunlight and shadow fell upon great bowls with star maps in their concave parts; they draped themselves over two huge sundials that dwarfed the nearby houses; they striped two glimmering metal astrolabes as tall as a man; they highlighted tall precision-made walls whose marble quadrants and arcs revealed such secrets as the maximum declination or obliquity of the sun's ecliptic.

Circles, discs, dials, bowls, walls, towers. Crossman and King walked amongst these vast instruments like two small boys. These were India's answer to the pyramids. These were holy temples to practical science. These were the secret-sharers of bygone giants.

King spoke in low whispers, of zeniths, equators, meridians, azimuths, altitudes, eclipses, declinations, ascensions, longitudes, latitudes, equinoxes, solstices. The fantastical magic words of the science of measuring. Spellbinding words that pointed at the solar system, tracked the stars in their courses, kept the sun's pace and used it to chart the precise movement of time. The sun, moon and stars – their rotational and elliptic motion, their fiery tracks through the sky – were captured by these towering devices which glittered their timely cryptic messages to men who knew their use.

This wondrous park, this garden of science, was a holy shrine to men like Sergeant King who measured the length, breadth and shape of the Earth. If it would have been appropriate to pray, he would have fallen to his knees. Here was the equivalent of the mystic's gateways to other worlds. And they worked, they worked! The Kranti Writta, the Yantra Raj, the Chakra, the Ram, the Shashthansa and the Dhruva. They worked as in dreams. They did as they were asked to do, close to perfection, their scales providing measurements which turned the man of science into a wizard of the universe.

The pair climbed the steps cut into the gnomon to the top of the ninety-foot sundial and surveyed the lesser world.

'Well sir, what d'you think?' asked King.

Crossman replied gravely, 'These people – we give them no credit for science, yet they surpass us. Explain to me again when these instruments were constructed.'

'I was told they were built by Maharajah Sawai Jai Singh during the first half of the eighteenth century. He was a warrior-astronomer and built other observatories at Delhi, Ujjain, Mathura and Benares, as well as this one. He studied Ulugh Beg's tables – a royal astronomer of Samarkand – and Portugal's De La Hire's too, finding errors and correcting them. This man was brilliant. Euclid, the syntaxes of Ptolemy, Flamstead's works, De La Aire's tabulae, nothing was beyond his reach . . .'

Crossman glanced at his sergeant, suspiciously. 'Where did you get all these names from?'

King looked shamefaced for only a second, then said defiantly, 'I was fortunate to be shown round the park by the maharajah's astronomer.'

'Ah, I thought your education had been somewhat expanded from this morning.'

'I'm not too proud to take lessons from others,' said King, not at all defensively. 'If a man knows more than I do, I admire him for it and listen hard.'

'But,' Crossman looked about him, 'you were right about this observatory. It's one of the wonders of the world for men like you and me. I feel humble in such a place. The size of these devices alone! Why they almost touch the sun in a physical sense. Marble and stone! What I would give to have been here when they were constructed. I wonder if the workmen who built them knew what they could do? I mean, you build a palace and know that someone is going to live there – but to build something unique, something quite strange

76

which has never been built before! Why, man, that must stir even a bricklayer's mind.'

The two men went back to their quarters in separate quiet and contemplative moods. Crossman was so impressed he immediately wrote about the 'astronomical observatory' in his diary, noting that even though these were works of science, they had a mystic side to them too. Nothing which was fashioned in the orient could be wholly practical. Astrology would be part of its function, as well as astronomy. So too would be aspects of the Hindu and perhaps Buddhist religions, which would influence the design and use of these instruments. Crossman had been in India long enough to learn that, though the meanings and subtleties of any shapes or symbols would be beyond him. He knew next to nothing about Hinduism, even less about Buddhism, and just a smattering of Islam. The park would pay homage to a god or gods, of that he was sure, but just how escaped him.

'Sahib, you work to the candle!'

It was Sajan, his dusty face coming between page and eyes.

'What do you want, young man? You should be asleep.'

'I sleep this afternoon, sahib. Now I stay awake to serve you. Shall I make you chocolate? Ibhanan tell me how to do this.'

He smiled at the boy. 'If you're truly not sleepy.'

At that moment the child's expression changed to one of alarm and he gripped Crossman's sleeve with a clawlike grasp.

'Cobra, sahib.'

Slowly, slowly, Crossman turned his head to see the snake which had slid into the room, under the large gap beneath the door. The lieutenant was relieved that the serpent was not rearing, nor was its hood wide, but any movement from him or Sajan could have the creature up and ready to strike, of that he was certain. The pair stood like statues for what seemed a very long time, though indeed it was only moments, Then suddenly the door flew open and Raktambar stepped inside. The Rajput had a stick in his hand the end of which he hooked under the cobra to flick it through the air and out of the open window at the end of the room. It was neatly done.

'I saw it enter,' explained Raktambar. 'You must guard against Indian snakes, they do not like *firinghis*.'

It was the first time anyone had used the derogatory term for a European directly to Crossman's face.

'I'm sure cobras aren't choosy,' he said, mildly. 'They'll bite anyone they fancy a threat.'

The sullen Rajput shrugged. He left the room. Sajan, now that the fear of being bitten had gone, was back to his chattering self. He made the chocolate on a small stove and carried it gravely to Crossman who thanked him and told the boy to get to his bed.

Then the lieutenant had a thought. He went to the box of arms, which Gwilliams kept close by him at all times, and told the corporal he was taking one of the Enfields. Carrying this weapon and an ammunition pouch, he went to the Rajput's quarters. The Indian appeared to be asleep. He placed the rifle at the foot of the man's mat, hoping this gift would buy Raktambar's acceptance of the situation.

The next morning, when Crossman woke, he found the rifle back by his bedside. Annoyed, he sought out Raktambar, determined to take issue with him. He found the Rajput washing by a well in the courtyard. Sajan was nearby, watching the warrior at his ablutions, seemingly entranced by the water droplets, that flashed like diamonds in the sun.

'What's this?' he said, taking the same tone the maharajah had used on him. 'You refuse my gift?'

'I am washing myself!' protested the Rajput, sulkily. 'This is my moment for cleansing.'

'Never mind that,' snapped Crossman, determined not to be put off. 'I'm talking about the rifle. I gave it to you as a gift in good faith. It's the very latest firearm.'

'I don't want it. It's no good.'

'It's a *very* good weapon. I used it myself on my last campaign. You couldn't get a more accurate rifle.'

Raktambar looked at the officer darkly.

'It uses the cartridges with grease.'

Crossman frowned, remembering the murderer in Chundore market had said something similar. 'Yes, the cartridges are greased with tallow. And what of it? I don't understand.'

'I have heard about this. The rifles are not good. I will not fire your rifle. I have my own. Please do not bother me with this, sahib. Know that I will *never* use this Enfield. I will use my own rifle. It is a *good* rifle. Listen, sahib,' he said, sitting on the stone flags of the courtyard. 'Please sit with me and talk. I will tell you about Rajputs. Please, sit.'

Crossman was in an undershirt, but he sensed an opportunity to get closer to Raktambar and learn something of the man. So, to the amazement of King's chain-men and perambulator-wallahs he too sat crosslegged on the hard stone floor. The chai man who was passing by saw an opportunity not to be missed and provided both men with a cup of tea. They sat there, impassively for a while, until Crossman prompted the other man.

'So,' he said, gently, 'tell me about Rajputs.'

'Sahib, I am a Rajput, a very proud race. You might say that all races are proud and you would be right. The Englishman is proud. The Pathan is proud. The Bengali is proud – perhaps not so proud as the Rajput – but proud just the same. We have our honour. Honour is the most important thing in the whole world. Men live for it, men die for it. Rajput means "son of king" which is what all my people are – sons of kings. We are a warrior caste who prefer to die on the battlefield than live a life of dishonour. The Mughals did not defeat us, nor the British. We are Rajputs.'

'Yes, but Raktambar . . .'

'No, sahib, you must listen. I am not one of your soldiers, to be ordered to be silent. I have been given by the maharajah to watch over you. I must tell you the Rajputs are not concerned with victory on the battlefield. No. They are concerned by bravery only. And they will fight for five things. The first is to protect the kingdom. This I will do. The second is for my religion. Yes? The third is to right any wrongs. The fourth is for women and the fifth is for cows.'

'Cows?'

'Yes, for cows. Now, I have given my word to protect you, sahib, while you stay here in India. This I will do, but only because of my word you understand. I do not like you. You are a *firinghi*. I am an Indian. This is not said often to the British, but I must tell you. Since you are also a Christian you are therefore a *Mleccha* – an untouchable. I am of the *Ksatriya* caste. That is a very noble caste, sahib. It must not be corrupted.'

'I understand that – I know that. I wouldn't wish to corrupt you.'

'Good, then we understand one another.' The Rajput stood up. 'I am glad, sahib, that we have had this talk.'

'So am I,' said Crossman, really not comprehending why he felt so relieved. 'Very glad.'

He stood up and walked back to his room. There he stood for a few moments in the shafts of sunlight that poured through the window. Outside the world was awakening. Smells of dung and cooking were coming through the open window. Three elephants

79

were passing along the track, one of them making snuffling noises with its trunk. Somewhere cymbals were being played, probably in a temple. There was the clatter of pots and pans, the grumbling of dogs, the snort of camels. Chatter from the local children reached up to his window and entered the room. A woman screamed at an ox, trying to get it to move from her vegetable patch.

'The rifle,' said Crossman to himself. 'What about the rifle?'

He had just learned that he was not personally liked, that his race was despised by the Indians, that he was an untouchable, that his new bodyguard couldn't give a damn about him. He had just been told all these things, his gift of a rifle refused – God only knew why – and he had come away from the conversation, the *telling*, with a smile on his face. No wonder the Indians thought the British were stupid. They *were* stupid.

The party remained all that day and the next in the quarters at Amber which had been given to them by the maharajah. Crossman was very reluctant to move. Beyond the small hills of Jaipur lay the wide dusty plains of Rajputana. Their journey so far had seen all three soldiers gather suntans to themselves. Gwilliams never took off his shirt, so he was probably as white underneath as when he started. Crossman and King, however, quite often exposed their bare upper bodies to the sun. They were becoming acclimatized to the temperature as well. Not so long ago they would have been gasping like stranded fish in the midday heat, but now they could actually move around and do things, physical tasks.

Crossman was lying on his bed writing in his official journal, the one Lovelace told him to keep in code. There was not a great deal to write. He had seen only one band of dissidents and that was the group that had attacked him and his men. There was this business of the two travelling chapattis, being passed from village to village. What was all that about? A signal of some kind? The mystery of the travelling chapattis which was something Lovelace would have liked solved was still a great secret. Crossman had talked with Ibhanan, his chain-men and others of the party and they confessed themselves to be just as ignorant as he was himself. That was not to say that they were, of course, for they might be lying or at least reluctant to reveal things.

However, there were indications of unrest amongst the Indians, which had been hinted at both by peasant and king. Crossman also believed he sensed an underlying disturbance in the mood of those natives he met. But it was difficult for him to gauge the nuances,

80

being a newcomer to India. He was still coming to terms with an alien culture which was incredibly complex and complicated. There were thousands of castes and subcastes about which Crossman knew nothing, nothing at all. Only the other day he had mistaken a *bindi* mark for a caste mark. There was a multitude of languages, some of them tribal, others national. There were the several religions, perhaps more than several, only two of which he could understand. Not only that, there were different ethnic groups and clans, some of them mixed, others determined to remain aloof and 'pure'. There were strange men who travelled as priests, yet were not true holy men, along with whirling dervishes and hermits and troglodytes and myriad other homeless beings. In a land such as this, where everything was strange, it was no wonder that Crossman had difficulty in gauging such things as a mood among men.

Yet, he felt there was something there. It was as if he were a fish and he sensed ripples passing over the surface of the water. Something was bothering *most* of the local people with whom he came into contact. They were in some cases unnaturally aggressive and rude. He had been treated with great kindness by those Indians he knew, yet strangers had called him names and verbally abused him without reason or provocation. He knew this was not normal, that Europeans were not ordinarily subject to such taunts, from the embarrassment of his carriers. If this had been common behaviour, the Indians in his party would not show they were shamed by it.

'Lieutenant, I believe this is where thee and I part company. We have had our differences, but I hold no grudges. The Lord insists on forgiveness and I extend mine to thee. Shall I leave thee some of my embrocation?'

Jack looked up from his writing to see John Stillwell standing in the doorway to his room. The man was just tall and wide enough to fit the doorway perfectly. A fly could not pass by him.

'Er, no – that won't be necessary.'

'As you wish, as you wish. But please don't blame me in my absence if thee has an attack of the prickly heat or some other horrible skin rash. We tender-skinned British are prone to such, as thee know. Our bodies are not fashioned for the heat and dust of India.'

'I shall bear that in mind.'

'And Lieutenant, when and if thee ever get to Delhi, please look me up. I am a member of the Delhi Mutton Club and will gladly take thee along as a guest.'

'The Mutton Club? I don't think I've heard of it. Is it similar to White's?'

Stillwell laughed. 'Not at all like a London club. It's the sharing of a roasted sheep carcass. A kind of social gathering to devour meat which reminds us of home. Of course, in an English town or country village, we would follow it with an apple pie, but the only apples thee will get here, my friend, are custard-apples, a poor substitute for the real thing.'

'I see. Yes, thank you. And you are taking the road north-east?'

'Yes. I am sufficiently rested now to continue my journey to Delhi. I thank thee for allowing me to join your party. I hope I have not been too much trouble.'

'No, no,' lied Crossman, who had found the minister a source of great irritation, 'you've been the model passenger.'

'Well, sir, I hope my prayers have assisted us in reaching this point and I will endeavour to continue to place thy welfare in front of the Lord. Thee will agree I'm sure that such requests can do no harm, even if the intended recipient is a non-believer.'

'Oh, I didn't say I was an atheist nor even an agnostic, sir. I simply don't proclaim my beliefs to the world.'

'Ah, then thou art a good Christian.'

'I didn't say that either.'

Stillwell shook his head.

'Thou insists on remaining enigmatic, Lieutenant. Well, that's thy right, I suppose. A man true to his beliefs would shout it from the rooftops, but perhaps thou art one of the quiet men of faith? Perhaps thee moves like the Lord, in mysterious ways, yet underneath are quietly as firm as a rock in thy following of Christ?'

Crossman lost patience with this raven-like man.

'Stillwell, I'm an assassin. I couldn't in truth be both slayer *and* a good man, now could I? It wouldn't fit.'

The minister stared at Crossman for a long while. It seemed he was trying to gauge whether the lieutenant was joking or not. When the minister decided that the remark was serious he gathered even more gravity to himself and with solemn words pronounced that Crossman was a lost soul.

'Indeed I am and have no wish to be found.'

'I shall still pray for thee, sir,' cried the minister, leaving the door-way free for the hot air and flies to enter again. 'Thee can be sure of that.'

Crossman watched him go, the lines of a recently written poem which Jane had read to him leapt to his mind.

If the red slayer think he slays,
Or if the slain think he is slain,
They know not well the subtle ways
I keep, and pass, and turn again.

The title of the poem was *Brahma* by an American called Emerson and Crossman was inclined to think it must have come out of an Indian experience. One further line had haunted the lieutenant ever since he had heard it fall from Jane's sweet lips.

And one to me are shame and fame.

The spy, the assassin, the gatherer and sower of information, drew both in equal quantities to himself. His fame was amongst his peers and he was admired for all the wrong things. His shame was within himself and it flourished there with every deed or action that drew fame. One day, Crossman knew, that shame and fame would mingle and become lost in one another, and he – poor man – would not be able to tell them apart.

The pen began to scratch on the page once again, the wrist-stump holding the book still enough to write in.

Now there was Gwilliams there. 'When are we movin' on, sir? Ain't you getting kinda bored here? I am.'

The pen was placed carefully down in the crease between the two sides of the journal.

'Tomorrow, I think, Corporal. How are you bearing up? Is India all you expected?'

'Between cockroaches the size of bats and red ants that bite great lumps out of your ass, yeah, pretty much as I thought.'

'Good, I'm glad you like it.'

'My favourite place, bar none. Hows about you? You happy with the way things are turning?'

'So far we've all three managed to avoid malaria, typhoid, yellow fever and a host of other illnesses. No one has managed to put a knife or bullet in us. I think we're doing pretty well. All we've got are sore feet at the moment. Are the horses refreshed?'

'All except that lame mare which I had to put down – I got us a new one, but she ain't a patch on the old. There's good horses hereabouts, but you can't lay your hands on 'em. The only thing for sale is nags.'

'We'll make do.'

A lizard – a gecko – ran across Crossman's book, pale and with eyes like large black beads.

'Smudged my ink, you little beast,' murmured the lieutenant. 'All right, Corporal, yes we'll move on in the morning. I'll check the provisions and stores tonight, just in case we've forgotten anything. That flour which we bought in the market is full of weevils, by the way. It seems that you can't buy maize flour which isn't, so we'll have to pick them out of our bread, or add them to our meat ration.'

'The local eggs smell bad too, when you break 'em in the pan,' said Gwilliams, 'but I don't think they's rotten eggs. It's just the way eggs is out here. Got us a case of pullets, for fresh fowl on the road. Bananas, but no oranges. Dates and stuff. Mangoes, guavas. Lots of dried peas. Little itty-bitty peas that you make up in a mash. No potatoes. I took the liberty of drying and salting some of that mare. Horse meat does in times when you ain't shot deer nor gazelle. Some nuts. I bought some nuts. And some beets that look like turnips, only they ain't.'

'Good, sounds as though we're well provided for, Corporal. I'll still have a look myself, in the morning. What about the Indians? Most of them don't eat meat, you know. Have we plenty of vegetables? They like their spices too . . .'

'Ibhanan's doing the buying for them.'

'Good, good. What can I say, you work wonders, Gwilliams. Now, a haircut would be fine, and possibly a shave if you wouldn't mind. This beard's starting to itch like hell.'

'That's what I'm here for – that's my trade.'

'Just imagine I'm wild Kit Carson,' said Crossman, remembering one of the names that Gwilliams bandied about, 'and you want me to look like your President.'

'Slick you up, you mean?'

'That's the idea.'

Later, all slicked up, Crossman went out to check the livestock. The camels seemed happy enough, staring at him with big eyes while they chewed. He was reminded of Betsy, the camel he had requisitioned in order to have a zumbooruck in the Crimea. She had eyes just like these two. The horses seemed fine now. It was a shame about the mare,

Bathsheba, but apparently she had not departed from them completely. She had been a good ride and now they would dine on her at some time in the future. Finally, Crossman checked on the dog that Sergeant King had found and cleaned of ticks, so that the beast could keep the camp clear of scavenger birds. There were buzzards and kites that descended upon anything that even looked like food and bothered the horses and camels. The hound, which always looked tired and miserable unless it was chasing and scattering feathered creatures, seemed in reasonable health, and had been fed and watered.

As he was leaving the stables Crossman saw a trio of women passing by. As always he admired their colourful saris, which were in stark contrast to the dismal red-brown brickwork of the party's quarters. They were chattering, the women, as they went through a rusted iron gate that hung from one hinge, into a walled garden. One of the women, the middle one, looked back at Crossman and suddenly glared at him. He straightened under the baleful eyes, wondering whether it was because he was a European. Then, through the opening of the gateway, he saw who was waiting for the women in the garden. It was Ishwar Raktambar, his bodyguard.

So, now the bride-in-waiting knew what her enemy looked like. A tall *firinghi*, a dark-haired man with one hand. With her expression she picked him, popped him in her mouth, and swallowed him like an overripe plum. He was left feeling wretched and wanting to beg her forgiveness. Such a very lovely lady, with eyes to drown in. Ishwar Raktambar was a lucky man to have won the heart of such a beautiful woman. Or had he? Perhaps, as was the custom, his father had chosen her for him?

'Out of the way! Out of the way!'

The shout came from a mahout guiding his painted elephant along the track which ran through the cluster of buildings.

Crossman stepped aside and the mahout looked down at him with annoyance written all over his face. This was the kind of thing that had Crossman wondering. After all, there was plenty of room either side of him. Why had the driver urged his elephant over the very spot where the lieutenant was standing? The lieutenant had the feeling that he could be anywhere in India and that mahout would have found him to be in the way.

85

12

There were strong contradictions. The countryside was a wasteland of flat endless dusty plains scattered with sullen-looking bushes and burnt leafless trees. Oppressively dull. The scene pressed down on Crossman's spirit, threatening to mangle it. A still air of lethargy pervaded over all. This torpor, reinforced by the listless appearance of the cattle, the slow movement of figures on the landscape, weighed upon him. Yet, now and again, here and there, was vibrant colour, vivid life. It was in the swift flight of birds, in the flocks of multi-hued graceful women in saris who drifted through the heat haze, in the darting gazelle, the water-blue skies. It was these occasional hazy clouds of colour and streaking creatures which saved him from drowning in a lake of melancholia.

'Do you see someone back there?' asked Crossman, still plagued by the idea that there was someone following in their wake. 'Look, King, back along the trail, by those wampi shrubs. See? See? There, he's slipped in behind them. Raktambar, be so good as to ride back there and challenge the man. He's been pestering us for quite a while now.'

The Rajput did indeed do as the officer requested, riding over the dull plain to the wampi patch and investigating, but he reported back saying there was no one there.

'Are you suggesting I'm seeing things?' asked Crossman.

'No, sahib, but I cannot invent someone to please you.'

'Of course not, for there *is* someone back there.'

'I am saying, sahib, that I saw no one.'

Jack peered back through the heat-haze again, unsure of himself, a little worried about the effect of heat on the brain.

Raktambar had changed his palace uniform for white cottons and finally Crossman and King had followed suit. The temperatures on the plains were often 120 degrees or more. When it was a still day they sweltered on their horses. When it was a blowy day the wind was hot and burned their skins. The two guides, taking turns to ride ahead and scout the terrain, worked at half their former speed.

King had not done a great deal of mapping while on the march, though he had produced those linear maps which a foreign army prized. His sketching hand was quick and talented. He drew the roads and tracks they took, and the landscape either side, using shading, contours and symbols where necessary. Fords over rivers, passes through mountains, other physical barriers that could hinder an army were important. What came out at the end was a snake of a map which would enable an army on the march to find its way north or south without too much trouble. It mattered not to a general leading a forced march what lay beyond six miles either side of the road. He needed to be shown any distant hills or forests which could hide an enemy, and gorges which could conceal an ambushes, but as long as these were clearly marked and he could take cognizance of them, the easiest, straightest road was what he needed to reach B from A.

King showed his maps to Crossman one night. They were in the lieutenant's tent, bothered only by the moths which battered against the glass of the lamp. Crossman studied the efforts under the lamplight and was quite impressed.

'These look excellent,' he said, 'though before you puff yourself up too much, I'm no expert.'

'Thank you, sir. I'm grateful for your opinion.'

Crossman lowered the sheaf of charts. 'My father was a good artist, you know.'

One of the men came to ask King a question, which took the sergeant some time to answer.

Crossman, waiting for his attention again, drifted off.

13

Betty went to a cabinet hanging on the wall by the back door and opened it with a small key. Inside were larger keys. She took one from a hook and handed it to him. Then fetched him a lamp from another cupboard.

'It'll be a bit dark and stale in there, sir. I've not been in there for an age. I was told to stay out, by your father. I said that to the mistress . . .'

He knew she meant Jane.

'That's all right, Betty. I understand.'

Crossman went out of the kitchen into the hallway. He shivered. It was very chilly there, the draughts coming straight under the door which led on to the street. He could not bear the cold after that long winter in the Crimea where many soldiers froze to death for want of adequate clothing. It was one of the reasons why the Punjab was so appealing to him. There would be times, he knew, when there would be snow and ice in the North West Frontier, but he understood the winters there were short. The winters he had known seemed to last for ever and a day.

Climbing the stairs he put the key in the lock to the mysterious room, turned it, then opened the door. He stepped inside. It was gloomy and smelled musty. Thick curtains kept out the light and kept the smell and dampness within. He crossed the room and drew back the curtains. Then he opened a window despite the fact that the weather outside was worsening. There needed to be some air in the place to freshen it.

It was now about three o'clock and it was already growing dark outside. He lit the lamp and held it up to survey the room. The place was indeed a mess, with too many chairs and overstuffed sofas. Underfoot was bare of carpets and splashes of oil paint decorated the wooden floor. He saw bunches of brushes in glass jars, standing as if they had been used just yesterday. He counted at least seven easels, one or two with half-finished paintings still mounted on them. Two other paintings, with slashed canvases, littered the walking space: presumably his father had not been satisfied with the way they had been going. Leaning against one wall were a whole stack of finished works, some of people, some of scenes.

One or two of the scenes he recognized. They were of the Crimean landscape he knew so well. Crossman began leafing through the rest of them. There was one of his brother in full uniform, holding his shako under his left arm. And one of his mother in a ball gown. Then there were the nudes, obviously painted here in this room, the subjects draped over one or another of the overstuffed sofas. Crossman had to consciously stop himself from disapproving. Not because he did not appreciate fine paintings – though actually he did not, since he preferred to think of himself as a man of science not of art – but because of his father's history with women. He wondered how many of those voluptuous nudes had been seduced by the old man. How many had received extra money on top of their modelling fee?

He knew he was being prudish, but he felt with good cause. His father had caused misery in the family with his philandering. Crossman himself was a natural child, not a legitimate one.

Finally, Crossman came to a painting which made him start backwards and catch his breath.

'What?' he muttered, astonished. 'When did the old goat do this?'

He found himself staring at his own image in full 88th sergeant's dress uniform. His father had painted him! And with his NCO rank. The major had hated the fact that one of his sons had joined the ranks. It had made him breathe fire when forced to acknowledge it. Yet – yet clearly he had viewed his bastard son from afar: had actually painted him in that uniform. Crossman felt both angry and amazed. He was angry because he did not understand and he was amazed at the enigmatic character that was his father.

Why did the old man have to be so complicated, so complex? Why couldn't he just be a damned ale-swilling libertine with nothing to him but loose morals and a gluttonous appetite for sex? Why should there be pretensions to anything fine in his character? Why couldn't he be bad through and through, so that his natural son could feel happy and justified in feeling contempt for him and everything about him?

'You bloody old goat,' Crossman swore, harshly, 'damn you to hell, man.'

A shadow drifted away from lamplight in the doorway.

Crossman went to the doorway quickly and caught Betty halfway down the stairs.

'I was just talking to myself,' he said, weakly. 'It was not intended that anyone should hear.'

Betty's expression was one of a frightened woman. He realized how he must have sounded. Like a madman, of course.

'I – I'm sorry, Betty. You were not meant to hear that. I was ranting you know, but it was not anything to do with you or Tom.'

'I know,' she said. 'It was your father.'

'Yes.'

'Forgive me if I say out of turn, Master Alexander, but times are passed and it's better to forgive and forget.'

'Thank you, Betty. I'm sure you're right.'

She continued down the stairs now and Crossman went back to collect the lamp and lock the door. The painting could stay where it was. All the paintings could. His brother would know better what to do with them. Either they would go out with the rubbish or be stored up in Scotland. He couldn't imagine James selling them. Not that one, anyway. He and his brother loved each other as brothers should, but even James had not approved of Crossman's running away and joining the infantry as a private. Only his step-mother understood. She was a woman and women saw into souls.

14

'You say your father *was* a good artist?' said King. 'Is he dead then?'

Crossman came back with a jolt. 'No – no, senile. His mind has gone. But in his day he could do you a watercolour of a proposed battlefield so that you could imagine yourself in there. Generals loved him for it. Of course, most army officers can produce reasonable sketches or paintings. It's part of the job. But some of them actually find they're quite skilful artists. I've seen some landscapes to rival the best of our so-called genius painters, even surpass them. Take that chap Turner, for example. My father's paintings could knock his into a cocked hat.'

King was having none of this.

'Oh, come, sir. Joseph Turner is England's pride. They're brilliant in their composition.'

'Brilliant, yes,' argued Crossman. 'Too brilliant. All that blinding light. What you want is something highly representational, not something that looks like it's rising from the mist on a winter's morning. I can't be doing with the man. I think his work is highly overrated. Constable, now there's a painter for you. Trees look like trees and rivers like rivers.'

'But your grandfather would not have approved of Constable.'

'What does that mean?' Crossman swatted a mosquito on the back of his neck and felt great satisfaction in his success.

'I'm afraid it means you have reached a point in your life where you are looking back to old heroes, sir.'

'Careful, Sergeant,' protested Crossman, 'I'm only a few years older than you.'

King sighed. 'But it's in the mind.' He quickly changed the subject as he saw his commander beginning to bristle. 'We're straying from the subject. I expect your father was, as you say, sir, an excellent artist. So, you approve of the maps then, sir?'

Crossman's attention went back to the charts.

'Very good, yes, very good. What are a mapmaker's instructions for route surveys such as these?'

King's chestnut hair bobbed over the map as he poured out his enthusiam.

'To observe everything on the road, or that is visible from it, which can be considered of any importance, particularly hill forts, remarkable peaks, mountains, hills, ghats, passes and towns. Rivers or nullahs – all that sort of thing.'

'Well, you've done that. The detail is quite extraordinary.' The lieutenant looked up. 'But have we used any of our men in producing these? Can you justify the expense to which I have been put?'

King felt flattened for a moment. He rallied.

'The perambulator-wallahs, yes sir.'

'Using the measuring wheels. But the others, no?'

'Well, that time you were sick and down with some fever, I did do some wide-scale mapping in which all the men were used.'

To King's relief Crossman accepted this as his justification.

'Fair enough, Sergeant. So long as they have not been wasted.'

'And they're with us for the time when they'll be of great use, sir, once we reach the north-west. There are areas there which have no maps at all. I doubt I could recruit such men in the Punjab.'

'As you say.'

At that moment there came sounds of a great commotion going on outside. Crossman snatched his revolver out of its holster and King rushed through the tent flaps empty-handed. They were just in time to see one of their tents flying through the night, heading away from the light of the fires. It looked like a fleeing phantom. One or two of the Indians chased it for a short distance, then it turned on them and headed back to the camp. The pursuing Indians turned too and raced ahead of the streaming canvas. The pursuers had now become the chased.

'What is it?' cried King. 'Is there a man inside?'

'No man, sahib,' yelled Sajan, his little legs carrying him to the nearest tree, which he proceeded to climb. 'Big pig.'

It seemed there was a massive humpbacked boar caught in the folds of the tent, which now came hurtling into the camp again, over the campfire scattering the burning logs, and crashing into yet another tent. The boar was shrieking now and thrashing like mad. It rolled over, found its legs again, and went thudding into one of the Indians. The man was knocked aside, fortunately only winded and bruised. The boar thundered on, shaking his unwanted garment, trying to free himself from its embraces. A pole with a lamp on top was its next victim, the lamp sailed into the night, smashed, and burning oil scattered on the grasses. Little fires began to spread over the stubble-grass, which was naturally very dry at this point in the season.

Crossman thought that enough was enough. He took aim at the flailing tent and shot through the canvas. His first shot did not kill the boar, but his second and third finished it off. It sank to its knees with a sigh. After a few more moments the tent was still again, but heavily pregnant.

Men were running around now, grabbing water containers, using coats to flail out the flames. Once the fire was under control, King extricated the boar from the tent. He found it was his own accommodation and was somewhat aggrieved to find two of the bullet holes were on the ridge of the canvas. Moreover, the boar's tusks had pierced the tent too.

'We're not far away from the monsoon rains,' he complained. 'A patch is never as good as the original.'

Once the camp was put to rights again, the fire was relit and the lamps in place again, they assessed the rest of the damage. One of the poles to King's tent was also broken and his personal items scattered over a wide area. A few things were broken. His precious instruments, however, were in another tent and had not been touched. The second tent which had been uprooted belonged to some chain-men. It had been ripped all down one side. The men were not overly concerned. They could sleep out in the open just as easily as under canvas and often did.

Sajan was fascinated by the dead boar. He poked it with a stick and remarked how stiff were its bristles. Crossman said the boy could have one of the tusks but Sajan shook his head when the bloody-ended tooth was presented to him. It was a bit too grisly for his liking.

'Damn fortunate it wasn't a tiger,' Crossman said to Raktambar, 'for I doubt my little revolver would have stopped a big cat. How did it come to enter the camp anyway? I thought the fire was supposed to keep them out.'

'It was chased in here, sahib,' replied the Rajput in a smug voice, 'probably by a big tiger.'

Crossman stared out into the night. Raktambar might have been trying to worry him, but it seemed a likely story. The boar must have been panicked by *something* out there and boars of this size were not frightened by mongooses. A leopard or a tiger was the most likely explanation, and of those two the tiger more probable. Thus it followed that out there in the night there was no doubt a tiger of fairly large proportions.

'Take the carcass,' he ordered four of the men, 'and throw it well away from the camp. If there's a tiger out there, he'll smell the blood and come for it and we shan't be troubled by him – or her. Once the beast has fed he won't bother with a few scrawny humans.'

'We'll keep a few choice cuts though?' said King. 'It's our boar, after all.'

'Butcher it quickly, then. Don't leave it until morning.'

For the remainder of the night most of the camp lay awake listening for sounds of some large creature ripping their tent with its claws. Gwilliams slept soundly enough. So did Sajan, who could not have kept his eyes open if God were having a tantrum. But for the most of them, they remained conscious, their imaginations running away into the realms of horror.

The next two days were fairly uneventful. The party continued its ascent up to the Punjab. Yes, the land was flat, but they crawled along at climber's pace, as if they were indeed going up a sheer face to a summit in the Himalayas. The heat bore down on them with a ferociousness that left Crossman aching in every limb. Insects bothered them continuously. The flies were large bloated creatures that crawled into their mouths, up their noses and into their ears. Then there were the massed midges that stuck to their sweaty faces in their thousands. Blood-sucking bugs went into their veins at night, leaving nasty little wounds that took time to heal. Snakes, rats and other low creatures of the field added to their misery.

Happily there were few mosquitoes, since the land was parched and the monsoon rains had yet arrived.

15

On the morning of the third day after the tiger scare, Crossman was woken by a wild-eyed Sergeant King.

'Run off!' cried King. 'Stolen them!'

Crossman sat up with his head buzzing. Sleep had not come until two o'clock and he was not totally *compos mentis*. There had been reports to write and some sort of clicking insect, much louder than any clock Jack had ever heard, was trapped somewhere in the tent and kept him awake. Halfway through the night the sound changed from clicking to a loud harsh continuous note: the noise of a saw driven by an engine. The creature was then distracting the lieutenant so much he had searched for it, only to find the beetle had wonderful powers of ventriloquism. Going to one spot in the tent where he was certain to find the creature, the sound actually switched to another corner. It was both amazing and frustrating. Yet even though he stood, concentrating, and listened very hard he did not catch the insect. It could truly cast its voice to several feet away, thus fooling its hunter.

Jack tried to concentrate now. He was suddenly aware that King must have been speaking before he had actually woken up. The sergeant was staring, waiting for an answer to a question. The he started gibbering again: not making sense at all.

'Calm down, Sergeant. What's the trouble?'

Gwilliams stepped through the flap then. 'Gone,' he said. 'No trace.'

Crossman rubbed his head.

'Please, Corporal, Sergeant – can I have a full report? Two seconds ago I was fast asleep. I am not a mind-reader.'

'One of the Indians,' blurted King, 'has run away. He's taken three of my instruments with him.'

'Which of them?'

'The two chronometers and a sextant.'

'Both of the timepieces?'

'Yes.'

This was bad. Chronometers were very expensive items. Eventually they would have to be replaced or paid for. By rights any non-personal equipment in the field was the property of the 'regiment' and it was the quartermaster's job to find the money to buy new. Crossman was thousands of miles from his battalion: he imagined the quartermaster and, indeed, the colonel of the 88th Foot might justly feel indignant at receiving a bill for two chronometers stolen on the Indian subcontinent. Sometimes a regiment short of funds would raise the cash by selling one of its captaincies, or even majoracies. There was clearly no chance of that, though at that precise moment the lieutenant would have dearly loved to sell his sergeant.

He rose and began to pull on his boots, forgetting for once to check for scorpions. Luckily the boots had not been occupied during the night.

'We'll have to track him down then. Chronometers are quite valuable and I'll be held accountable.'

'Not forgetting the fact that I can't make maps without them,' said King, in rather resentful tone.

'Sergeant, I'm afraid I've no time to fight with you this morning over your hurt feelings. You see, we have had a thief in our midst.'

King stuck out his jaw but wisely kept silent after this, realizing that the important thing was to retrieve the instruments.

Gwilliams said, 'I'll get the rifles.'

'Sergeant King, you will remain in the camp,' ordered Crossman, splashing water on his face from a copper bowl. 'We don't want to get back and find the place ransacked.' He allowed Sajan to wind his turban for him, still not adept at doing it himself.

'They're not all thieves, sir. Ibhanan . . .'

'Is an honest man, I'm sure. But he's also an elderly man and can easily be overpowered. Besides, if the thief has accomplices out there, you will be of no use to us. You can't shoot for toffee. Gwilliams,

96

Raktambar and I will set out after the burglar and hopefully bring back the goods.'

Raktambar was already waiting with the horses. Without being asked he had supplied each man with a waterbag and some bread. He had his own weapon with him, a long-barrelled flintlock musket, along with tulwar, two single-shot pistols and a curved dagger stuck in his belt. Unlike the two white men, his appearance was immaculate. He was clean-shaven except for a large black moustache, the ends of which were waxed to a needle sharpness. His clothes had no creases, his boots were gleaming, and moreover he was bright-eyed and ready for the ride.

'Ah, well done, Raktambar,' murmured Crossman, taking the reins of one horse from him. 'You know what we are to do?'

'Yes, sahib. We have to kill the man who has stolen the sergeant's treasure.'

'Well, we may not have to kill him. Gwilliams? Are you mounted?'

'Just about – yeah. I'm ready,'

Raktambar, being the local man, should by rights have been the tracker, but he was not country bred. The Rajput was town born and had become a palace guard in his youth. He had no useful skills out in the wild in hill, forest or plain. Crossman had learned to track in the Crimea and Gwilliams in the American West, so between them these two men picked out the trail. The thief had taken no horse, presumably because he could not ride, and had set out on foot. From the length of his stride it was clear to Crossman that his man had begun running but after two miles had dropped to a fast walk, then a little later, to a slower walk. He tried to point out these signs to Raktambar, thinking the Rajput would like to learn.

'What do I care if a man runs or walks?' said Raktambar, sulkily. 'It means nothing to me.'

'The more information you can gather on your quarry, the better,' explained Crossman. 'Then when you find him there'll be less surprises to encounter.'

'Humph. I see his marks in the dust, I follow them, I kill him. What do I care about surprises?'

'Could be he might be waitin' to bushwack you,' Gwilliams argued. 'Could be that's a surprise you ain't gonna be ready for. Mebbe he'll shoot you deader'n lump of rock on a mesa. Then you can stick that nose up in the air and tell ole Gwilliams he's only a barber and don't know pigeon poop from cobra shit.'

'How can he shoot me with no firearm?' asked the Rajput.

Crossman said nothing to this, but Gwilliams fell into the trap with a triumphant, 'How do *you* know he ain't took one from the camp?'

'I count them, before I leave. There is no weapon missing.'

Crossman stared at the Indian for a minute, as they rode along, his mind half on the tracks in the dirt and half on this argument.

'You counted all the weapons in the camp?' he said, incredulously. 'How did you know how many there were in the first place? What about the Enfields I keep locked in the strongbox?'

'Since the arms' box was locked, and the lock not broken, Raktambar believes the Enfields must all be there. As for the others, I know how many there are because I counted them the first night I arrive in your camp and I count them *every* night since. This is how one stays alive, to know where each weapon is at all times. My master, the Maharajah Ram Singh would be dead a long time ago if I did not keep a tally of where are all the weapons and who is armed with what. You, sahib, and you,' he flicked his nose at Gwilliams in a gesture of contempt, 'both follow these footmarks in the dirt, but I know the man has only one weapon. A long knife women use for scaling fish. When I catch him, for he is a stupid fellow to go on foot, he will run at me screaming, knife in hand, and I shall shoot him dead.'

But when they found the man, whom Jack immediately recognized as a quiet, mild fellow called Sitakanta, he was already dead. The body was lying naked in a crop of rocks, this thief having fallen foul of other thieves. There were many footprints in the dust, indicating a group of at least five. King's instruments were gone, of course, and so were Sitakanta's clothes. Sitakanta's throat had been cut and he would have bled to death over a relatively short period of time. His hands and feet were bound with grass rope. There were marks on the binding around his wrists indicating that he had probably tried to gnaw his way through the rope, even as the life drained from him and the world faded away before his eyes. There were also signs that scavengers had been around, probably rats and kites, no doubt scared off when sounds of approaching humans were heard.

'I wouldn't have taken this man for a thief,' said Crossman, as they wrapped the body in a blanket and draped it over the rump of Gwilliam's mount. 'He didn't seem the type. He was always so cheerful and eager to please. When King wanted someone there, Sitakanta would be among the first to volunteer. I'm genuinely surprised.'

'You never can tell,' Gwilliams replied. 'Mebbe his daughter was bein' held hostage by a bandit chief. Could be his father was in a blood feud with another family an' needed money to buy 'em off. You can't tell what's in a man's head. He could be smilin' like a crescent moon, day in, day out, and still be eaten away inside with worrit 'n' woe. These people ain't our people, Lieutenant. We ain't got halfway to knowing their ways in the time we been here. Maybe he hated our guts for some reason? These people are deeper'n any I've met on any shore.'

Crossman acknowledged that the corporal, whose insight was sharper and keener than that of most men, was probably on the right track.

'Then again,' said Gwilliams, 'it's only money. No malice needed, when you think about it. Just a case of you've got more'n me, so I'll have some of yourn, thank you kindly sir.'

They picked up the tracks of the new robbers and followed them for about two miles. Eventually they found themselves approaching a plains village which stood high on a bridge of land with deepening hollows on either side. The rains had not yet come and the lakes had dried up to bowls of dust where white cows and dark buffaloes roamed listlessly in search of scant green leaves on miserable shrubs. There were dark shells of fishing boats lying stranded on the barren earth, lifeless as dead turtles in a desert.

It was obvious that people were desperately poor. Crossman began to wonder what the village near his own home would be like if Loch Eileen dried up every so often and the sheep and cattle were dying of thirst before the inhabitants' eyes.

'Now Raktambar, I don't want you killing everyone in sight,' said Crossman. 'Curb your enthusiasm for blood, if you please.'

The Rajput grunted something which might have been assent.

Gwilliams said, 'I might remind the officer that a murder has bin committed.'

'We're not judge and jury, Corporal. We can't hang half a dozen men for something which might have been done by one or two. The

99

man who has the instruments now might not be the man who took them from Sitakanta and ended his life. We also don't have the time to sift through evidence. We'll take our goods and go, leaving dire threats in our wake. If we meet resistance, of course, it'll be a different matter.'

They were now at the entrance to the village, which was a sprawl of huts either side of a dusty track, some fifty or sixty habitations. Dirty, naked children were standing, staring at the visitors. Old men and women, many squatting their haunches and stirring tiny fires, looked up with red rheumy eyes probably wondering whether they ought to be as interested as the young. Cattle stood or wandered between the shacks or mud dwellings, harried by the occasional scrawny dog. One younger man stepped out of a hut and then immediately vanished again in the blink of an eye.

Crossman called his party to a halt.

'Raktambar, your Hindi is obviously a hundred times better than mine — please tell the villagers they must bring our goods out now, or suffer the consequences. Tell them if they don't do what I say we'll burn the place to the ground, kill all the cattle, hang the murderers, and sell their female children into slavery before nightfall today.'

Gwilliams whistled under his breath. 'Jeez.'

'Corporal, I don't intend to carry out these threats, they're merely to save us the time of searching the place.'

'Never make a threat you do not intend to carry out,' said Raktambar, wisely. 'Not in India, sahib.'

'I'm sure that's wise advice, but we'll try it my way this time.'

Raktambar did as he was told, bellowing out the words while waving his tulwar and snarling ferociously.

He added the lies that the goods had been stolen from members of the Maharajah Ram Singh's column of guards, that the instruments belonged to the court magician and were devices for conjuring demons from beneath the earth and if used by the uninitiated would culminate in the users going to a horrible afterlife where their souls would rot and dribble away into drains that led to the fetid sewers of the underworld.

'Very imaginative,' murmured Crossman, sitting aside his restless mount. 'Very colourful. You have my admiration.'

A short time later, a small trembling boy with round fearful eyes came to them and led the party around a section of the huts to an

100

open space. There on a ragged sack lay the glittering treasure. Both chronometers seemed intact, but the sextant was in pieces. Someone had carefully unscrewed it and taken it apart, bit by bit. There was no telling if all the parts were there or not. Gwilliams gathered up all he could see on the sacking and put them in his saddlebags. The corporal then patted the trembling village boy on the head and gave him a biscuit.

Crossman ordered the party to leave the village.

No one looked back.

As they rode back to camp Raktambar remonstrated with Crossman.

'You should have burned the village. That place is full of murderers and assassins. Other travellers will not thank you, sahib.'

'I'm aware that there are bad elements within the place, but I can't kill women, children and innocent men for the sake of retribution. Had we time enough I would've done my utmost to find who was responsible, but we're short of the stuff, and there it is.'

'The soldier administrators in the Punjab would have chosen ten men and hanged them without question, to teach the village a lesson.'

'I am not an East India Company Punjabi irregular, Raktambar. I am a officer in the British army. We do things differently.'

Raktambar shrugged. 'Some of you do, some of you don't.'

Which left Crossman thinking. Without a doubt many of those North-West Frontier men were a rougher breed, a more ruthless sort of soldier than he was himself. He had heard stories, of Harry Lumsden, John Nicholson and Herbert Edwardes, warrior-clerks belonging to John Company, who if they had not had their own way of doing things on the frontier, would probably be dead men now. Some of them, Nicholson especially, were revered by the Pathans and the Sikhs almost to the point of deification. Nicholson had made a similar journey to Crossman on landing in India at the tender age of seventeen and had gathered rough glory to himself ever since, defeating all who came up against him. Some of those Punjabi men were already double-stamped, with greatness and with ruthlessness, the one hardly possible without the other.

Those soldier-clerks, these collectors of revenues, had carved an empire out of a divided subcontinent, out of its collection of independent states, pitting one ruler against another, leaving some still nominally in their places but removing others and usurping them. The pen may be mightier than the sword, but in this case the pen and the sword together were invincible. They had taken from the Mughals what the Mughals had taken for themselves several hundred years previously. They had marched in with little more than themselves, formed armies out of Bengalis and others, and had wrested yet further empire from the Sikhs. They were the new Akbars, the new Ranjit Singhs, the latest in a long historical line of conquerors and overseers.

Yet they were not monarchs or even warlords: they were Company men, employees, salaried personnel with managers in distant cities. They were uncompromising men, they had to be to survive the dangerous half of their job, that of being a warrior in a warrior's world. Pathans, Gurkhas and Sikhs, especially, had an affinity with such men. There was mutual respect between them. They lived a life where honour on the field was everything.

Crossman was not such a man, this much he admitted to himself. He *was* ready to compromise. He was not as ruthless as he should be for the work he was given. It would probably cause his death one day. But he could no more be one of those warriors, famed among other things for being able to split a man down the middle from crown to crotch with a single sword-stroke, than he could be the priest of a small parish church in Norfolk. He was a hybrid: someone not wholly convinced by the violent lifestyle of the soldier, certainly not inexorable, yet someone who would die of boredom in an ordinary life back home. His main fault – and it was a fault in a man of his stamp – was that he could be moved to unnecessary mercy.

That is also to say he was no great administrator either. Nor decisive judge, nor iron-willed negotiator, as these Company men had to be. Their talents were many and varied and their characters impressive. Jack's charisma was limited, though his charm was above average. As a pioneer on the frontiers, he would have been sorely tested. But since he was coming up behind those men, now that things were established, his skills might be enough. Nathan Lovelace could have been another John Nicholson, but not Jack. One needed to be steel from the backbone out, even to the farthest reaches of the mind. One had to be a manipulative genius.

He entered the camp to see Sergeant King's face suffused with relief at being handed his precious instruments. The glow was short-lived, as King looked at the pieces of his sextant in dismay.

'Who did this?'

Crossman stiffened at the implication. 'Not I, nor any member of our party, Sergeant.'

King was distressed. 'Oh, I did not mean . . . how am I to do without my instrument? Look at it! It's been shattered.'

'Not shattered, simply taken apart.'

'As good as shattered,' wailed the sergeant.

'Look, Sergeant, I'm sorry for it, but there it is. Perhaps we'll come across someone who can put it back together again. You've not used the thing all that much, anyway . . .'

King walked away clutching the sacking with its precious pieces jingling inside, hardly even bothering to listen to his commanding officer. He became over the next two days even more self-absorbed than he had previously been. He used all the rest stops and even worked by lamplight at night. So engrossed was he that he did not respond to Crossman's demands to take duty watches. This was a serious omission, but the officer did not chastise his sergeant, recognizing that here was an occasion like no other, which would not be repeated. The death of a family member could not have obtained more grieving-time than was given to that broken sextant. On the third day, after two hours' rest had been passed at noon, Sergeant King emerged triumphantly. He held the sextant up in two hands, as if it were a crown about to be placed on a monarch's head.

Crossman was on a canvas chair, sitting in the shade of giant thorn tree. He praised his sergeant grudgingly. 'Well done, King. Gwilliams and I have had to cover your duties over the last forty-eight hours, but we did it without complaint, and do not require any thanks. No, really,' he continued, seeing that King was paying absolutely no attention to what he was saying, 'please don't swamp us with gratitude. We're happy that things can now get back to normal.'

'I did it,' murmured King, seemingly more amazed with himself than others appeared to be. 'I reconstructed it perfectly.'

'It's hardly a beam engine, Sergeant, and if I may say so, the pieces probably only go back together one way. It was simply a matter of time and perseverance. You managed it because we gave you the time.'

But the sergeant was not going to be done out of his glory. He went about the whole camp, showing the sextant to anyone who would pay him any attention. The chain-men and perambulator-wallahs, of course, praised him to the heavens, as they were wont to do on any occasion whatsoever. If he had showed them a lump of clay with twigs stuck in it they would have exclaimed their delight and amazement at his creativity. Why not? King had employed them to do next to nothing except walk the length of northern India, and to them he was a saviour.

Gwilliams was something different again, pointing out that telescopic sights were back to front. King looked at the corporal in annoyance, as if it were the corporal's fault that a mistake had been made. He disappeared again for half-an-hour, then came out with the instrument not only correctly aligned but polished to gleaming. Holding it up to the sky he might have been a chief of some primitive tribe about to perform a sun ceremony.

Raktambar and Gwilliams went off to shoot *chikor*, game birds, so that there would be something for the meat eaters. This left King first enthusing to his commanding officer, but growing ever more mournful, using poetic language to describe how the survey of the Great Arc of India had been like the opening of a flower as the mappers slowly worked their way northwards, the triangles its petals, the line of longitude which was the 78 degree meridian, its stalk.

'I was born too late,' moaned King, realizing that he still had not yet used his sextant in anger. 'I was born too late for the blossoming.'

16

They entered the land of the five rivers, the Punjab, knowing their journey was now nearing its end. A few days previously the countryside had changed to lush jungle, except where it had been cleared along the banks of the rivers themselves, for agriculture. Looking at the tangled thick foliage it was not difficult for Jack to understand why 'jungle' was a Hindi word.

Although this new vegetation held hidden dangers for the travellers, by way of tigers, wild boar and snakes, Jack Crossman was pleased to see thick foliage again. It filled his heart with green joy and his letters to Jane were suddenly lifted out of the despondency which, despite every effort to keep them positive, had filtered into their pages at times while on the Rajputana plains.

He was looking forward to seeing a familiar face again too. Colonel 'Calcutta' Hawke was apparently waiting for him in Ferozepur. Hawke had been born in Surrey, but had an Indian mother, the wife of an officer of the East India Company. There were derogatory epithets for Anglo-Indians here, but Crossman could not imagine anyone using them to the colonel's face, or even behind his back. Hawke was a lean, iron-man, the hardest man Crossman had ever met, and it would be a brave warrior who insulted him. He was not alone in his mould, of course, for in the Company army were generals who had Indian mothers and British fathers.

'We'll need to ford the river further down,' said Crossman, having spoken to one of his guides. 'The current's too fast at this point.'

It was indeed too fast for them to negotiate a crossing. It was a rushing torrent. Over the other side of the river, dhobi-wallahs were bashing white cottons with stone and spreading them on rocks to dry. A tame elephant was washing itself in the shallows, sucking up gallons of water and spraying its own back. Chattering children were picking amongst the stones, looking for creatures in the mud. The scene was one of peace and calm, except in the middle of the river, where the water was raging and running amuck. It was intolerable to have to take the long route to reach the other side.

They trudged along the south bank, eager to be amongst humanity again. As they walked they saw one or two dark lumps like thick logs floating down with the current. Raktambar told them they were bodies: he did not seem disturbed by the fact. However, one particular sight did anger the Rajput. A human corpse went by, out in the middle of the flow, with a jackal standing on its chest. The creature was eating flesh. Raktambar fired his musket, but missed the raft's passenger. By the time Gwilliams took his shot, the human carrion and its live cargo were gone, far downriver.

'I've sin buzzards do that,' said Gwilliams, shaking his head in disbelief, 'but never a cur.'

'Where did you see something like that?' asked King.

'After an Injun battle,' replied Gwilliams, then upon reflecting for a moment, added, 'diff'rent Injuns.'

There had been a storm the previous evening, one which ripped tents and tore poles out of the ground. A ferocious swirling thing. In the morning the ground was covered in what Ibhanan called *beerbahutis* which were like little bits of red velvet littering the place. There was also a multitude of frogs, which no one could help treading on, the British amongst them grimacing squeamishly when they squashed the creatures underfoot.

At one point along the riverbank they came across a group of men carrying huge objects on their shoulders which turned out to be the inflated hides of buffaloes. The ballooned skins were so obscenely strange in appearance, something like dumb blind animals with stubby limbs, they frightened young Sajan. Crossman was told by Ibhanan that the skins were used to float goods and people over fast-flowing waters such as this river by *mussock* men. The *mussock* men tried to engage Crossman and persuade him to avail himself of their services, but the lieutenant could not see what they were going to do with the camels and carts. King was terrified of losing his instruments in the flood. The sergeant argued that if his cargo of brass sank here it would never be recovered.

106

'Tell them no,' said Crossman to Ibhanan, reluctant to get into a hassle with them himself. 'Say we don't wish to cross here.'

The ford was eventually reached and the party crossed the river to an army camp on the far side. They discovered the camp belonged to a Frontier Punjabi force known as Stuton's Rifles. Irregular units often took their name from their commanders – Hodson's Horse, Brownlow's Punjabis, Wilde's Rifles – and the commander himself was in residence. Crossman went to pay his respects to John Stuton himself. He walked through a camp full of Sikhs, Pathans and Dogras, whose hawkish eyes bored into him when he was not looking at them directly, but were politely removed from his person when he did. They wore indigo blue-black coats with trousers and turban to match. In consequence they were known locally as the *saih post*, the 'black coats' and they had the honour of being the one of the first irregular infantry regiments raised in the Punjab.

Colonel Stuton greeted Crossman amiably enough, but the commander's mind was obviously on other things. He was a large man with thick black hair and a bushy beard and his gruff tone indicated to Crossman that he was a straightforward infantryman with no frills. Jack liked this in a man. He waved Crossman into a bamboo chair and asked him who he was and what he was doing travelling towards the infamous Khyber Pass.

'Please excuse the whites. I shed my uniform back on the road, finding it too burdensome to travel in. My name's Crossman, sir. Lieutenant Jack Crossman, of the 88th Connaught Rangers . . .'

'Bit far from your regiment, lad? Lose your way?'

Crossman explained that he was now only loosely attached to the Rangers. He was working for Colonel Hawke, who was waiting for him in Ferozepur.

'I see no reason to hold this back from you, sir. I'm here to help gather intelligence, a spy if you will but not one of those fellows who go sneaking about in false beards, looking in private drawers . . .' The attempt at a little humour was lost on Stuton who simply drummed a rhythm with his fingers on a table in front of him until Crossman got back to basics. 'No, more a man who travels under another guise picking up bits of information as he does so, hopefully dropped by unsuspecting speakers.'

'You speak other languages?'

'Yes, sir, I do. And I hope to become more proficient as my time here goes on.'

'What guise?'

'Mapmakers. We're posing as a party of mapmakers.'

Stuton grunted in a non-committal way. 'Hodson's always on about this sort of thing, intelligence gathering. And what have you learned on your journey, sir? Where are you come from?'

'Bombay.'

'So, what have you discovered?'

Crossman told him everything he knew, seeing no reason to hold back before this powerful Punjab commander. While he was un-ravelling his information, along with his theories, a servant entered the room with two glasses of water. Crossman stopped his narrative to thank the man in Hindi, before letting him leave and continuing.

At the end of his telling, Stuton said severely, 'You spoke Hindi to my servant.'

'Oh' Crossman suddenly realized he may have made a mistake. 'Was he a Pashto speaker?'

'No, but do you also speak to your own men in their language?'

'Some of the time, yes, though many of them have some English. I have a Rajput bodyguard who is an excellent English speaker.'

Stuton stared through the opening of his hut, out at the clear sky above the forest. 'If I were a spy, I should keep such a talent hidden,' he said, 'so that those around you would think they were safe when they opened their mouths to their friends. You might learn more that way, don'tcha think, Lieutenant? Take my advice, don't trust a Rajput or Bengali at the moment. They're frying fish we might not want to eat.'

Another officer entered the hut then, a captain, and Colonel Stuton told him to 'see to the lieutenant, if he would' and Crossman suddenly realized he had been dismissed.

The captain, a tall thin man with heavily hooded eyes and a sour twist to his mouth led Jack out of the hut.

Crossman was horrified with himself. Of course, John Stuton was right, he should have kept his knowledge of the local languages secret. What a fool he had been. It hadn't occurred to him until now, he'd been so full of the fact that he could converse with Indians, probably hoping to impress them with his skill. It was such a simple thing. Why hadn't he thought of it?

'What did he mean by that?' asked Crossman. 'Did you hear what the colonel said about Rajputs and Bengalis?'

'No,' replied the captain in a reedy voice, 'but I can guess. There have been four Bengal regiments disbanded recently. Some talk of mutiny amongst the sepoys.'

'You think it's serious?'

'Serious? In what sense?'

'You think it'll spread?'

The captain took off his cap and shook his head. A spray of sweat went out from his thinning hair, which Crossman avoided. The cap was replaced and the captain peered down his narrow nose.

'Not to my way of thinking. Lot of fuss about nothing, if you ask me. Come down hard on these Pandies and they'll respect you for it. My guess is it'll all peter out. They've seen what happens when there's an odour of mutiny in the air and I doubt we'll see any more trouble. Those that have been naughty have lost their livelihood. If I had my way . . .' But the captain did not expand on this, having to return a havildar's salute.

When the sepoy had passed by, the captain suddenly turned and faced Crossman. He put his hands on his hips, revealing the perspiration patches beneath his armpits. His manner was almost confrontational.

'Well, what d'ye think of India, Lieutenant?'

'I haven't really had time to gain an impression yet, being a new boy here.'

A snort of derision greeted this answer. The captain cried, 'I was in India a week before I knew I *hated* the place. It stinks. You either love it or you despise it. There are those who tell me they find England dull after here, but I ain't one of 'em, I can tell you that. To my way of thinking the food is disgusting, the heat is unbearable and the social life intolerable. I am bored to the very roots of my soul. I can't wait for my time to come.'

He rubbed his right shoulder hard with his knuckles.

'Took a bullet there,' he explained, wincing. 'Plays the very devil when I get out of sorts with myself.'

Crossman didn't know whether the man meant death or repatriation, but it was clear from his vehement words and the ugly expression on his face that he loathed every aspect of life at the moment. For his part, Jack had not really thought very deeply about whether he himself loved, hated or was indifferent to India. There had been days when he had been very low and there had been times when he had felt lifted by the sheer intoxicating breath of his new

109

environment. He thought about it now. To hate a subcontinent? Was that possible? There were so many diverse regions and peoples you couldn't put them all in one bag. Yes, the food took some getting used to and the heat was not good to someone from a temperate climate, but he felt that time and usage would help to smooth these into place. As for a social calendar, when had he ever had one of those?

'Well,' he said, 'I may be one of the first to fall between your two extremes, Captain. May I know your name? Mine is Crossman – Lieutenant Jack Crossman of the 88th Foot.'

'Queen's army, eh? You may get out of here quicker than me. I see you're travelling in cottons. Good idea. Damn stock.' He ran a finger around the inside of his collar as if it were strangling him. 'Name's Butcher. Captain Douglas Butcher.' He stuck out a hand which, when Crossman grasped it, felt as limp and slippery as a basted fish. 'See you around, Crossman.'

The captain marched off, his hand clenched by his sides, looking drab and unhappy.

Jack went back to his tent and found King waiting for him. When he told King about Colonel Stuton's criticism, the sergeant scoffed.

'Sir, you don't really think these natives would open up in front of you, do you? It doesn't take long to learn a smattering of the language. I'm not bad at it myself now and I didn't do any formal learning, like you. I just picked it up as we went along. If they had anything important which they wanted to keep from you, they wouldn't say it any language. They'd wait until they were sure you were out of earshot. I expect men like Stuton and Hodson and Nicholson all speak the local languages like natives themselves and wouldn't think of holding it back.'

Crossman was relieved. 'Of course, you're right, Sergeant. Thank you.' Still, he resolved that in future the fewer people who knew that he could understand Hindi, Pashto and Urdu the better. He would keep himself to himself and not seek admiration for his skills. 'It's just that Stuton . . .'

'Look, sir,' said King, 'I've been talking with a Scotch sergeant while you've been out. You know what this commander's maxim is? *The way to deal with a Pathan is to first knock him down, then pick him up.* That's the kind of man you've been talking to. He sounds a rough sort, if you ask me. A raw-knuckles man. I had a sergeant-major, just the same sort, in training – he would put you on your back as soon as look at you and then tell you it was for your own good.'

'Perhaps the frontier needs men like him to hew it into shape?'

'Yes, sir, but we don't need to admire them for other things, do we? All I'm saying is, he's probably not the man *you* ought to be taking lessons from, in your line of work.'

Crossman was grateful to his sergeant for these words.

King could be irritating in the extreme, but there were aspects of his character Crossman was finding admirable. The blacksmith's son was driving prejudices from Fancy Jack Crossman by the day. The lieutenant's direct dealings with classes lower than his own birthright had opened him to new revelations. His father had taught him that common people were not very bright, had no proper understanding of manners and morals (which was rich, coming from him) and were all right if told what to do. The easiest way for the upper classes (and indeed the middle classes) to ensure superiority was to equate station with intelligence: the lower the station, the lower the intellect. Jack Crossman had learned on his own account that it didn't work like that and he was going to make sure he didn't make the same mistake with people of another culture, which it seemed many Europeans were apt to do in India.

While they were in Stuton's camp, Crossman studied the local men under British command. They looked a fierce, tough breed, some of them undoubtedly from the Afghan hills, others from the Punjab itself. Crossman saw a variety of weapons displayed, including the dreaded long Khyber knife and, apart from the tulwars, the shamshir swords with their lighter hilts. It was wise to recall that the British had suffered one of their worst defeats when Afghan tribes slaughtered a column of more than 4,000 British troops and a far more numerous band of camp followers on their way from Kabul in '42. A promise of safe passage by the Afghan ruler had been ignored by the hill tribes, many of whom were autonomous. Only one man had survived, a surgeon, who had witnessed the last stand of the 44th Foot, men of the Essex regiment, who had refused point blank to surrender to the enemy.

Besides native troops, attached to the Rifles, for the march they were making, was a contingent of EIC European soldiers As with many regiments there were different groups and one or two loners. The loners were mostly lying on their beds in their tents, reading or simply laying

111

back with their hands behind their heads staring at canvas. Down by the river was a bunch of men who obviously enjoyed physical exercise, playing long-bullets, a game which Crossman had seen only once before, where a ball was hit along the ground with one hand.

A few clutches of men were wandering the bazaar. It did not matter where the British set up a camp, whether they be billeted in the middle of a town or out in the desert, a bazaar would spring up next to it within hours. There would be women in one of the tents, selling themselves, and there would be bars and pepper-steak grills and all sorts of entertainment for those who had rupees to spend. Barbers, tailors, shoemakers, coffee sellers – their tents were up and running alongside the army. When the regiments were in the process of striking their camp, so were the camp followers.

Crossman passed a group of British soldiers on the edge of the jungle. They were in shirtsleeves, lounging on a grassy sward. Crossman heard one of them say, 'Billy Stink, if it please you, Johnson . . .' The lieutenant paused, thinking they might be referring to him in some way, but he saw a bottle being handed from one man to the other.

'What's that?' he asked. 'What's in the bottle?'

'This?' One soldier said, smirking. 'This here's Billy Stink. You want a taster, chum?' The bottle was held out to him. He did not take it and for a moment he thought he was going to be abused for failing to drink with them, but something must have triggered their caution. His accent, perhaps, or his demeanour, his confident approach. They sensed authority.

One of the men whispered hoarsely to his friend, 'He's the officer.'

'Beg pardon, sir,' said the man who had offered the drink, 'didn't know you in them cottons.'

They did not jump to their feet. Soldiers were never as concerned by an officer not of their regiment and even less so of one not of their army. They knew him now for who he was, for in such far-flung lands such a party as his would be the sole subject of conversation for at least a couple of days.

Crossman asked, 'What's Billy Stink?'

'Blimey, you 'aven't bin 'ere long, 'ave you, sir? Arrack, it is. So cheap we use the dregs in our lamps at night.'

There was laughter amongst the men, which encouraged the comedian.

'It burns so bright and fierce you'd think an angel of the Lord had landed amongst us. Sometimes it don't do us no good, 'cause too much of the stuff make you wake up blind in the mornin'. Just now it's burnin' our bellies, bright and fierce as you please.'

'That's if you wake at all,' said Crossman, 'for you might as well drink quicklime as that fermentation.'

The soldiers roared at that. One of them suddenly broke the conversation with a whooping sound. He reached into the grasses where a line was pegged to the earth. He grabbed the cord and began reeling in a large black crow, which fluttered and flapped as it fought against the pull. The line was hooked at the end like a piece of fishing tackle, but obviously laid out to catch scavenger birds such as this one.

'Got you my little beauty,' cried the soldier. 'Now we got a goer, eh, Smedge? You get yourn and we'll set to soon as you like.'

Crossman walked off. He had seen this before, in Bombay. The men would tie coloured rag collars to the crows and set them on to each other like fighting cocks, gambling on the winner. Unlike in cockfighting, the crows did not kill each other, but usually one saw the other off. The troops called it 'mortal combat' but rarely did the birds suffer serious harm, except when the disgruntled owner of the losing crow shot his bird. Sometimes a soldier who had lost a lot of money also shot the winning bird in a fit of pique. It had also been known for the owner of one bird to shoot the owner of another. Who knew what would happen when you mixed rot-gut alcohol with gambling in a bunch of tough, bored soldiers let loose in a foreign land?

When Jack was a short distance from them, though, an Irishman among them called out in a strong Ulster accent.

'That sergeant of yours – I know him for a runner, sor.'

The man stood staring darkly at Crossman and nodding his head slowly. The remark was significant. Jack thought about questioning the man, but decided against it. The Irish soldier then turned back to his friends and joined in with encouraging one or the other fighting bird.

Later, when one of those soft evenings came in, black-and-red velvet curtains over the silhouetted jungle, Crossman asked King to join him at his tent. They sat outside on their canvas chairs like two explorers of an untamed land. Jack had opened a bottle of whisky which he had been saving to celebrate the end of their journey. He now offered the sergeant a tot '. . .or a chotapeg, as they say here,' said

113

Crossman. King accepted the offer gratefully and was soon mellow in his mood. As Crossman had guessed, Farrier King was not a hard drinker, finding his work more intoxicating than any leisure pursuit. It did not take a great deal of amber liquid to make him merry.

'So, Sergeant, tell me,' said Jack, as they listened to the sounds of the crickets and other jungle inhabitants, 'have you seen any action? Anywhere?' He rubbed his stump involuntarily as he spoke and King seemed to notice this and appeared to be a little embarrassed by it.

'Oh, never as much as you, sir,' came the reply. King sipped his whisky. 'You were in four or five battles, I understand, in the Crimea? It's not easy to survive just one. You must have a lucky stamp on your soul.'

'Perhaps, perhaps. So, you have seen some fighting. Where was it? You weren't in the Crimea?'

'No, but in the same war, sir. I was at Kars.'

At that moment they were interrupted by Ishwar Raktambar, who came into the light of their lamp. He was dressed in splendid attire and gleamed from head to foot. Crossman was tempted to joke about the Rajput going to a ball, but knew it would not be taken in the right humour.

'Sahib,' said the Rajput, 'one of my cousins has asked me to visit him this evening – he is here in this camp.'

'Certainly. Permission granted.'

The dark brown eyes of the Indian gleamed in the lamp light.

'We may talk a long time.'

'If you wish to remain with him for the night, I have no objection. However, I would like us to be ready to leave at six am.'

The Rajput bowed his head and backed away, his two palms together in that prayerlike attitude the locals often adopted.

'Now,' Jack said, 'you were saying? You were at Kars. With General Williams?'

'Williams Pasha, as they called him. Yes. I was there with some sappers,' confirmed King. 'We dug trenches – dirty work like that. Nothing so glamorous as what you were doing as a sergeant in the Crimea. No famous charges, no blistering infantry attacks. It was a war of sorts, I suppose, but nothing to write home about.'

King had reminded him gently that they had both been of the same rank at one time and were therefore brothers-in-arms. Crossman was beginning to realize that this otherwise roughly-hewn man, from low beginnings, had natural subtleties in his character. King could also

114

manipulate, for the constant reminders that Crossman had fought a hard and bitter war in the Crimea would have tempted any old campaigner into launching into stories. The lieutenant did indeed appear to fall for this ploy, telling King about one of his exploits, that of tracking down and killing deserters. The young sergeant was obviously a little shocked by the tale of the massacre at the end.

'You executed them?'

'We fought them on the beach. They were just as likely to kill us as we were to kill them. The corporal who was their leader had indeed "executed" some of his own rebels. It was a dirty business, not at all like digging trenches, it dirtied the soul not the hands.'

King was still a little shaken. He stared at his lieutenant as if seeing him in a new light.

'Did you do work like that all the time?'

'All the time. That was our job. To infiltrate the enemy lines. To spy, to commit acts of sabotage. To assassinate . . .'

'To assassinate? To *murder*? Sir, forgive me, but you sound – I don't know – you almost sound proud of such work.'

'It was thrust upon me. I did it to the best of my ability. That's what a soldier should do. One gets used to the grit. One swallows it. I admit it took me some while to come to an acceptance of it, but lives were saved because of that which me and my men achieved.' Crossman began to move in for the kill. 'But tell me, have you never done anything of which you were ashamed? In war, I mean. What about Kars?'

King said, 'No – nothing like that. I have never killed a man in cold blood. Of course, I've killed in battle, but . . . you know my ability with a weapon, sir.' He laughed lightly. 'I'm an engineer. That's what I do best . . .'

'Digging holes.'

'Not just that. As you are well aware, I'm now a mapmaker. That's a very noble occupation – isn't it?'

Crossman conceded that it was better than digging holes at any rate. Then he went on to say that he had also fought in and survived those battles that King had mentioned. Firefights that were open and above reproach. They were legitimate killing grounds where men could shoot men without any stain on their souls. On the battlefield a soldier could kill and not have his name go up in his parish church as anything but a hero.

115

'Did you ever fear that?' asked Crossman, casually. 'A note pinned to the board in the parish church? A note with your name on it?'

Despite the mellowing effect of the whisky the sergeant suddenly smelled a rat. He stared out into the night. There were comforting sounds out there, of animals eating fodder; of men conversing quietly in the light of other lamps; of the clink of horse brass and other metal objects. He did not answer Jack's question, remaining silent, listening, watching.

Crossman said quietly, 'Did you ever run away?'

King tried to get to his feet, but was a little drunk and fell back in the canvas chair.

'Well, did you?'

The sergeant said, 'I don't know what you mean.'

'Yes you do. I was told you ran away. The man who told me might've been lying of course. Or even mistaken. But that's what he said, without malice it seemed to me. Was it true? I need to know. I need to know because I have to understand how far I can trust you in tight conditions. It doesn't matter to me otherwise. I'm not here to judge. Others have presumably already done that, it being common knowledge amongst some. Did you, Sergeant King, leave your post, desert the battlefield?'

King's struggling now paid off. He finally managed to get to his feet, though he was swaying dangerously. The sergeant looked down at his commanding officer.

'It wasn't like that.'

'What was it like? That's all I'm asking. I'm not looking to twist knives into old wounds. I know what a hell the battlefield can be. I've been there. Sometimes men become disorientated, lose all sense of direction, or are simply out of their minds with fear. Others simply become confused by the noise and the smell of human blood. It's not always a straight case of cowardice . . .'

King flushed at the word to the very roots of his hair.

'I'm no coward!' he shouted. 'Whoever said that was a liar.'

Talk in nearby tent suddenly ceased. Other ears were now listening.

'Calm down,' said Crossman. 'Sit down. Keep your voice low. D'you want to rouse the whole camp? I'm trying to understand.'

King flopped down in his chair again. He took a large gulp of whisky and held out his glass for more. Jack filled it, sympathetically.

'There were seven of us,' said King. 'We were digging a mine, under an enemy position. The idea was to put explosives in the end and blow a gun emplacement to the heavens . . .'

Jack wondered at the difference between this kind of warfare and his own sabotage which King had decried, but said nothing. He also wondered if King's objections to such an action had put him at variance with his superiors, but this did not appear to be the case.

'. . . but the materials for the mine's supports were hard to find. The wood we took was either rotten or not good — not hard and strong — and the weight of the mine's roof — well, it was heavy, full of rocks and stones. I said to the ensign that the mine wasn't safe, that I didn't want to go down.' King licked his lips after taking another swig of his drink. 'But I did go down, for a while, then I came out again. Have you even been down a mine, sir? It's hot and smelly. You get that closed-in feeling.'

'No, but I can well imagine how such an atmosphere might cause feelings of panic.'

'I didn't panic,' snapped King, indignantly. 'That's just what I didn't do. Because I was last in, with arguing with the ensign, I was at the back. I heard the props cracking. I yelled at the others to get out too. But I was in their way. I was just the corporal then. There was a sergeant. He was up at the front. We were passing stuff, munitions and other equipment, from my end up to the front chamber, where they were laying it, ready to light the fuses. I heard something. I heard a creaking and shouted it was going. Then I got out of the way quick. I had to be quick or there wouldn't be enough time, see. We had to crawl backwards swift as we could. The roof was so low we were almost on our bellies, so it wasn't easy. I had dirt in my nose and mouth and there was water in the bottom of the tunnel. It wasn't easy, but I'm certain sure I didn't knock a prop out. Not with my elbow, not with my leg — nor any bit of me. Look, if all of us were to get out at all, I had to get out of the tunnel first. That makes sense, doesn't it?'

It did indeed make sense and Crossman nodded thoughtfully.

King had bitter words to spit out. '*They* said I panicked. They said I somehow caused the fall by scrambling backwards in a funk. That wasn't so.'

'The tunnel collapsed then?'

'It fell in. I was the only one who got out. We tried to dig to them, but they'd suffocated, or was crushed by then. I didn't do any good.'

117

King slumped back in his chair, the misery apparent on his face. He was vociferous in his proclamations of innocence, but Jack could see the man was in an agony of torment at the remembrance of the incident. Was he so sure of himself? It appeared to the lieutenant that his sergeant was still questioning his own motives, still wondering whether *they* were right. Had he panicked? Or had he simply been more aware than the others of his team of the fragility of the tunnel? Certainly his ears would have been tuned at that point to the slightest sound from the support timbers, having raised the fact with his officer. But his refusal to go down in the first instance must have fuelled the suspicions of those who believed it was his fault that the mine collapsed, that he knocked something in his haste to get out which triggered the falling of a whole domino line of struts and props.

'Thank you, Sergeant, I understand now.'

'It wasn't my fault.'

Crossman said, 'I haven't any right to judge you guilty or other-wise — of anything at all. I wasn't there.'

A silence fell between them during which a harsh laugh of some soldier or other rent the peaceful evening air. It was probably nothing to do with either of these two men. It was simply campfire humour, out there in the night, where men without heavy consciences could alight on something funny.

'Were you punished?' asked Crossman, out of curiosity.

'Yes, but not for getting out — for refusing the order before we went down.'

'I see. But you kept your stripes?'

'No, sir. I lost them. I got them back later, when I transferred.'

'And was promoted yet again, up from corporal?'

'I went straight to sergeant. If you must know my father had a little money he saved. He bribed an officer to promote me. And before you say anything, sir, I must tell you I don't see the difference in that to officers like you purchasing a lieutenancy, or a captaincy, whatever. It's just the same thing. Money for rank. I'm not ashamed of *that*, that's certain.'

The inference was that he was ashamed of something, but whether the incident at the mine, or some other aspect of his army life Crossman was not going to know. The lieutenant said he had nothing further to say on the subject, except to tell the sergeant that he had not bought his lieutenancy, that he had been promoted in the field.

'I knew that – I wasn't meaning you, personally, sir. I was talking of the purchase system in general.'

'Just so. Well, I'm going to turn in, Sergeant. I'm glad we had this little talk. I'm sorry if it opened old wounds, but I needed to know what was behind that remark I heard. Thank you for being honest.'

'You do believe me, sir?'

'I'm in no position to comment.' He could see that King was desperate for support. 'I'm sorry, Sergeant.'

'No, you're right.' King hung his head a little. 'You can't absolve me – no one can. Good night, sir. Early wake-up?'

'I think so, Sergeant.'

Once King had gone Jack poured himself another whisky, knowing he would suffer for it in the morning, but feeling a need to re-enter that gleaming old-gold world where even if everything is not all right, one doesn't care that it isn't. He leaned back in the creaky chair and allowed the balmy evening to cosset him as it never would have done at home. Warm soft air wrapped itself around him making him feel better than he should.

The extra imbibing didn't work of course: whisky will not do the same job twice in one evening. Second efforts are always disappointing. Yet he enjoyed the gentle breezes on his back and the rustling of the palms. It was a tranquil atmosphere. Jane, he knew, would find India a joy. She would be one of those who fell definitely into the adoration yard. The exotic sights, scents and sounds of the orient would beguile her.

Jack missed Rupert Jarrard, to talk with. He and Rupert, an American war correspondent, had shared many quiet hours during the two years Crossman had spent in the Crimea. Rupert was a good man to bounce things off, even if in the end you did not take his advice, which was often applied in a forthright manner. They were soulmates, he and Jarrard. Jane was the love of his life but she did not understand military problems, or if she did she did not care to enter into a discussion about them. Her advice over King would be to let bygones be bygones, give the man a fresh start. Forget what had gone before and begin with a clean sheet.

That was too dangerous for a soldier to do. Rupert would understand that more was at stake than mere forgiveness. There were other lives to consider. If King was a military recidivist then Crossman would feel duty bound to get rid of him, even if Hawke or Lovelace insisted the sergeant remain. Neither the colonel nor the major had to go out into the field with Sergeant King. Crossman and his men did.

Jack no more wanted to judge his sergeant than King wanted to be judged. There was a thinner line between cowardice and courage than there was between sanity and madness. If a man be afraid and fall under the spell of that fear it need not be a sin. It is only a wrong if others are relying on the sinner and he runs and leaves them to a terrible fate. Then, of course, in the eyes of the army it is a monstrous wrong, worthy of a death sentence. To leave King behind a desk would not injure anyone but King, who would wrestle with his shame and either win or lose. There would be no external effects. No group of men would suffer because that struggle.

It all came down to this: did Jack believe Farrier King when the sergeant said he had not panicked?

'I'm turnin' in for the night, sir. Should you be wantin' me for further duties, I'll be in my own tent. Your kit's all up to the mark. I seen to that earlier. Boots is shined. Coat is brushed. Got to get some shuteye now.'

'Thank you, Corporal,' said Crossman, turning to see Gwilliams coming out of his tent. The lieutenant had not seen him enter it. 'Er, Gwilliams, did you hear the conversation?'

'Atween you an' the sergeant? Couldn't but help it. Didn't stay intentional to hear it, but once the sergeant started in, weren't nothing for it but to listen in.'

'I'm not accusing you of eavesdropping. Since you did hear, what do you think? You know what I'm talking about. I need to make a decision very quickly. It affects you as much as it does me.'

'He was then just a boy. Things done then is all part of the learnin'. Youth is impulsive. It jumps where it should wait a second. Youth don't take time to calculate, it works by intuition. Once it's jumped the wrong way a coupla times, it starts to settle some. Our boy is at the settling stage to my way of thinking. He's done jumping.'

'Yes but we can't let him practise on us, now can we?'

'I think he's up and done his practising. I think he knows what's what now. Didn't he do good at that last skirmish? He'll be fine. He's a square kind of a fellah, ain't he? Square body, square feet, square fists, square head, square mind. I think he's all squared away now. All

120

the points is worn down and he'll do, I reckon.' Gwilliams spat at a big black beetle that was crawling under the tent flap and success-fully drowned it. 'That's my opinion, sir, take it or leave it. I'm off to my bed.'

Jack was surprised. He had expected Gwilliams to come down hard on King. Instead, he had given an honest considered opinion. Jack's admiration for Gwilliams increased from that moment. He knew the American did not like the sergeant, yet he had not used the opportunity to get rid of him. Nine other men would have gone with their feelings, not their minds.

Crossman gave it another half an hour, which he wiled away watching the Punjab soldiers huddled around their fires. To a man they squatted on their haunches and the lieutenant finally went to bed wondering why such a position was so difficult for Europeans. Was it just because they were unused to putting their body in that shape? It looked so comfortable. It looked as if the human form was meant for such a position. Yet he had tried it himself and found his calves aching within a few minutes.

A morning filled with drums and bugles came too soon and sure enough Jack's head was troubling him. He had been dreaming, for shame not of Mrs Jane Mulinder Crossman, but of the gyrocompass, which probably had something to do with his head feeling as if it were full of liquid in which his brain spun this way and that, search-ing for the True North of knowledge. He took his morning coffee from the chai man, fingers trembling, with a feeling of gratitude that bordered on benediction. Through the open tent flap he could see the morning parades in progress.

Once he was up, washed and dressed he felt a little better. Bugles were still blowing, and when they were not the gaps were filled by cockerels and the squeal of hungry pigs or the snort of cows. Some-how all these religions with their different eating rituals managed to live side by side without too much trouble. Jack went first to see the horses and found Raktambar grooming them. The beasts had already been fed and watered and looked very happy to be pampered.

'You don't need to do that,' said Jack. 'One of the guides' duties is to groom the mounts.'

'I like to,' came the simple reply.

Crossman left the Rajput to it and went on to the camels, where he found Ibhanan with a lame dromedary. She had picked up a thorn and the wound had festered, leaving her in pain. The thorn itself had been removed, though she was still upset. She moaned on seeing Jack, as if she recognized someone who could something about her problem. He stroked the matted hair on her head and asked Ibhanan if they could get another beast and let this one rest.

'She can't draw a cart like this. Where's the sergeant, by the way?'

'Out far-looking,' replied the Hindu, which meant the sergeant was playing with his theodolite or sextant somewhere.

'All right. Can you get another camel from the village?'

'I will try, sahib, though they be very poor creatures in this part of the world.'

All the men from Bombay were disparaging of the Punjab flora and fauna. In fact they didn't think much of *anything* up here. Which was counteracted of course by the general local feeling that anyone from outside the land of the five rivers was an inferior being.

'How many rupees will you need?'

Ibhanan told him the amount and was given it.

'Take Sajan with you. Teach the boy how to haggle.'

'Yes, sahib, it is a very necessary thing here in India.'

'Here or anywhere,' said Crossman, remembering how he had to haggle with his laundry woman in London.

A fakir and a snake charmer, who had entered the camp that morning, now tried to catch Crossman's eye. But he was becoming adept at looking into the middle distance as if studying the horizon. The pair chattered at him as he passed them, but he knew he had to ignore them. You couldn't help the whole of India and there were a lot of needy souls here. Many millions in the Punjab alone and that was but a small part. Sometimes he found himself buying things he did not want, or paying for services or entertainments he did not need, but today he was steel.

'Sergeant?' he shouted, seeing King moving between some far tents. 'We need you. We're soon to be on the move.'

King, glimmering instrument in hand, walked towards him. At that moment the captain Crossman had met the previous day passed by. The captain said, within King's hearing, 'I'd get rid of that one, if I were you, Lieutenant. I hear he scuttles at the sound of a gun.'

Until that moment Jack had not made up his mind about his sergeant. Until now there had still been nagging pictures, imagined confrontations with tribesmen in the Afghan mountains, ending with

Sergeant King deserting his post, riding away on the only available horse, yelling hysterically that he was going for reinforcements. But the captain's words had blasted all those images out of his head. Infuriated, he said in a very even voice, 'I'll thank you to leave the men under my command to me, Captain.'

The captain whirled on his heels, gave Crossman a very nasty look, and muttered something about 'regret' which Jack did not quite catch. He gave the captain the benefit of the doubt, preferring to believe that the other officer had expressed regret at interfering in his business, rather than prophesying that Jack would later regret his words. There must have been something in Crossman's expression which made the other man hesitate to repeat his statement, for he turned again and walked on. The captain's weak right shoulder slumped as if this incident, on top of having to bear burden of life in India, was just too much for one man to carry.

King said in a quiet voice, 'Thank you, sir.'

'I suggest we get about our duty,' answered Crossman, sternly, without looking at his sergeant. 'Others have been up and about for hours, preparing for the march while you've been playing with that thing.'

King stiffened a little, but then seemed to realize his officer was trying to disguise an acute embarrassment.

'I have been up and about too, sir,' he finally said, mildly. 'My kit is packed and ready to go, as is that of my men. The tents are all in. I've just ordered one of the chain-men to strike your tent.'

'Very good, Sergeant,' replied Jack, briskly. 'I expect another camel to be here soon, then we'll be on our way.'

As they rode out of camp, an hour later, the *mussock* men were back wandering the banks of the river, carrying their inflated buffalo hides on their backs, only their legs visible beneath. They looked very, very strange, resembling giant plucked birds strolling around. Blind, mouthless, with bare stubby wings and cropped claws, they seemed to drift along the bank of the river like shapes from a horrible dream painted by Hieronymus Bosch. Crossman could not help but let a shudder go through him, though he knew there were but men beneath, anxiously hoping for river passengers and cargo: men with their work on their backs, looking to make a few annas.

17

Plunging into forests of ebony and teak, some of the trees nearly a hundred feet high, Ibhanan told them this region was infested with tigers and large crushing snakes. Understandably, this made everyone nervous, and the hardwood forest, sometimes impenetrable, had to be negotiated one way or another, mostly by making detours where necessary. Eyes flicked from overhead boughs in search of slithering giants, to umbriferous bushes which might harbour burning-bright beasts bearing claws and fangs. When they came out the other side, neither Crossman nor anyone else had seen a tiger or a boa constrictor. Ibhanan believed this to be a miracle, saying many of the compass-wallahs whom he had served had been torn to pieces by tigers.

Crossman confided in Gwilliams. 'I don't believe there are wild tigers in India,' he said. 'I think it's a myth perpetuated by those who think they *ought* to have seen one, therefore they make up a story.'

'You could be right,' muttered the corporal, nevertheless looking around at shadows dancing under the palms. 'Fisherman's tales to impress.'

The pair of them convinced each other that, like men's stories of sexual prowess, tales of tigers were nine-tenths fiction.

They were not four days out from Stuton's camp when Jack fell foul of Punjab fever. He felt ill during the afternoon and took to his bed before evening swept in. His stepmother had never been a sympathetic nurse with her children, lovely though she was in many other ways, and had always advocated that fresh air and a strong

124

constitution would defeat most ailments, applying her philosophy to herself as well as to her husband and sons. It was her idea that illness was an unwanted invader and could be driven out with a stout stick. Thus when Jack was ever laid on his back he felt guilty for being so weak in allowing the invader to get the better of him.

He tried ignoring the fever by occupying his mind. Unwisely, he chose to read, by the jaundiced lamplight, a small volume given to him by Rupert Jarrard: twice-told tales written by the American author Nathaniel Hawthorne. The first story he read was the ghastly tale of a young lady who grew poisonous plants and whose very breath imbibed that poison, not affecting her, but eventually killing her youthful lover with their toxic fumes when they kissed. It was not a good subject for an invalid and the tiny print of the pocket edition was soon swimming before his eyes, making him feel dizzy. Once he had vomited over his sheet, had it changed, then immediately vomited again, he knew it was time to surrender. His mother would have disapproved, but he could not fight it any longer, and lay back on his bed with a spinning brain to sweat out the worst of it. Very soon his fevered mind was racked by images of the poisoned garden and its mistress.

The headache was excruciating and the feeling of nausea horrible, but in the morning he asked to be laid in the back of the camel cart, so that they could continue the journey.

'No, sir – you're much too sick to be moved,' pronounced King, adding, which he subsequently realized was a great mistake on his part, 'and there are a series of shallow valleys here, shrouded with vegetation, which have not yet been properly mapped. It'll give me the opportunity to prove myself at surveying an unknown and thickly jungled area. You must rest, sir. Leave things to Gwilliams and me. We'll manage well enough.'

Crossman went up on his elbows, his yellow eyes wild-looking and rolling in his head. 'Sergeant! Sergeant, I order you . . .'

The lieutenant's breath was foul and King winced, backing away from the exhalations.

'Sir, you're in no condition to argue. Gwilliams is coming to give you a wash and try to make you as comfortable as possible. We're all very concerned for your welfare. Ibhanan is making up a herbal potion which he says will help with the fever. We must trust to his judgement, he having been born in this country. No – don't try to

\text{}
125

get up. Sir! Sir! I mean it. I'm sorry, but this requires firmness on my part. Please remain in your bed, Lieutenant, or I'll have to call Raktambar and have you restrained!'

'You— Damn you, Sergeant . . .'

'Your mind isn't your own at present. You're in the grip of fevered delusions. I've assumed command of the expedition, which after all has mapping as its main aim. You know I did tell you this when we met in London, sir, and I still believe it to be true. It was in my orders. You say you've been told something else. Well, be that as it may, now that I am in charge I must carry out the orders given to me.'

Gwilliams entered the tent with Sajan carrying a bowl of cool water and a compress, just as the lieutenant's fingers scuttled crab-like under his pillow, presumably searching for his revolver. When he couldn't find it he reached up with his other hand, the missing one, for his sword which hung from the central pole. Naturally there were no fingers to grip the hilt, though possibly in his fevered state of mind he imagined them back. Frustrated by the uselessness of the appendage, Crossman wailed.

'I shall kill you, damn you.'

King unhooked the belt, scabbard and sword to keep them away from the distraught and demented lieutenant.

'Corporal Gwilliams, please note that the officer is completely out of his mind,' said King, 'due to the maddening affect of the illness. I've taken the liberty of removing any weapons from his tent, should the said officer – in his delusional state – accidentally injure himself or someone else. We must keep him under constant watch lest he cause any harm.'

Gwilliams looked at King hard. It was always difficult to know what the corporal was thinking, due to the fact that his face was almost completely enveloped by a magnificent mane and beard, both worthy of an ancient Assyrian King. Crinkled hair and full set were all the colour of burnished bronze and spread like the sun's rays away from the little patch of flesh in the centre of its mass. Gwilliams had an awesome countenance.

'You figure he can't be moved?'

'I'm certain of it, Corporal,' said King, trying to subdue the lower rank with an officious air. 'He's much too sick. We could damage his brain with too much jigging about on the cart.'

126

Here Sajan came to King's rescue. 'Sahib,' cried the boy, tugging on Gwilliam's beard, 'we must seek to give him rest.'

'The boy is right,' continued King. 'Rest is important, don't you agree, Corporal? Now, I'll inform the rest of the camp that we'll remain here until the fever breaks properly.'

'No,' croaked Crossman, but then he fell back on his pillow – a folded coat. His mouth, encrusted with dried white saliva, was a testament to how ill he was.

A few moments later the convulsions began. They held Crossman down, Gwilliams ramming a ball of rags in his mouth to stop him from biting through his tongue. His eyes were frightening to behold and, once the convulsions ceased, King was glad to leave the tent. The lieutenant was now yelling hoarsely, but not at the sergeant. His shouts were apocalyptic prophetic nonsense, right out of the Revelations of St John. Had the minister, John Stillwell, been there, he would have said the lieutenant had been struck by the hand of the Lord and was speaking in tongues.

Sergeant Farrier King was in bliss. He tried to feel guilty about his happy state of being, but couldn't succeed. Of course he was worried about Lieutenant Crossman's illness and hoped his officer would recover, but since he, King, couldn't do very much about it then the time would be usefully employed. He made his way to a nearby hill and once on top climbed a tree like a young boy. Once at the crown he viewed the countryside. It was ripe for mapping. To his knowledge only one map had been published of this area, and that was by Baldwin and Cradock of Paternoster Row, April 1834. It had been published under the superintendence of the Society for the Diffusion of Useful Knowledge, a worthy body, but it had been surveyed in a time of conflicts and upheaval, by amateur mapmakers.

This particular map, which the sergeant had in his possession right now, had been surveyed and drawn by two gentlemen turned adventurers. They were a restless scholar and vicar, sometime water diviner, named Jones whose parish in Haslemere Surrey had finally proved too dusty for his lively mind, and a River-Master Baxter, the pilot of a russet-sailed Thames barge who yearned to be on the big oceans of the world and had crewed on a ship which was wrecked on the shores of northern India in '29. Their work was adequate but not entirely professional, and King was glad of that.

127

Raktambar sauntered over to him when he arrived back at the camp. King suddenly realized he was now the centre of the world for all these people. It was a new experience for him. As a sergeant, of course he had had men under him, but there was always someone else around to take the final responsibility. Now he was the ultimate authority in this little band. It might have gone to his head if he had not other fish to fry.

'Yes, Ishwar,' he said, as the Rajput approached him. 'What can I do for you?'

'You will call me Raktambar. My first name is for my family and friends.'

Nothing could spoil the sergeant's mood today.

'Forgive me. Well, what is it?'

'Is he really sick? The lieutenant?'

'Yes he is,' King replied, gravely. 'Very sick I'm afraid.'

'Will he die?' There was a note of hope in the Rajput's tone which the sergeant could not miss.

King was suitably shocked. 'I don't think so. If we can break the fever he'll find his way back to health. I'm surprised at you, Raktambar. I thought you Hindus had a great respect for life?'

'Some life, it is true.'

'All life, I thought.'

Raktambar shrugged and then said, 'I think he will die. He has the yellow look. You *firinghi* die like flies in our land. You have pale weak bodies that do not like the heat and the smells. You get sick very easily and you die very easily. I think the lieutenant will die and I will go back to the maharajah and take myself a wife.'

'Flies don't die that easily,' muttered King. 'You have heard Englishmen use that saying, but it's not true. Flies take a lot of killing, that's why there're so many of them. That's why the bloody things are always around to bother us so much.'

Raktambar blinked. King realized that the Indian was confused by his ramblings. The Rajput had been expecting an argument about the lieutenant's health, not about the durability of flies. King knew what the man was thinking – that there was no fathoming these *firinghi*, that they had minds which flitted back and forth like butterflies. Well, thought King, it makes a change. The boot is on the other foot for once. He regarded the tall man before him and saw a disgruntled palace guard, taken away from his own and given to

128

another he neither knew or cared anything about. Raktambar's spirit was in a sorry state and he was homesick. On top of that he had to tramp halfway across India with a group of mad British soldiers, suffering all the indignities and inconveniences, all the discomforts of life in the field.

Raktambar was not used to the dirt, the direct heat of the sun, the proximity of horses and camels, the long marches, the snatched poor-quality meals, water from a different well or stream. The outdoors was anathema to him. He despised the jungle, having known only well-ordered gardens. Muddy streams had replaced his marble fountains which sprayed crystal waters. He now slept on the grubby ground in a tent, whereas before he had known a *charpoy* in a cool room swept clean every day by palace servants. In fact, this work he had been given, to protect this Englishman, was a living hell to him and it was no wonder he hoped the man would breathe his last.

'I'm sorry, but I doubt the lieutenant will die, Raktambar. I know it's very disappointing for you, but there it is. You never know, he may take a turn for the worse very soon. These diseases have a habit of revisiting us pale weak-bodied creatures and finishing us off later. You might have to delay just a *little* longer before you get married, but it will be all that much sweeter for the wait. Now, I have work to do . . .'

He stepped around the Rajput, leaving the man staring off into the jungle.

Back in camp, for the first time King laid out on a makeshift table all the instruments of his profession. They were of course in prime condition, since he had lovingly oiled, polished and kept them so. Ibhanan of the elephant face had assisted him in this task. Both men were in a state of joy, knowing they now had time to do the work in which they took pleasure. The bright chains were out, the men in a state of anticipation.

Sajan, sent away from the lieutenant's tent by Gwilliams with the instructions to 'play some games, boy' – something the child had not done since the day he had been old enough to pull the cord of a punkah – arrived at the table with round eyes.

'All your gold, sahib!' said Sajan in a tone filled with awe. 'You are a very rich man.'

'Your English improves by the day,' King said, approvingly. 'Ibhanan, the young learn so quickly, don't they? I wish my Hindi was coming on as fast.'

Sajan reached up and stroked one of the shining brass chronometers. 'So much gold,' he said. 'So much riches.'

King saw a danger in this. He said sternly to the boy, 'You mustn't keep calling it that, baba,' using a fond word for a child. 'We'll have dacoits, badmashes and Goojurs queuing up to steal my instruments. They're not made of gold. They're made of brass – the same as the metal used to make Ibhanan's washbasin. Do you understand?'

'It shines like gold.'

'So does Ibhanan's basin.'

'Yes, sahib, but Ibhanan's *chillumchee* is just one piece. Your treasures have many pieces and much magic in them.'

King saw a way out. 'Yes, they're real and proper magic, and they will destroy any man who does not know their ways. Inside each of them is an evil djinn and a good genie. If they are stolen, the evil djinn will turn the instruments into monsters, which will up and eat the thief.'

Sajan's eyes narrowed. 'I think you tell a lie, sahib.'

'Look what happened to Sitakanta. Did he return after stealing my instruments? No, he was eaten by that one there.' King pointed to the sextant. 'It swallowed him whole and spat his bones and teeth on to the ground.'

Sajan eyes shot to the device in question.

'It is not possible, sahib. It is too small.'

'It grows, to an enormous size,' King's eyes climbed up the sky, knowing the boy's eyes were following, 'then like a giant metal crab, it leaps on its victim and devours it, crunching it to pulp.'

'You said it spitted out the bones and teeth.'

'In splinters and bits and pieces. Now, if you are very good, I'll allow you to polish my magical instruments. The bad djinn will allow you to do this, without harming you, because he likes his shell to be bright and sparkling like new. See that soft cloth over there? Fetch it and rub the casing of this solar compass with it until you can see the sun inside the metal. If you rub hard enough the good genie will reward you with an anna.'

Sajan's disbelief was faltering. 'Will I see the good genie, sahib? Will he appear?'

'The good genie, like the bad djinn, is invisible. He visits you when you least expect him. My guess is he will leave the anna under

130

your pillow tonight. That's what he does for me or Ibhanan, usually, when we polish the clock. Later still, when I have time, I'll show you how to use the sun compass properly, with the sextant that devoured Sitakanta, and you'll get to know how to work the magic of the stars. Would you like that?'

'Yes, after I get the anna,' replied the child, prioritizing. 'Then will I wish to know the work of the sextant.'

Sajan took the cloth and then gingerly began rubbing the casing of the solar compass, without lifting it up. He would do this for hours if required now. His years as a punkah-wallah had inured him to the boredom of tasks which by their nature were repetitive and dull. Yet he still had a lively mind, which the Europeans were further enlivening with stories and information, not necessarily for any philanthropic reasons, but because they found the boy entertaining. He was like the gardener's lad on a British estate: simply there, around and about, without having any real duties. Thus he wandered from one person to another, asking questions, helping in a childlike way, and learning quickly. They taught him things because it amused them to see how quickly he grasped them and repeated the words or tasks. He came out with such delightful quips. The adults retold them to one another, like jokes, or rather more like a grandfather quoting an amusing grandchild.

By midday, Ibhanan and King were measuring the elevations of the hills, using the differential method of levelling. Ibhanan had charge of a wooden levelling rod, marked in numbers with graduations. He took it and held it on a point of assumed elevation. King, holding a telescopic device fitted with a spirit level, sighted on the rod. The line of sight on Ibhanan's rod established for him the relative elevation of the telescope. Ibhanan then moved the rod to other positions for similar readings, thus establishing the difference between the separate points. King was also teaching Ibhanan how to use the solar compass – which required no needle, relying on the position of the sun to give them their compass points.

The pair were as happy as they could be and soon the angle instruments came out, the chains were used (and where they could not be employed, the perambulators) and vertical and horizontal measurements flowed on to the pages of Sergeant King's notebooks.

In the evenings, he sat at a table working out his calculations by lamplight, with Ibhanan close by his elbow, assisting him. This was how he had imagined it would be, when he was stuck in those miserable garrison towns and country billets back in England. This was what life was supposed to be about, charting the unknown – or failing that the inaccurate known – in a fascinating foreign land ripe for pen and coloured inks. There, laying down those wonderful symbols and marks which told men where they were, what was around and about them, and how to get to some other distant place. Writing exotic sentences such as, *A high ridge separates the Suthij from the Indus* and making an art, a beautiful representation of the landscape on paper, out of the science of mathematics and measurements.

When the night was clear, which most of them were, the stars came out in their shining millions. King had never seen such encrusted heavens, such a mass of glistering stars. He was absolutely lost in the wonder of it all, like a child seeing them for the first time. However he was not too awestruck by their beauty to use them for his purposes. Pouring mercury from a metal-encased bottle into a dish, thus manufacturing an artificial horizon, he used the level reflecting surface to calculate the angular altitudes of the stars, determining latitude, timing his observations with one of the chronometers for absolute accuracy. His heart was full. Here the work he loved went hand in hand with the splendour and magnificence of celestial lights.

To give him his due, Gwilliams left King to his work during the lieutenant's illness. The corporal didn't mind supervising such onerous tasks as digging the latrines, gathering wood, fetching water, and all those other chores necessary in a camp. Gwilliams did a lot of the cooking too, mostly because he didn't like spicy food, but partly because he enjoyed the task. King disliked cooking intensely, though he too was not used to some of the spicy food the Indians prepared, so was grateful for the dishes Gwilliams put before him. The lieutenant, on the other hand, had grown to love curry. But then, thought King, look where he was now – lying on his sick bed.

King knew that Gwilliams did not like him much. But then the sergeant suspected that the corporal did not like anyone very much and would have been astonished to find that Gwilliams had even been fond of his own mother. The corporal often surprised King with the depth of his learning, though it was delivered in that slow drawl which grated on King's nerves much the same as a West Country

132

accent did. Apparently, according to Lieutenant Crossman, the American had been raised by a preacher who had an extensive library which Gwilliams had digested book by book.

But there was also a tiresome corner to Gwilliams' nature. He tended to brag about being on the American frontier and quote 'famous' men King had never heard of. The sergeant was not interested in people like a Mr Wells or a Mr Fargo, or anyone from the other side of the Atlantic unless they had something to do with mapmaking. Gwilliams had mentioned Mason and Dixon once, but only in relation to a 'line' which ran east-west between two states, the inhabitants of which Gwilliams had shaved to a man, apparently.

But there had been no vital discussion on the profession of these men. The fact that George Washington himself had been a surveyor did not seem to arouse any patriotic fervour in Gwilliams. And when told that Thomas Jefferson's father had produced an authoritative map of the southern colonies, Gwilliams simply made a farting noise with his mouth and said, 'Jefferson sided with that Frenchie General Napoleon aginst you Brits. How about that then?' When King, whose knowledge of American politics was zero, later mentioned this to Crossman, the lieutenant told him that Jefferson had not actually supported Napoleon but had advocated neutrality during the Napoleonic Wars, which was a different kettle of fish entirely. But it was Lewis and Clark who were the sergeant's real heroes from the New World. Adventurers, explorers, like himself he thought, who, though not refined mappers, went on journeys and voyages of discovery down rivers, over lakes, through wilderness plains and mountain ranges, taking astronomical observations and plotting their positions as they went. Backwoodsmen like Davy Crockett, and Jim Bowie – Gwilliams' heroes – left the sergeant cold. What did they ever do to understand the world?

'Do you think we did good work today, sahib?' asked Ibhanan after several blissful days. 'That nuddy, it was not easy for following.'

'We did *excellent* work. The lieutenant will be pleased with us, once he's back on his feet again.' King had a flash of conscience as he remembered he had not called in all day to see how Crossman was faring. 'I shall speak with the corporal in a minute, to find out how he is.'

'The lieutenant is lucky to have a caring soul such as yourself, sahib, for his sergeant. Many sergeants do not like their officers and wish them ill. I know this. I have seen it.'

'Yeeeess – well, I'm . . . Ah, here's Corporal Gwilliams now.'

'His lordship wants to see ya,' said Gwilliams with a wicked smile. 'Says to go immediate.'

'Yes, thank you, Corporal,' replied King, not looking at the messenger, 'I'm a little busy at the present, but . . .'

'I'd go now if I was you, Sergeant. He ain't in the mood for waiting. He didn't even want a manipulation today.'

Unable to wipe the glow of pleasure from his face, King finally confronted a rapidly mending lieutenant. Crossman looked thin and wasted, with a very wan complexion and pale-looking eyes, but his faculties had at last left the realms of fancy and were back within the strong fences of reality. Weak and still unable to raise himself beyond a sitting position, the lieutenant glared at his second-in-command.

He said in a hoarse voice, 'I'm still unsure whether or not to have you flogged.'

It was a sharp reminder that Crossman could do this to him. He could order such punishment. The lieutenant had the power to order a hundred lashes. He could even hang him if the crime was judged awful enough to warrant it, so long as the right paperwork was done and the right procedures were followed. Lieutenant Jack Crossman was his commanding officer, the senior rank on this assignment. He was captain of the caravan: a ship which across sailed the land.

'I did what I thought best for the expedition,' replied King.

'You did what you damn well wanted to do, that's what you did.'

This time the sergeant made no reply. He was a good manager of people and knew when not to speak. His silence allowed the lieutenant the idea that his sergeant accepted the rebuke, without actually giving the officer the words to write down in any report. *He remained silent* was far less damning than *He agreed that he had been in the wrong.* King knew he could always argue later that the lieutenant was still far from rational when he was questioned and he thought it best to humour the officer.

They stared at one another for a short while, during which Crossman obviously realized that everything had been said on the subject, unless he was prepared to take disciplinary action. It was clear to both men that since Crossman had been ill to the point of having delusions, the edges were very fuzzy. The officer could take action on his own, without recourse to higher authority, but King knew that the lieutenant was a fair man. If there was a question that things were not clear cut, he would not take disciplinary action. Once Crossman had fallen too ill to command, of course, the decisions had become the sergeant's. King could with all conscience and right countermand any order previously given once he was the commander, especially those orders he considered had been issued during a wild fever.

The hollow-eyed and ravaged-looking lieutenant waved his good hand.

'We'll take it no further,' he said, 'but let me say I'm very disappointed in you, Sergeant. Very disappointed.'

King was quietly relieved. 'Yes, sir. I'm sorry.'

'No you're not,' came back the lieutenant with a little more fire in his tone. 'You're a self-satisfied, jumped-up little prig, who thinks the whole world revolves around your own interests.'

'If you say so, sir, though I should have to disagree.'

'You're not permitted to disagree. I'm your commanding officer.'

'Yes, sir.'

'Get out of my damn sight.'

'Yes, sir.'

Sajan was waiting outside the tent. That morning King had been showing the boy the largest chain measure, taking the shiny metal link-bars from the custom-made hardwood box and laying them out on the ground. There was a hundred feet of blistered steel consisting of forty-two-and-a-half feet links. The steel bars could have been made from silver as far as Sajan was concerned. He was wide-eyed with wonder at being allowed to touch such a treasured object. Now, though, obviously having heard the raised voices coming from within, he seemed concerned for the sergeant. King ruffled his hair as he passed. The boy turned and trotted beside him.

'Our master is very angry with you, sahib?'

'Yes, our master is definitely very angry with me, Sajan – but he'll come round, given a little time.'

'He will throw away our maps.'

'No, no he won't do that. But we mustn't mention maps for a little while, just to be on the safe side.'

'Today you will show me how to do the sextant?'

King stopped and smiled down at the eager face. Yes, here was a willing disciple, one who had taken to mapmaking as if it were his chosen calling. He had been instructing the child on the use of the

135

instruments. One day soon this small boy would be a man full grown and perhaps be the first mapmaker to enter Chinese Tartary to gather the facts and figures on the Tibetan mountains? If King couldn't do it, one of his followers might yet be able to. Dress Sajan as a Buddhist monk and send him in with a measuring wheel disguised as a prayer wheel, a rosary to use as an abacus and a begging bowl in which to put his reflective mercury in order to carry out astronomical calculations. King's heart beat faster when he thought of it.

At the present time, and for the foreseeable future, the Chinese emperor's edict held sway – *No Mughal, Hindustani, Pathan or* firinghi *shall be admitted into Tibet on pain of death*. Nepal too, was a land forbidden to foreigners. Oh, what a great achievement if Sajan were the first to calculate the true height of the mountain which the British had called Peak XV up until last year, when it was renamed 'Everest' after Farrier King's hero, George. An astute Indian surveyor, Radhanath Sikhdar, had calculated the height of this great mountain from readings taken at six stations on the plains, but the measurement was not accurate of course.

If he were one day to go into the forbidden zone, Sajan would have to risk his life, for he was a Hindustani and therefore subject to the emperor's edict. But with the appropriate disguise who would know his identity? Surely the grown Sajan would realize that the risk was worth the ultimate prize?

'Yes, I'll show you how to use the sextant, if the officer isn't up and about by then. You must come to me at noon, Sajan.'

'I will, Sergeant-sahib,' said the boy, happily. 'Noon.'

18

Crossman actually did not drag himself from his bed until another day later and then felt very shaky on his legs. He staggered out of the tent and went on a tour of inspection around the camp. He found it in good order and grudgingly commended his sergeant and corporal.

'We must be on our way tomorrow morning,' he told them. 'We need to reach Ferozepur.'

The lieutenant had survived so far on Gwilliams' soup. He did not trust the local cooking while he was still feeling so fragile. The day of their departure he ate his first solid meal and felt better for it, even though he had to drink a lot of water with the food. He could at least sit on his horse without falling off and allow the beast to saunter along the trail at its own leisurely gait. Around him the natives chattered incessantly, which drove him half-mad, but to his credit he did not bellow at them. By midday he was feeling physically weary but his mental state had improved somewhat. Spotting an eagle similar to those which flew over his Scottish home, he took this for a good omen, and felt better cheered by it.

During the stop he swallowed his pride and asked to see the map that had been drawn by Sergeant King.

There was no actual map, but there were several pages of figures and writing, which meant nothing to Jack.

'Well, show me on your *rough* map the area you have covered.'

King, happy to be of service in his real work, beaming all over his broad square face, showed the lieutenant.

Jack was at first astounded, then not best pleased.

137

'What? That *tiny* strip of land?'

The beam vanished from King's face. 'It's a whole valley.'

'A very *small* valley. A minuscule valley.'

'Sir, how much do you expect for just over a week's work? It takes years and years to map a large area. Decades. We could only do a very little in the days that were available to us.'

'I went through that hell of a sickness for *this*?'

'Sir, forgive me but I was not responsible for your illness. I didn't give you Punbjab fever. You caught it. I merely used the time available during the period of your sickness.' King was very stiff and starchy now. 'And if I may say so, the time was well used.'

'You may not say so,' fumed the lieutenant. 'I get to do that because I'm the commanding officer. It seems I have to keep reminding you of that fact. I'm not sure your time was well used. We could have been halfway to our destination by now.'

Both men parted on the worst of terms.

Two days later the party was attacked. They were crossing a stream which tumbled out of a ravine high above them when something smacked into a rock by one of the camels. Then came the sound of a shot and Gwilliams noticed a puff of smoke in a cleft between two rocks. The corporal always carried a loaded rifle, in case of tiger, leopard, or emergencies such as this one. He took aim from his saddle and fired back at the attacker. Three figures then sprang from the ground around the rocks and made their way up a goat track with rapid movements. One of them was wearing the red coat of a sepoy.

'Did you see that?' asked Gwilliams, riding over to Crossman. 'That was the army.'

'Could be they stole the coat,' said Sergeant King. 'Or they might belong to one of them disbanded regiments.'

Crossman dismounted. 'We'll find out,' he said. 'King, Gwilliams, follow me. Raktambar, you stay and guard the camp.'

The Rajput had also dismounted and he nodded, then urged the men in the carts to jump out and take cover. The Indians were not slow to do this. It was difficult to tell who was fastest on his feet, young Sajan or the much older Ibhanan. Raktambar took up a position facing the goat track, but told one of the chain-men to keep his eyes on their rear.

In the meantime the three soldiers ran up the track.

138

'Sir, you ain't yet strong in your constitution,' argued Gwilliams. 'Let me and King go after 'em.'

But the lieutenant would have none of it. If there was action to be had, he wanted to be there.

'Just don't shoot anyone on our side, Sergeant,' he said in between laboured breaths, 'keep the weapon pointing to the front.'

'I'm not *that* bad,' protested the sergeant.

They raced up the track, but when they came to a bend, with a sheer drop on one side and a cliff on the other, they were met with a hail of rocks. Higher up the path their attackers were hidden behind some boulders. One or two shots came zinging down, keeping Crossman and the other two behind the corner. Now the ambushers were calling to them, taunting them, inviting the *firinghi* to come and get them.

'You will all die,' came a clear shout in English. 'We will cut your throats and throw your testicles to wild dogs.'

'Well now,' muttered Gwilliams, 'that ain't exactly where I keep my balls but you ain't gonna get to find out anyways.'

A figure then presented itself, just as Gwilliams was taking a bead on the boulders ahead. The man wore a white pillbox cap and red coat with naik's stripes on the sleeve: a corporal just like Gwilliams himself. Gwilliams thought nothing of it. He shot the figure in the chest. The Indian let out a yell and fell backwards, causing a great commotion amongst his fellows.

'Nice work, Corporal,' murmured Crossman.

Rocks were again flung blind over the boulders, but clattered uselessly down the hillside. It seemed to Crossman that there were quite a number of men up there, though they appeared to rather lightly armed. It seemed there were three or four firearms, though doubtless their attackers would have knives and perhaps swords too. Crossman and Gwilliams could hold the path indefinitely, but that would keep them there too.

'King,' he said, 'go back down to the camp and bring two men with casks of powder, if you please. Leave your Enfield with me. I take it the weapon is loaded? You'll find my Enfield in the second cart.'

'Yes, sir. Right away, sir.'

The sergeant withdrew after propping his weapon on the rock face. At least, thought Crossman, the man can obey orders without question under fire, which was good.

Gwilliams took another shot at a fleeting movement amongst the boulders. Crossman had not yet fired his revolver since the distance involved was too long for his weapon. Now he fired twice, not in order to hit any target, but to let them know he and his men had plenty of firearms. Then he took up the rifle and rested the stock on his left forearm, the fingers of his good right hand employed with the hammer and trigger. The grip was of course not firm and it would take an age to reload, but he could soon revert to his revolver if the men up above charged them.

'We will kill you,' came the same voice again. 'We will cut out your eyes and throw them to the birds.'

'Original beggar, ain't he?' said Gwilliams.

Jack called out, 'This is Lieutenant Crossman of the 88th Foot. Who is that up there? Why are you firing on us?'

There was another commotion for a time, then the voice came back, 'Here is Jemandar Prithviraj Suraj. We have been disbanded, sir. I am no longer of the BNI, for my livelihood has been taken from me. I was a commissioned officer, like you, and now I am nothing. My wife and children will starve. It has all been taken away. You are now my enemy.'

There was a plaintive tone to the shout, underlined with a defiant note, which Crossman might have found himself sympathizing with, if he had not guessed at the reasons behind the disbanding.

'You mutinied!' he called back.

'No, sir – we did not mutiny. Not at all. Those bad men in Meerut, they were the mutineers. Yet we have been reduced, sir, to men of no consequence. It is unfair. My name means nothing now.'

'There must have been a good reason for disbanding your regiment. No doubt the risk of mutiny was there. But that is by the by, Jemandar Suraj, you have fired on us and I'm sure you do not intend to let us go without a fight.'

'Go. Go. You have killed one of us, now go.'

'You won't follow us and try to kill us?'

'No, sir. We have had enough of the fighting . . .'

At that moment a small stone, dislodged from the cliff, struck Crossman lightly on the shoulder. He glanced up to his left and saw three or four armed figures slipping along the ridge above his him. It appeared they had climbed over the high point, which looked formidable even for goats, while Crossman and Gwilliams had been distracted by the Indian jemandar. The sepoys were now dropping down behind the two soldiers. Crossman raised his left arm, levelling the rifle, but when he fired the Enfield kicked violently off its forearm rest. The shot missed its target. Gwilliams was more accurate with his shot, spinning one of the figures round like a ballerina. When the victim had completed his pirouette he fell sideways from his perch and dropped down into the ravine without a sound escaping from his lips. His comrades slipped down the other side of the hill.

Shots now came from above again and those left up the hill attempted a charge. Crossman reached for his revolver and shot one man dead, the following man tripping over his body. Gwilliams had now reloaded and hit a second man in the head. Two more charged on, yelling at the tops of their voices, wielding blades. Crossman's revolver refused to fire, even when he skipped chambers. He dropped his firearm and drew his sword, slashing at the first man who tried to force his way round the corner. He caught an upper arm, the attacker lost his balance and he too dropped over the edge into the deep ravine, to smash on the rocks below. Gwilliams felled the next man with the butt of his Enfield, crunching bone.

No more followed these foolhardy few into the narrow bottleneck. A scrambling sound above them told the two soldiers that the remaining Indians were making good their escape over the pass. Crossman sheathed his blade and picked up his revolver.

The sound of shots came from the camp below.

'Let's get back,' said Crossman. 'They may have been surprised by those two who went over the top.'

The pair raced back down the path, but when they reached the camp there was a dead man lying near one of the camel carts, and a live one being efficiently trussed by Raktambar with some raffia.

'I shot this one,' said King, standing over a prone body with a cavernous hole in its back. 'Got him in the belly with your Enfield, sir. He came straight at me. Couldn't miss. Three feet away when I fired. Went through him as if he were butter. Nasty hole, that, though. Amazing. A cannon ball couldn't make a worse exit hole.'

'Sergeant,' said Crossman, who could not help but be aware of King's agitation, 'are you all right?'

King did not lift his head to reply, seeming to be mesmerized by that ball wound in his victim's back.

'All right? I should say not, I think.'

The sergeant then went behind one of the camels and vomited quietly on to the ground.

Crossman and Raktambar interrogated their prisoner. He refused to say which regiment he was from, but he was full of venom for the British and their treatment of him. He kept addressing his remarks to Raktambar, ignoring the lieutenant. Finally, Crossman called for Gwilliams to take the captive and put him in one of the carts. Once this was done, Crossman and Raktambar spoke together.

'He says he did nothing wrong and his livelihood was taken away from him by the Company army – do you believe him, Raktambar?'

The Rajput nodded. 'He is telling the truth, sahib, but not *all* the truth.'

'What do you mean by that?'

'He would have mutinied, later.'

'How do you know this?'

Raktambar's dark eyes bore into Crossman's. 'Because, sahib, all India is ready to revolt against the British rule. It is a pot just reaching the boil. Everything is simmering, ready to bubble. I know this because I am Indian. This man,' he flicked his hand at the doorway, 'is a Rajput like me. He is of the same caste as me. We are brothers of the same blood.'

'You know him?'

Raktambar's patience was thin. 'No, I do not know him. He is a sepoy, not a palace guard. His name means nothing to me. He is one of millions. But I know his feelings.'

Crossman stared at his protector. 'You have the same feelings?'

'Of course. I am a Rajput. I am an Indian. We share the same feelings, the Rajputs, the men of Oudh. We all have an anger which will not go away. You try to change us. We will not be changed.'

'You mean we are interfering with your religions?'

'That and many other things.'

'If you feel the same as that man we have in the cart,' said Crossman, sadly, 'I can no longer trust you.'

The Rajput's face gave nothing away. 'You must think as you will, sahib.'

Crossman sighed. What was he to do? Send this man back to his master in Jaipur? That seemed the most sensible course of action. Otherwise they would all have to sleep with one eye open. And Raktambar might decide to let their prisoner loose, while no one was

142

looking. Both Raktambar and Crossman knew that the man would be hanged, once they got to Ferozepur, providing the British were still in command there. And that was another thing. Just how stable was the situation? Some regiments of doubtful loyalty had been disbanded – Colonel Stuton had told him that – but surely not the whole of the Bengal army? Getting rid of four regiments was not going to do it, if the whole show was festering. That would just add fuel to the fire and Raktambar's pot would indeed boil over. The jemandar who seemed to be the leader of their attackers had mentioned Meerut. *Those bad men in Meerut.* He had spoken of them as mutineers. So perhaps the disbanding of Bengal regiments in the Punjab was a reaction to a mutiny elsewhere?

None of these thoughts brought him any closer to knowing what he was to do about Ishwar Raktambar. Crossman called for Sergeant King and Corporal Gwilliams. They came to him and the three white men stood by a rock and looked across at the Rajput, who must have known he was the subject under discussion. Crossman told his two NCOs what he knew and said, 'I'm thinking of giving Raktambar his marching orders.'

'What about my men?' asked King. 'They're Indians too.'

'I don't know. They're from Bombay, not Rajputana or Oudh. Also they're not sepoys and are of low caste. Most of them are just coolies. Perhaps if a mob were to attack us their loyalty might be suspect, but for the moment I think we'll have to keep them with us. Otherwise we'll have to abandon your instruments, King, and just the three of us ride out.'

'I agree,' said King, quickly. 'And the boy?'

'Oh, he'll stay with us, of course,' replied Crossman. 'I can't think he'll give us any trouble. Besides, he dotes on you, King.' The lieutenant paused for a moment in thought. 'I tell you this, men – if we can't trust *some* of them, then we're all dead men. There are millions and millions of people in this vast subcontinent, and very few of us.'

A few minutes later he called Raktambar to him.

'You are free to go,' he said to the tall Rajput. 'Go home and marry your bride.'

Raktambar gripped his sword. His face, under his turban, was impassive. 'I cannot go. It is not for you to say, but for the maharajah, who asked me to protect you.'

143

'I don't want you here. I don't trust you any more.'

'Did you ever trust me, sahib?'

'No, to be truthful, not really.'

'Then what has changed?'

Crossman couldn't answer this for a moment, then he realized that yes, things had changed a great deal.

'There are men out there who agree with you. How can I be sure you won't cut the my throat and those of my men?'

Raktambar's eyes blazed. 'I have my honour!'

'So did that jemandar. He gave his oath to the East India Company army. That didn't stop him trying to kill me.'

Raktambar shook his head sorrowfully. 'You will not let me stay? Even if I say I will be your good and faithful servant?'

'No. I'll write you a letter to give to the maharajah, which will exonerate you from all blame. I'll tell him it was entirely my fault that you were sent back, that your work for me was exemplary and that you were a good and faithful protector for the time you stayed with me. Raktambar,' said Jack, in a change of tone, 'we both know why the maharajah told you to accompany me. It was to spy on me, was it not? To watch me and gather information for a report? Surely you don't think me stupid?'

'You are not stupid, sahib, and I do not need your letter.'

'Right then. Gather up your belongings and leave, if you please.' Crossman held out his good palm. 'I would like to shake your hand, if you will, before you go, and to thank you for your services to me.'

Raktambar ignored the hand and turned on his heel. He went to his horse and mounted immediately. Leaving all his gear behind him, he rode off, along a jungle path. Crossman watched him go with mixed feelings. Despite the questionable loyalty of his erstwhile 'protector' Jack was sorry to see him go. There was much to admire in Raktambar. Yes, he was a little petulant and peevish, but that was the young man in him. What bridegroom torn away from his bride so close to his wedding would not have revealed the same character deficits? Yet, there was also a steadfastness in Raktambar and a great sense of honour. And as for his loyalty, why, if Britain had been taken over by Indians there would be no question where Crossman's loyalties lay. It certainly would not be with newcomers who governed his land.

The party moved on, towards Ferozepur.

19

The town was sombre. Clearly something had happened here. Crossman told Sergeant King to find billets for the men and hand their prisoner to the authorities. He himself then made enquiries as to the whereabouts of Colonel Hawke. Calcutta Hawke was not a hard man to find. Crossman discovered him in a dwelling not far from the barracks. Tanned and looking very much at home in his Indian bungalow, the colonel appeared to be in a grave mood when Crossman saluted.

'Ah, Fancy Jack – you made it.'

Crossman smiled at the colonel's familiarity.

'Yes sir, not without incident. But I imagine it would be difficult to travel this land without something occurring. We gathered one prisoner on the way: a sepoy from a whole party of them who attacked us.'

'Quite so.' Crossman felt the scrutiny of those piercing eyes as the colonel openly appraised him. 'Yet here you are. Good. Good. And how's the hand?'

Crossman looked down at his damaged wooden appendage.

'No trouble, sir. I've invented an iron hand, which I've yet to try out in anger.'

The colonel smiled. 'You were always a one for your devices and machineries, Lieutenant. And Sergeant King? Are you two getting on all right.' The colonel's tone suggested he only wanted one answer.

'The sergeant's with me, sir,' he couldn't help himself, 'now about this mapping business . . .'

'Ah yes,' the eyes lit up, 'quite so. Mapping. Very useful to us in our business, Lieutenant. Two birds with one stone, eh? We can be about a legitimate business, yet do our own work at the same time. And − and, mark you, the maps we make can help us in our future operations. There's no advantage more useful than knowing where one is, where the enemy is, and what lies between, now is there? Now, down to political business. Have you any intelligence for me? What did you pick up on your way?'

'Not a great deal, Colonel. Anything we did discover will be redundant now that mutiny has actually broken out. All I managed to obtain were inferences and warnings, veiled threats of an uprising, all of which it seems have been fulfilled prior to my arrival.'

'Quite. I thought as much. Events have overtaken you. Fact is,' the colonel stood up, a tall lean grey-haired man with a sharp edge to his profile, 'I know far more than you do at the moment.' He laughed a little. 'I should be reporting to you.' He began pacing up and down behind his desk. 'There've been uprisings all over, and more will come, without a doubt. A full-scale mutiny at Meerut. Several regiments of sepoys and sowars turned against us. There are many dead. Women and children slaughtered as well as officers and men. The mutineers have now left Meerut and marched down to Delhi, gathering sympathizers on their way − many of them badmashes and other flotsam − and the reports from Delhi are appalling. Massacres. Babes being put to the sword before the eyes of their mothers. The mothers then killed and mutilated. Ugly. All sorts of thugs joining the sepoys, swelling their numbers, committing foul deeds.

'The old Mughal emperor in Delhi has been dragged into it − the mutineers are claiming him as their leader − but the poor old fellah's a feather's flight away from death as it is, so he can only be some sort of symbol to them.'

The colonel paused in midstride, then, after a moment or two, continued his pacing.

'We've had a little uprising here in Ferozepur, but we put it down very quickly. The facts, when you look at them in stark figures, are not very encouraging. The East India Company army has something like three hundred thousand men − have you eaten by the way?' The colonel's hospitality, Jack remembered, was always ten paces behind his work.

'I'm fine, sir. I ate, and drank, not two hours ago. Do go on.'

146

'Right. Anyway, of those three hundred thousand only fourteen thousand are Europeans. The rest are native troops. We do have over twenty thousand Queen's army stationed in India, quite a lot of them here in the Punjab. You can see by those numbers that if the Company's native regiments as a whole decide to rise up together we won't stand a chance. They'll cut us down and roll over us like a wave. Our only hope is that some of the Bengal regiments, and those of the Bombay and Madras armies, will remain loyal to the British. It's a fragile time, Lieutenant. The Company might shatter to pieces if we don't manage to keep some friends.'

'We've fought greater numbers before and won, sir.'

'But not from within. This is akin to civil war. Any help we get will be from the brothers of our enemies. We're entangled, Lieutenant. Fortunately, I don't think they *will* all rise up at once. Many of them are waiting to see what happens. Our reputation, as conquerors, will hold many of them back until – I hope – it will be too late for them to commit themselves.' He sighed. 'This damn Company army has gone to ruin in the past few years, Jack.' Crossman was startled at the use of his Christian name into being even more attentive to the colonel's words. 'European officers have become lazy and indolent. Their men hardly ever see some of them. When they're not lying on their *charpoys* they're out pig-sticking or playing polo. Decadence. It's brought down great empires before now.'

Hawke paused to take a drink.

'These Company officers, they've come to thinking that the machine will run on its own. You're interested in machines, Jack. You know you have to look after them, lubricate them, replace worn parts, repair them. This damn machine has been allowed to run on without anyone bothering to look to its servicing. Oh, there are good officers out there,' he threw a hand in the air, 'but for every good officer there's a dozen bad 'uns. Fat colonels, gin-soaked majors, idle captains. Yet even now – even now – many of them won't disband their regiments, saying their men would never mutiny, never go against them. And what's happening? The sepoys are shooting them out of the saddle of course. Just because they've been in India half their lives – *all* their lives in some cases – they think that entitles them to be loved.'

He whirled on Crossman. 'The causes of all this are numerous – it's not just the grease on the cartridges – it goes much deeper . . .'

147

'I've been told,' said Crossman, hoping now to add something to this debate, 'that the annexation of Oudh didn't help things. Also this business of sending high-caste sepoys overseas.'

'Oh, those and others, Lieutenant. The whole pie has been crumbling at the edges for a long time now. You know I am Anglo-Indian myself. My mother, bless her soul . . . Well, I have half this continent in me. I understand the frustrations of the people. The fact is, this has been caused by stupidity. Nothing else really. Plain stupidity. Ignorance. These people are used to being conquered, used to being ruled by invaders, and for the most part settle for what comes, so long as their culture is *respected*. Even the great conquerer Akbar knew that. He was a Muslim but he did not try to convert the Hindus to his religion.

'So long as they do not feel their religion threatened. It doesn't take much,' the hands went up, fluttered like birds, 'just a bit of common sense. Once you start trying to change them against their will, then the dove becomes the tiger.' He stopped, poured two glasses of water and offered one to Crossman. 'You've listened to me long enough, Lieutenant. What questions do you have?'

'Obviously, sir, I want to know how we can help, my little team and me. What's happening here, in the Punjab? I understand we have several Queen's army regiments stationed here at the moment.'

'Yes, we do. Also, the Punjab Irregulars. Five cavalry regiments and ten infantry battalions, and the Corps of Guides of course'

'Are they all likely to remain loyal to the British?'

'I think so, yes, yes, I do,' the colonel seemed to be convincing himself even as he spoke. 'They aren't Bengalis of course – the regiments here are made up of Pathans, Sikhs, Musselmen, Gurkhas, Afghans and Baluchis. None of these feel any sort of kinship for the Hindu or Muslim sepoys of the Bengal army. The Sikhs are dead keen to have a go at them, in fact. You may recall it was with the Bengal Army that we conquered the Sikh empire. They owe the Bengalis a thump or two and they're raring to get at them. No, I'm pretty sure we're secure here on the North-West Frontier – with one possible exception.'

Crossman had the feeling that here was where his duty lay.

'Yes, sir – that is?'

'The local Afghan tribes to the north. No one can be sure what the thinking is on the other side of the Khyber Pass. Do they see this as

148

an opportunity to shed themselves of the British? It's a distinct possibility. Or will they simply sit and wait for the outcome of this insurrection? Also a possibility. General Reed is heading what they call a Movable Column, out of Peshawar, but we do not want a rising in the hills to take advantage of the absence of our troops in the region, nor do we want anyone attacking our rear. You may recall we've got a bloody nose from the Afghans once before. I need you to ride north with all speed and assess the situation amongst the hill tribes, gain an assurance of their loyalty if you can.'

Crossman blinked and remained quiet.

'Lieutenant? You seem a little puzzled by your orders.'

'To be frank, sir, I am. There are surely more qualified people here to do that kind of work. It is *my* work, but aren't there others who've been here since Adam who could do it better? Pathans and Afghans, and British officers who have formed bonds with the local tribes?'

'There is – there are. They *are* all working. The number of tribes in those hills, which show as much aggression to their neighbours as they do to strangers, is legion. Even to cover the most important of them would take an army of agents. You're a welcome addition, despite your lack of local experience. Your help will relieve some of the burden we face. Major Hodson is the big man around here for political activity, although he's down in Amballa at present. Anyway, he's happy for us to use you, and anyone else we can get. All right? I suggest you go can get yourself a bath, and a good meal, then I'll send someone over with details of your mission.' He chuckled, despite the gravity of the situation. 'Not so much a fox hunt out here, as a tiger hunt, eh Lieutenant?'

'Yes, sir.' He paused before he said, 'There won't be much chance for King to do any mapping, will there?'

Hawke gave him one of his iron smiles. 'No, and I take it you're pleased about that.'

'He is rather obsessed. Keeps going on about a man called George Everest. Some Surveyor-General or other. I gather he would follow the man into hell's fire.'

Hawke said, 'Met Colonel Everest once. Didn't like him. Not many people do. Now Lambton, I understand, was the better man.' The colonel sighed. 'These mathematicians and science-wallahs are all right in their place, but they start to think the world revolves around their work. Who cares whether India is mapped to the inch,

149

so long as we have charts which guide us over unknown ground. But there you go, they are — what was the word you used? obsessed? — they are obsessed with precision. Well, back to soldiery matters . . .'

The colonel then gave Jack a detailed appraisal of the situation in Meerut, Delhi and other stations, as he understood it, and then gave the lieutenant leave to prepare his men for the ride.

Jack left the bungalow with mixed feelings in his breast. There were a couple of junior officers on Hawke's veranda. Crossman managed to speak with them for a short while, to gauge their feelings at this momentous time in the history of the Company. What he heard was not encouraging. There was a great deal of spleen and very little calm thinking. Jack only hoped that the big names in the region — Nicholson, Chamberlain and Edwardes — were more rational. From the junior officers he heard threats of wholesale slaughter of the population, of retaliatory massacres, of razing towns and villages to the ground. The general rage of the British seemed somewhat out of control.

The task ahead of him, as a gatherer of information, was daunting to say the least. To go immediately up into the northern hills to assess the situation there was a frightening thing for someone so new to India and even newer to the North-West Frontier. He had imagined he would enter the water gradually, getting used to the temperature by degrees, submerging himself slowly and carefully. Yet, here he was, being forced to dive in without knowing anything of much use to him.

Of course, these were desperate times, what with massacres of not only men but also wives, daughters and sons. Infants being hacked to death. Babies being murdered. Even from just looking about him now, at the faces of officers and men in the barracks, he could see the incandescent fury in their eyes. British women and children! And European continental families, along with Americans, Australians and Canadians, for the British were not the only traders in this rich and profitable land. They felt it was a monstrous act, an unpardonable act, an act which required not justice but wholesale vengeance. Someone would have to contain this rage or it would explode with terrible consequences and the sickness move into following generations.

When Crossman arrived back at the quarters King had secured for them, he found Ishwar Raktambar sitting by the doorway. The

Rajput's horse was tethered near a water trough not far away, the foam from a hard ride shaping where the saddle had been. Raktambar stood up as Jack approached. He looked as contrite as Jack had ever seen him. There was a sober expression on his face. For once he did not appear aggressive nor sulky, only attentive and ready to talk.

'Sahib, I see the furrows on your face. You are not pleased to see me. Yet I have come back to honour the promise made to you in front of the maharajah, to protect you for your time in India.'

'I admit I'm surprised to see you. I thought we understood you were to return to your master?'

'Once out in the country, I had much time to think,' said the Rajput. 'Please do not make me beg to come back. I have my honour, sir. I have my honour. It means more to me than anything. If I go back to my home, I go back without that honour. I offer you my hand in friendship,' he extended his arm, 'and my loyalty. I will give you my loyalty and you will give me yours. It is only fair, sahib, to have your oath as you have mine.'

Natives were always throwing this word 'fair' into any bargain, knowing it to be an important one amongst the British.

'Can I trust you, then? What made you change your mind?'

'You can trust me with your life, sahib, as I expect to trust you with mine.' Raktambar clearly wanted this to be a two-way bargain, in order to be *fair* and *honourable* to both men. 'We are brothers of the blade.' He touched the hilt of the sword at his hip.' He paused, then continued, 'What made the change of my mind? The sunset. I looked into the sunset and saw my pride draining from the sky like blood. For a Rajput there is nothing so important. We must put aside our loyalties to the rest of the world, you and I, and we must look to each other. These are uncertain times. This is what I saw in the sunset. You looking to me and me looking to you.'

The arm was still out. Jack finally took the hand and shook, grimly.

'I hope neither of us will regret this, Raktambar. We are different men from different worlds.'

'Different in many ways, but not the most important.'

Crossman smiled. 'I believe you're right. Now, see to your mount, then join us for some food. There's a lot to discuss.'

The Rajput heaved a sigh, possibly of relief, but more likely of resignation, then he too grinned. The tall man walked away, leaving

Jack wondering what was going to become of the two of them. Was he making a mistake? He did not blame Ishwar Raktambar in the least. Certainly not for having loyalties to his fellow Indians, nor for wishing to be safe at home in the arms of his beloved, but the fact was the Honourable East India Company was in crisis – the British were in crisis – and reliable men were needed. One had enough to do without having to watch one's back for signs of treachery amongst one's own men. Better to let the danger go away, than to keep it with him. Even as he was stepping through the doorway, Jack was beginning to regret his decision to keep Raktambar.

20

They were gathered in Crossman's bungalow, a small but adequate dwelling which had come – to Gwilliams' great disgust – with a manservant. This cook-bearer was at that moment making them mango drinks in the small kitchen off the back of the building. They had clustered on the veranda, the room behind them being stifling hot. On hearing of the arrival of newcomers, flies had come in their thousands from surrounding areas to greet them. King was at the moment engaged in a wholesale slaughter which did not seem to reduce the numbers of the unwanted visitors in the least. Around his chair, like a spilt box of dried blackcurrants, were the bodies of the dead. King still wielded his swat, becoming adept at hitting flies in the air, as well as those which had settled on arms, legs and furniture.

'We're to receive orders to go north-west, to a place known as Piwar,' Crossman said. 'To assess the danger of an uprising amongst the hill tribes. We leave in the morning. You may have heard on the grapevine that there's been trouble all over India – outbreaks in Aligarh, Mainpuri, Etawah, Bulandshar, Nasirabad, Moradabad, Shahjahanpur and many of the smaller stations. In others, Lahore, Agra, Lucknow, Peshawar – as you know – native regiments have been disarmed. But many British officers are refusing to disband their regiments, believing they will remain loyal. We all hope that's the case, but we must prepare for the worst.'

Sergeant King rose from his wicker chair, which had been protesting noisily with each violent movement of his body as he attacked the enemy.

'I'll go and get the men ready,' he said. 'We'll probably need to purchase another set of camels – ours need a rest.'

'Stay where you are, Sergeant.'

The sergeant blinked and sat back down again.

Jack explained, 'We're not taking your retinue, King. This is a proper military expedition, not a mapmaking jaunt.'

'Very funny,' muttered Gwilliams. 'Retinue. King. Yes, a humorous note has entered the proceedings.'

'What?' cried a hurt Sergeant King, predictably. 'Why can't they come anyway?'

'Because,' the lieutenant explained, 'I say so.' He had never thought he would use those words – words which he had treated with contempt when he had been a private and on the other end of them – but they saved a lot a time. 'Speed is important. It's vital. They'll slow us up. Do as you're told for once in your life, Sergeant, or I shall get very cross.'

'. . .man,' said Gwilliams, grinning.

'And that's enough from you too, Corporal. This is a serious business. I've just been briefed by Colonel Hawke. There's been a full-scale mutiny at Meerut. Several regiments of the Bengal army have shot their officers, and others, set fire to barracks and bungalows, and then – gathering a lot of badmashes on the way – set out for Delhi. So far as I can gather they've got control of Delhi and whole families are being cut down. The plight of our people in Delhi is dire. A column is setting out from Peshawar, but they're concerned about the tribes beyond the Khyber. We have to join others in paying a visit, gaining assurances from the hill tribes that they have no intention of attacking our column from the rear, or using the absence of our soldiers to create havoc in the hills and down here in the Punjab. How far we can trust their word, once we've got it is anyone's guess, but at least we can gauge the mood and the numbers. Any questions.'

'Only about a thousand,' said Gwilliams. 'Ain't there regiments of British soldiers at Meerut? Europeans? Why ain't they followed the mutineers an' cut 'em down on the way to Delhi? Come to think of it, why didn't they stop 'em leaving in the first place? They queer in the head, or what?'

Jack sighed. 'Meerut is under the command of a General Hewitt. It seems he failed to act, despite having two British regiments and several batteries of artillery at hand. He and his colonel allowed three regiments of mutineers, infantry and cavalry, and a growing rag-tag mob of followers to get away in the night. They took Delhi by surprise, gaining control of the city. Other sepoy regiments are now joining them. They hunted down and killed any British or Eurasian families, foreigners of all kinds. The telegraph operator managed to get a message out with the bad news, before the line went dead. It seems those survivors of the slaughter are now on a rocky ridge north of Delhi attempting to defend themselves.'

A silence fell on the proceedings for a few moments as these events were visualized in each of the three minds.

'So you can see,' continued Crossman after a moment, 'we need to move with all possible speed.'

'I think we ought to volunteer to join the column and relieve Delhi,' answered King. 'Women and children . . .'

'This is not a democracy, Sergeant. You'll do as you're told.'

There was a great deal of steel in Crossman's voice which made King's head jerk back. After a moment, the sergeant nodded. 'Yes, sir, of course, sir. A reaction to the news.'

'Fine. Now, does anyone want to know where we're going? Ah, here's Raktambar – and the drinks.'

The cook-bearer was leading Raktambar on to the veranda from the rear of the house. Gwilliams and the servant glared at one another for a moment before the drinks were handed out. Raktambar fetched a wicker chair from the other end of the veranda and placed himself next to Crossman. The lieutenant waited for the servant to get out of earshot, before he briefed his men.

'As I said, our destination is Piwar. In the hills around there's a tribe called the Kafirisi. They're also known as the Wolves of Paktia, but don't let that worry you. Just about every tribe in those hills is called the wolves-of-something-or-other. That doesn't mean they're not a fierce bunch, but they're no different from their neighbours so we haven't been given the hardest chore. Our task is no different from any others going on the same mission. We need to find the chief, obtain assurances from him, and return, hopefully in time to join the column from Peshawar.'

Sergeant King was sent back to his own quarters. He returned with some tubes of maps. He took one out and spread it reverently on a table so that they could study it. They had some hard riding ahead of them: some 250 miles or more. The country was rough and there was no telling who they might meet on the way. Crossman was not so much worried about mutineers, for the Punjab British officers – unlike many of their Bengal counterparts – had acted decisively in disarming their own doubtful sepoys and sowars. The Punjab force was a newer and fresher entity and sentimentality did not get in the way of stripping any regiments of uncertain loyalty of their arms. No, his main concern were other tribes or groups of hill men they might meet on the way: people who might simply resent their presence.

'Right,' said Crossman, rolling up the maps, 'we've rivers to cross and mountains to climb, so I suggest we all get a good night's sleep and be ready to ride at six in the morning. Raktambar, perhaps you'll stay for a while after the sergeant and corporal have left? Thank you, men.'

King and Gwilliams left the bungalow. Raktambar remained.

Crossman said, 'I wanted to give you one last chance to change your mind.'

There was a firm shake of the head. 'I wish to come.'

'What about afterwards, when we advance to Delhi.'

'Then too.'

'I accept your offer then.'

Raktambar left. Crossman went into his bungalow. He was feeling tired and washed-out. The servant had given him some tamarind seed case to chew, which was now going sour in his mouth. He spat it out, through the window. There was a stream of white ants on the window-sill, marching back and forth, a group of them triumphantly carrying the corpse of a cockchafer on their shoulders. Jack mused on the fact that even further down the chain of being there was not much respite from war and the acquisition of territory. That poor cockchafer had probably wandered innocently enough into a region where he felt he might find food and found savage inhabitants instead. It was best, when all was said and done, to stay in your own back yard. If you didn't bother your neighbour he wouldn't bother you.

'Sahib,' said a voice from the kitchen, 'you like guava?'

'Don't think I've ever tasted one, but thank you, yes,' said Jack, who loved fruit of any kind. He was given one by the bearer, who smiled when Jack bit into it. 'Faint taste of strawberries, I fancy,' murmured Jack, thinking of Jane and home for a few flourishing thoughts.

Outside in the compound, bullocks were drawing water which gardeners were channelling into flowerbeds of jasmine and oleanders. Inside, pockets of the heat of the day lingered as invisible clouds in random patches. Jack sat at a wobbly table on which stood an ink-stand, a paperweight made of a tiger's fang and a half-filled page of a letter. The bearer brought in the chairs from the veranda and placed them about the room: one by the oriental cabinet whose lacquer was peeling away from its wood; another by the bookcase containing ragged volumes – some text books, a very few novels; the third by a weapons stand, a huge ceramic pot in which there were some pig-sticks, two very old shotguns and an even older regimental sword. The owner of the bungalow, a captain, had died of sunstroke just two weeks previously. Jack imagined that the sword belonged to the man's father, or even grandfather, being of a style which had gone out of use many years ago.

When Jack moved he heard something crinkle and found he was sitting on an old copy of *Bell's Life*. He leafed through it, listlessly, then went on a tour of the bungalow. In the adjoining room he found the bed he was to sleep on, a wooden frame crossed with ropes for springs and a padded cotton quilt for a mattress. There was, at least, a new-looking mosquito net draped over a line which crossed the room over the bed. There was also the ubiquitous punkah frame with the matted fan suspended from it and the cord at the moment attached to a hook on the wall.

All in all, though, it was a pretty dismal place in which to spend one's leisure time. A few friends round for cards perhaps, once in a while? Or drinks? Otherwise Jack imagined the captain would be in the mess, playing billiards on that moth-eaten table he had seen there, or out hunting some wild creature or other. Surely, Captain – what was it? Cox? That was it. Surely, captain Cox did not spend more time than he should in this place with its worm-eaten furniture and its dreary air of deadness?

It was a shabby life to be sure, even though attended by many servants. On arrival Jack had found that there was no less than thirteen of them on Captain Cox's payroll, including a sweeper, a water-carrier, a dhobi-wallah, four punkah-wallahs, a tailor, khitmutgar – a kind of butler – and several others. Crossman had informed these disappointed people that he was only staying a very short time and would not require their services. The cook-bearer had refused to go

157

and said he would work for nothing, since his bed was in a corner of the kitchen and he had no wish to sleep in the open. There were many who did, of course, some out of choice, but he had his patch. The rest of them disappeared into some baked-mud huts at the rear of the bungalow, presumably to await a more promising occupant, someone who would stay until death, like the last one.

Crossman went to bed after sitting up late planning the journey to Piwar. He took some time in getting to sleep, what with the heat and the mosquitoes along with night noises. Even the geckos were particularly loud in their calls to each other as they skated up and down the walls, and over the ceiling, on their peculiar-looking feet. Nevertheless he eventually dropped into a fitful doze which lasted until the early hours. At about five o'clock he felt a warm soft body next to his own. Unsure whether or not he was dreaming he gradually came to consciousness to find a youngish woman in bed with him, smelling of incense and perfumed oils.

'What?' He sat up abruptly. 'What's this?'

The woman turned over and looked up at him with large brown eyes ringed with kohl to emphasize their seductiveness. She said nothing, simply lying there in the flimsiest of muslin which hid none of her charms. The aroma which came from her smooth skin was maddening to Crossman, who had not been this close to a female for several months now. It played like music on his brain, captivating him. Where had this enchantress come from? Did she go with the house? Had she been sent by one of his own men? Ibhanan? Raktambar? Or perhaps – his blood ran cold for a moment – she was the cook-bearer's wife or daughter? Dear God, would the man rush in wielding a tulwar any moment and accuse him of adultery? These people were passive most of the time, but just occasionally they went berserk. Then they killed without mercy.

'You must leave,' he said, hardly convincing himself let alone her. 'You must go. You can't stay here. Go home.'

She spoke in a husky voice. 'Sahib Cox would not tell me to go. He would tell me this *is* my home. I have done nothing wrong. I have come to the same bed I have visited every night for two years. Would you have me go to another? Whose? I think I must stay. You will regret sending me out into the night. I can be a very loving woman you know.'

There was a note of panic in Crossman's voice.

'Ah, Cox, yes. But I'm not Captain Cox. You've noticed that now. Perhaps at first you thought I was? Is that why you came to my bed? You had not heard of his death? The funeral was last week.'

Her eyes grew moist. 'I have heard of it. I was there. Sahib Cox was to marry me soon. He spoke of it many times.' She turned her whole body towards him and her heavy warm breasts rested against the bare skin of his right arm. 'What will happen to me now that he has gone? I come to you, sahib, because I have nowhere else to go. My family will not have me now that I have been with a *firinghi*. I will starve.' She stroked his cheek with surprisingly rough fingers. It reminded him that he was used to the silken touch of Jane's fingers. 'You will look after me, will you not, sir? You are a kind man. It is in your look, in your eyes. I do not believe you could send me away to be beaten by my father and brothers.'

'I can't help you,' he said. 'You must find another man.'

'You are a man. Do you not like women?'

'Of course I like women, but my wife – I love my wife – this would hurt her if she knew of it.'

'She need not know of it, sahib. Can you not afford a missy *and* a memsahib? Where is she? In England? How can she know of us? This is India. We can live together without *anyone* knowing, anyone at all. Even the commander did not know of Sahib Cox and me.'

'Didn't he? That's extraordinary.'

Her voice grew deeper and huskier. There were bangles on her wrists and ankles, which jingled with each small movement of her body. Now he saw the jewel in her navel, a red ruby, bright as blood. Suddenly she shook her head and a cascade of jet hair fell to her shoulders, past them, down almost to her narrow waist. Her white teeth parted a little.

'This is India where there are secrets. I am the hymn the golden oriole sings. I am the whisper of insects in the dry grasses. I am the cry of the hawk that circles the blue sky. You are my warrior, sahib, courageous and full of honour. You deserve to have my bee-honey love, sweeter than any tasted in that cold country from which you came. Here is the passion that burns. Here is the heart of heat you seek. You are the lord of all you survey. Here in India I am yours to command, my deep strong soldier. You are quick, like the burning snake, to take what is yours by right. You strike when I am ready.

159

During the day I bring my sticks for your fire. During the night you bring your stick to my fire . . .'

Murmuring this nonsense she entwined herself around his torso, a contortionist with a suppleness nothing short of miraculous. Her legs plaited with one of his own up to her thighs. Her arms wound around his head, pulling it down, burying his face in her belly. When he tried to move away from her midriff, she lifted his face to her own. Her scent was almost overpowering now, as she arched downwards, so that her lips were almost brushing his cheek. Jack felt himself weaken. Certainly he was aroused – he could not help but be aroused. That in itself was not a moral wrong, but it was a persuasive influence. He groaned when she linked an arm around his neck and stared deep into his eyes. Her breath was cloying. The soft touch of her breasts on his chest drove him crazy.

'Look,' he began, with a catch in his voice. 'I have to leave today, for an unknown destination. I might never come this way again . . .'

At that moment Sajan walked into the room, carefully carrying a cup of tea in his small hands.

'Sahib,' he said, his attention wholly taken up with his balancing act, 'I bring you your wake-up chai.'

Jack was brought back to earth with a jolt.

'Thank you, Sajan. Please put it on the small table by the bed.'

The boy looked up after he had done this deed. A frown crossed his face. 'Who is this woman?' he asked.

'You mind your Ps and Qs,' said this woman, petulantly. 'Little boys should be seen and not heard.'

'You don't tell me what to do,' said the boy with some asperity. 'I take no orders from the likes of *you*.'

'Cheeky monkey. I shall give you a clip ear, if you're not careful.'

Jack said to the woman, 'You'd better go. I shall leave some money with the quartermaster. You won't starve for a while.'

'Huh!' she cried, haughtily. 'Keep your money.'

She gathered up the bottom sheet and wrapped it around herself like a sari, before striding from the room with her chin in the air.

'Sajan,' said Crossman, 'I think we should keep this to ourselves. You're to tell no one, you understand?'

'Can I come with you to Piwar?'

'No, you may not. You will stay with Ibhanan, here. But don't think you can blackmail me. It won't work. I always have the upper hand, because I'm a grown man and you're a small boy.'

160

Sajan made an ugly face. 'I do not like you, sahib. You do not want me any more.'

'It's not a question of that.'

'You send me away!'

'No.'

'Then I come with you?'

'No.'

'I hate you,' cried the boy, his face contorted with anger. 'I hate you. One day I will grow to a man and kill you.'

He then burst into tears and ran from the bungalow and Jack sighed. What was he to do with the boy? Were children always this much trouble? He would have to remind himself of the fact when he and Jane talked about a family.

Jack rose, dressed hurriedly, and then methodically went about the chores necessary before setting out on a long journey. He shaved himself this morning, preferring to do without Gwilliams, who came later and remonstrated with him for doing so. However, the corporal had other tasks himself and left the lieutenant to get on with his packing, another chore he preferred to do himself. If there was some important item missing from his luggage later, he would have only himself to blame. In an hour he was done and gathered his men about him. He said goodbye to a sullen Sajan and requested Ibhanan to look after the boy.

'And see to the sergeant's precious instruments, Ibhanan.'

'I will, sahib. They are safe in my hands.'

'The sergeant trusts you with them and so do I. I'm very impressed with what the sergeant says about you, Ibhanan – your growing skills as a mapmaker . . .' He suddenly realized how patronizing this sounded and he added, 'Though there's no reason why you shouldn't be skilled at such things,' thus making a bad speech even worse.

A little later Jack and his men were out on the trail, heading north-west in the general direction of the Khyber Pass. They intended to enter the high country through a narrow valley further south of the pass, closer to their destination. Sergeant King, Corporal Gwilliams and Ishwar Raktambar were the other riders. They each had led a pack horse which would also serve as an alternative mount. The mood was sombre. Normally a British officer going on such a mission would have a troop of cavalry with him, or a a few companies

161

of infantry. Jack was relying on the fact that he had no army protection to impress the tribal chiefs.

However, hill men were hill men, and they might just decide to decapitate all four of them to teach the British army some kind of lesson. Who knew whether or not the head of the Kafirisi tribe had not lost a son in a battle with the British? Or perhaps had been insulted and humiliated at some time by a pompous major? Crossman could well imagine that his own father, in his time, might have called tribal chieftains by dirty names. Major Kirk had considered himself to be superior to most British, let alone foreigners. (Though such prejudice did not prevent him from accepting the title of Knight Commander of the Portuguese Order of the Tower and Sword.) Had he been let loose in Asia, Jack could well imagine his father starting several wars with his arrogance.

Jack hoped his own arrogance, for he recognized that he had a little of his father within him, was under control. He was the son of an aristocrat and an officer in what he believed was the greatest army in the world, so the potential was there. He tried always to remember Burn's line, *A man's a man, for a' that*. Whether the great poet had meant what Jack took it to mean was neither here nor there. The line did its job when Jack was feeling particularly pleased with himself.

At this moment in time, as his horse trod resolutely forward with its load, he was not feeling anything but humiliated.

Before leaving Ferozepur, Jack had visited the quartermaster of Cox's regiment and given him some money for Cox's courtesan. It had been humiliating, having to suffer the hooded knowing eyes of a grizzled sixty-year-old quartermaster, when Crossman tried to explain that absolutely nothing untoward had taken place, but since the captain had omitted to leave the woman provided for, he had taken the duty upon himself. Clearly the major had not believed him. Why should he? *Oh, yes young man*, the elderly quartermaster might as well have said, *I understand. Good luck to you, you randy little devil. Get it where you can is my motto.* His eyes and demeanour said as much, even if the words had not come out of his mouth.

Jack's mind was still taken up with the woman. What would have happened if he had woken to find her beside him an hour earlier? The thought was both terrifying and thrilling. He knew that, now, after the event, he would be regretting any indiscretion, yet he also knew that he would have experienced a short time of forbidden ecstasy, when all guilty thoughts would have flown from his mind and he would have been free of himself.

The four men rode until evening when they came across a vast mangrove forest which would need the light of the following day to see their way. They had brought a single tent with them, a small bell, which they put up between them. Then Raktambar went looking for wood to make a fire, while King saw to the horses. Pasture was found for the beasts and they were hobbled and left to roam for the night. Gwilliams scouted the immediate area, looking for any possible hazards, whether in the form of hostile men, savage wild beast, inclement weather or physical geography. Crossman found himself fetching water and laying out the beds. There were no servants to do the chores out here, he reminded himself, and strange as it might have been to other officers he felt churlish simply sitting around waiting for others to finish the work. He preferred to be doing something himself.

Once they were all set up for the night, poor young Sergeant Farrier King wandered around looking lost and naked having no precious instruments to play with. He did walk off to a nearby rise, without his rifle-musket which seemed a little foolish to his lieutenant. Crossman said nothing however. It would not improve their relationship to be *always* criticizing King for something. Better to let some things float by without bringing them to notice.

When he did return, the others were sitting around a small campfire and he joined them in eating the stew Gwilliams had cooked.

An evening near jungle is never a peaceful affair, what with all the myriad noises the forest creatures make, but a traveller in any new land soon gets used to particular sounds and blots them from his consciousness. Gwilliams was aware that he was scraping his tin plate with his spoon and begged the pardon of the others.

'Not a concern,' murmured Crossman, leaning back. 'Look at those damn stars! Have you ever seen so many? I swear they multiply every night. And that moon. Have you ever seen so fat a moon?'

'That moon,' agreed King, 'is fatter than my last landlord. He drank fifteen jugs of ale every evening, without fail, and it all went to his middle. At about ten in the evening his shirt would part company with his breeches and his belly would appear, white and round, just like that moon.'

'So, what was she like?' asked Gwilliams of Crossman, casually. 'This mornin' I mean?'

Jack straightened. 'Who?' he asked, hoping there was some other explanation for the question.

'You know,' replied Gwilliams. 'The woman.'

'None of your damn business, Corporal,' snapped the lieutenant. 'How the hell did you know, anyway?'

'Got eyes,' replied Gwilliams, smugly. 'I seen her. Fine pair of haunches, from what I seed. Good set of shoulders.'

Fortunately for Lieutenant Crossman, newly married and concerned about fidelity, King was so engrossed in the heavens, in the stars and their courses, he had not followed the conversation. The young sergeant did not look quite real in the fading light. Jack wondered whether the sergeant *was* real. Any other ranking soldier would have got himself as drunk as a bishop the previous evening, their final night before going off on what might prove to be their last jaunt into the wilderness. But not Farrier King. He had spent the evening carefully wrapping lightly-oiled rags around his instruments and giving Ibhanan last minute instructions about their care and servicing.

Gwilliams, on the other hand, had soaked his brain in the local gin, but fortunately for the corporal he had the ability to surface the following morning as if he had been supping on spring water.

Only Crossman, the officer in charge, had something to hide and, as usual, it concerned women.

King was something of an enigma to Crossman. After all, he was only a blacksmith's son and should have had no pretensions to anything but an ordinary soldier's life. Yet the young man had a purposeful air about him, as if he knew exactly what was his role in life and it certainly wasn't serving army officers or shoeing horses. It was not that he regarded himself as special, but that he considered himself lucky to have found work that he knew to be special. Farrier King was a surveyor and it was the job that should really bear the capital letter, not his name. He was quietly genteel in a less than lofty way. Not the gentility associated with an English aristocrat, but the kind that settled on men of knowledge who have no time for frivolous pastimes such as drinking and whoring. It seemed to Crossman that King would rather go to a lecture on the use of the Dip Circle Device, than swill ale or bed a willing buxom milkmaid. He did not know how to enjoy himself: or perhaps he did, but his joy was of a deviant variety, resting in cold metal instruments and strings of mathematical theories.

'I shan't let you down on this mission, sir,' said the sergeant. 'You can be sure of that.'

'What?'

'You were staring at me, as if assessing my worth, sir. I know I've been a disappointment to you in the weapons area, but I'm sure I'll get better with a firearm with practice. Gwilliams here has had a lifetime of shooting squirrels out of trees – he told me he *barked* them – isn't that right Gwilliams? You bark squirrels by shooting at the tree limb on which they sit so that the bark flies up and hits them in the head and stuns them. Remarkable.'

Jack said, 'I wasn't assessing you, Sergeant. I was dreaming. Staring into cold space. Now, what's all this about squirrels? Why would you do that, Gwilliams?'

'So's not to ruin the meat and pelt. You shoot 'em square on and you make a mess of the cadaver. Damn great hole in it, the ball blastin' right through on occasions and taking good meat with it. If'n you just bark a squirrel or chipmunk, you don't wreck its hide, so to speak.'

'One learns something every day. What about bears and cougars?'

'Straight a-tween the eyes, sir, every time, or you might as must end up with raked back and ragged pants.'

'I thought as much. No barking bears, then. Remember that, King.'

Later, when they went to bed, a rota system for guard duty went into operation. Jack had to take his turn: there were only four of them. Two hours each was not a great chore. The officer worried when it was Raktambar or King on duty, feeling the only one he could really trust to be alert or loyal was Gwilliams. But when it came to his turn, in the early dawn with the grey light leaking from the forest around, he realized he had slept *some* of the night away. Beasts and birds were moving in the sunrise, some out looking for food, the nocturnal ones looking for a bed.

Jack had heard so much about tigers before coming to India he had expected to meet one on every corner. So far the only ones he had seen were on the walls of a rajah's palace, though there had been spoor and other evidence. Still, he did not feel so threatened by tigers as he did by elephants. They might seem more benign, the bigger beasts, but they were just as unpredictable. He saw a herd of them go past in the dawn now, silent as creeping mice, down towards a river's edge. As they crossed a ridge, some dozen of them, their silhouettes

165

were stark against the sky. One stopped to defecate and Jack could distinctly hear the thud of dung hitting ground on the drum-hollow forest floor. Then the great grey beasts were gone, into the forest, without treading on so much as a twig.

An anteater came next, shuffling down a narrow path in the grass, followed a little later by some sort of largish feline – not a leopard or any that Jack knew – though whether one was hunting the other was a mute point.

Finally, a snake slithered over some warm boulders, into the sunshine, to bask with the lizards and get some heat into its bones.

Jack had heard much about cobras, but apart from one or two encounters, had not been too bothered by them. There were a lot of snakes in India, despite the fact that the natives and foreigners alike killed them willy-nilly, whenever they saw one. But for the most part – perhaps cobras excluded – they were pretty shy creatures. You don't bother me, I don't bother you. It was a philosophy he agreed with.

Gwilliams was first up, followed by Raktambar.

The corporal got the fire going again, blowing on last night's embers, while Raktambar went down to the stream for water.

It was an hour before Jack realized the Rajput had not returned.

'Has anyone seen Raktambar?' he asked of king and Gwilliams. 'Is he back yet?'

Gwilliams looked along the jungle path. 'Ain't seen hair nor hide since he went for water.'

'I haven't seen him at all this morning,' answered King, rolling up some bedding. 'He was gone when I got up.'

Crossman walked down the animal track towards the stream. He found it was further away than he'd first imagined. There was no sign of the Indian on the trail down to the water. When he got there though, Jack found the water skins lying on the bank, draped over a stone. A half-filled one was up to its belly in the shallows. But Raktambar was nowhere to be seen. Jack picked up the skins, dipped his stump into the cold water for a few moments to soothe the constant irritation, then walked quickly back to camp.

'He's missing,' the lieutenant told the other two men. 'No sign of him.'

'Skipped?' asked Gwilliams.

Jack shrugged, genuinely mystified. 'But why? He came back of his own accord. Why would he duck away now?'

'Mebbe he knows where we're going now? Could be he doesn't like our chances? Or mebbe he's gone to get men, now he knows the trail and where he can attack us?'

'I can't believe he would betray us so soon after his speech to me at Ferozepur – I just don't believe it.'

King said, quietly, 'How well do we know these people?'

'I take your point, Sergeant,' replied Crossman, 'but the sincerity in his tone, in his very demeanour, was not faked, I swear. I'm not sure what we should do now. We could track him down. I'm sure you could follow him, couldn't you, Gwilliams? Or we could push on without him.'

Gwilliams, bushy beard glinting like copper in the morning sunlight, shrugged off his present task of saddling the mounts.

'Take me to the spot, sir. Give me a look.'

Jack took the corporal down to the stream. Gwilliams spent a few minutes looking at the ground there, and at the surrounding bushes and trees. He then gave his opinion.

'There's bin more'n one man down here. Look at the prints in the mud on the far bank. Two others have come. And you can see where the shrubs is broken, the leaves disturbed, out that way.' He pointed. 'I reckon he was met by someone, mebbe even took. You want my opinion, I say we go after him. It may slow us down a piece, so it's your call, sir.'

Jack did not hesitate. 'I'm sure this won't be the last time we'll have to deviate from our path, Corporal.'

The pair walked back to the camp and assisted King with the final packing. Then the three riders with two extra horses in tow, set out to follow the trail left by the people who had met with Raktambar. It could be he was known to them of course, even that the meeting had been pre-arranged, but Jack wanted to be sure that Raktambar had not been forced. His own thoughts were that the Rajput had gone willingly, for who would bother to abduct an Indian in a country of millions? Had it been Gwilliams or King who'd gone missing, Crossman would be certain of an ambush.

After an hour's riding through the forest the trio came upon several mango groves, clearly planted by farmers. A little further on still and huts came into sight, surrounded by cultivated fields. There were no workers in the fields, nor any around the village itself, which seemed strange. Something had frightened them away, probably only temporarily. Once again his thoughts naturally went to tigers. A man-eater? Surely not the whole village though? It had to be something other than just a wild beast.

It was not long before they came across the real reason for the temporary evacuation. They came to a place where something ghastly had happened. There was a giant tree with wide-spreading strong-looking limbs. Dangling on ropes attached to the limbs were five hanged men, all Indians wearing only loincloths, some in turbans. They swayed there grotesquely, one or two of them spinning slowly like plumb-bobs. Jack inspected the corpses and was relieved to discover that Raktambar was not among them. This set of executions had obviously frightened the locals out of their wits, and probably in their eyes had defiled their orchards. It was as if an apocalypse had passed through like a foul wind and left these symbols of death behind it to dirty the landscape.

'Rough justice?' murmured Gwilliams. 'Or mebbe a raid from bandits?'

'I think you were right the first time,' answered Crossman. 'Let's push on. Can you still track them?'

'Easier, over the fields.'

In another hour the three soldiers had caught up with a troop of Sikh irregular cavalry led by two British officers. The heavily bearded sowars wore long black boots, red kilts and reversed animal-skin coats, with dark-blue turbans. The two officers were dressed much the same, except for decorations on their uniforms and helmets in place of turbans. They were riding in good order, but there was a solemn air about them. The officers had been speaking to one another, but they stopped when Crossman approached.

Jack was aware he was not in uniform, having opted for white cottons for the ride north-west. His eyes swept up and down the line of horsemen and noted that they had three prisoners with them. One of these was Ishwar Raktamber, who looked as if he had been beaten. His head was hanging down and his clothes were torn. Crossman rode up to the two officers, who watched him coming through narrowed eyes.

'Lieutenant Crossman of the 88th,' he said, coming abreast. 'You have my man there. I want him back.'

The two officers were subalterns themselves. One of the pair, the senior by the look of him, for the other was not much more than a boy of seventeen, glared at Crossman. They were clearly taken aback by his abrupt manner and looked affronted.

'Who the hell are you, sir, to make demands?' questioned the big cavalry lieutenant in an accent Jack recognized as East Coast Scotland. He appraised Crossman, looking him up and down. 'You're not even Indian army. Giving me orders! Whatsay?'

The cornet looked at his senior and grinned.

'Wipe that smirk off your face, Cornet,' snapped Crossman to the youth, then keeping his voice to an even tone he said to the older man, 'I've told you who the hell I am, now who the hell are you?'

The retort came back. 'Mind your own damn business.'

'I am minding my business. My business is that Rajput you have there. You took him from my camp, sir, and I want him back. I don't know what your orders are but I'm sure they don't include abducting one of the Maharajah Ram Singh's palace guards, a man who has been in my employ for the past several weeks and who has nothing to do with insurrection.'

While they had been talking a Sikh officer – a subedar – had walked his horse up alongside Crossman's. The Sikh had his hand on his tulwar sabre, as if ready to draw it at a command. Jack turned to stare into the man's eyes, finding nothing comforting there.

The cornet piped up, 'These prisoners are all mutineers – they're scum. We caught them all together, running south. We've already hanged the worst of 'em and this lot will meet the same fate, once we've questioned them as to the whereabouts of their fellows . . .'

Gwilliams had now moved up and was nudging the subedar's horse with his own, forcing it away from Crossman's. King, who was the only one of the three in uniform, had come up on the other side. His Enfield rested across the saddle of his mount. There was an uneasy shuffling amongst the cavalry horses, as if their riders were wondering what was going on. It must have been unusual to see British officers arguing so hotly amongst themselves, even if one of them was in mufti. The subedar had now moved behind the two British officers. Raktambar had his head up and was looking anxiously at the confrontation.

Gwilliams said to the cornet, 'You're a damn liar, sonny. You never caught our man with those others.'

Raktambar shouted, 'They came to the stream while I was getting the water – these two,' he nodded at the other captives, 'and fell on their knees to drink in front of me. Then the troopers came . . .'

'We are not mutineers, sir,' cried one of the two prisoners. 'We are simple travellers, sir. We are holy men, not soldiers.'

'Shut your rotten mouths,' shrieked the cornet, clearly embarrassing even his comrade, 'or I'll shut them for you.' He then whirled back and addressed Gwilliams. 'I'm not a liar and you'll answer for that remark. If you're an officer like your friend here, which I doubt, I'll have satisfaction. If you're not, I'll see you flogged.' He was still a little hysterical. 'You hear me?'

Gwilliams made a farting noise with his mouth, his usual rejoinder to someone he regarded as an upstart and not worth his time.

Everyone ignored the youth after that and the conversation continued in a calmer mode between the two senior officers.

'What, Lieutenant Crossman,' said the senior cavalry officer, 'do you think you can do to wrest this prisoner from us? We are about a legitimate business, sir. If he's innocent, as you say, you can collect him from Ferozepur, after we've given him a trial.'

'A trial similar to the one you gave the hanged men we saw?'

'The cornet here was a little over-zealous, I admit, while I was out searching with the rest of my troop. One can't blame him after all that's being going on, can one? There will be a trial for these others . . .'

'I can't wait for any trial,' interrupted Crossman. 'I'm on a mission to the hill tribes and this man is one of mine. I've told you this, repeatedly, yet still you stand here and argue. What kind of officer are you? All the EIC officers I've met so far have been reasonable men, but I seem to have come up against two buggers who don't know their arse from their elbow. Sergeant, cut our man out, will you? I've no more time to waste on these fellows.'

A dreadful tension was strung like invisible wires in the air. The Sikhs felt it. The British knew it was there. Incredibly, it seemed to all for one taut minute that there might be a fight for Raktambar. That British officers – and NCOs – should attack each other was of course unthinkable, yet here it was in their minds. It was indeed only there for one savage minute, when searing emotions almost overrode common sense, that insanity was loose.

The first blow, especially with a weapon, would have been disastrous for all concerned. To explain such circumstances at the inevitable courts martial, would have been impossible. One could never recapture such a sharply-honed mood again in a dusty courtroom. It would have been one of those cases, like the mutiny on the *Bounty*, from which no one would have emerged with any honour intact. Infamous was the word which sprang to mind, as they sat in their saddles and for a few vicious seconds contemplated their own self-destruction. Then it was past. King rode up and took the reins of Raktambar's mount from a Sikh's hand.

'Thank you, Lieutenant,' said Crossman. 'You may wish to report this incident when you get back. I should tell Colonel Hawke, as well as those you wish to inform, if I were you. He is my superior.'

'Calcutta Hawke?' muttered the officer. 'Why didn't you say so, man?'

'I wish I had, now that I see it impresses you.' As Raktambar was led away by King, Crossman turned his horse and faced the still furious cornet. 'And you, young man, you might want to reflect on something other than your own feeling of importance. I have no idea of your orders, or what you regard as your duty, but you're going to have to live with your deeds and you'd better have some good answers in that head of yours to the questions you'll ask yourself in the future – or God help you, boy.'

The four rode away, back towards their camp.

'What about us, sir?' came a plaintive cry from the same captive who had spoken before. 'Take us with you. They are shooting men from guns. They will fire us from their cannon. A man should die honourably, sahib, not be blown to pieces. Sahib, sahib, we will be good servants, to you, we will be faithful . . .' Further words were lost on the wind.

Jack could do nothing for the other two men, even if he wanted to. It was entirely possible they were guilty of the crime attributed to them, in which case they were doomed. Mutiny had only one punishment, be it in various forms. Death. Death by firing squad, by hanging, by other less honourable means. British officers, men and civilians had been murdered. In such turbulent days it was certain that innocent men would go down with the guilty, for chaos and confusion reigns in such times and some men will regard the flimsiest of evidence as damning. Some, indeed, would not need any evidence at all, preferring indiscriminate revenge over specific justice. British families were being slaughtered. There would be madness in the wind for some time to come, on both sides of this new war.

Raktambar was up behind Gwilliams on the corporal's horse.

'Are you all right, Raktambar?' asked Crossman, going up alongside. 'Were you beaten?'

171

'A little.'

'I'm sorry for that.'

The bedraggled Rajput shrugged, as if to say, these things happen.

'Are you badly hurt? Do you need to stop?'

'No, I am not hurt. I am ashamed. I did not fight hard enough.'

'You were taken by surprise. They would have killed you.'

Raktambar shrugged again, then his expression hardened. 'If I see that boy again, I will kill *him*.'

'That's not advisable. He's a nasty brat, to be sure, but no good will come of retaliation. His father's probably an important man, back in Britain, and he thinks he's invincible. He isn't. He'll get his come-uppance one day, fairly soon I imagine. These arrogant little pipsqueaks always do. It'll all be in my report, when we return to Ferozepur.'

'Until then he will hang many men.'

'I think his lieutenant will keep him reined in, from now on. I believe the lieutenant was as shocked as we were by those bodies in the tree. Was it he who stopped the executions?'

'Yes, the boy had ordered his men to hang us all. If the lieutenant hadn't arrived back, I would be in that tree.'

Once back in the camp they gathered up their equipment and set out once more for Piwar. A dark mood hung over the whole party. It was bad enough that they should be riding out on such a dangerous mission, without interruptions such as this one, from their own people. Sergeant King rode up alongside Crossman and spoke with him.

'Did that prisoner mean what he said? Will they fire him from a cannon?'

'We're new to this country, sergeant. We shouldn't make any snap judgements.'

'Nothing to do with being new,' snorted King. 'That would sound barbaric to me anywhere.'

Jack sighed. 'I agree, but my name's not Lord Canning, I'm not the Governor-General of India. If this mutiny spreads further, which seems likely, I doubt even he can contain things. What we have to concentrate on is our small sphere of duty – do our job as best we can without compromising ourselves. We can't stop the mayhem. It'll just roll right over the top of us and crush us. I'm not saying we should join it, I'm saying to a certain extent we have to isolate ourselves from it. There's a canker here which has been growing, I think, for many decades. We've come fresh to the shores of India and find a festering land. You have your opinions, and you're entitled to hold them. Mine probably accord with yours. But don't destroy yourself by going against unstoppable forces. It'll just be more waste.'

The subject was then dropped. It was not something that either man felt able to carry forward with any chance of resolution. Jack certainly felt that he would exhaust himself both mentally and spiritually if he were to delve too far into it all. He had chosen the profession of soldiering, not that of the study of politics or ethics. He knew what was right and wrong for him, even for his men, but when it grew to nations he felt overwhelmed.

'Who's for a song?' cried Gwilliams, later in that gloomy day. 'How's about one of them English songs o' yourn? *The White Cockade?*' Without waiting for a yay or nay he burst into it with a rich timbre that went with his magnificent bronze beard and hair. King tried to join in with him, but his voice was drowned by Gwilliams. Ishwar Raktambar looked away, embarrassed by this breakdown in discipline, waiting for Crossman's expected intervention. Then Jack cried, 'That's it lads, roar it out, louder now. Put a bit of backbone into it. *'Twas on a summer's mornin' as I crossed o'er the moss, I never thought to tarry till some soldiers I did cross. . .'* The voices roared out. *'. . . he is a handsome young man whose blade will serve the King . . .'* Then Raktambar realized that the illness was catching and fell back, lest he became a victim too. When it was all over, the soldiers looked much better, more refreshed. Clearly this strange yelling had clarified their minds, their blood, and had given their spirits a lift.

In camp that evening, Jack found himself alone at the fire with Gwilliams, who was darning a sock by the poor light.

'What are you really doing in our army, Gwilliams?' asked the lieutenant of his corporal. 'What's someone from the other side of the world doing with an officer like me, in India?'

Gwilliams looked up and grinned through that mane of his.

'Me? I just washed up, like driftwood on the beach. I bin up and down my own damn continent so many times it made me dizzy, so I came lookin' for some new ones. Don't you like to travel, sir? Ain't that one of the things that makes you join the army?'

'Travel? Not for the sake of it, no.'

'Well, I do. I just like to walk on different dirt. As a youngster I was stuck in this preacher's house, night and day, readin' the ancients. Oh, I told you I ain't got no languages, but neither did the preacher. He had all these translations in English: Horace, Plato, Juvenal, Homer, Plutarch, Plautus and the rest of the Roman and Greek crew. I got to thinkin' about how it was in them olden days, when the world was small. I came down gradual to thinkin' how lucky it was that world got bigger by the time I came to it and that it weren't there just to sit and do nothin', but to be walked on. So I started walking. Then ridin'. Then sailing. Till I fetched up in some marvellous places and some terrible ones. This is one of the better ones. Whole different way of livin'. Somethin' no one in Nebraska even dreams about.'

'But to join the British army, and to sing about being a soldier of the King, like you did today? Isn't that against your American philosophy?'

Gwilliams grinned, holding up the bright needle to the firelight in order to push the wool yarn through the eyehole.

'Just cause I sing it, don't mean I live it. The reason I'm in this man's army, is cause o' you. I knew you'd take me to places I ain't got the money to go to. Sure, I could've joined some navy or other, but they work the bejesus out of a man, kill him with it, then flog his dead body for asking for a bit o' cheese to eat on his way to hell. The navy's no life for a man who likes to walk on foreign land, only for someone who likes water – a lot of it – and bein' alone with a band of stinkin' sailors. They take you away for two years 'n' more, out on the wet, then when you get off the damn boat they leave you for a couple of days before knocking you on the head and draggin' you back to the ship's hold agin. That ain't no life. Sure, there's parts o' this one I could do without, but nothin's perfect in this here world.'

'Well, I admire you men who know what you want from life. King seems to have the same gift. Me, I'm still looking for my slot. I really don't know where I belong.'

'Sir, there's excitement in that too. The eternal quest.'

'I'm glad you think so.'

The next morning, shortly after they set out, Jack's horse threw a shoe. Gwilliams had suggested, and Crossman had agreed, that they carry spare shoes for all the horses. The last time they had visited an army farrier, at Ferozepur, the mounts had been re-shod and spare shoes had been provided. Here, in the foothills of an approaching mountain fastness, the ground was becoming rougher the whole while, so it was necessary they replaced the lost shoe fairly swiftly. A charcoal fire was lit to heat the shoe before pressing it on the hoof and nailing it home. Gwilliams did it, but all the while he berated his sergeant, the son of a blacksmith.

'How in the hell did you escape your pa's trade, Sergeant? You surely watched him at his work, when you was a sprat?'

They were in a rough circle in a clearing, the fire at their centre. King was sitting on a rock nearby smoking a stubby clay pipe, this object a very poor cousin of his leader's long-stemmed chibouque, purchased in Constantinople a few years before. Crossman was at that moment smoking his wonderful curved pipe, straight out of the Arabian Nights, blissfully switched off from the conversation between the other two and more interested in what Raktambar was doing to occupy his time during this leisure halt.

The air was thick with smoke, from the charcoal fire and the two pipes. Gwilliams – stripped to the waist and wearing leather chaps on his legs – had his back to the horse with its rear leg between his own. Raktambar, who had no interest in shoeing or smoking, was busy playing some sort of game with his hands. He seemed to shuffle his fingers as if they were a deck of cards, then he shook his hands and stared at the result, as though he expected the fingers to be in different positions after this exercise. Crossman stared through the smoke, obviously puzzled by these machinations.

King said, 'I sometimes watched my dad at work, but I didn't take it in. I was more interested in learning my schoolwork. My dad didn't *want* me to be a blacksmith. He wanted me to be more interested in my studies. He sacrificed a lot to give me some sort of education. You've got to remember my dad didn't like being what he was. He said the work was gruelling hard. The heat from the forge, day after day, burned him something fierce. All up his arms and on his face he had these little black pits where white-hot sparks of iron had flown up and buried themselves in his skin. And lately he's been complaining that his strength is giving out. You've got to be mighty strong to be a blacksmith of any kind.'

Gwilliams, struggling with the restless horse, looked up from his work. 'Do tell,' he retorted, sarcastically.

Suddenly Crossman shot off his seat and whipped his pipe from his mouth.

175

'How did you do that?' he cried at Raktambar.

The Rajput smiled, flicked his right hand, and held it up for Jack to inspect.

'All back to normal now,' said Crossman. He repeated, 'How did you do that?'

King said, 'What did he do, sir?'

'His fingers were back to front,' said Crossman. 'He somehow twisted them on their joints so they faced the wrong way.'

'I seen you do that too, Lieutenant,' said Gwilliams, grinning, 'with that woody hand o' yourn. Don't you kick me, damn you madam,' this to the mare, 'or I'll slap your arse for you.'

King stared at Raktambar's hand. 'An illusion,' he said after a while. 'He fooled you, sir, by mesmerizing you somehow.'

'No, no,' insisted Crossman, 'I saw him do it.'

'Whole point of an illusion,' grunted Gwilliams. 'Hell lady, if you don't stop shiftin' your rear I'll whop you so hard . . .'

Finally the shoe was on and Gwilliams himself could relax and join in the conversation. Crossman was saying to Raktambar, 'Did you do it?'

'You saw me do it.'

'But was it real?' asked King, 'or did you hypnotize him?'

'Watch!' replied the Rajput. He began the strange shuffling movements with his fingers, which flashed up and down, crossing each other a dozen or more times, then he flapped his right hand and held out his left. The fingers were all back to front on the left hand, though the eyes of his audience were continually distracted by sudden movements of the right hand. Then just as quickly, after another swift flick, they were back to normal again. The eyes of the audience went back and forth between the two hands, amazed that this man before them was able to do such a trick, whether it be a physical displacement or an illusion of sorts.

'Double-jointed,' growled Gwilliams, 'most definite.'

'No, no,' said King, 'it's a trick of our eyes, not his hands.'

'Do it again,' cried Jack, 'I almost had it that time.'

Raktambar shook his head. 'Too many times is not good. This is not the way.'

'He's right, sir,' King said, 'magic tricks lose something in the repeat.'

'It's not a magic trick – he's got these here funny joints,' insisted Gwilliams.

They were still arguing when they were out on the trail, later, which helped them disregard the heat which bore down on them.

In the middle of the long days they rested in the shade, riding only in the mornings and the late afternoons. Crossman avoided villages and indeed people where he could. All India was not in turmoil but it was simmering at the edges. This was a land in which news moved swiftly from one region to another, there being many travellers – wandering holy men, pedlars, itinerant men of strange sects who painted their bodies with yellow ochre, dancers, musicians, a whole host of rootless people who needed to keep on the move to survive – and the word was that the British were vulnerable and ripe for being driven from the land. Some Indian recipients of this word were indifferent to the news, others were glad and rejoiced, a few whose businesses would be affected, were concerned.

This mixed reaction was dangerous in itself. Crossman could never be sure of any they met. The best policy was to keep out of the way of any habitations and avoid groups. Of course they met men and women on the trail, out about their daily business of collecting wood and water, or one of those nomadic types who walked barefoot over the world. But often as not they passed by without a word, or offered a simple greeting, nothing more. Crossman had to hope that by the time those individuals could pass on the news of the strangers, he and his men would be out of reach of any vigilante groups or organized bands of brigands.

Ishwar Raktambar had said very little about his ordeal in the hands of the two British officers and the Sikh irregulars, but opened up one time when he and Crossman were changing guard. It was coming on dawn and Crossman had decided not to go back to bed. He sat with the Rajput and watched the stars fade into the light blue early-morning sky.

'I wish to thank you for saving my life,' Raktambar said. 'Someone should kill that boy before he is made into a general and has power to destroy many hundeds of men without being called to answer.'

'There are others like him, at this time, I'm afraid. This is not a civil war, but it is like one. In such wars emotions have more force than do rational minds. It is a time when the bullies are able to do what they like doing and not be held to account. If the pot boils over, neighbours will attack neighbours, hiding murder under the cloak of patriotism.'

177

Raktambar said, 'I do not understand *all* of that, but – yes – some of what you say is true. But it must happen. You British try to change us too much. We do not want to be changed. We do not want to become like you. When the British soldiers first came here, they did not despise us, they took our women to wife. But now they bring their pale wives with them, haughty women who look down their noses at Indian wives of the British soldiers. This is hard to bear. And the soldiers too have changed. They wish to make us all Christians. We do not want to become Christians. We do not want to fight your wars overseas. I do not want to corrupt my caste by going over the sea.'

'I'm sure we don't want to make you Christians, do we?'

'Some of you do. There are generals who visit my maharajah who ask him to become Christian as an example to his subjects.'

Crossman nodded. 'Well, not me.'

'Some are also like you,' conceded Raktambar, 'but not all. And we are afraid. We are afraid we will be changed. In India there are many religions. All of them believe they are the right religion. But we do not try to change each other.' Raktambar paused, before going on, 'You and I, we are bound to each other in honour. I did not wish this. I tried to stop it from happening. But it has happened and we are brothers of the blade – there is no help for it. My blade protects you, your blade protects me. We must try to make our way together through these troubled times. If the British are driven from India, then you must go and our bond is at an end. If they defeat their enemies, then you will stay and we will remain locked in honour. You have saved my life, but my life would not have been in danger if you had not taken me from my home. I will save your life, sometime. It will happen, I am sure. Perhaps we will do it many times, one for the other, and will die together in some lonely place, overwhelmed by enemies.'

'That's a pretty gloomy end you envisage there – a romantic one, but a little drear.'

The Rajput shrugged. 'If it must be . . .'

Crossman thought about his old comrade-in-arms, in the Crimea, the Turk Ali. Now Ali had been loyal, steadfast and true. He had loved Jack as a real brother and would have died for him. For his part, there was nothing Jack would not have done for the Bashi-Bazouk, Yusuf Ali. Now here he was with another foreign comrade who did not particularly like him, was not enthusiastic about being one of his number and would have just as soon put a bullet in him if 'honour' permitted it. The only thing which kept them together, Raktambar and he, was this adhesive idea that seemed to prevail over all in this land of the eastern sun. Men here, everywhere, seemed so fiercely attached to the word they made allies of invaders.

'Can we ever be friends?' asked Crossman, as the light of the day drove out the night. 'Must we always be reluctant allies, you and me?'

The Rajput sighed. 'I do not know. You will always be the man who took my bride from me.'

'Surely the maharajah did that?'

'No, you chose me from the line.'

'That's true – but how was I to know?'

'Another Rajput would have known,' said Raktambar, nodding. 'It is all the same with you British – you do things with closed eyes.'

'Then Rajputs must be mind-readers.'

'No, they read faces. It is easy to do, with open eyes.'

And Crossman conceded that Raktambar was probably right. If he had been a little more aware that day and not wrapped up in the pomp and circumstance of his visit to His Highness Ram Singh, he might have taken more notice of Raktambar's expression, of the reluctance which must have been written there, plain for him to see, if he had only *looked*.

'Well, as you say, neither of us can do anything about it now. You are sorry for it. I am sorry for it.'

Unexpectedly, Raktambar grinned. 'Never mind,' he said.

'And now,' Jack asked, seeing that the other two were still fast asleep, 'can you teach me that trick with the fingers? I would love to know it.'

The Rajput laughed. 'Sahib, you are so foolish!'

This nettled Crossman, both as an officer and a man.

'Am I? I might not be the cleverest person in the world, but I think I'm capable of learning a parlour trick.'

'But sir, you have not the right equipment.'

Crossman was flummoxed. 'I beg your pardon?'

'Sahib, you only have one hand,' laughed Raktambar. 'How can you do such a trick with only one hand? One needs both, to take away the attention of the watchers. To control those who would see.'

179

Crossman looked at the empty socket of his sleeve and burst out laughing too.

'I hadn't though of that. I was hoping to impress Jane when I saw her again. Damn, I'll never be able to do that trick, will I?'

'No, sahib – never.'

'Damn.'

Gwilliams, huddled in a blanket on the other side of the fire, opened bleary eyes and glared at the two men.

'Beggin' your pardon, sir,' he said in a deeply sarcastic tone, 'but could you shout just a bit louder – I'm not quite awake.'

'Time you were up and about anyway, Corporal – come on, shift your backside man. We need to be on the trail. Yes, you too, Sergeant. We're not on a jaunt, we're on a mission. I've been far too soft with you two recently. I'm thinking about morning kit inspections followed by a parade. When did we have those mainstays of the army in this regiment, eh? Inspections and parades? Something to think about, while you fetch the water Gwilliams. This is the army, after all.'

Neither Gwilliams nor King thought their commanding officer very funny as they dragged themselves out into the day.

21

At last they were in the rugged mountains of Afghanistan having crossed the River Indus. Gwilliams had likened the action to that of a Roman army crossing the Rubicon or the Israelites the River Jordan. It was immensely symbolic. The Indus had fed romantic travel literature of the West since the time of Alexander the Great and actually washing one's socks in its waters was almost a spiritual affair. The Ganges belonged to the Indians, Gwilliams told the others, but the Indus was one of those roots of mankind which belonged to everyone, white or brown.

'I tell you, Sergeant, it brings a lump to my throat,' the corporal had said, as he paddled his dirty feet in the shallows. 'This is as much my water as the Potomac or the Colorado. Kings have come here to bathe. Nations have rose from its banks and marched across continents. The Indus. Who'da thought it, that one day I would've trod in its hallowed ripples?'

King, who had no emotional feelings at all for the gushing torrent and had drawn a section of it on his maps, was baffled by Gwilliams' sentiment. A river was something to be charted and this particular watercourse, being braided, shifted its channel sometimes by as much as six miles either way on a regular basis. No matter how accurately King drew the Indus on his maps the next time he came through this way, even be it only weeks between, the river would be in a different place. It therefore represented something a little too unstable. If he had anything to do with it, he said, he would plant willows down the banks to contain its wild wanderings, so that it behaved like sensible

English rivers and stayed in more or less the same place, year in, year out.

Now they were in the mountains, where around every corner lurked a hill man with his *jezail* – the long ornate musket with its carved stock – and a *chora* – his long Khyber knife – stuck in his cummerbund. They were deadshots, one and all, as good, if not better, than any sharpshooter in the Crimea, be he Russian, French or British. The word 'fierce' might have been coined for these wild tribesmen, with their pale eyes and their tangled beards.

Crossman and his men passed the odd one or pair on mountains paths, dressed in *angarka* tunics, turbans on their heads and sandals on their feet. They replied to no greetings and only a slight flick of their eyes indicated they recognized the presence of others on their trail at all. Crossman never looked back at them, but he guessed that once they were at a distance they turned round to stare at this unusual sight. Strangers, especially Europeans, were not often seen in these mountains except when they were collecting revenues for the Honourable East India Company, and on those occasions were accompanied by at least a company of soldiers.

No man ever passed them going the same way, yet when Crossman and his men arrived at a particular pass, it was defended by a hundred or more tribesmen. It was as if the eagles and falcons that circled above them carried the news of their coming. As Gwilliams said, the hills fair bristled with the barrels of firelocks and knives were thicker'n porcupine quills. A shot between the front legs of Crossman's mare stopped him in his tracks. He waved his good hand in what he hoped was a sign of peace. Now he was going to get his chance to speak Pashto with a live Pathan.

'Are you the Kafirisi?' he called. 'I would speak with the Kafirisi.'

'No,' came the reply, 'we are the Bochura.'

Crossman was relieved to hear that because the Bochura were supposed to be friendly towards the British.

'I am Lieutenant Crossman, of the British army,' he called again. 'I would ask for safe passage through these hills.'

A volley of shots answered his shout, none of the actually hitting a target, but frightening the horses.

'So much for friendship,' muttered Crossman to King and Gwilliams. 'I was told the Company paid these people to be on our side. I was assured by Colonel Hawke there would be no trouble.'

'Well there ain't bin yet,' offered Gwilliams, ''cept for a little crazy shooting.'

A group of men then came out of the rocks like beetles emerging from their holes. They did indeed look a rough band, their cheeks windburnt and scarred, their beard hair stiff with white dust. They walked up to the horsemen and stared hard at what they were carrying, as well as openly inspecting the mounts and the riders. One of the Afghans peered closely at Crossman's leather gloves, a present from Jane, which he had taken to wearing in the mountains. Beneath the left one was the metal hand he had invented with Tom. He was getting accustomed to its foibles and could now do fairly simple tasks with it, including skilful use of the reins.

This same man grabbed the bridle of Crossman's horse and demanded gold.

'Gold?' asked Jack. 'What gold?'

'You will give me fifty pieces of gold,' snarled the tribesman, who was clearly a chief of some kind, 'as payment to go through my pass.'

'*Your* pass?'

'This is the land of the Bochura. You will pay me this gold.'

'Has the Company not given you money for our passage?'

The man's eyes were the colour of a wolf's, yet they had not even the compassion of that wild creature's. They were as hard as flints as they bored into Crossman's. Money for passage may well have been given sometime in the past, they said, but that was then and now was now. Negotiations were in progress again, all other payments had been eroded away by time. It was as if word had already reached these people that the British were on their way out and one must fleece them before it was too late. Crossman realized that he would need to purchase his progress through the land. Either that, or fight his way through, which might prove more expensive. Whole regiments had tried that and had failed or had been held down for months. He'd been given some gold by Hawke. Now was the time to start using it.

'Of course we have the tribute,' said Jack, suddenly smiling, 'but this must be done in the proper way, with tea around a fire. We have ridden many miles to visit the Kafirisi, who, as you know, are the most numerous tribe in the region and who hold sway over all others.'

'The Kafirisi will not begrudge us our share of your money.'

'No, I didn't mean that,' lied Jack, who had been hoping that

183

mention of the greater clan might cow this lesser one, 'I simply tell you what is our goal so that we are open and easy with one another.'

'What's happening?' asked King who, like Gwilliams and Raktambar, had not been able to follow a word. 'Are they letting us pass?'

'Not yet,' murmured Jack. 'We need to drink tea with them first.'

They were taken to a place where the ground was reasonably flat and where there was a deep cave which went into the rock face. A fire was soon lit and tea boiled on its flames. Everyone sat cross-legged in a circle around the fire, the Bochura splitting the four intruders by forcing themselves between them, so that they were sitting apart. In between each of the soldiers were two or three of the tribesmen. The one to the right of Crossman grinned into his face with blackened teeth. They were indeed a tough-looking bunch with hard elbows that dug into the ribs of the newcomers.

'So,' said the chief, to the right of Crossman, 'where is my gold?'

The lieutenant reached inside his poshteen and withdrew two purses each containing twenty-five gold pieces. He handed these solemnly to the chief, who was doing his best to peer inside the poshteen to see if there were any more bags where those came from. Crossman glared at this effrontery, stroking his chin and murmuring, 'For shame'.

The chief stood up in front of the lieutenant, who also got to his feet, at the same time as warning his men to stay seated.

'You would fight with *me?*' cried the chief, his hand on his Khyber knife, a weapon which Crossman had been told could be used in an instant to disembowel an enemy, with an upward thrust that sliced through belt, clothes and belly, all in one movement. 'Is *that* what you would do?'

Crossman said, coldly, 'I have given you the payment for our passage, yet you remain hostile. This is not the code of the hills. Is this the honour I have been told to expect?'

'You would teach me honour too?'

'I have been told,' said Crossman, picking up a rock with his left hand, 'that the men who live here are as hard as stone.'

The chief frowned, studying the fist-sized rock Crossman had in his hand, as if he expected it to be used against him as a weapon. Several of the other tribesmen were now on their feet, their *jezails* pointing at the lieutenant. Ignoring Jack's order, his NCOs jumped up, beating Raktambar to his feet by only a second. The situation was tense. No one was quite sure what was happening. Still the chief did not draw his *chora*, though his hand was on the hilt.

'If you have been told this, it must be the truth,' growled the chief. 'We are of these hills, of these mountains.'

'This,' said Crossman, 'is what I do with stones.'

The chief and his clan stared, wide-eyed at last, as the lieutenant crushed the rock to powder with his gloved hand. It fell as dust from his fist to the ground beneath. A truly remarkable show of strength. None of the watchers said anything, but the air was taut with amazement. The chief bent down, picked up a similar rock and tried the same feat. This attempt was a failure and in the end he threw the stone to the ground.

'It is a trick!' he cried. 'Your stone was weak!'

Crossman then stooped and, after a long moment, picked up the chief's stone: it crumbled like the first under the grim fingers that enclosed it.

'Now,' said Crossman, quietly, in English to his men, 'walk slowly towards your horses, mount, and ride out with me in good order.'

He then deliberately turned his back on the chief and walked to where his mare was tethered to a bush. He and the others swung themselves up into the saddles, took the reins of their packhorses, and left the place in single file. No one looked back. Not one of them spoke a word. They each could feel wolfish eyes boring into their backs, but Crossman sensed there would be no firing. He had made his point and the tribesmen could go back to their homes and tell a strange story unsullied by blood. ' There is an Englishman', they could say, 'who is at this very moment riding through these hills, who looks as weak as a puppy, yet is stronger than a bear. We took his gold for we are the Bochura, who are afraid of no one, not even wizards.'

'By God,' said Gwilliams when they were out of earshot, 'I don't mind telling you, sir, the sweat is running down in my pants.'

'There's more than sweat going down my breeches,' gulped King, who appeared to be teetering on the edge of a swoon. 'I thought we were goners that time – I had my prayers ready and loaded – my weapon would have been no use – I was shaking too much to hit anything.'

'You cain't hit anything even when you're steady,' growled Gwilliams.

Raktambar was grimacing, his teeth together and his lips curled back.

'I too was praying,' he finally admitted, 'very, very hard.'

Crossman looked back at his men and smiled. 'I'm glad about that,' he said, 'because at one point I thought I wasn't going to get my metal fingers to open for the second rock, and that would have spoiled the show. Those prayers obviously worked, because the fist unlocked right at the moment I was beginning to panic. Now look,' he held up his left hand, 'this was a fine glove and it's soiled. I shall get hell from my wife if she ever finds out. I'm sure they cost her a great deal and are impossible to replace.'

'I'll stitch you a new one myself,' promised Gwilliams, 'the minute we come to a market with some good leather for sale.'

'What concerns me,' said King, 'is that the Bochura are a small tribe while the Kafirisi are one of the largest. If this is the kind of treatment we're to receive, we have no life to look forward to.'

'Little tribes are often more aggressive than big tribes, having to assert themselves to make themselves heard,' answered Crossman. 'Just like little people.'

King frowned and looked at his leader. 'Is that meant as a barb for me, sir?'

'Not at all. At least, I don't think so.'

They rode on. Birds of prey roamed around the sky overhead, no doubt purposeful yet seeming uninterested in the ground beneath. Indolent lizards basked on the rocks. The heat in the mountains was not as fierce as it had been on the Rajputs' plains, but the scenery was just as dreary. Sandy stone everywhere, with the occasional reddish-coloured rock. Dust devils swirled in pockets, scattering their contents. Goat bells were occasionally heard but they saw no goats, nor indeed any goatherds. The lone men who had passed the soldiers earlier like separated beads on a string had now ceased to do so. The landscape was empty, arid and bitter. It bore the presence of new men with resentment, never temperate in its mood.

'I got called a *griffin* in Ferozepur,' King told Gwilliams, as they trailed on at the rear. 'What that means, I've no idea.'

'Yeah, me too. Only I asked the man who called me it – very politely – just what he meant by it. It only means fresh meat.'

'Newcomer?'

'Yeah.'

'Oh. I thought it might be some sort of insult. Well, I suppose it is in a way, but you can't really insult a man with the truth. We are fresh to India.' King moved forward in the saddle, having uncomfortable sores on his buttocks from previous riding. He looked about him at what he considered to be a miserable scene. 'God, I wish I was home now. Down there,' he nodded backwards, 'in the jungle it was different. It was lush and green, and noisy, and, well, exciting. This place is like the land of the dead. Everywhere old bones of dead animals – maybe humans for all I know. Nothing but dust and carcasses, mouldy fur and feathers.' He swung round in his saddle to face Gwilliams. 'What do you miss most about England?'

'Not a lot. It ain't my home. It's a foreign country.'

'Oh yes, I forgot. Well then, what do you miss about your own country? Canada, isn't it? Or the United States?'

'Let's just call it North America, 'cause I bin everywhere on it 'cept some small towns what ain't worth the visit. Guess there's a few more o' them sprung up since I bin away. What do I miss? Girls, I guess. Good ole girls with lots o' flounces and plenty o' warpaint. God they used to smell so good. Enough cheap perfume to drown a rat. Legs up to their necks. Great big boobies spillin' out of their dresses, white an' creamy. Black stockings with red garters. Nuff to make a man sweat in Eskimo-land. You take 'em to a room and what's the first thing they do? Take out a powdy-puff and create a whole blizzard of pink scented snow on the sheets, nuff to drive you wild. I once had a girl, she weren't more'n forty-five, which is young when it comes to them ladies in the new western towns, I tell you. She was some woman, that's a fact. Almost got married that one time. Narrow squeak.'

'Tavern girls, you mean? Good lord, Gwilliams, you can't marry a tavern girl.'

'Why in hell not? I like taverns myself. Homely places where a man can drink and talk to his heart's content. Better'n being stuck in an empty room with a bottle. How about you, Sarge? What d'you miss?'

King smiled. 'Oh, I don't know. Apple pie and custard. My dog, Hammer, a big black mongrel who sits around my dad's forge when I'm not there, pining for me. Oh, stovepipe hats! They're greatly in fashion at the moment. Everyone's wearing them. I bought one before I left, but haven't had time to put it on and go out in public.'

187

'And by the time you get back home again, they'll be out of fashion. I guess you like them 'cause they make you look taller. You should wear your shako, that'll correct the deficit just as good.'

The sergeant frowned and wheeled his horse to confront his companion.

'That's the second time today. I am *not* short.'

'Just a wee bit, next to the lieutenant an' me, that is – oh, and Raktambar. I tell you one thing, you ain't shorter than Sajan.' Gwilliams grinned.

King pulled his mount back into line feeling aggrieved.

'I'm as strong as any man here. Two rupees says I can lift a heavier load than you or the lieutenant.'

Two rupees was equivalent to four shillings in English money. Gwilliams did not consider this a worthy wager for a man of his stature and suggested they should raise it to ten rupees. 'That'd be less mean.'

'Ten rupees?' cried King. 'Not on your life.'

'No, on your strength, Sergeant. Damn man, it's only a third of your monthly pay. You can afford that. Nothin' to spend it on our here.'

'I have far better things to do with my money, Corporal. I withdraw the wager and consider the matter closed.'

He trotted his mount and packhorse on, to show he meant it.

Raktambar had heard this conversation and was impressed by the amount of money Gwilliams was prepared to bet. He waited for a short while before asking Crossman, 'I would be able to join the British army, yes?'

'Not the British army, as such, but certainly the East India Company's army, as you well know. Three out of four men in the Bengal army are Hindus like yourself. Rajputs and Brahmins. Or, if you liked, you could join the Madras or Bombay army. Much the same thing, though. No difference. Better to be with friends, I would have thought. Rajputs and men of Oudh.'

'How much money would I receive?'

'I understand a sepoy gets seven rupees a month.'

Raktambar drew a sharp intake of breath, before saying, 'The sergeant gets much more. I heard the corporal say so.'

'Yes, but he's Queen's Regiment. You would be with John Company.' Crossman paused before adding, 'Of course, a European soldier in the Company army also gets more, but then he *is* British.'

188

'And this is the fairness of which you people speak so much? A man's life is worth the same, wherever he comes from.'

'I expect you're right, but you won't get the Company to agree. You see the Company's managed – that's to say, controlled – by a dozen old men called "directors" who sit around a table in far-off London. I doubt they've even seen an Indian sepoy, let alone spoken with one. As I understand it, there's over three hundred thousand sepoys and sowars in John Company's army. If they raised the pay to that of a British soldier it would cost the Company another – oh, maths, maths – four to five million rupees a month. I doubt they would ever agree to do that.'

'But,' said the astute Raktambar, 'they must make many riches from revenues in India.'

'I'm not much interested in finance. I wouldn't know. I suppose you're right, but there it is. It's always appeared to me that the greediest of people are men who sit around small tables in London, talking profit and figures that seem to come out of fairy tales. Nothing seems to satisfy them. I doubt they'd give a sepoy *one* rupee more without a huge battle around that small table. Certainly the British soldier doesn't consider himself well paid. I myself, as an officer, must use my own money to keep up appearances, for my army pay doesn't cover what I need.'

Raktambar's eyes swam around in his head for a moment.

'You *pay* to be here, in these forsaken hills?'

'Well, not here, exactly. I go where I'm sent.'

'I think I will *not* join the Bengal army.'

'Wise. Very wise. Remain in the royal household, once you've got shot of me, of course. The maharajah's palace is probably a haven of delights compared with being out here, in the field, or back in one of the camps. You get to live in the palace, do you not? With marble floors and walls, curtains and what not? In the Bengal army you'd get a barrack room full of noisy coughing sepoys, with a floor of rammed earth covered by watered cow dung to keep away the insects. I know, I've been in similar barrack huts, though not in India. They're ghastly places. They stink of the worst of human smells. They're noisy beyond belief. There's drinking and fights – all the worst kind of characters you can imagine.'

'Oh, sir, sir,' interrupted King, coming up alongside his commanding officer, 'not all bad, surely? There's also backgammon,

189

draughts and sometimes even a coffee-room in which one can relax. Why, I've known barracks with libraries attached.'

Crossman smiled and nodded. 'There you have it, Raktambar, the worst and best of barrack-room life.'

The Rajput nodded, clearly thinking it all over. Then he was uncommonly candid. 'Palace life is not all fragrance and flower petals,' he said, hinting at things more dark.

'No?' said King. 'Do tell. I love gossip.'

'In the palace,' Raktambar said, 'we have *hasad-wa-fasad*.'

Crossman translated. 'Jealousy and intrigue.'

Raktambar continued with, 'The maharajah is not well-loved by all. Others wish for his power. Brothers will plot against him. Sons will war against him. He must always have a food-taster or be poisoned. He must sleep in a room where the boards sing like larks when trodden upon by approaching assassins. The favourite of today is tomorrow's condemned man. I will serve my lord, but if his son kills him, I shall die for that faithful service, for the son is jealous of all that was the father. A new palace will be built to show a new beginning. Fresh palace guards will be recruited and the old put to the sword in case they foment revolt. No one is safe. Everyone looks under his pillow for the planted scorpion. Everyone unfolds his clothes carefully in case a deadly snake has been put there. There is a book, the *Arthashastra* which tells maharajahs how to hold on to their kingdoms, how to defeat their enemies, how to perform magnificence. This book has a thousand deaths for men like me, who are close to the rajah.'

'Sounds like Machiavelli's *The Prince*,' muttered the well-read Gwilliams, trailing on behind. 'Every culture's got one.'

'Nowhere is safe,' said King. 'Life is full of danger.'

'Not as much as we seem to seek,' Crossman answered. 'If you'd stayed with your father and had settled for a blacksmith's life you'd be safe enough.'

'Maybe, but who's to say that blacksmiths will always be a wanted trade. Perhaps in the future they won't need farriers any more? When I was at school our master told us that in some countries they make wooden shoes, like Lancashire clogs, to fit horses' feet. The people carve them out of oak or some other hard wood and just put 'em on the horses' feet like shoes.'

'I can't ever see *us* not needing farriers,' said Crossman.

'You don't know,' replied King. 'It could be that one day we'll all ride about in steam trains and not need horses any more. What about that then? A world of steam trains! It's not impossible.'

'Of course it is,' scoffed the lieutenant. 'Totally impossible. Perhaps more than most men I prefer steam trains to horses, but I can't see machines ever forcing horses out of our lives. You only have to look at history. The horse, like the dog, has been with men from the beginning. That's not a union which could easily be put asunder, as they say. Mankind began life with the horse and when the end of the world comes, the horse will still be with him, you mark my words. Not that we'll be there to see it, but just the same.'

Gwilliams said, 'I agree with the lieutenant. Horses is permanent. I don't know where you get them warped ideas from, Sergeant, but you sure oughta do somethin' to straighten 'em out one day.'

'I still think it's possible,' replied King, stubbornly, though he sounded less convincing now. 'It *could* happen.'

'Never,' chorused the other two men, with Raktambar adding, 'Not ever.'

As they progressed into the hills and mountains their situation worsened by the day. The paths became less distinct, the way more rugged and parched. Dust rose to fill their mouths, noses and ears. The heat of the day was intolerable. The nights were cold, bitter. There were snakes and scorpions and blinding relentless hot-wind storms. Crossman had a constant headache that robbed him of his concentration. It pounded from within and there was a terrible pain across the ridge of his brow that threatened to split open his skull. His water stung when he peed and his anus burned with raw fire. On the bottoms of his soles and on his single palm the skin had cracked, letting in sweat and dirt. He festered with sores on his buttocks and elsewhere. And waves of nausea came and went irregularly, swamping his gut with bodily sewage.

They all suffered equally on that march.

The maps King had brought were entirely inadequate and the group became lost in this khaki-coloured world where everything blended into one. Watercourses which were supposed to be there, were not. On one stretch, one interminable four-day slog, they had very little water and thirsted as they had never done before. They went along as if in a dream, their heads full of visions of waterfalls and streams, their horses stumbling over rock and stone, one of them falling to its knees in the dust and having to be put out of its misery with a single shot that echoed through the emptiness of the landscape around them. They were blind men in a blind land. Nothingness was behind them and nothingness ahead. All trained soldiers, they had experienced thirst before, had been on route marches that had torn the souls from their frames and left them flapping in the wind, but nothing compared to this unholy arid landscape where nought but dry lizards lay panting on stones, staring with unpitying eyes as they passed, and spiders scuttled from shade to shade, offering only a momentary distraction from their woes.

'How can you be lost?' grumbled Gwilliams at his sergeant, echoing the thoughts of them all. 'You're supposed to be the map man. Damn me, you can't shoot, you can't do much of anything. The one thing you're meant to be good at is follerin' maps, Sergeant.'

King flapped the chart angrily, staring about him as if some rocky outcrop might suddenly leap forward and offer directions.

'They don't match up. I can't help it if the maps are wrong.'

'So much for your bloody Everest,' muttered Crossman. 'A two-year-old could have drawn a better chart.'

'Everest didn't map this region,' growled King, defending his hero, 'these are much earlier maps. They were probably done by some addle-brained lieutenant sent out here to quell the tribes.'

'That sounds a lot like insubordination to me, Sergeant,' rasped the dry-thoated lieutenant. 'Be very careful.'

They were all past the point of exhaustion, screamingly frustrated, and sick to death of each other's company. Raktambar had withdrawn from the group completely. He rode and rested apart from them. Gwilliams' sympathies at this time were as close to the Meerut sepoy mutineers as any living white man's could be, he having a very low opinion of the British army in the first place. His lieutenant hated the very sight of his sergeant and the sergeant despised the lieutenant. It would have taken but a small spark to set them all on to each other with boots and fists. In fact it was probably only fatigue which did save them from a brawl.

At least, Jack thought, as they struggled along, that mysterious pursuer would not be with them. Surely? To follow them into such bad country would be foolish indeed. Perhaps he would be waiting for them, if they ever came out alive?

Crossman's control of the march had sadly seeped away. Occasionally he had an insight into his own inadequacy and stared at it with horror, seeing the equivalent of a demon sitting there, mocking his self-confidence. Any arrogance he had owned was laying back there in the dust somewhere, dead on the ground. Aware of his failure, he fought to retain some sort of grip upon his own self-discipline. So far he had not actually cracked in public, even though there were myriad internal fissures. However, if they did not get water soon – one of them at least was drinking his own urine filtered through a sock – there would be serious consequences to the expedition.

And they had to find their path! They *had* to.

Then a blessed thing happened. He caught a movement in the corner of his eye. What was that? His head shot round and he studied a craggy hill to his right. Was that a man? The rock face seemed bare of life. Nothing moved. Despair entered his soul again. More delusions? More false visions? There had been several over the past week. Wait! A slight movement again. The clack of a hoof on stone. A mountain goat? Something like it, yes. There it was, camouflaged, blending beautifully into the rocky background. Yes, a goat, perhaps a wild antelope of some kind. It skittered over the ridge and was gone, down the other side.

'Stay here!' he yelled at his men, startling them and the horses as he dismounted. 'I'll be back in a minute.'

He scrambled up the hillside in his filthy white cottons, the end of his turban fluttering in the airless regions. Up the slope he went, raising dust, sending scree and shale flowing down behind him. When he reached the top he stared about him, expectantly. At first he tasted bitter disappointment. Prayers that had been washing through him suddenly dried at source. Then, finally, he saw it. A glint of silver. Down below in a deep bowl-shaped valley, was a thin stream like a string of mercury. Water!

'Water!' he yelled, hoarsely, through cracked lips. 'Water!'

Then his eyes shot back, fearful that he had seen but a mirage and knowing what effect that would have had on his men. They might have killed him if they had climbed up and found a lie. But no, it was still there, and not dancing in the haze in the manner of *fata morgana*. A stream. A blessed stream. He could taste the water from here. It was cool and sweet: made in heaven by the angels from their own dewy teardrops.

Of course, when they reached it, it was a dirty little brook full of grit and sand, but it was still the best water they had ever tasted.

They stayed by the watercourse for a whole day, reluctant to leave it and go out again into blistering oblivion. But having found it, King was able to trace it on his map and now had a rough idea where they were again. Gwilliams shot some pea fowl which were drinking further down the bank and a fire made to cook them on. The rancour of the previous few days suddenly melted away. Raktambar rejoined the group. It was not the jolly party which had started out – there were still wounds which would take time in healing and scars which would remain for ever – but at least they were back on speaking terms again. When they finally left the place, to travel north in the cool of the evening, they found they did not have to say goodbye to their newly-found friend just yet. They could walk alongside it. Even the horses were back nudging each other, though eight were now seven.

In order to try to further close the rift, Crossman opened a conversation with King on the sergeant's favourite subject.

'Your measuring chain, it is a marvel of engineering, is it not? A hundred feet of blistered steel, I believe. Precise to an inch, so Colonel Hawke tells me.'

'Sadly that's not so, sir,' replied King. 'It's a very old-fashioned chain, which expands in the heat. They wouldn't let me have what I really wanted – compensation bars being too expensive, so they said.'

'How massively disappointing for you.'

King glanced at his leader, looking for some hint of sarcasm in the remark. 'It may seem a little selfish to you, sir – me wanting all this highly expensive equipment – but one needs to map accurately, or not bother at all. This trip must have given you proof of that. Colonels Lambton and Everest, now they mapped to a thousandth of a decimal place. They saw that as the only way to do the work we do. Surveyors will all tell you the same thing, sir. Oh, I know I'm soaring a bit high for a sergeant. I've been told that by other officers. But men have come up from lower and have done great things. Captain Cook, you know, came from very humble origins.'

'Yes, but he was a navy man and therefore doesn't count.'

Again, King realized he was being made fun of, but did not rise to the bait. He breathed loudly, as if pulling in fresh clean air. 'The Himalayas, sir. Some of them have been done, but not all. Certainly not all. The ruler of Nepal, the King in Kathmandu, has closed off the borders again. We can't get in there and we can't get into Chinese

Tibet. Someone, some day, is going to do it. I wish it could be me. I want to train Sajan as my artificer, my assistant, and map the unknown regions. Is that flying too high?'

'Every man should have his ambitions, his aspirations, and the grander they are the better for his spirit.'

The stars were out now as the horses placidly plodded on. Gwilliams and Raktambar were also listening mutely to this conversation, interested in spite of themselves. Entertainment had been sparse over the past several weeks and this was as close to it as they were going to get.

'I wish though, they had given me compensation bars.'

Crossman asked, 'What makes them so expensive?'

'The brass, I suppose. They're fashioned of two bars, one of brass, the other of iron, fixed side by side, bolted together in the middle. Somehow the two metals expand differently and cancel each other out – I don't know exactly how, for no one has explained that part to me – but what you get is a sort of adjustment going on all along the chain.'

'You seek this precision like a philosopher seeks the meaning of life.'

'Oh, yes – yes, I do,' replied the eager young man, 'as I have said to you. It is so necessary to the work. Do you know, until Lambton we did not know the shape of the Earth? Think of that! Our own home and we did not know its contours – not exactly.'

'And what shape did he find it?'

'Sort of roundish, with a flattening at the poles, I believe.'

'Well, having made this astonishing discovery, mankind's knowledge will no doubt advance at a tremendous pace. Are there other things – other than metals improperly expanding – which bedevil the profession?'

Once again King looked askance at the lieutenant. This time he said, 'These frivolous sarcasms do you no justice, sir.'

'I'm sorry. You can take it, King. I am listening, after all.'

'I suppose. Yes, yes there're other devils. The worst of them being refraction. Refraction of the light. That's the most terrible of the demons. Let me explain to you, sir . . .'

'I had the idea you were going to.'

'. . . you may think that a mountainous region, or a jungled area, is the worst kind of terrain to map. Not so. Not so at all. The worst

195

kind of country to map is a wide plain. You remember those droogs we saw in the south?'

'Those hills like puddings dumped upon the landscape?'

'That's them, sir. Well, they're excellent for setting up flagpoles for sightings across an expansive plain. Or Hindu temples, with their tall towers. One must have a trig point, sir, in order to sight from the base line. You will recall on the Rajputan plains there was nothing. Not so much as a high tree. One has to build towers oneself in such circumstances. It slows down the work enormously, as you can imagine. And out on those plains you remember the haze – the haze from the heat, from the smoke of thousands of cooking fires, from the dust swirled up from the earth – all those cause a refraction in the light when one is trying to sight through a telescope. This bending makes for imperfections in the readings and – well,' King threw up his hands in a gesture of horror, 'so we get inaccurate maps.'

'So how did they map the plains accurately – or did they?'

'Yes, they did. Colonel Everest invented a lamp and flares, which he used at night, thus beating the refraction. They would build a tower, use a lamp flanked by fires, and sight on the artificial light. He's a most brilliant surveyor, Colonel Everest. I admire him a great deal.'

'But a bit of a martinet I understand.'

'All *great* men are entitled to lose their tempers, sir.'

Crossman thought wryly of the times over the last few days when he had lost his and how King had regarded that loss with utter disgust. Obviously he was not great enough to carry the sin.

'So, heat expansion and refraction. Horrible devils, eh?'

'There are many more. One has to have an accurate reading of one's altitude when measuring the landscape. An aneroid barometer is the best instrument for this work.'

'Which you haven't got, I imagine, being too expensive?'

King played the game now, satisfied with having Crossman's attention for once. 'Exactly, sir. They wouldn't let me have one. I have to make do with an ordinary barometer, or by taking the temperature of boiling water, a very primitive method. Sometimes we surveyors have to mark our position with astronomical observations, for which plumb lines need to be used. There's another devil for you. The surrounding hills and the density of the earth beneath our feet cause plumb line deviations. Wicked things, deviations, as you can well imagine, sir.'

196

'Perfectly ghastly, I'm sure. But tell me, didn't the natives regard your man Everest as some kind of sorcerer? It smacks of witchcraft, all these midnight fires on towers, pointing things at the stars, dangling lobes of lead over the earth. I know if I were a local person I should be very suspicious of some pale-skinned stranger walking past my village wielding strange devices and artefacts, muttering oaths and curses, stopping to inscribe odd symbols in a book of magic. It's a wonder they didn't burn him.'

'Oh, it wasn't like that at all. He was like some far sultan come from a distant land. Why, on one occasion alone he reported having four elephants, forty-two camels, thirty horses and seven-hundred natives with him. He travelled with a huge retinue, sir. No expense spared. He was not a witch, he was one of the wise men, seeking the knowledge of a star!'

Crossman retorted pleasantly. 'If you think my wife's dowry is going to stretch to elephants and camels, you're sadly mistaken, Sergeant. You were right earlier on. You need to rid your head of all those high ideals. Crossing the Himalayas like some modern day Hannibal? Better to settle for doing route maps which will aid the army on its marches. Elephants indeed! Do you hear this, Gwilliams? Elephants and camels. Ah, here we are at a bend and there's a cloud over the moon. I suggest we stop and camp here. Never mind, King. If it's meant to be, it'll come to pass.'

The next morning Gwilliams shook Jack awake and he opened his eyes to see the camp crowded with heavily-armed men. *Jezails* and *chora* knives were much in evidence, but there were one or two matchlocks such as Jack had seen Hindus and Muslims carrying in India. The intruders were squatting around the campfire or simply standing around leaning on their muskets. There was little to differentiate this group from the Bochura they had encountered, except for an air of absolute confidence. It was clear these warriors came from a tribe which was used to being feared.

Crossman rose to his feet, splashed water on his face from a bowl, and addressed the company in Pashto.

'Who is the chief here?' he asked. 'Or the chief's first man?'

They seemed startled to be addressed in a language they understood. One very tall lean man, all skin and bone, stepped forward. He was a good half-head taller than Crossman who was no dwarf. Two startling blue eyes looked out from a leathery face covered with more creases than a well-used map. He wore a loose smock and cotton trousers, much the same dress as Crossman himself had on, but his *lungi* was wound round a pointed cap which Jack knew was called a *kullah*. His tulwar sabre was richly inlaid with semi-precious stones, but the most magnificent thing about him was his waistcoat, which was of richly embroidered black cloth covered in gold and silver thread designs. He saw Jack looking at this last item, looked down at himself, and when his head came up again his expression was just as richly patterned in smiles. Obviously he was proud of his waistcoat and nodded at Jack as if to say, *Pretty impressive, eh?* His face was, however, without the necessary intellect which a chief would need to rule here.

'You are the chief's man?' said Crossman. 'I am Lieutenant Jack Crossman of the 88th Connaught Rangers, a mighty regiment which has left death and destruction in its wake wherever it has been.'

'You are British army?' the rasping cigarette voice replied in surprise. 'Where is your red coat and your tall hat?'

'I left them at home, as did my soldiers. A soldier's uniform is not made for travel in these hot, dusty regions. One needs the comfort of loose garments which let in the breeze. I commend you on your waistcoat, sir. Where did you get such a beautiful item of clothing, if I may make so bold as to enquire?'

Again the tall skinny man looked down at himself, but this time he fingered a hole no bigger than a pea in the front of the waistcoat.

'I killed a man for it.'

'With a single shot, by the look of it.'

'Of course.' The head came up again. 'Otherwise I would be dead too.'

At that moment a crow-like bird, perhaps a black drongo, flew overhead. The warrior whipped his *jezail* to his shoulder and shot the bird in flight. He looked at Crossman and his eyes widened in another faint smile, as if to say this time, *Just like that, eh?* He loaded his weapon, slowly and deliberately, while staring at the handle of Jack's revolver. His Tranter would be a prize here, in the hills, where such firearms were seldom seen.

While the pair were talking, one of the tribesmen began prodding Raktambar in the chest, forcing him backwards, seemingly trying to intimidate him. It was a challenge. Jack moved instantly to defuse the situation, especially not wanting them to pick on the only Hindu

198

in the group. Gwilliams and King would not act without his orders, but the Rajput might very well decide to give as good as he got. Raktambar glanced his way, his expression saying that he was been patient long enough.

'Stop that!' ordered Jack in a very haughty English accent, one such as these hill tribesmen might have heard before from visiting officers of the Queen. The tone of his loud authoritative voice was enough to halt the tribesman in his tracks. 'Keep your hands to yourself, you grubby man. If you wish to fight, we shall accommodate you later.'

The man stiffened, looked at Skinny, then moved away from Raktambar, glaring at Crossman.

'You, one-hand,' said Skinny, 'you do not shout at a Kafirisi tribesman in such a way, unless you wish to die.'

Jack pushed his face forward and said in Pashto. 'I am an officer of Queen Victoria's army abroad. The greatest army in the world. You will not threaten me.' Skinny edged away a foot or two. Jack continued briskly, 'Now, Kafirisi you say? You are the people we have been seeking these many weeks. You will take me to your chief, Akbar Khan, for I have business with him.' In English he added, 'Men! Strike camp. Pack the horses. Do it in the most busy fashion you can muster, swiftly yet not with overdue haste. Make it seem as if their presence means nothing to us.'

Gwilliams immediately kicked sand on the fire to put it out, eased his saddle out from under a tribesman who was sitting on it and began to saddle his horse. King began to roll up his blankets, despite the fact that a man was standing on the end of them. When he reached a pair of feet in dirty sandals he gave the blanket a little jerk, not enough to topple the passenger, but enough to make him stumble backwards. The man gave a shout and put his hand on the hilt of his Khyber knife while staring hard at the sergeant. King took no notice of him whatsoever and began packing his equipment into a cotton bag. Raktambar too went quietly about his business. Crossman stepped around Skinny and attended to his own packing.

The tribesmen stood watching and waiting until it was all done. They gave no indication as to whether they were going to go along with Jack's request to meet with their chief.

The tribesmen mounted their horses and kept them in a rough circle around Crossman and his men. There was still a great deal of tension in the air. Who knew what the relationship of this group was to the rest of the tribe? Perhaps they were a rough outfit, operating on their own? Certainly there was more autonomy within one of these tribes than in a regular army, with subchiefs and subsubchiefs taking much on themselves. There would be no reason to suppose they would not shoot all four intruders and steal their horses and goods before the rest of the tribe got their hands on them. Just because Crossman knew the name of their paramount chief did not mean he had free access to the region. Skinny and his followers might well have the authority to act on their own without necessarily going back to their head.

The first shot of course would lead inevitably to the deaths of Jack and the other three. They were surrounded by at least two dozen tribesmen, all of whom were undoubtedly crackshots. All of whom would think nothing of carving their bellies with those long Khyber knives.

Skinny sat patiently waiting as Jack was the last to mount.

Jack then said, 'Oh drat, wait a minute, I haven't performed my ablutions yet, have I? How stupid of me. I suppose it was the fact that we had guests this morning which drove it right out of my mind. Gwilliams, would you mind shaving me?'

The corporal's bushy eyebrows shot up, but he dismounted.

Crossman then apologized in a smiling frank way, in Pashto and Urdu for the delay.

With everyone ready to move, Gwilliams deliberately took out a tin mug and filled it with water placing the mug on Jack's horse's rump so that it balanced there. Then he took out of his saddlebag one of those gentlemen's travelling toilet packs, the kind that have pockets all the way along. He untied the strings and unrolled it. He lay it over the horse's behind, alongside the mug of water. Next from the pack he took a mirror which he hooked to the lieutenant's horse's bridle, so that the officer could see what was happening to his face. He then took out a shaving brush, wetted it and soaped it, before beginning to lather Jack's cheeks, chin and under his throat.

The horse, used to this morning procedure, remained perfectly still.

The tribesmen watched both men carefully with narrow eyes.

Next, Gwilliams took out a cut-throat razor from the pack and, opening it, carefully began to shave the officer. His hand was as

200

steady as stone, the honed edge of the razor glinting cruelly in the early light. He started with the officer's left cheek, scraping carefully down to the chin, then washing the foam from the razor in the mug water. Then it was the turn of the right side of his face, a more awkward movement. Finally he scraped under the chin and around the mouth, requesting that Jack bulge his cheeks with air for the best effect.

Gwilliams then took a small towel from his saddlebag and wiped away the residue of the soap, very carefully, and asked his lieutenant to inspect his face in the mirror, feeling over it with his hand for smoothness. A last satisfying scrape at a missed patch and all was complete. The toiletries were then placed the pack and the pack rolled. Gwilliams gave the remainder of the water in the mug to his horse and placed the items in his saddlebag.

Finally both men mounted. Jack took his horse up alongside Skinny's.

'Are we ready then?' he asked in Pashto. 'Shall we ride?'

'You do not want to bathe and have a shit first?' asked Skinny. 'I am sure we all have plenty time.'

'No, I never loosen my bowels before noon, then it's best I bathe afterwards, my English stomach not being used to Afghan food.'

This brought a howl of laughter from the tribesmen and they moved forward, the tension having filtered away during the wait.

'What are they laughing at?' whispered King to Crossman. 'What was all that about? The shaving, sir?'

'I wanted to show them I wasn't afraid. That I had not a care in the world.'

'And had you?'

'Of course I had. Inside I was shaking like an aspen in a Suffolk breeze. Funny thing, having only one fist, King. A single does not react in the way two hands do. My knees were knocking together, but of course they couldn't see them. I think we're going to get to see Akbar Khan. It was touch and go.'

'Was it?' The sergeant went pale. 'Would they kill us for nothing?'

'Probably not for nothing. We are rich men beside them, even though we have brought little with us. Colonel Hawke was telling me that a Captain Williams was out with a party not far north of here just six months again. They were riding around a ravine and had to go single file through a gap between two cliffs. Williams was a little ahead of the others and went through first. His companions were quite close behind but by the time the first of them came through the other side Captain Williams was lying dead, covered in knife wounds, his upper body stripped of clothing and his horse and weapons gone. They never did find the killers, though they only had three or four minutes to perform the deed.'

'Good Lord, sir! You would have thought he would have put up some sort of fight. Surely he had a loaded weapon with him?'

'If he had, he had no time to fire it. These men live by plunder, Sergeant. They kill more swiftly than a snake. We're not out of the woods yet, by any means. However, we have one thing in our favour, they're fascinated by eccentricity. I can give them that, if need be. Another show like the shaving one, perhaps. I have an inventive mind, as do you.'

'But is that the only thing between us and oblivion, sir?'

'Probably. Perhaps. Who knows? I'm not one of those officers to exude confidence just to keep my men in good spirits, King. You'll have to sweat it out alongside me. Give me a hand, if you will.'

At that moment Gwilliams began whistling a tune, which startled a hawk from a nest up on a cliff edge. The hillmen laughed. They whistled, of course, but to signal, rarely to entertain. They sang in those rough whisky voices of theirs, played their mountain drums and flutes, but whistling was not their forte. The hawk did not seem to like the melody and screeched, the sound echoing around the rock walls of its home. Gwilliams stopped whistling and mimicked the raptor's cry perfectly. One or two of the hillmen did the same and soon the valleys were ringing with the sounds of false hawk cries. Then came the sound of another bird, this time the cry reminded Crossman of a ptarmigan. Gwilliams copied it exactly. King tried but failed miserably, tried again, got better, until he too had it. The game continued, all the way along the trail, right up to the walls of a natural fortress.

Crossman left his men to take care of the horses. He himself was taken by Skinny to a tall tribesman who was clearly linked to him by blood. They were obviously cousins or even brothers. This was Akbar Khan, the paramount chieftain of the Kafirisi, a man with an incredible nose. In profile this magnificent organ looked almost square, the bridge jutting out at a right angle from Khan's forehead into a sharp corner which then fell steeply to his mouth. If it had not been for the hard eagle's eyes, the nose might have dominated the whole face. As it was, the eyes impressed Crossman more. They cut into him like blue diamonds.

'*Salaam-ali-kum*,' said Crossman.

There was not a responding greeting. Instead, Khan said in English, 'Why have you come here?'

Crossman began to reply in Pashto, but this seemed to irritate the leader of this large tribe, the men of whom were now milling round, listening to the conversation. He switched to English, realizing that Khan did not wish his followers to understand what was passing between them.

'I have been sent to obtain some assurances,' replied Jack. 'I would be grateful, sir, if you would hear me out.'

There was a great deal of noise going on around them, of men and animals. Cooking fires filled the bowl of rock with drifting smoke which smelled of herbs. It was not certain whether this fortress in the mountains, surrounded by walls of rock, most of it natural but reinforced in places with some mud-and-stone brickwork, was the real home of the tribe. There were no women that Crossman could see, though they might have been in one of the many caves. Dogs and horses, camels, chickens, other livestock were in evidence, hobbled or wandering around, rooting amongst piles of rubbish. There was a Muslim cemetery on a patch of hard earth in the western area of the fortress. Apart from the lack of females there were also no children. It was possible this place was the tribe's main fall-back defence, while their villages were scattered throughout the region.

Akbar Khan nodded towards a cave entrance.

'We shall talk in there,' he said, 'but you will not call me "sir" – this is a term used by the British, not by us. You will call me Khan.'

When they entered the cave it took Crossman a good ten minutes to adjust his eyes from the brightness outside to the dimness within. There were lamps though, filled it seemed with scented oil. Tapestries hung on the walls of the cave, giving it a homely feeling. On the packed-earth floor were carpets and cushions and the odd brass-plate-topped 'table' on which stood ornate brass jugs and containers. It was simple and elegant.

In here there was indeed a woman, but whether young or old was impossible to say, for her black garment and veil covered all. Jack thought she moved like a mature younger woman, but tried to avoid studying her which would have been impolite and most likely construed as insulting. She drifted like a shadow in the background, not even allowing the stranger to look into her eyes. Whether she was curious about him was difficult to tell, though she did appear to be startled when he first came in.

Both men sat cross-legged on the floor. It was a position Jack was becoming used to, though it still felt awkward. He then smelled the fragrance of fresh coffee, heard it being poured, and his eyes closed in anticipation.

'You have had a hard coming,' said Khan in an amused voice. 'The coffee smells good?'

'Delicious,' murmured the lieutenant.

'Then the taste will be disappointing, for coffee always smells better than it tastes. Now, to get down to business. You are Lieutenant Crossman of the 88th Connaught Rangers, so my brother tells me. I know why you are here – it is very obvious. What you must tell me is what you have brought me to persuade me not to rouse the hill tribes and attack the British while they are concerned with their rebellion from their lackey troops.'

'The mutiny . . .'

'Some would call it an uprising. I myself have no love for those tribes over there, whether Hindu or Muslim, Jain or Sikh – they are all jackals and dogs so far as I am concerned – but I can understand why they have come to a time when they wish to shake off the fleas that live on their back.'

Crossman did not particularly like the British being likened to fleas but it would have been counterproductive to his mission to argue such.

'The mutiny or rebellion, call it what you will, has left us with a vulnerable rear. Make no mistake that if you seek to profit by our misfortunes, Khan, we will eventually overcome. You might, at the outset, make some gains, but the Honourable East India Company army will be strengthened by the British army itself and in a very short time those gains will be wrested back. We will always prevail. We are invincible . . .'

Khan grinned. 'You were not invincible on the retreat from Kabul. A namesake of mine slaughtered twenty thousand soldiers.'

Now Crossman bristled, his national pride wounded. The coffee tasted bitter in his mouth. He could not let this go unchallenged.

204

These people of the mountains respected only one thing besides honour. Strength. Strength of fighting men. They lived by it. They died by it. Weakness was considered unworthy and there was no point in being self-effacing or modest when talking to one of the strongest chieftains of the ferocious and fierce hill warriors.

'Not twenty. There were four and a half thousand troops and twelve thousand camp followers. It's true all were killed, except one. However, you and I know how easy it is to attack travellers through this land, especially a straggled band of refugees. Many of them died of the cold. Victory was Kabul's, I grant you, but it was no true test of the might of the British army. We have conquered, we are conquering, we will conquer again. You may win a few battles, here in the hills, but we will win the war.'

'Why do you think that is, Lieutenant?'

'Because we are a highly disciplined fighting force, whose men are drilled and trained to an exquisite sharpness. We have generals who are skilled in greater warfare, who can command vast numbers of men and retain control over them even in the heat and confusion of battle.' Jack paused, seeing something in Khan's eyes, then added, 'As individuals our men are no braver than hill warriors, who fight with great courage and motivation in their rugged homeland, but you cannot always choose the battlefield, Khan. If you are to retain any gains over us eventually you have to come out and meet us on our terms. You, each of you, fight with great intensity and with great honour, but you don't have our control. You're also a loose federation of tribes, who fight amongst yourselves with as much fervour as you fight against the stranger. We will exploit the more treacherous among you. We'll turn tribe against tribe. We're good at such warfare. I can assure you that if you do attack our rear someone will come and take retribution. Whether you care about this or not, is of course entirely up to you.'

Crossman paused again, before adding, 'These words may anger you, but I am here to speak the truth, not to stroke you.'

Crossman's heart was beating fast as he spoke. Some of what he said was bluster and bravado, but much of it he believed to be true. Both he and Khan knew that if the uprising in India spread to include the Bombay army and the Madras army, it would be all up with the British. They would be driven out of India ignominiously. On the other hand, if the mutiny was contained and held down, it

205

was also true that the British army would pay back with interest any who had taken advantage of the situation. He was speaking the truth, sour and ugly as it seemed, and there was no point in saying things he thought the chieftain might want to hear.

There was a long period of silence between them before Akbar Khan finally said, 'You would not be here if you did not fear us.'

'Very true,' replied Crossman. 'You could hurt us.'

Khan nodded. 'And so, on a lighter note, what have you brought me, Lieutenant?'

Crossman reached inside his garment and withdrew a heavy money belt which even his own men did not know existed. He laid it in front of Khan.

'Gold, and the promise of revenues from the other side of the border, once this trouble is out of the way.' There was a bad taste in Crossman's mouth, but he repeated what he had been told to say by Colonel Hawke. 'A blind eye might be turned by the British towards raiding parties crossing the Punjab into Kashmir.'

Akbar Khan nodded. 'And where is your piece of paper?'

He meant the treaty which Crossman had brought with him for Akbar Khan to sign, giving assurances of non-hostility.

'Here,' said Jack, taking it out of his shirt. The woman refilled his coffee cup. 'And so it was . . .' He tore the treaty in half.

Akbar Khan looked surprised for the first time during their meeting.

Jack explained, 'All I want is your word of honour.'

Now Khan smiled again and wagged a finger. 'You are very clever, Lieutenant. If I signed this paper it would mean nothing to me. But if I give my word of honour and later break it – why, that would bring shame on me and on my sons for generations to come. Clever. Well, I do give you my word, but not because I fear the British army. What are they but a lot of little men in red coats, doing as they are told? No, I give you my word because I like you. I like you as a man. How did you lose your hand?'

Crossman felt the exhilaration of triumph wash through him, as he answered the last casual question.

'My hand? Ah, it was crushed by a ladder.'

'How very disappointing. This is no story. You must learn to lie about such things. I thought perhaps a sword in battle . . .'

'It was in battle. A terrible battle with the Russians where we lost many men and few survived. I had been shot through the face, bayoneted, and a great ladder, which needs a dozen or so men to carry it, and is used for scaling fortress walls fell on my arm.'

'They have ladders for that? Ingenious. I simply make my men climb up the brickwork like monkeys. So, you were wounded many times in this battle, yet you live! Now that is *almost* a story.' He leaned forward, the huge nose almost touching Jack's cheek. 'If I were you, when someone asks about the hand, tell them you fought with Akbar Khan's champion to obtain his word of honour. You slew the champion, who sliced off your hand with his *chora* at the moment of death. Thus did you win the admiration of a great hill-tribe chieftain, who gave you his word that he would not attack and annihilate the British army once its back was turned. Now that is a much *better* story and one worth losing a left hand for.'

'Your brother perhaps?' said Jack, entering into the spirit of the thing. 'That tall lean warrior who brought me in?'

'My brother,' Akbar Khan replied with heavy contempt, 'is no champion. He is an idiot, born with the brain of a tapeworm. You must invent someone far more worthy than that infestation of the gut. Now, while you finish your coffee I shall tell you about the Kafirisi. It is very interesting. Come, drink – there is plenty more. There was once a chieftain named Karam Fatteh Khan, whose tribe, the Kafirisi, invaded the north of India in what you call the eleventh century – not ours, of course, for we Muslims have the proper calendar – as part of a greater force of a huge and mighty Afghan army. At first they settled in the Attock and Fatehjang region of the Punjab, but Karam Fatteh Khan was assassinated by his half-brother, who eventually fled with some of the tribe into these hills. This is where he settled and the tribe has flourished since those times. Those who remained in the Punjab have since become weak and are of no real account. But we in the hills have thrived on the harshness such arid landscapes offer. Since then we have lived as warriors and raiders, extracting dues from weaker tribes and quelling all those who have set themselves against us. Now, what is the history of your tribe?'

Jack said, 'My father is a clan chieftain, like yourself. Many years ago the clans fought amongst themselves but were then invaded by the English and so they joined to battle the invaders. Sometimes the Scots won, sometimes the English, and things remained much as they were. Then the English lost their king and wanted ours to rule them, which we agreed to, thinking that a common king would unite us.

207

I am half-English myself, so this arrangement is quite acceptable to me, though there are many on both sides of the border who harbour distrust. The two great tribes of the English and Scots joined together under a new banner. There have been troubles since, but we remain as we are, for the time being, together.'

'So,' said Khan, sipping his coffee, 'now you must return to Peshawar?'

'That way, yes, if we ever get there. We had some little encounter with the Bochura on our way here. They may not let us go back through their passes without a fight.'

'The Bochura!' Khan spat into a corner. 'The Bochura are cockroaches. I will give you some men who will take great pleasure in killing a few of the Bochura. It is time we paid them a visit and taught them a few lessons in who are the rulers of these hills.'

'Thank you, Khan. I will not hesitate to accept.'

Akbar Khan thrust a hand forward, smiling, to grasp Jack's.

'We are friends now, you and I. We would die for each other.'

'Naturally,' replied Jack. 'Of course.'

22

The battle for the passes through Bochura country was a fierce one in terms of ammunition used, though loss of life was minimal. None of Colonel Hawke's four was killed, but two of the Kafirisi died. They fell mostly because of their rashness and impatience. The passes were indeed heavily defended and it took a week and several days to force the way through. How many of the enemy fell, Crossman had no idea. Any Bochura who were hit were dragged away by their comrades, either to recover from their wounds or to die.

The daily battles went through a routine which rarely varied. Usually the day began with an exchange of jibes. They started with insulting families, the names of which seemed to be known to both sides, and ended with challenges to single combat. No one was foolish enough to respond to these challenges of course, except with a further challenge. Then the shooting would begin with everyone ensconced neatly inside a sangar, thus presenting the flimsiest of targets to the enemy. The idea, it seemed to Crossman and his men, was not to actually *hit* your man directly, a virtually impossible task given the protection, but to aim at a particular curve or overhang in the rock and hope to strike him with the ricochet.

'Barkin' squirrels,' said Gwilliams, with satisfaction. 'This is how it's done, sir. Now you get my meaning.'

One morning they woke and their insults were not returned in kind. A spyglass was useless in this kind of country, unless you were looking at hawks, so the subsequent investigation had to be physical. A tentative probing suggested that the pass was now open and clear.

This may have been the prelude to a trick, but thankfully for Crossman it was not. The Bochura had retreated back into their mountainside hideaways again. The Kafirisi escorted their charges up to the border and a little beyond, before retiring back the way they had come. Crossman's mission had been successful so far. It remained to be seen whether Akbar Khan would be a man of his word, but the lieutenant had a gut feeling that Khan would not attack. Although Jack had seen nothing like the number, Hawke had said that Khan could muster ten thousand men within an hour, the Afghans being ever ready for war. He had loaned Jack two hundred of his hillmen and, having fought with them, the lieutenant was heartily relieved they were not going against them.

Once again they plunged into the jungles of the Punjab, frightening the hornbills so that they clattered in the canopy. This time they beat the same path back again. When they had set out from Khan's fortress the month of July had just been entered. Raktambar had celebrated the Hindu festival of Ratha Yatra, the chariot journey, on his own. The monsoon had reached up into the Punjab and the season which in India they called the Wet had arrived with hundreds of inches of rainfall. Rain fell from the heavens like none Jack had seen before: it was as if they were travelling through waterfalls. For the first time in his life Jack knew what a 'deluge' was and it slowed the party down tremendously. It was not that it rained all day – on the contrary, the periods of rain were relatively short – but so much came down in so short a time streams became rivers, rivers floods, and any paths turned to quagmires which swallowed the horses' feet.

With the rain came a different wildlife: amphibians by the million – and leeches. Like all white men the three soldiers detested leeches. They knew the best way to removed them was with a lighted cigar or twig, but everything was so soggy they could not produce fire and they had to pinch them off 'at the arse' leaving behind a head that festered. Raktambar was no more a lover of leeches than were his companions and he too suffered. It was a miserable coming they had of it, with mud to their eyebrows and a jungle that hung limp and fetid around them. The days when they had almost died of thirst – not so very long ago – in a dry arid landscape mocked them in their memories. Here was the Wet, at which even Noah and his sons might have marvelled.

All the while they travelled they had no idea what was happening in the rest of India. When they had left, the garrison at Meerut had mutinied and there had been several other uprisings in other places in Bengal. For all they knew now the British might have been wiped from the face of the subcontinent, or the mutinies quelled and things returned to what was normal for northern India. However, one night they met two mounted *Akalis*, Sikh religious warriors, who had become detached from their irregular Punjabi regiment during a night march. The two men were – as was their wont – carrying an excessive amount of weaponry each, including musket, two swords, several knives and steel-throwing quoits with razor edges which served as bands around their turbans.

'How far have you travelled, sir?' asked one.

When he told them they had journeyed the whole length of northern India and had then gone on to Afghanistan, the Sikhs pursed their lips.

'How unfortunate for you, sir.'

'You do not like to be on the move?'

'The Punjabi for *I am travelling* is *I am suffering.*'

'I suppose the answer to my question then, is no, you do not – whereas we British love to journey through strange lands.'

'Yes, sahib, but this is not a strange land, it is a common one.'

He had no answer to that. Instead, he asked them what was the state of affairs now in the rest of India.

'Sir,' said one, 'there has been many more mutinies. We have had rumours from Cawnpore of a terrible massacre. Also in Lucknow, where our forces are besieged. No one knows what is really happening but the news is not good. There are stories of many deaths and some of escapes, but who can tell what is going on so many miles away?'

He reeled off a staggering list of names, where the uprisings had taken place, and Crossman listened with a lump in his throat. It did indeed sound as if the whole of India had risen with one hand on the sword and the other on the throat of an intruder. However, later, Raktambar went over the names with him and told him they were almost all in Bengal, and that it did not seem as if the other two Company armies, the Madras and Bombay, had yet joined with their brothers in the north of the country.

'Also, sir,' said the second Sikh, 'there has been a British defeat at Chinhut.'

'Chinhut? Where's Chinhut?'

'It is near Lucknow, sir. A very bad defeat.'

Gloomy news indeed. Crossman stirred their first fire for two weeks with a stick and contemplated the future. It all depended on the size of the force that had been crushed of course, if that's what they had been. The soldier seemed certain that it was a terrible blow to the British, but then, when an army had been viewed as invincible for so long, any defeat was looked on with great anxiety by one side and great joy on the other. Such victories were thus blown out of proportion by both sides. At such times few could take a step back and view a battle objectively. This, coupled with rumour and mis-information running amuck over the land, served to produce no really accurate picture of the events. Crossman suspended judgement.

They ate a meal together consisting wholly of vegetables, since Gwilliams had not been able to shoot any game for days. The two Sikhs said they would accompany the lieutenant and his men to meet the Movable Column 'under General Nicholson, sir'. So far as Jack could remember John Nicholson had still been a captain when he had left Ferozepur.

'Are you sure about him being a general?' he asked.

'Yes, sir – brigadier-general.'

'Ah, a brevet rank, no doubt, to meet the occasion.' Still, it was quite a leap, from captain to general. Someone had great faith in John Nicholson.

Later, Sergeant King came to Crossman and whispered in his ear, 'Can we trust these people, sir? They are natives after all. I have nothing against them, as such, but we're fighting for our lives here.'

'I know what you mean, King, but you have to make a distinction between Sikhs and Bengalis. They're traditional enemies. So far it's only been the Bengali sepoys who've mutinied. We'll keep a close watch on them and hope they're not of the same mind as the Bengal army.'

They were back in their saddles as soon as they had rested and as they rode Jack questioned the Sikhs further.

'What's happening in Delhi?' he asked. 'Do you know?'

'Yes,' said the tallest of the two, 'Delhi is in the hands of the rebels, many thousands of them, but there is a ridge to the north-west which has been captured by the British. I do not remember the name of the general sir, but I know of one officer sahib they call

Major Hodson. They are the Delhi Field Force who have captured the ridge and now fire guns into the city and also the Corps of Guides is there, sir, to help them. This is where General Nicholson is going now – to Delhi, to kill the rebels. I do pity them, for General Nicholson is a most ferocious man. It has been my privilege, sir, to see him cleave a man's skull in two with one stroke of the sword.'

This man Nicholson was a demi-god in the eyes of some of the local people. Major Hodson's name was also known to him, but in connection with Colonel Hawke. Hodson had formed a network of informants and was therefore in the same business as Crossman himself. The spying business. Jack and his men would have to hurry now, if they were to catch the Movable Column at Amritsar, where the Sikhs had put Nicholson's camp.

They rode all that night and the next day and when they arrived at Amritsar the young General Nicholson had just left, on his way to Gurdaspur to intercept a rebel force of over a thousand horse and foot – sepoys and sowars who had killed their British officers at Sialkot – on their way to join their comrades in Delhi. Nicholson was hoping to defeat this small but dangerous enemy force and thus strike a psychological blow. Any victories, however minor, were worth their weight in morale.

Crossman reported to Colonel Hawke who seemed quietly satisfied with the success of their mission.

'Well done, Lieutenant. You have opened your Indian journal and the first page has been written. I am very pleased for you and Major Lovelace, your mentor, who is now on his way to India, I might add. Now we must join with our countrymen and do some ordinary soldiering. You have heard that a flying column is on its way to Gurdaspur?'

'Yes sir, I was going to ask if we could catch it up and join it?'

Hawke frowned. 'You surely want to rest up first?'

'Sir, we've been travelling almost non-stop since we left you in Ferozepur and a few more miles will make no difference.' Crossman shrugged. 'It's become a way of life. My backside is now the shape of a saddle. Once one is used to it, it ceases to weary one. I should not know what to do here, waiting. If there's any action to be had I would like to be there, rather than sitting on my . . .' He stopped, suddenly, embarrassed by the inference. After a short silence, during which Hawke looked out of the window, he continued with, 'I'm sorry, sir, I didn't mean – that is . . .'

213

'That's all right, Lieutenant. I'm quite happy to be sitting on my arse, for the moment. You go off and join Nicholson's column. Do you wish to take your sergeant and corporal with you?'

'If they want to go, sir. I'll give them the choice.'

'That's a little too democratic for my taste, Lieutenant – the army was different when I first joined it. So be it. I'll see you when you get back. By the by, here's a bunch of letters for you.' He tossed Jack a bundle tied around with a rough piece of string. 'They arrived two days ago. The mail still gets through, despite the empire teetering on the brink.'

Crossman took them eagerly, noticing the top one bore the handwriting of his brother James, but certain others were from Jane.

'There's two in there for King and one for Gwilliams, also.'

'I'm sure they'll appreciate them.'

'Let's hope they all carry good news. One is so far from home. If anything untoward occurs there is little we can do from here.'

'Yes sir, thank you.'

King's mouth set when he was asked if he wanted to accompany his lieutenant, but Gwilliams volunteered straight away. The sergeant, after letting out a very audible sigh, said he would join them. Raktambar was not asked, but when the fresh mounts and provisions had been obtained, he was there waiting for the other three, as if there was no question of him staying behind. Where Crossman went, Raktambar went. It was as simple as that, though he kept stressing he was not the 'faithful servant' of the officer. He was simply doing his duty as ordered by the maharajah.

There was over forty miles to cover to Gurdaspur. The four horsemen soon realized that they would have to pace themselves, for General Nicholson was pushing his men hard. The 'flying column' that Nicholson had taken with him was composed mostly of the Queen's army 52nd Light Infantry, mounted Pathans and Punjabis and – Crossman had been told – around a dozen guns of the horse artillery troop. On the ride, however, the four kept coming across fatigued and sick men of the 52nd who had dropped out of the march and were either on their way back to the main camp at Amritsar or waiting to be picked up when the column hopefully returned.

'How far ahead?' Crossman called to one group of three, resting in the shade of a tamarind tree.

'Not far,' came the reply. 'Two miles at a guess. They'll be a halt at Patiala.'

The four had so far ridden quite a distance before they caught up with the flying column. The infantry was a bedraggled looking sight, but Jack could read determination in the mouths of the marchers. Here for the first time he caught sight of John Nicholson, a very imposing figure, tall and straight in the saddle, grim-faced, broad-shouldered, with a black beard and a seemingly isolated air about him. It was if this stern Irishman rode alone, the men around him mere wraiths that followed his aura. He rarely seemed to acknowledge anyone except a huge Pathan who rode to his right and was no doubt the famous bodyguard Jack had been told about by Raktambar. There was the suggestion of enormous strength in Nicholson's frame and not only physical. There was a spirit lodged in there which was indeed carved from the same granite as his physical stature. He appeared to be just a few years older than Crossman himself.

Crossman rode up and reported to the brigadier-general, who inclined his head slightly as the lieutenant spoke.

'Lieutenant Crossman, sir. 88th Connaught Rangers. On special duties in India. Beg permission to join the column.'

Grey eyes flicked over Jack's Pathan clothes, but no mention was made of the fact that he was not in uniform.

'Granted, Lieutenant.' There was a pause during which Jack knew something else was coming. Then, 'Welcome.'

'Thank you, sir.'

Jack reined his mount and fell in with his men to the left of the marchers. He saw one man drop to the dust, going down like a toppled log. Then a little later, another keeled over sideways, held up by the man next to him until he could be shuffled out of the column. These casualties of sun and sickness were carried and laid in one of the carts drawn by ponies, of which there were many. It seemed that General Nicholson had bought a number of these before setting out, to carry men and provisions.

The column moved on, the men quite obviously very thirsty, for they were licking slaked lips and their eyes revealed their distress.

Jack counted nine guns, not twelve as he had been led to suppose. The 52nd themselves looked a very depleted force of men. The Pathan and Punjabi cavalry seemed in better condition.

An artillery officer was summoned to speak with Nicholson and afterwards rode over to Crossman. He nodded at Ishwar Raktambar.

'Your man,' he said. 'Where's he from?'

'He's not Indian army, if that's what you mean,' replied Crossman. 'He's an ex-palace guard, from Jaipur.'

Raktambar kept his eyes to the front, not revealing his feelings of being spoken about as if he were not there to hear it.

The officer said, 'The general's not keen on Hindus at the moment.'

'Understandably,' replied Crossman, 'but this man is completely trustworthy. I will vouch for him.'

'Not good enough. Colonels have vouched for men who've turned on them and shot them from their saddles. A few hours ago we disarmed half the 9th Bengal Light Cavalry, who were also protesting that they too were completely trustworthy. The other half of their regiment is up ahead waiting for us and ready to cut us down. Fact is, old chap, you can't trust any of 'em at the moment.'

'You're speaking of sepoys and sowars of the Bengal army. This man is my personal friend, not a Company soldier.'

Raktambar now intervened. He drew his sword and took his carbine from its saddle holster. These, along with a pistol and a dagger, he handed to Gwilliams. 'Now you have disarmed me, sahib,' said Ishwar to the artillery officer, 'just like the 9th Bengals. Is that satisfactory?'

The officer's face took on a sour look. 'Is he being insolent?'

Crossman said, 'It didn't sound like it to me. It sounded like he was complying with your request.'

The officer gave Raktambar one more suspicious look then rode back to report to his general. Jack wondered whether Nicholson would still demand they rid themselves of the Hindu, but there were no other approaches.

Gwilliams, so bundled up with arms he couldn't hold his reins, said, 'What do I do with this lot?'

'Wrap them in a blanket and strap them to your horse,' replied Jack, then to Raktambar, 'We'll return them to you later.'

Raktambar nodded, obviously satisfied his dignity was intact.

The march continued with no further incidents befalling the four additions to the column.

When they finally reached Gurdaspur, Crossman could see that there were only around just over 200 infantry still on their feet. Heat stroke and sheer fatigue had taken a heavy toll. A velvet black evening was coming in and the exhausted troops rested for the night. There was milk and rum, and bread rations, which were handed out.

216

Jack and his men had brought some dried meat with them, some of which they gave away. Now that the march was over the soldiers seemed a little more cheerful as they spoke in whispers around their fires. Why they kept their voices low was one of those common mysteries, but this often happened on the eve of a battle. Nicholson strode among them, giving them heart. He rarely spoke, but his presence was enough to strengthen the spirit of fighting men.

The artillery officer came to Jack and said, 'Sorry about that, back on the march, old chap. Orders, you know.' It was an apology of a kind and Jack graciously accepted it.

'Of course. My man understood.'

'Fine. See you in the melee tomorrow?'

'I'll be there,' replied Jack. 'Not much else on. I've already cancelled my game of tennis.'

The officer smiled. This was the kind of banter which army men approved of, before going out to die. It was very British.

A little later, King said, 'Sir, how many enemy are we facing?'

'I was told a little over a thousand.'

'But we're down to a quarter of that number.'

'And? You would like me to ask the general to call it off?'

King shivered, uncomfortably. 'No – no, I was just remarking, that's all. I'm not worried. We've been outnumbered before.'

'Many times,' said Gwilliams, 'and it ain't gonna be the last.'

Raktambar said, 'I will not be able to fight.'

'Do you want to?' asked Jack. 'They are sepoys.'

'I feel naked without my weapons.'

'Gwilliams will give them back to you, just before the battle – only, Corporal, do it discreetly. I don't want the general down on my head afterwards.'

'Right.'

They slept fitfully, as men always do before a battle, if they sleep at all.

In the sharp morning light, Nicholson took his flying column a dozen miles to the edge of the Ravi River at a ford known as Trimmu Ghat. There they discovered the mutineers lined up ready to fight. The enemy infantry were in order of battle with the other half of the 9th Bengal Light Cavalry on their left flank. If they had left as a mob when they had mutinied, they were back to being disciplined soldiers again. One has to admire them, thought Crossman, for this was no rabble but an organized group of rebels. They made a proud and colourful sight, some of them still in their Company uniforms.

'Spooky,' muttered Gwilliams. 'Like fighting our own.'

'You were right about us being outnumbered,' Jack murmured to King at his side. 'There they are.'

'But we have the Enfield,' King replied. 'They don't.'

It was true the superior rifle was in the hands of Nicholson's troops, the Indians scorning the weapon which needed greased cartridges. The enemy was still armed with the old Brown Bess. Jack recalled how the Russians had been slaughtered by the British Minié musket-rifles, back in the Crimea, the Russian smooth bore muskets similar to the Brown Bess. The new rifled barrels sent a conical ball out with such devastating force it was accurate up to a thousand yards or more and would pass through four men if they were packed in a column one behind the other. Such fire power gave heart to men who were lined up in inferior numbers.

It was the enemy who fired first and then, bravely, thought Jack, charged the British guns with their bayonets. At the same time their cavalry spurred themselves forwards, into the hastily made squares which the 52nd formed to repel such attacks. Harsh volleys thundered from the Enfields, then rattled along the lines after the reloading. Guns fired swarms of grapeshot into the oncoming charge. The British delivered a stern lesson to the sepoys, whittling down their ranks as they came on. Once again the air was full of whining, whistling metal, seeking targets. Crossman saw a sepoy fling up his arms as he was struck somewhere on his body, his thrown musket coming down bayonet first into the back of one of his comrades.

The battle was quite a short affair. Crossman had only time to discharge one set of chambers on his revolver, while King and Gwilliams used their carbines. The Enfields and the field guns took a swift and merciless toll of the charging enemy troops before bayonets were crossed. In a quarter of an hour the mutineers' ranks had been broken and they were in full retreat, running back towards the river. King whooped loudly and rode off to join Nicholson and his Pathan and Punjabi cavalry, chasing the rebels. King's sword was out and he was waving it above his head in the wildest fashion, riding in the wake of the young general.

Out on one of the flanks, there was a private duel going on. Nicholson had a motley band of tribesmen on wiry horses who followed him wherever he went: a large gathering of volunteer bodyguards. It seemed that two of these dedicated horsemen had challenged a duo of sowars from the mutineers to single combat. These four men rode at each other, two against two, the sowars with their swords straight out in front of them pointing like lances, the Pathans swishing the air with tulwars, ready to slice. At the last minute before any of them struck, the Pathans appeared to vanish, the sowars' swords passing over empty saddles. Then the Pathans suddenly reappeared from under the bellies of their mounts and swept around, beheading the passing Bengali cavalrymen each with a single stroke.

Crossman, Raktambar and Gwilliams had witnessed this startling duel and its astonishing outcome.

'I seen Injuns do that,' muttered Gwilliams. Then looking at Raktambar, added, 'Other Injuns, o' course, with bows.'

Down by the river the mopping-up was in progress. The remnants of the mutineers' army had retreated to a thicket-covered island, where they were trapped, the river flowing too fast on the other side. Those who tried to cross it were swept away and drowned. Those who remained hidden on the island had nothing left to give. Crossman saw that General Nicholson was not inclined at this time attack them. Instead, he posted troops along the bank, ready to shoot any who tried to escape from their hiding places. No British had been killed in the battle, just a half-dozen wounded.

A jubilant Sergeant King returned in a state of high elation.

'That was a *glorious* charge,' he said. 'I never knew battle could be so exciting.'

'How many did you kill?' asked Raktambar.

The sergeant was crestfallen for a minute.

'Well, I don't think it matters. What it was, was the ride. The gallop. By the time I reached the river they had all crossed to the island. I hadn't any chance of using my blade. If it had been needed . . .'

The lieutenant said, 'You charged, that was the main thing. It's quite an experience, so I've been told.'

King said, surprised, 'You've never charged?'

'On foot, yes, but not on horseback of course. I'm from a foot regiment, not cavalry. I believe an infantry charge is far less intoxicating. I remember feeling nothing except fear, my legs shaking so much I wondered how they managed to keep me upright. It's really not so much a charge as a stumbling run, trying not to trip over. You're aware of men being blown away on either side of you, the gaps appearing in the line, having more time to observe what's going on around you. But I imagine that on the back of horse, waving a sabre, it would be a different experience.'

'Oh, yes it is,' said King. 'Very different.'

Crossman decided that since he was exhausted now, so were the others, and ordered his little group back to Amritsar, where Nicholson's Movable Column was waiting to march on Delhi. General Nicholson and his troops remained in the battle area and the word was that few of those mutineers on the island would escape the general's wrath. General John Nicholson, it seemed, was not much interested in taking prisoners. He had decreed that 'the penalty for mutiny is death' and that's what he intended to mete out to any rebels who came within reach of his fury.

Back in Amritsar, Crossman bathed and let Gwilliams attack his face. Once he was clean and shaved, he put on his uniform and went off to find Calcutta Hawke. The colonel was in conference at that time, so Crossman waited outside his quarters until he was free. He was called in just an hour afterwards.

'Sorry to keep you waiting, Lieutenant,' said Hawke, gesturing to a bamboo chair. 'A rider from Delhi arrived just before you.'

'That's all right, sir. Good news?'

'Not especially. There's news from further abroad – General Havelock's force is advancing from Allahabad hoping to relieve Cawnpore. Apparently they're having a pretty savage time of it down there. The ridge is holding at Delhi, but making no great strides. More and more mutinies in more and more places. Not all of them significant, but the pot is boiling merrily now.'

'Who's to blame for all this, sir?'

'Blame?' Hawke watched a moth batting its wings against the glass of his hot lamp. 'Do we have to apportion blame? I suppose we do. The blame must lie with those who're responsible for the running of things here – the senior officers of the East India Company. If they had been a little more circumspect we might not have this mess, for mess it definitely is. A little less arrogance wouldn't have gone amiss, I tend to feel. The Company is a large body, larger than the governments of many countries, and such bodies often lack foresight and sensitivity.' He sighed. 'Well, we're in it now and we have to extricate ourselves with the minimum of destruction. Has General Nicholson returned yet?'

'No sir, he remained with his troops to mop up.'

'The tone of your voice suggests you do not approve of the methods being used, Lieutenant.'

Crossman hadn't realized he was injecting any feeling into his words at all, but he replied, 'It's not for me to approve or disapprove.'

'You think, though, that the general is too ruthless.'

'I believe he thinks he's right in his actions, but perhaps a little mercy might go a long way. This country's vast but word travels quickly. What we do today sets the rules for tomorrow's engagements.'

'Well, when all's said and done, this isn't our show, Jack. It belongs to John Company, though how long they will remain the power here, after this, is anyone's guess. I believe Her Majesty's government will think twice before leaving them with their auton-omy once it's all over. If things continue the way they have been doing, there won't be a British India to fight over. We'll all be shipped somewhere else to begin again.'

'What now, sir?' asked Crossman. 'Any special duties?'

'I think we'll stick with the column for the time being. Once the general has finished his mopping up, we'll be on our way to Delhi. At least this victory has offset the thrashing at Chinhut. As you say, word will spread, and this will be a great boost to our troops, small as it is.'

Jack went to the billets to make sure that King and Gwilliams were comfortable and found them both fast asleep on their cots. Ishwar Raktambar was waiting for him near the compound. Jack told the Rajput to find himself a bed and then went looking for one himself. He found an empty bungalow which had obviously be-longed to a European family. There was a portrait on the living-room wall of an elderly-looking man in civilian clothes sitting in a high-backed chair. A woman – no doubt his wife – stood behind him with her hands on his shoulders. At his feet were two pretty-looking maidens, daughters, in puff-sleeved frocks and ribbons.

The door to the bungalow had been broken off and lay out in the yard. Someone had forced an entrance, but whether the family had remained in residence Jack had no idea. Nothing else seemed dis-turbed: ornaments were still on sideboards and clothes in wardrobes. There was a letter lying on a coffee table in a language other than

English. It appeared to be Swedish or perhaps Norwegian: somewhere in those regions. Jack was not familiar with Scandinavian tongues. Some businessman or other who had come to India to make his fortune under the umbrella of the Company.

Jack fell, fully clothed, on one of the beds and opened the first of his letters, one from Jane, but he had only got as far as *My Dearest Husband* before he was fast asleep.

In a few days they were on the march again, heading towards Amballa. Crossman and his men were asked to ride on ahead, to act as scouts in fact, though there were already plenty out there. They came across many Sikhs, who stood by the roadside asking when 'Sahib Nicholson' was going to pass by. Jack felt that all that was needed were palms to lay on the road. It was here, on this very road, that Crossman once again had the eerie feeling of being watched and followed. He thought he glimpsed a familiar face amongst a crowd of villagers, but on riding over the man quickly disappeared into the rainforest behind the huts. Why would someone run from him? It was a most uncomfortable feeling, a mystical experience he could do without. There was enough going on without being spooked by a stalking man.

As they were ahead of the column, they encountered many disturbing sights. On riding through a village one day they were accosted by an elderly Indian woman who gripped King's trousers with claw-like fingers and led him on his horse to the doorway of a hut. When he entered, King found a British woman and her child cringing in the corner, half-hidden in the dimness of the interior. She was in a filthy dishevelled state and even when he identified himself as an Englishman, she remained cowed and whimpering. Her child, sucking its thumb, stared wide-eyed at King when he offered her some water.

Going outside he asked the old woman, 'Is that your memsahib in there?'

She shook her head and on being questioned by Crossman they found she was the owner of the hovel. The white woman had come wandering into the camp one night with a baby and a child. The baby turned out to be dead and the old woman had buried it behind the house. She had then given the white lady some peppery soup and water, and left her to sleep. The visitor and her child had not spoken since entering the village.

The lieutenant thanked the local woman for her kindness and followed King into the hovel to speak with the one she had rescued. With coaxing the white woman told them her name was Susan Fletcher and that her husband had been a clerk for the Company. Their house had been attacked and burned, but the mob had only driven them away, without harming them. Her husband had secured a horse and had told her he was riding for help. When he did not return she followed in the same direction and found him bleeding to death, torn to pieces it seemed by thorn bushes through which his horse had dragged him. He was still attached to the grazing mare, his ankle caught in a stirrup, his life draining away from him.

'Where's my baby?' she asked. 'Is it outside?'

'I'm afraid your youngest child is dead,' King replied, stroking her head as he would an anxious horse about to be shoed by his father. 'I'm sorry.'

She turned to the wall. 'We had no water.'

Crossman said, 'Your daughter is well enough, though.'

The two men comforted her as well as they could.

Gwilliams took the woman and child back to the column and then rejoined the other three later that night.

They also saw and heard, of British revenge, with makeshift gallows decorating the landscape and stories of rebels being shot from cannons. It was, as Hawke had said, a great mess. A mess which grew bloodier and less savoury by the day. Yet even here, in such circumstances, there were stories of great courage and tales of great kindnesses, from both sides of the conflict. There were also, incredible as it seemed to those who experienced it, some lighter moments.

Several days after the discovery of the woman and her child Crossman and his men were four abreast, walking their horses down a long and dusty road which seemed to stretch for ever. Suddenly, out of the haze ahead, a swaying elephant with a howdah appeared, shimmering in the heat haze. The closer they came to the rolling beast, the more they were impressed, it being highly decorated with designs painted on its hide. The howdah itself was richly ornate, a four-poster, the spiral supports covered in gold-leaf, the roof stretched over with a satin cloth that had been bleached somewhat by exposure to the weather. Curtains hung from the rim of the roof and shielded whoever was inside from direct sunlight.

223

The mahout was naked to the waist but wore an enormous red turban on his head and yellow silk pantaloons with fringes at the ankles. Hooped brass earrings the size of soup plates hung from his lobes and sparkled in the light.

The mahout forced the horses to the edge of the road, two on either side: he and his elephant walked imperiously between.

'Hold hard,' cried Gwilliams, annoyed at being treated in such a peremptory fashion. 'Who's the captain of this rig?'

The mahout seemed not to hear until he was aware of the barrel of Gwilliam's carbine pointing at his chest. He halted his elephant but remained staring ahead of him.

From inside the howdah came a high-pitched shriek in Hindi. 'Go on! Go on!'

'You stay where you are,' growled Gwilliams, who now knew enough Hindi to understand the order. 'Who's in there?'

'It is a powerful nawab, sahib. Please do not make him angry.'

'A nawab? Of where?'

The mahout looked very unhappy and confused. 'I do not know, sahib. He did not tell me. He gave me money for the hire of my elephant and for the use of the clothings which my uncle keeps for festivals and weddings.'

King took his mount alongside the elephant and then stood on the saddle to reach up and pull back the curtains. By now Crossman had come round to their side of the elephant and witnessed the unveiling. Sitting on a stool in the howdah was a fat man dressed indeed like royalty. He stared out from a brown face with wide pale eyes ringed with black paint. His lips were rouged, which made his teeth seem very white. Then, on seeing that they were British soldiers who had stopped his elephant, he threw up two chubby hands covered in jewelled rings. His jowls quivered, revealing it seemed, his immense relief at discovering they were not bandits or rebels.

'Oh, I am saved. Thank the Lord for His deliverance. Lieutenant, thou art my saviour. God has been kind to his loyal servant . . .'

Crossman peered at the man. 'Reverend Stillwell? Is that you under all that cocoa powder and rouge?'

'It is indeed, Lieutenant. I have been through great trials, but I have overcome. I *am* overcome, now being under thy protection.'

'I'm afraid, Mr Stillwell, you will need to go further before you find the protection you require. We are merely the advance scouts for a column led by General Nicholson. If I were you I would divest myself of the fine garb, wash my face, and prepare to meet the column with dignity. There will be life after the mutiny and you might not wish to be the butt of subsequent humiliating stories.'

'A wash, yes.' The reverend licked his finger and ran it down his cheek, leaving a white mark. 'Yes, of course.'

'And get shot of those garments.'

'You're right, Lieutenant.'

They left the reverend clambering down from a kneeling elephant, anxious to find a well in which to wash. King, Gwilliams and Raktambar were roaring with laughter as they trotted their horses down the road. It was not something they could control. Crossman tried not to smile but he couldn't hold back either, though he knew that Stillwell was in earshot. The image of the reverend would stay with them for some time, they knew, a little ray of humour in the murky atmospheres of an India in turmoil.

Jack's letters had been a blessing. He had now read all of them several times over, mostly by poor lamplight at night. Britain was a whole world away from insect-plagued India. His brother James had written that the estates in Scotland were beginning to repay their debts. Management of them had been poor during their father's time, he being more interested in hunting (and other manly pastimes) than talking with tenant farmers. Caleb McNiece, their father's servant, had toned down his aggression towards James, but still lurked like a dark phantom around their senile father. Their mother was well and in good spirits, though she was concerned by news from India.

Jane's letters had very little substantial news in them whatsoever. They were mostly full of descriptions of the countryside as spring had come upon them. Jane was a painter with words, rather than informative, and her prose was almost poetry. They were light and airy and he could hear her laughing as she penned some incident or other. There was one describing a walk she had taken along a country road, when she had come across what she thought was a cat attacking a shrew. Having a stick she shooed the cat away, whereupon the shrew began attacking her foot. It now occurred to her that the tiny hedgerow mammal had been bothering the cat and not the other way around. *Shrews are known as aggressive creatures,* she had written, *and I should have guessed by the indignant attitude of the cat.*

She had ended the letter pleading to be allowed to come to India, *whatever the state of affairs there, to be at least in the same country as my husband, even if we meet only occasionally.*

Jack sighed. It was impossible at the moment of course. And even if this unpalatable war were to end tomorrow, there would still be simmering pockets of resistance. Not that any of that would worry Jane, who had been with him in the Crimea as a guest of her friend Lavinia Durham, a captain's lady with a romantic history linked to Jack's, making it an uncomfortable trio for him. Jane had seen war close hand and though she did not relish it – unlike friend Lavinia who saw in war only the greater glory and élan of dashing men – it did not deter her from her purpose. Jane believed her place was beside her husband, wherever he was, for had they not promised one another to be in that place, until death do them part?

The dust rose from the road as their horses walked on.

'King,' asked Crossman, 'you had one or two letters I noticed.'

'Yes sir,' replied the sergeant. 'From my father. All's well, I'm glad to say. Business is brisk. He made a set of gates for the new manor house which has given – which will give him – a considerable income. The squire hasn't paid him yet, of course,' a glowering look, 'but my father usually gets his money in the end. The squire will need more wrought ironwork soon and my father's the best in the county at his trade. Bills are paid one behind. Father gets the money for the last job when a new one comes along. It's how things work amongst the rich, isn't it?'

There was no hint that Crossman fell into this category in the sergeant's rancour. He was simply telling it how it was. And Jack knew the man was right: the wealthy did not pay their bills until they were absolutely forced to.

'Have you no brothers or sisters?'

'A younger sister, a very sweet girl, married to a tavern landlord who works her to a frazzle.'

'But she is well cared for?'

'Oh yes, she wants for nothing, really. I suppose, being my sister, no one was good enough for her. Her husband's a lot older than she is, but then she chose him, I didn't. I must admit she seems happy enough. Whenever I visit she seems pleased to see me, but isn't demonstrative.'

'Does she not write to you?'

'Unlike me, she's had no schooling, though she can do figures well enough, in her head.'

'And your mother?'

'Ran off with an Irish tinker.' He paused, then, 'Or she might be dead.'

Crossman was naturally surprised. 'You don't know?'

'Gone before I was old enough to understand. My father is a close man. He rarely speaks of her.'

Jack made no further enquiries, feeling he had overstepped the boundaries as it was. To delve into another man's family history was not dignified. Things had simply trundled on a little too far.

'Gwilliams! You had a letter too! From your President, no doubt?'

'President Franklin Pierce kept out a Whig, but that's the best you could say of *him*.' He frowned here, before adding, 'That's if he's still in office. Mr Buchanan, now, he's different. I give him a shave once, and one of them body rubs I give you from time to time. He was very appreciative, Mr Buchanan. Gave me ten dollars and told me to keep the change.'

'Not a Whig I take it?'

'Nope, nor a damned Republican neither. Good ole Democrat.'

'I hesitate to ask then, who your letter was from, it being your private business.'

'Yep, it is, but I don't mind tellin' who. It's from a cousin o' mine, Jake, down in the state of Kentucky. Seems if I see a Clegg I gotta shoot him, cause the Gwilliamses is having trouble with the Cleggses down that way.'

'Any Clegg?' cried King. 'It's not an uncommon name in England.'

Gwilliams stroked his chin. 'Well I guess an English Clegg might be different. I'd have to think on it first. I ain't come across that problem before. There's a feud on, see, and family is family. Do you know any Cleggs?'

King and Crossman looked at each other and raised their eyebrows.

'No, I don't,' replied Crossman, 'and I wouldn't tell you if I did, Corporal. I'm not going to be responsible for you murdering some innocent soldier simply because he's had the misfortune to be born with the wrong surname. Sometimes I wonder about the American culture.'

'Tain't the American culture, so much as round about Kentucky and Tennessee.'

'And that was the extent of your letter?' said Crossman. 'No news from home fields?'

Gwilliams shook his head. 'Nope. Just that. Jake did ask after my health, which was damn good of him. *How's your health?*' he said. *And by the by, if you see any Cleggs, be sure to shoot 'em.*'

'A man of words,' muttered King.

'No sense in rattlin' on about nothin' in particular,' replied Gwilliams, not at all put out. 'Ain't nothin' important going on, I guess.'

When a red-clouded evening came around and trees became silhouettes on the skyline, they rode back to the main column to report. Crossman was summoned to Hawke's tent after he had eaten. The colonel had a new man guarding his entrance, but when he heard Crossman's voice he said, 'I'll come out there, Lieutenant, it's getting stuffy in here.'

Hawke indeed came out a minute later, a smouldering cigar in his right fist.

'Would you like one?' he said, taking out a cigar case.

'Thank you, yes.'

The first pull on the cigar made Jack's head swim and he had to steady himself on the branch of a tree. Hawke smiled. 'You haven't smoked for some time I take it?'

'I enjoy my chibouque, when I can get good tobacco. I thought the tobacco was rough in the Crimea, but it had nothing on the sawdust that parades itself as tobacco in India. This is a good cigar, sir.'

'By way of Singapore. Not sure where it came from originally. Now, Lieutenant, I've got some Hindus under guard. They wandered into camp earlier today. Their leader, an elderly man, says they're Sergeant King's chain-men, or somesuch.'

'Is his name Ibhanan?'

'Yes, that was it. They're lucky I was around. You know how suspicious and jumpy everyone is at the moment.'

Jack's heart skipped a beat, as he thought momentarily of a horrible scenario: Ibhanan and the other perambulator-wallahs dangling on gallows.

'Thank you, sir. Where can I find them?'

'At the south end of the camp. Here.' He handed Jack a card with something scribbled on the back. 'Give this to the guard commander and he'll release them to your charge. You're sure they're loyal?'

'Even if they weren't,' Jack replied, 'they're harmless. They wouldn't know one end of a musket to the other. They're just coolies and lascars. I'll take Sergeant King with me. They'll be more pleased to see him than me. He's their man, really.'

Crossman collected King and they went together to the compound where Ibhanan and the others were being held. There was an ensign in charge, who seemed flustered. When shown the colonel's card he said, 'I'm not sure General Nicholson – I mean, I've been told to keep all prisoners under tight guard.'

'The colonel will answer to the general,' said Jack. 'And as you can see, I'm a responsible officer too.'

'All right then, but I hope I don't get into any trouble.'

Ibhanan was delighted to see the two British soldiers. His face was covered in creases as he smiled.

'Oh, Sergeant sahib,' he said to King, 'so happy to see you alive. I hear many stories, terrible stories.'

'I'm equally happy to see you are all safe too,' replied King, while Jack stood in the background, not at all put out to be second best. 'Are you all here? No one missing?'

Ibhanan hung his head. 'I am sorry to report, sahib, that one of the men run away to go with the badmashes.'

'Badmashes?'

'Yes, sahib. Dacoos who would join with the sepoys.'

'I'm sorry to hear that, Ibhanan, but it's not your fault if a man runs away.'

At this moment, Jack's eyes were sweeping the group of Hindus who were clustering around King. He then said, sharply, 'Where's Sajan? Where's the boy?'

'Unfortunately, sahib,' replied Ibhanan with sorrow in his voice, 'the boy went with him – with the dacoos.'

King cried, 'He did? Was he taken?'

'No, sahib, he went of his own choosing. He steal the sun compass, sir, I think because it is the most shiny of the instruments.' Ibhanan raised his hands in a gesture which asked them to think leniently. 'A boy, just a boy. An orphan. He knows no better.'

'The sun compass,' said King, hopefully. 'Perhaps he thinks he can find Nepal? I spoke often of Nepal to him. Is that what he's done? Gone to Nepal?' Jack realized King was grasping at very thin straws.

Ibhanan said, 'No sahib, I think he takes it to polish, so the good genie leaves an anna under his pillow very night.'

'Oh, how disappointing for the child,' King said, genuinely distressed by this news. 'I shouldn't have told him such fairy tales.'

'The boy Sajan say he want to fight the British, to make them go from our country. I told him that the sergeant and his officer are very good to him and save him from being punkah-wallah all his life, but he talk to many Hindu people in the village through which we pass. They tell him the British are bad people and he listen to them.' Ibhanan could see the distress in King's eyes and it upset him. 'I am sorry, sahib. I try to stop the boy, but he escape in the night. I think he go to Delhi with the badmashes. What can I do?'

'Nothing,' replied Jack, intercepting a sharp reply from the sergeant. 'You did what you could, Ibhanan.'

Seeing the Indians begin to cluster around King, Crossman left them to supervise the putting up of his tent by coolies. Once it was done he sat outside and relit the cigar given him by Hawke. It was an awkward business with one hand, but eventually the thing was glowing. It tasted better with every draw and he tried to enjoy it but he was feeling more upset than he was likely to admit to anyone about Sajan's defection.

How old was the boy? Eight? Nine? Old enough anyway to know right from wrong. Could he blame the child though? Crossman's mother had always told him to put himself into the other man's shoes. Now, if he was a young boy and the French were tramping all over Scotland and England, taking what they wanted, would he throw in his lot with the invaders? He knew he wouldn't. Yet, he *had* taken a risk in accepting the boy into his care and yes, he did expect a little gratitude for that gesture. It was all very unsavoury. He was a soldier, going where he was told to go, doing what he was told to do. Was that good enough? Were there times when a soldier should go against authority? He had never heard of such a thing and was inclined to think that chaos would be result.

He sighed and tried to get his mind on other things. Around him was activity. The Punjabi and Pathan irregulars tended to gather in natural groups of eight or ten men around fires not lit for warmth but to act as a focus. Horses, camels, bullocks and other livestock were either tethered near to their owners or in makeshift corrals within the camp, usually under guard, for there were still thieves out there in the night. The mixture of smells, both exotic and foul, thickened the atmosphere. Perfumed oils were in there somewhere, but also horse and camel dung. In a place where weapons were carried there was always the clatter of metal striking metal, metal hitting wood, wood knocking against wood. With over four thousand men, their mounts, and their baggage train, however light, there was bound to be a constant noise going on. It became like waves falling on the beach, something there in the background, but hardly worth the brain's attention

More interesting was the talk from his neighbours, tents having thin walls and withholding no secrets. It seemed that now that they were getting closer to Delhi, fugitives were dribbling in. A magistrate from one of the outlying districts had wandered into camp a few hours previously in a daze, completely naked, covered in dozens of tiny incisions. When asked how he came by his wounds, he said he could not remember. A young man and his sister came in both disguised as local female labourers. The pair had arrived in India just seven weeks ago from Gloucester and were as cool as if they had been in a pageant back in their home village. The woman and her little girl were mentioned. And, inevitably, the story of the minister.

'. . . came in on a bleedin' elephant, he did, like some bloody maharajah. You could see where he'd put the colourin' on his skin, it bein' streaked and running down his face. What a sight! A vicar he is, or somesuch. Said the Lord had delivered him into the hands of his people. Like some bugger out of the Bible reachin' the promised land.'

'You watch your blasphemin' tongue, Oakes, mentionin' religion and buggery in one breath.'

'Well, so does the Bible, with Sodom and Gamborrow an' all that,' came the protest. 'I'm just tryin' to paint the picture.'

There were more tales of fugitives, stories of the punishments meted out to captured rebels, prophecies of what was to come.

'It'll be all over by Christmas, you mark my words.'

'I should bloody well hope so – it's only bleedin' August.'

Suddenly Jack was aware of Sergeant King approaching him and he stubbed out the remains of the cigar on the rock which made his seat, scratched his stump to relieve the constant itch, and greeted his visitor.

'King? Any problems?'

'No sir — just came to talk about the boy.'

'Ah yes, the boy. Unsettling business.'

'Sir,' said King, firmly, 'there's talk of Brigadier Chamberlain blowing mutineers from guns. If Sajan should fall back into our hands, we must protect him from such barbaric punishment.'

'Must we?'

'Sir, you *know* we must. He's a child, easily impressed. I impressed him with my instruments and talk of mapmaking. The mutineers, or their followers, have done the same with their talk of liberty and wealth for all who support their cause. As I understand it, until now he's been a prisoner of a rajah, having seen nothing of the outside world. Now we took him from that prison, rightly in my opinion, but we exposed him to all sorts of influences which he couldn't possibly cope with, not all at once.'

'So he's still our responsibility? Even though he's betrayed us?'

'I think so,' said the sergeant, firmly. 'I hope you feel the same way, sir.'

'It might not matter what I think,' replied Crossman. 'If the Company army gets its hands on him before we do, we may have to witness his execution.'

King went pale. 'I could never do that.'

'You could if you were ordered to.'

'I'm one of Her Majesty's soldiers, not a damn copycat civilian in uniform,' shouted King. 'This Company army is just a collection of clerks playing soldier. I don't have to follow their orders.'

The murmured conversation from the neighbouring tent ceased abruptly.

Crossman said, mildly, 'Don't shout at me, Sergeant. Who the hell do you think you are? Find yourself a suitable stone and sit down . . . and you, sir, go back into your tent and mind your business.'

This last was directed at a man in braces, trousers and vest, who had emerged from the tent next door. When he heard the authority in the voice and subsequently saw by the lamplight that he was being addressed by an officer, he muttered something and reluctantly did as he was told. Low threatening voices then came from that tent, but no one else felt like taking on the toff and his man further down the line.

'Now just calm down,' said Crossman as King sat moodily down on the ground. 'We must try to get to Sajan first, though I have to

232

say I'm extremely angry with the boy. It won't be easy. If we have to storm Delhi it will be a bloody and confusing business. I know about these things. I've been involved in urban fighting before, in the Crimea, and it's nothing like a battle on open landscape. There's casualties from friendly fire as well as from enemy fire. No one's quite sure who's who, especially in darkness. The best we can do is hope to sort through any prisoners before some revengeful major or colonel gets his hands on them.'

Crossman sighed. 'You've got to remember, King, that many of these soldiers have family here, some of whom have been cut down in their homes. You can't expect things to remain on a cool and rational footing. Atrocities will occur, on both sides. There're some who'll take little notice of the fact that he's just a child, especially if they've lost children themselves in this unholy conflict.'

King screwed his forage cap with his hands. 'I just don't want him to die needlessly.'

'Nor do I. We'll do what we can. Now, where're your instruments? What had Ibhanan to say for himself?'

'Ibhanan stored them with a merchant at Ferozepur. He says he thinks the man is honest, but of course we can't be sure. Those instruments are worth a lot of money. If we lose India, of course we can't expect to see them again, but the merchant has many holdings in Ferozepur and he won't simply disappear or he'll lose his business. I think Ibhanan did the right thing.'

'It sounds reasonable. Tell Ibhanan I'm very grateful. And King?'

'Yes sir.'

'Don't ever raise your voice at me again.'

The sergeant looked down at the ground, still twisting and turning his cap in his hands.

'I'm sorry, sir. I was overwrought.'

'Don't get overwrought. Don't even get wrought. You're a sergeant in Her Majesty's army. Conduct yourself with dignity.'

'Yes sir.'

King got up and bade the lieutenant goodnight. But as he walked away he had to pass the neighbouring tent. A remark came from within. King gave answer. A tall dark-haired man flew from the tent and began raining punches on Crossman's sergeant. Far from conducting himself with dignity, King returned the blows with fiery temperament. The two men went at it like prize fighters, trying to

233

punch holes in each other. King was very stocky, a square man with fists like hammers. Without question the other soldier had been drinking: the smell of arrack was in the air. Alcohol and hard physical exercise do not go together. Arrack may help to numb the blows from an adversary, but it slows action, and destroys balance and judgement. King gradually began to take the other man apart, parrying strikes, delivering body-shattering blows.

Crossman was at a loss to know what to do. As a responsible officer he knew he ought to intervene, but since he knew that it would be beneficial all round for King to let off steam, he was inclined to hang back in the shadows of his tent. He finally did the latter, while King proceeded to paste his taller opponent, getting under the man's longer reach and thumping him in the ribs and gut until the soldier fell on the ground, groaning.

Other men had come out of the tent to watch. One of them began to go forward, but seeing King's stance, decided that valour was not worth the effort. He and his friends helped the broken soldier to his feet. Yet, being upright again, the man suddenly got a second wind and decided he was not yet beaten. His rage fuelled another foolish attempt at victory. He shrugged off his fellows and flew at King once again in fury. King landed a solid punch to his jaw, as he came on, and the soldier went down like a felled tree, to crash amongst some kettles and pans on the ground.

At that moment another officer, a major, appeared on the scene.

'What's going on here?' he cried, imperiously. 'Fighting?'

No one answered him.

'I ask you again, are you men fighting? Is that you Sergeant Collins? Answer my question, if you please.'

'No sor,' replied the sergeant. 'It's all a bit of fun, if you like.'

'Fun? Then what's that man doing amongst the pots?'

The sergeant grinned. 'He's a little worse for the drink, sor. Not drunk, you understand, but a little overheated. Just the daily grog. Fell over, he did, in the dark. We'll put him to bed, sor, and no more rumpus. Roight!' The sergeant became officious, addressing two of his comrades, 'You twos, put Jacobs in his cot, on his belly so he don't drown if he sicks. Jump to it then, whot are yous, princes or privates? I've given yous an order.'

There was a *little* alacrity in their response. They lifted the beaten man and dragged him inside, the victim still mumbling something

234

about, 'I'll murder the bastard, so I will . . .' the reply being, 'Oh yes, you'll murder him all right, Jacobs, once someone's taught you to duck a wallop.'

'That man has been fighting,' said the major, firmly.

'Respectfully, no he hasn't, sor,' replied the sergeant, with just as much firmness. 'No witness, sor. None at all.'

'What about you?' snarled the major, turning on King. 'What's your story?'

'Man came out of the tent,' replied King, 'stumbled against me. Tried to steady him, but the fresh air went to his head. Made him groggy I believe. Fell away from me as I tried to catch him.' King looked the other sergeant directly in the eye. 'Hope he's all right by the morning.'

'Oh, he'll be roight as a biscuit, Sergeant, don't yous worry.'

'Good, well then, with your permission, sir,' King saluted smartly, 'I'll be getting back to my tent.'

'Cocky little man, aren't you?' said the major.

'No, sir. I hope not, sir.'

Suddenly the major seemed to see Crossman, hovering in the shadows not far away.

'You sir, did you see this fracus?'

'Who, me? No, major, I don't think so. I heard a commotion and came out of my tent to find a man battling energetically with some kettles and saucepans. I assumed it was some sort of game.'

'Game?' cried the furious major. 'This is no game. This is war, man. Who are you?'

The reply was delivered in a cold and crisp manner.

'Lieutenant Crossman of the 88th Connaught Rangers, on special duties with Colonel Hawke. And you sir, are . . .'

'Never mind who I am!' thundered the major, thoroughly put out. 'I'm conducting this enquiry. I'll tell you who I am when I'm good and ready.'

'That's a little discourteous, if I may say so.'

The major was about to be indiscreet. 'You . . .'

'Not,' interrupted Crossman with sharpness, 'in front of the men, if you please, Major. Have some decorum. We are officers of the Queen.'

The major seemed to realize he was about to overstep the mark. He struck his thigh with his palm, stood for a moment regarding

King with blazing eyes, then strode off into the night. Sergeant Collins heaved a sigh of relief.

King said, 'Sorry, for that. Didn't intend the wrath of God to descend on you and yours, Sergeant.'

'Arrgggh,' the sergeant waved him away. 'Never moind.'

King turned to Crossman and shrugged, as if to say, these things happen in the heat of the moment. Then he too left the scene.

Sergeant Collins, standing there in vest and trousers, finally saluted Crossman and said, 'It wasn't the criticism, sor, so much as the timing. He,' there was nod towards his own tent, 'lost his brother in Meerut.'

'I understand, Sergeant. I'm sorry for it.'

The sergeant nodded and went to join his fellows.

23

Delhi Ridge, August 1857

When it arrived outside Delhi, the column from the Punjab was
greeted by the foetid stink of an imbedded army and the noise of
guns blasting. Some of the guns were on a length of high ground
known as the Ridge, throwing shells and balls into Delhi. But there
were over a hundred of them on the walls of the city, returning the
fire. Only a thousand yards separated the two sides. The Kabul and
Kashmir Gates were within musket range. Around the walls of
Delhi, looking out towards the Ridge on which stood a tower known
as Flagstaff, was a huge army of sepoys now fighting for their king.
The last of the Mughal emperors had been dragged from retirement
and was now the figurehead of the sepoy rebellion. He was eighty-
two years old, his days as a warrior were over and he was now an artist
and a writer, but the mutineers needed him to give their uprising
some cohesion and centre. Forty thousand rebels had flocked to the
city and, with gunpowder aplenty, they planned to fight to the death.

On the Ridge was the hastily formed and hotchpotch army of the
British, consisting of Sikhs, Pathans, Gurkhas, Company European
regiments, HM European regiments, Baluchis and others. Their
numbers were at the moment Crossman arrived somewhere around
seven or eight thousand combatants. The column in fact had almost
doubled the number of men on the Ridge. Around the Ridge the
forest had been devastated by gunfire and foraging for fuel.
Conditions were appalling and disease was rife. This wallowing in

unsanitary muck, with tainted water and a shortage of food was not new to Crossman and Gwilliams, nor even King, for they had been through it all before.

'Well, here we are, Raktambar,' said Crossman. 'The sculleries of hell.'

Ishwar had never experienced anything like a siege before. He was utterly unused to such a filthy environment. He choked on the black smoke of gunpowder which perpetually hung in the air. He put his hands to his ears to block out the continual clapping of cannons as they punched their balls this way and that. He tasted the acrid fumes of war and could not but help smell its stink. The sights of death were in his eyes wherever he looked. Only his sense of touch remained unsullied by the destruction going on. A blue-jowled cholera victim, his eyes bugging, was gasping out his last breath not three yards away. The body of a headless Sikh lay propped against a wall, the raw neck covered in a black mass of flies. A dead bloated horse blocked a doorway, lodged there, immovable. Open graves shared a small stretch of ground to the rear with yawning latrine pits live with white worms.

'This is indeed a hell,' he said, staring at the chaos. 'I wish . . .'

'You wish you'd never come,' finished Crossman. 'It's a club we all desire to belong to, the one that isn't here.'

Out in the boggy marshlands, amongst the spear grass and cactus, lay the putrid bodies of young men. These were corpses of the dead enemy, out of reach for the time being. A lieutenant named Crawford, who, like many, had taken to wearing khaki-dyed cottons rather than his uniform, spent some time with Jack trying to convince him that the 'Pandies' were cowardly swines who were all much the same, yellow through and through.

'They don't much look like cowards to me,' said Jack. 'They attack on a daily basis, many of them are getting killed in brave if foolhardy attempts to overrun us. I really don't understand what you mean.'

'Oh, one of those are you? said Crawford, with a twist to his mouth. 'Still, you're new to India – you'll change.'

'I may do, but I doubt it.'

Crawford switched his subject to the generals.

'The mismanagement here is worse than in Crimea, almost,' complained Crawford. 'Doddering old fools who can't make a definite decision to save their lives. Sick bay's full of cholera victims and getting

238

worse every day. I tell you, if someone doesn't give the order to go into Delhi soon, there won't be any of us left to attack. We've bungled everything since we took over the Ridge, including command's stupid idea to burn the huts as an act of defiance. Act of defiance my arse! There's nowhere to shelter from the sun now. If I had my way . . .'

Although he was inclined to agree with Crawford about the command and staff, he was glad another attack cut short their conversation. Jack watched as the 60th Rifles and the Gurkhas repelled the attack. There were musket balls zipping everywhere, pinging from rock and brick, smacking into soft clay. A servant carrying a drink to Lieutenant Crawford lost his head to a cannonball. The same undiscriminating ball went on to lift a British soldier off his feet and carry him headlong into a wall.

A pair of coolies ran to the spot and retrieved the ball, still burning hot and with blood-steam rising from its surface. British ammunition was short and there was a reward for the collection of enemy shot. The two men passed the ball back and forth between them, it being still too hot to hold for long. Eventually Jack saw them get to where a bored sergeant was waiting to give them their two annas, one for each of them.

Jack wondered if the fact that Crawford's servant had been killed while discharging his duties would change the bigoted lieutenant's mind about 'Pandies' but apparently not, for a second servant was instantly dispatched through the hail of fire to fetch another drink. Crawford, like many, had become inured to death, especially the death of Indians, and bitterness had eaten away his soul. He was not alone in his views, though indeed there were those who despised such opinions. Many British soldiers thought a great deal of the Gurkhas and the Sikhs, if they found it hard to think kindly of the sepoys, and fast friendships had been made on the Ridge. There were even those who considered the mutineers to be worthy adversaries, though in truth they might admire good gunnery while hating the gunners.

When the attack abated, Jack went looking for his men. He found them at a stall which had been set up by 'Messrs Peake and Allen of Ambala' which sold everything from tobacco and soap to bottled beer. King had purchased some tooth powder and Gwilliams several small towels. Raktambar had increased his supply of tobacco, the constant use of which had given his magnificent dark moustaches a sort of ginger-stained fringe

'Well, men – keeping trade going?' said Crossman.

'These ain't fer me,' replied Gwilliams, holding up the towels. 'That there lady,' he pointed with the stem of his pipe at a crouching woman nursing a baby, 'just give birth to that infant on the back of that tumbril. I aim to give her these to help her by.'

'Very noble of you, Gwilliams.'

'Yeah, ain't it?' beamed the corporal. 'Makes me feel kinda warm inside.'

He went off to offer his gift to the woman. Her husband had just arrived back from fighting with the 9th Lancers and he looked with great suspicion on this soldier giving his wife presents, but soon the pair were talking like old friends. Gwilliams was able to do that with other men, gain their confidence within moments, though he could turn mighty nasty if his overtures were rejected.

'Well, Sergeant,' said Crossman as he squatted down with the other two behind a short wall, 'this is a pretty mess, isn't it?'

'It's not what I thought it would be, when they told me I was going to India,' agreed King. 'I expected hard times, of course, but this place is beyond anything I could have imagined. Will we win, do you think? They seem fairly well imbedded in that city – it's like a damn castle, isn't it? – and we don't appear to have the numbers to force them out.'

'We don't, at the moment. There's a siege-train on its way. Once that arrives, I imagine we'll have all we need to attack.'

'Except numbers.'

'Maybe not that, but you can't have everything.'

Again another conversation was cut short when rebels from the city tried to storm past Hindu Rao's House, a lone building directly in front of the British lines. This time Crossman, King and Gwilliams were directly involved in the fighting, having to defend a stretch of the wall first with small arms fire, then with swords. There was some desperate hand-to-hand combat going on for a while. Raktambar, after holding back for a while, suddenly flung himself into the battle and fought shoulder-to-shoulder with Jack, defending the lieutenant's left flank. It was baking hot under the midday sun and they were glad when it was over and the attack repulsed.

Jack immediately thanked the Rajput.

Ishwar shrugged. 'You are weak on that side, having an empty sleeve flapping like a flag. I simply act as your left hand.'

'You make an excellent left hand,' said Crossman, smiling. 'Better than my old one, bless its five fingers.'

240

'In future, I am your left-hand man.'

Over the next few days fighting hardly stopped. Certainly the guns boomed out continually and there were many attacks coming from various areas even in darkness. Musket fire took its toll, along with shot and shell.

Water for the Ridge came from a canal at the back which was used for many purposes, including washing. After he had been drinking from this dubious source, King's stomach decided to mutiny along with the sepoys. He began to shed weight rapidly, until Raktambar produced a powder. After he'd taken it, the sergeant began to produce solid stools again and his paleness retreated.

One evening Crossman was smoking his chibouque, now back in action after repairs, and a tall lone major strode past him. The man was dapper in appearance in comparison to many on the Ridge, and though he had a thick moustache his pale face was smooth and shiny. It was the hooded blue eyes which held his attention though as the major suddenly stopped, turned, and regarded him for a while.

'Do I know you?' asked Jack, removing the pipe from his mouth. 'Or perhaps you know me?'

The man removed his cap and wiped his forehead, lank blond hair falling over his ears.

'The latter, I think. I'm Hodson. You, I believe, are Crossman.'

Jack stood up. This was John Company's head of intelligence gathering, Major William Hodson. Although they were of the same rank, Hodson's authority was far greater than Nathan Lovelace's. Hodson had followed Harry Lumsden as commander of the famous Corps of Guides and had just raised an irregular cavalry regiment, Hodson's Horse. Hodson was a legend, not liked by many but admired for his horsemanship and his ability to organize spies. Hodson had already lived several lifetimes in India, had been accused of various crimes but never convicted, and was now an invaluable member of the force against the rebellion.

'You've spoken with Colonel Hawke about me?' asked Jack.

'Yes, I believe we may have use for you soon. How do you feel about going into Delhi tomorrow night?'

'That's what I do best,' said Jack, who had been into Sebastopol many times while it was under siege from the British in the Crimea. 'Do I take any of my men with me?'

'Who've you got?'

241

Jack told him.

'The Rajput might be useful. Is he trustworthy?'

'Yes, he is.'

'Excellent,' replied Hodson. 'As for the sergeant, you say he's not had much experience at this sort of thing.'

'None at all, yet – but he's willing.'

'Still, we'll leave him and your corporal behind this time. Tomorrow morning at ten, if you wouldn't mind coming to a planning meeting with Colonel Hawke? The hand give you any trouble?'

Jack looked at his empty cuff, surprised, as always, to see no appendage there.

'Not yet.'

'What about climbing walls?'

Jack shrugged. 'I hadn't thought of that. Possibly, I don't know. I wouldn't *want* it to make any difference.'

'Well, it's your hide. If you get left behind . . .'

'Then I must pay the consequences.'

'Right.' He began to walk away, then stopped and looked down at his left boot. It seemed there was a spur missing. 'Damn Goojars,' muttered Hodson. 'Steal your boot off your foot while you're riding past 'em.'

'It's there,' said Jack, pointing. 'In the mud. Fell off when you turned. I forgot to mention it. There, see?'

'No left hand,' Hodson said, stooping, 'but nothing wrong with your eyes.'

'Nothing at all. My vision's very good.'

Hodson left Jack in a thoughtful mood. He had vouched for Ishwar Raktambar but was actually uncertain of his loyalty. Raktambar had given his word to Jack, personally, but did that word extend to the whole British army? Yet, a man's word meant a great deal around here. One had to accept it with more confidence than the word of a Leather Lane market stall owner. If Crossman was there he was sure he could hold the Rajput to his promise. And if he was not, well then the world of the living would have to take care of its own, for he would be on his way to a better place.

'Now,' said Jack to himself, rising and tapping the bowl of his chibouque on the heel of his foot, 'let's go and see the sergeant.'

He found King washing his shirt in the canal and tackled him immediately.

'You're always talking about maps, Sergeant. Do you have any of this city?'

King looked up, quickly. 'Delhi?'

'I know of no other within musket range.'

The sergeant stood up and wrung his shirt as if he were strangling a live animal. 'It just so happens, sir, that I drew a very accurate map of Delhi myself, when I was here as a young man. It's eight years old, but even though I say so myself, it's one of my better compositions.' From the tone of his voice he might have been talking about a concerto. 'Do the generals need a map? Haven't they any of their own?'

'You were in India?' Crosssman was astounded by this news. 'You never told me that.'

Sergeant King suddenly looked abashed. 'Ah, no. But I was here, a very young man. The occasion to tell you never arose before.'

'It's arisen a thousand times,' snorted Jack. 'At any time on our journey you could have informed me.'

'Sorry, sir, I didn't see the need.'

'Didn't you, by God?'

'You're angry with me, sir, and I don't blame you. Perhaps I should have said something, but there are some things which remain private. Things – things happened to me. I wasn't here very long, but the experience was a telling one. When I went back to England I tried to forget, never realizing they would send me out again. I'm sorry, but there it is. There's no harm done.'

'No harm done,' repeated Jack. 'Well, I'm glad you think so. We'll speak more on the matter, later. Where's this famous map?'

'It's in my pack,' replied King, walking towards the ruin where he kept his kit. 'Over there.'

Crossman studied the chart with a keen eye for a long time. He was not in the mood for praise but he gave it anyway, nodding at the sergeant in approval. 'Well, Sergeant, this is excellent. I'm beginning to understand why others think you're useful now.'

King's features shone. 'Always glad to be useful, sir.'

In the morning, when Crossman went to see Colonel Hawke he found there, not Hodson, but his comrade-in-arms, Major Lovelace.

'Nathan,' said Crossman, pumping his hand. 'I didn't know you'd arrived in India.'

'I'm afraid so,' said the steely-eyed major, smiling. 'Not the best of times to be here, is it? How are you managing? Is he worth his salt?' he asked of Hawke.

Calcutta Hawke nodded his iron-grey head. 'Did a good job up in the Punjab, going into Afghanistan. Now, Lieutenant, I've spoken with Major Hodson and we've agreed you're to go into Delhi tonight. What we need is a survey of the inner walls, to find weak points. Hodson has his network of spies in there, but they're all local people with little or no engineering knowledge. What we want is a first-hand assessment from within. How do you feel about that?'

'As to going in, I feel fine about that, sir. But I'm no engineer either. Major Hodson suggested I leave Sergeant King behind, since he's had little experience of this kind of thing. However, on reflection, it might be better to take him. He's an engineer.'

Hawke frowned. 'I thought you had an engineering background?'

'No, sir. I'm interested in *inventions*, as a pastime, but I have had no training in engineering, none whatsoever.'

'In that case, yes, you'd better use the sergeant.'

'Thank you, sir. We'll choose our time tonight, depending on the moon. I've been studying one of the sergeant's maps – a very good, detailed piece of work by the look of it. I thought we might slip over to the River Jumna and swim to beyond the Kashmir Gate where we'll leave the water and crawl up the shore to a church which lies to the south-west of the gate, just inside the walls. We'll use the church as a centre of operations, going out from there along the base of the wall. I'm also taking Ishwar Raktambar, my Rajput. If we're stopped and questioned, he can answer for us, as my understanding of Hindi is fine, but my accent will give me away.'

'Is that wise, to use the Rajput? There're Rajputs by the thousand on the other side of those walls. Do you trust him?'

'People keep asking me that, sir, and I can only reply that my intuition tells me he will remain loyal. I could be wrong. However, if it does appear that he might betray us, I won't hesitate to kill him.'

Lovelace nodded firmly, believing that at last his chosen disciple had learned the art, or science, of expediency. The major would feel no compunction in killing a traitor. He expected his disciples to honour the same principle.

'Good. Well then, good luck,' said Hawke, shaking his hand. 'You realize that there's a good chance you won't get back. We've sent two teams in there already and both have failed to return.'

'No, I didn't know that, sir – but of course it makes no difference.'

'It can't, can it? You're a soldier. You must do your duty.'

Lovelace called to him, just before he walked away, 'Seen any tigers yet?'

'Not a single one. You?'

'Yes, two already. Shot one of them.'

The lieutenant felt he was probably going to be the only British officer never to encounter a tiger in India. Well, that was all right. He'd seen plenty of mounted heads and knew what they looked like.

Crossman left the two field officers feeling excited but also apprehensive. So, they had already lost men in Delhi? Company men, no doubt. Hodson's men. Well, they were probably amateurs. Jack now prided himself on being a professional spy. He'd had two fortunate years of it, in the Crimea. Of course the enemy had not been dark-skinned there, but actually after being in India for so long he too had darkened considerably. Not only that, his trekking had also weathered his hide so that now his sun-burned, wind-burned skin was the colour and texture of leather. King too, despite his freckles and reddish hair, had become darker. However, Jack intended to wrap the sergeant up, muffle him in swathes of cotton, to hide his features. There were Asians who did much the same with winding sheets.

He found the sergeant with Ibhanan, predictably discussing mapmaking.

'Sergeant King,' he said, 'a word with you.'

The stocky sergeant patted Ibhanan on the back and joined Jack under the lea of a wall.

'We're going into Delhi,' he said, in a low voice. 'I want you ready to move by midnight.'

'What? An assault?'

'No, no – not an attack. Just you, me and Raktambar.'

King looked slightly shocked.

'Isn't that almost suicide?'

'No, not if you obey orders to the letter. If you ignore your own initiative and just do as I say, you'll get out alive. If you don't, then be it on your own head, I *will* leave you behind if I think you're jeopardizing the operation or my own life. Do I make myself clear?'

'I – yes – yes, very clear. What time? Oh, yes, midnight.'

Jack left the sergeant with his thoughts on the matter. He went back to his own quarters, which consisted of a tent draped over the end of a wall to form a bivouac. He had decided to tell Raktambar what they were doing only at the last moment. If the Rajput was a traitor, then he would have no chance to warn those inside the walls, or arrange some convenient ambuscade. Jack hoped the Rajput was loyal, indeed was sure of it, but there were others involved. He trusted his own feelings, but it was right that he didn't allow that trust to enfold others.

Not long after he entered his bivouac there was a furious attack from the city, the sepoys using a building known as Metcalfe House, and the surrounding vegetation, as cover to get within musket range. Musket balls were everywhere, smacking into the brickwork of Crossman's wall, striking tree stumps nearby, and snicking off a nearby flagpole. Bugles were blowing and drums were rattling, calling various companies to arms.

The Gurkhas were the first to answer the call to arms in any great number, pouring from their resting places fully dressed and armed, some with kukris in hand. The picquets had already been overrun or forced back to the lines when the Gurkhas passed them, charging at the oncoming sepoys, the little men from Nepal true to their regiment and their salt. They were followed by a mixture of Sikhs and Pathans of the Punjab Infantry, who did not want to be seen lagging behind at such a time. European troops, some of them in a state of undress, came relatively late to the call.

Jack went out to assist, as many other officers did, though only as a soldier not as a leader. The native regiments had their own officers, both European and Asian, and did not need others to confuse them. Jack simply went down to empty his revolver at the sepoys. Once that was done, he stood with sword in hand, ready to repel any that slipped through the ragged lines of the defenders. In the end he was not needed.

Loss of life on this occasion was severe, especially amongst the sepoys. How anyone could accuse them of cowardice was beyond Crossman, when they threw themselves at their old rulers with such fierce effort. Back near the walls of the city, women could be seen, loading muskets for them, and if sepoys did retreat before it was necessary, these women drove them back into battle with abuse and sticks. How the Honourable East India Company had fallen, to have earned the fury of mothers and wives.

The attack lasted about forty minutes, then the bombardment started again, the shot falling like solid metal eggs from the gods.

In the early evening, the Reverend Stillwell came to visit Jack, having left enough time to regain his dignity.

'Good even to thee, Lieutenant, my old friend,' said Stillwell, 'and will thee be coming to my songs of adoration later tonight?'

'No, you must forgive me, but I beg to be excused. I have other matters to attend to, Mr Stillwell.'

'More important than praising Our Father.'

'Not necessarily more important, but being my duties I can't ignore them, I'm afraid. I do beg your pardon.'

Stillwell looked suitably affronted on behalf of the Christian deity.

'Well, if that's the case, I shan't try to persuade thee. I just wish thee would remember there is a higher duty, a higher calling, than that of the army.'

'Fortunately, God doesn't preside over courts martial,' muttered Crossman, 'or I might be argued into changing my mind.'

'I heard that, Lieutenant, it sounded very like blasphemy to my astonished ears. In fact thee might well suffer many lashes in that place to which the sinner goes. I hope thee might not regret thy decision.'

'If you're within earshot, Mr Stillwell, I shall hum along with you.'

The reverend was not absolutely sure that Jack was not mocking him further, but he contented himself with pursing his lips. He stood staring at Jack a long time before leaving him to his chores. Once he had gone, the lieutenant, who had only been fiddling with his clothes and boots in order to ignore the minister, lay down on his bed in relief.

'One more minute,' he murmured to himself, 'and we might've had Mr Stillwell's head on a plate.'

At midnight Crossman was ready to enter the city of Delhi. He took no firearms, since there was swimming to be done. A knife was his only weapon and that was simply a comfort blanket. His attire consisted of light cottons which he hoped would not hamper him in the current. He had darkened his skin with berries Raktambar had given him. The Rajput had suggested it, saying the stain would not come off in the water. When King arrived at his bivouac they did the same with him. Then Crossman explained the mission to his two comrades, before they set out for the river. Happily, the moon was a haze of dim light behind some cloud cover.

247

Their own picquets had supposedly been alerted to the fact that they were passing through their lines, but Jack took along the duty officer just to make sure. The last thing he wanted was to be shot by some eager sentry. It was less than half-a-mile to the water's edge, but it was possible there were sepoys on that ground and thus after they had passed the last picquet they crawled on their bellies, stopping every minute or so to listen for sounds of concealed men. Indeed, when they were within two hundred yards of the riverbank, they heard the clatter of a pot and heard whispers. Somewhere near, the enemy were squatting. They crept past a clearing in which seven men sat, their muskets stacked like a sheaf of corn between them.

They snaked their way down to the river and slipped into its waters. Raktambar was not a good swimmer and insisted on staying within his depth, close to the shore. Crossman and King were very competent in the water and were able to go further out, into the darker areas. Soon Jack too had to move in until his feet touched the bottom, his missing hand making the swim more tiring than he first thought it would. The current was with them going north to south so the task was not a matter of effort, but one of controlling stability and direction in the swiftish flow.

It was unfortunate that he had to go closer to the shore: he was in graver danger than his Hindu comrade. At least if Raktambar were caught they wouldn't shoot him immediately. Being a Rajput he could stall his captors for a considerable time. Fortunately, though there may have been sleeping sepoys on the bank of the river, none were awake enough to notice dark heads moving along just off the water's edge.

When they had passed the silhouette of the Kashmir Gate, King swam shorewards to join them. The three men crept up on to the river's beach and lay down in the black comfort of shadows, there to gather their breath and get their bearings. It was disconcerting to find there was a lot of activity going on in the streets ahead of them. This was no sleeping city: many were up and about. The smells of cooking assailed them, along with those of spices and woodsmoke. Even though the guns had been silent for hours there was the strong odour of gunpowder in the atmosphere.

'Let's get to the church,' whispered Crossman. 'We can move out from there when it becomes a little safer to do so.'

When they got to the church, however, they found it occupied. Sleeping bodies were everywhere. Instead of entering the building, they went into a small graveyard at the back. There they waited, crouched by some headstones, for the city to settle a little more. Crossman knew that Delhi never entirely went to sleep, but it seemed wise to remain where they were until the streets had fewer people wandering through them.

Indeed, about three o'clock in the morning there was a lull in activity. The soldiers left their hiding place and walked along the inside of the city wall, making mental notes all the time. King seemed a little nervous but Crossman noted that the sergeant did not allow his state of mind to interfere with his ability to assess the strengths and weaknesses of the defences. For his part, Jack too made notes, yet always remained alert for signs of Sajan. Like King, he wanted the boy back in their fold. He was a little more upset by the boy's defection than the sergeant, but he still did not want to see Sajan executed – and executed he would be, if caught by the British with rebels. His age would be no protection, any more than it was for a cabin boy on a man-o'-war or a drummer boy in an infantry regiment.

Of course, there were young boys everywhere. With the other homeless they littered doorways and the edges of the narrow streets, blocked the alleys with their slumbering forms, and were draped over rooftops. It was maddening not to be able to inspect each one closely, just in case, but that would have aroused great suspicion. As it was they were stopped twice by people wishing to talk. A Musselman asked if they had any bread and Raktambar was left to explain that they had no food and indeed wished for bread themselves. Then a staggering sowar halted them, clutching on to King's arm. It emerged after a few moments that the man had a terrible headache and was violently sick in front of them. He was not drunk, he was genuinely ill and was suffering badly with the pain.

King simply peeled away the sepoy's fingers and walked on, as any other Musselman or Hindu might do. If you met a sick man, you avoided him. If you came across a dead one, you ignored him. If a beggar accosted you, you either gave him half-an-anna or kicked him aside, depending on your religion and your disposition.

The three men walked the mile between the Kashmir Gate and the Kabul Gate. To go beyond the Kabul Gate was unnecessary, for the British would only attack on that mile stretch, it being the most accessible and directly in front of the British Lines. When they had

249

covered the necessary ground they turned back again, repeating the exercise in the reverse.

'I think I have it,' muttered King to Crossman. 'I think I know where the weak points happen to be.'

'Good, then we can get away from here.'

'We haven't seen Sajan,' the sergeant said, disappointed. 'He must be here somewhere.'

'Yes,' replied Crossman, his eyes scanning the packs of sleeping young bodies, '*somewhere.*'

'Sahib,' Raktambar said, 'can you not ask your friend Major Hodson's spies to watch out for the boy?'

'But how will they know the right one?' asked the lieutenant. 'There are so many.'

'They may have ways.'

Turning a corner they suddenly came up against a crowd which blocked the way between the buildings and the wall. It seemed a tall thin man was having visions. The mob had allowed him space inside their circle and he was spinning slowly staring out at the faces. The pupils of his eyes were dilated, as if he had been smoking bhang or some other substance, and he pointed outwards with one hand. A ragged skirt around his waist swirled about him as he spoke out in a high shrill voice, the crowd remaining stunned by the strangeness of his words, both awesome and entertaining.

Crossman and the other two could not force their way through the mob without drawing attention to themselves.

'There is fire,' shrieked the Hindu prophet, 'with writhing bodies in it. Serpents rise from the flames – serpents with wings – and all they gaze upon turn to stone. Tigers crawl from giant eggs and tiny crabs emerge from anuses of ordinary men to drop like scales from a lizard's back.'

On and on this self-styled prophet gabbled, about women giving birth to calves and men growing the heads of pigs.

'It is a time when all the world's terrible shapes are twisted and mangled into other forms and none know who or what they are . . .'

The man suddenly stopped and appeared to vomit into his hands – when he opened his palms he revealed to the crowd a knot of leech-worms bloated with blood, squirming, falling between his fingers to the earth.

King made a shocked sound of disgust and horror, but in the general reaction to the prophet's activities no one took notice.

'The end of the world comes,' cried the prophet, wildly. 'It is the *firinghis* who bring it upon us, dragging us into the fathomless pit along with themselves, down into the darkness of the damned.'

To Crossman's utter consternation he stopped twirling and pointed with an accusing finger directly at him, crying, 'Ha!', before swooning away in the dead faint of a frenzied man with an overheated brain.

Fortunately for the lieutenant, most of the crowd's eyes were on the limp form of the prophet on the ground. But two or three were staring at him, not with menace but with curiosity. Who was it that the man seized with visions had indicated, and why? Did he too have a message for them? Were they to learn more about how their fate was entwined with the foreigners to their land, who brought nothing but death and destruction with them?

Crossman's eye caught that of Raktambar, who seemed at a loss to know what to do next. Should they run before the mob realized they were intruders? Or should they draw their knives and fight their way through to the river? Either way it seemed they would be overcome. Then Crossman lifted up his empty sleeve-end and waggled it in the faces of the lookers.

'Alms?' he murmured, twisting his mouth so that the words came out strangely warped. 'Alms for one crippled by the foe?'

He thrust his good palm into their faces, demanding money, staring them right in the eyes with a pleading expression.

'Give. Give. Allah wills it. Give.'

A woman pushed his hand aside. 'Get away from me,' she said, 'do you think you're the only victim in this war? I have a son with no legs. If anyone should be pitied it is my son, who weeps for a lost brother and a father who will never see light in his eyes again.'

'Shame!' said Raktambar, suddenly, turning Crossman around and leading him away. 'Shame on you, woman. Pity my poor friend here, who has been robbed of his hand. I am sorry for your son, but here is a man who has given his limb for the cause, his wrist black with rot.'

The Rajput and King bustled Crossman away on the edge of the crowd, gently nudging men and women aside. Most of them were still only hungry for fevered images from the fallen prophet. His eyes were now flickering and they were urging him to get to his feet and tell them more about the end of the world. Would they defeat the *firinghis* and drive them from their land before they were all dragged into oblivion? Would they swarm over the infidels and cut them

251

down like corn stalks? Would they stamp the Christians down into the caked earth and spit on their bones?

The three made their way through the watchers to the other side, without being accosted further. Then they slipped into the shadows and along the city walls, down towards the river. It seemed they might make it without further incident when two sepoys, still in their Company army uniforms, stepped out of a house and came towards them. The sepoys carried muskets in the crooks of their arms and it appeared they had been drinking. Both small men, they stared at Crossman and the Rajput, who had the advantage of height. The sepoys sauntered over to them, looking them up and down.

'Where are you going at this hour?' said one of the sepoys.

Raktambar asked, 'Who is that wants to know?'

'We are the guard,' replied the other, aggressively. 'You should know us.'

'I know that you are of low caste,' Raktambar growled, 'so do not come close to me.'

One of the sepoys stepped back, but the other looked fiercely at the Rajput and came on.

'You think you are better than us?'

'Of course I am better than you. I am a *Ksatriya*. You are *Mleccha*.'

'I have a firelock,' reminded the sepoy, whose friend had now come forward again. 'You do not. You would be wise to hold that in your mind, before you come the high priest over us. We are good working soldiers who struggle for our bread. Do not mock us or insult us.'

The sepoy lifted his Brown Bess now and aimed at Raktambar's stomach. Whether or not he meant to fire Crossman never knew. Jack was not going to take the chance. He drew his dagger and drove it hard between the sepoy's ribs. A scream went wailing up from the man as he dropped his firearm and clutched at the hilt of the knife protruding from his chest. Then he sank to his knees and with a short sigh fell sideways onto the ground.

The second man gathered his wits, having at first been shocked into immobility. Now he began running away, a gargling noise coming from his mouth. Raktambar chased him, swiftly, grabbed him from behind by his hair, and slit his throat before he too could begin shouting. Then all three of the intruders ran down to the river, expecting a howling mob to come out of the streets and follow them.

Nothing of the kind happened, for whatever reason.

The trio reached the waterline and waded in, diving under when some people appeared, but the party on the shore was talking and laughing, and walked on. The moon had disappeared completely now as if it had fallen through a hole in the night. In the blackness the three men lost touch with one another. Crossman found himself battling against the current, the rippling rush of a swift flow causing him to exert great effort. He found he was floundering, his handless arm failing to give him the kind of propulsion he needed to beat the torrent. The river was a strong master, carrying him back down past Delhi, towards the south of the city.

The hazy moon came out again just as a line of boats appeared. Crossman dived and was swept under them. While under the surface he lost his sense of direction, not knowing which was up, down or sideways. This caused him to panic for a moment, thinking that the current was dragging him to the bottom, but then he felt his good arm break into air. He thrashed around for a bit, gulping down breaths, not caring that he was making a great deal of noise. All he wanted now was to be out of the watery clutches of the Jumna. He kicked his legs like mad to keep his head and shoulders above the surface, but the muscles were screaming now. Strong eddies caught him and began to spin his body round and round. Close to exhaustion, he cursed his missing hand. That small paddle of flesh and bone was sorely missed: he had not realized how much it would matter to him.

The twisting eddies then started to turn him upside down, savage in their playfulness, like a dog with a rag. He knew he must be near some sharp bend in the river, or the turbulence would not be so fierce. Out there in the middle it was a faster but smoother flow. Here on the edge, where the waves twisted in great cables, there would be logs and even whole trees, washed along by the greedy Jumna to be caught in a tangled corner. His last breath left his body and that aching pain in his lungs began building to a terrible crescendo. There was no chance now for new air. He was topsy-turvy somewhere in the foaming torrent.

A strong muscled limb came out of nowhere, gripped him under his armpits, and a struggle began to reach the shore. Crossman went limp, his life in the hands of another. When his head bobbed above the surface he snatched at blessed air, trying not to panic when he submerged again. It seemed longer than an hour, but was probably shorter than a minute, before he found himself crawling up the shore, spluttering and gargling warm river water from nose and mouth. All he could think of, with a gladness close to religious joy, was that he had survived the water. He was out of that damned river with its many-fingered clutching eddies and currents.

His saviour spoke to him. 'You all right, sir?'

'Sergeant? Was it you who pulled me out?'

'I'm afraid so. You owe me a great debt of gratitude now. It'll be difficult for you to discipline me in future, won't it?'

'No it damned well won't.' Crossman heaved himself up with his good right hand, until he was sitting. 'It's your duty to rescue your commanding officer, when he's in trouble.'

There was a serious note to their flippancy and neither felt like carrying it any further. They sat on the shoreline, hidden by a bank of reeds which stretched up to a small village of mud-houses and shacks. Neither felt like moving for a while. King confessed he was aching from top to bottom. That last effort had scoured the energy from him, leaving him fatigued beyond any exercise he had ever undertaken. Crossman was limp in every quarter, not even managing to summon the energy to remove a nest of twigs from his hair: a parting gift from the River Jumna.

'Did you see what happened to Raktambar?' asked the lieutenant, fearing that his man had been drowned. 'He was the weakest swimmer amongst us, after all.'

'Yes, he was not long out before he began struggling, even though the water was only up to his chest. I saw him wade back to the shore. He's back in the city again.'

Crossman wondered whether this had been a deliberate ploy of the Rajput, to get away from him. Being a Hindu he would be able to hide very well in Delhi. It was a huge city with many inhabitants. No one would be suspicious of a new face in a city into which new faces were appearing by the day. As to whether Raktambar had worked it on purpose, it did not on the surface seem likely, unless the Rajput were very devious. It was true he was used to – Crossman struggled to recall the phrase, but found it in the end – *hasad-wa-fasad* – jealousy and intrigue. It was the 'intrigue' part that interested the lieutenant. Could Raktambar have planned such a thing? It was surely too complicated a method of escape. An easier scheme would surely be to walk away from the Ridge in the middle of the night.

254

When he and King were sufficiently recovered they reconnoitred the area. Dawn was appearing now and in the greyness they could see they were quite a long way south of the Ridge. The sky looked as if it had been swept with stiff brooms, the cirrus clouds having streaked edges. There was a village in the way, and a number of small farms, but Crossman guessed they were about three to four miles from the nearest point of the Ridge.

'More like five to six, sir,' said King.

'I think you're wrong, Sergeant.'

King was firm. 'Who's the surveyor? You or me.'

'Don't be impertinent.'

'I simply ask the question, sir, without the intention to irritate you, which seems to be a very easy thing to do.'

'You didn't need to add that last clause to your sentence. Do not think that saving my life makes us bosom friends. I can't ignore insolence. I don't dislike you, King, but you're my sergeant, not my chum.'

'If you don't mind me saying so, sir, you don't appear to have any chums at all.'

'That is surely my business and yes I *do* mind . . .'

They kept this up as they made their way over the uneven ground to the Ridge. Avoiding habitations and cattle corrals they encountered no serious problems. A man with a bullock cart out on a road seemed mildly surprised to see them. A gaggle of women going down to the river with their laundry giggled as they passed them. Whether their disguises, as Hindus, worked in the light of day neither man knew. Crossman was inclined not to trust it except at distance. In the main there were very few people about in the early morning. They swung west to come towards the Ridge from the rear, passing Eed-Ghur and going under the aqueduct to join the canal. They then followed the canal in a north-easterly direction, crossing the Kurnaul road, calling out for the benefit of any picquets that they were British and not Indian, as their appearance suggested.

'Don't shoot!' King kept crying. 'Scouting party coming in! No itchy fingers, lads. Keep it in the barrel. I'm as English as you.'

'That'll keep the Irishmen from shooting you,' muttered Jack.

However, they managed to enter the camp when they came level with the old racecourse, where some fusiliers were collecting water in their kettles. Weary, the two men made their way to Colonel Hawke, who greeted them with a cheery good morning and bade them welcome. Major Lovelace was called and King gave his engineer's report first, while Crossman relaxed and let waves of drowsiness wash over him. Then, the important information out of the way, he gave his own report, which terminated with the story of Ishwar Raktambar re-entering Delhi.

'You don't think he's defected?' enquired Lovelace. 'I simply ask the question, you understand.'

'I don't believe so – I'm sure he hasn't,' Crossman replied. 'In any case, he has nothing to tell them that they can't learn from their own spies.'

'I'm sure you're right, Lieutenant.'

After passing on their information, Crossman and King went back to their quarters. Crossman was awoken from a deep sleep by two soldiers talking outside his bivouac. One was telling the other that the long-awaited siege-train was nearing Delhi, elephants and bullocks drawing the heavy guns and ammunition wagons. The rebels had sent a force of seven thousand men from Delhi to intercept it and destroy it. Brigadier-General Nicholson had been asked by the commander-in-chief, General Wilson, to take the field again. Nicholson was to pursue the rebel column and crush them before they reached the siege-train. The British force was to consist of 2,500 Punjabi irregulars, three troops of horse artillery and two companies of British infantry taken from the Queen's Regiment of 61st Foot.

'We're in it,' said the soldier with the deeper voice. 'It's our company what's going out.'

'Sooner out than in, with this lot coming down,' replied his comrade, speaking of the continual rain of shells and shot from the mutineers in Delhi. 'A breath of fresh air, at least.'

Crossman dressed and went straight to Colonel Hawke.

'Shall we join General Nicholson's force?'

'Not this time, Lieutenant. You need a rest.'

The colonel did not expand on his reason and the lieutenant did not seek to question his superior further. Jack knew that one of Hawke's friends, John Coke, who had formed the Punjabi 'Coke's Rifles' had been severely wounded and it had upset him, so the colonel was in no mood for any arguments. Jack left his commanding officer in a thoughtful frame of mind, returning to tell Gwilliams and King that they were staying put. King seemed rather relieved, though Gwilliams, feeling stifled and oppressed in the Ridge encampment, would have liked to take the field.

'I thought one time we was going to join with Coke's Rifles,' said Gwilliams. 'Had we done, would we have got to go?'

'I doubt it,' replied Crossman. 'When the colonel says no, he means it. Well, we must make ourselves useful here. God knows, there's plenty to do and we're short of men now. They'll need us to help defend the Ridge while the column is out.'

Indeed, attacks continued to come, mostly over the ground on the south-west corner known as Subzimundi, where the rebels were able to use dwellings to shield themselves from rifle fire. Some were bold, some were timid, but many were willing to lay down their lives. They had fought for the British for many years, now they were fighting for themselves. The reason seemed enshrouded in fog. It did not appear as if they had any grand plan and senior British officials were mystified as to what was going to replace their system. Many Indians were waiting to see what the outcome was likely to be, before committing themselves one way or the other. Some of the princes thought they would get their power back. *Zaminders*, the land owners, hoped to increase the size of their properties. The poor had been promised much by the glittering rich. The rich hoped to get richer. All of this seemed vaguely desirable, but remained woolly and loosely woven.

Brigadier Nicholson achieved a commendable victory. He returned to the Ridge having fought and defeated a vastly superior enemy force at Najafgarh. Almost a thousand of the rebels had been killed in the battle at the cost of thirty lives in Nicholson's ranks. Guns were seized and the rebels routed. Those in the camp on the Ridge were jubilant. For his part Nicholson praised his troops, saying they had behaved very creditably.

Crossman could not but help feel the same joy as others on hearing of the victory. There was a certain pride in his nation and the satisfaction of knowing that those people who were even now pounding the Ridge with guns had been thrashed by a force inferior in numbers. He felt their morale must be suffering after this second drubbing by Nicholson.

One sweltering, humid evening, Jack was sitting on an empty powder keg smoking his chibouque to rid the air of insects, when he saw a man slinking along the bank of the canal. Visibility was poor since the sun was rapidly sinking into celestial foam, but Jack studied the figure, seeing in him something familiar. Then the man passed under the light thrown down by a lantern which stood on the spot where water was scooped in jugs and pots. His features under the lamplight, the man became instantly recognizable. Jack saw it was the willing assassin who had approached him just outside Bombay. Yet the man was here. What was his business on the Ridge? Had he come on a professional footing? Since his work was killing people, 'any persons you choose', then one had to assume he was here to do just that.

Suddenly Jack realized that this was the shadowy figure who had been following them across half of India. His aspect on the situation changed to one of deep alarm. This sinister man, this self-confessed murderer, was now surely after *him*, for why would Arihant trail him this way and that, if not seeking an opportunity to kill him? The man's profession bespoke of dealing out death at a price and it could not be purely coincidence that their paths had crossed so often in the last few months. Jack was now sure his own life was forfeit to some unknown third party, who wished him dead.

Crossman rose swiftly, intending to go and question the assassin, but the moment he stood up the dark figure was gone. It almost seemed as if he had vanished into the canal itself. Strolling down to the spot where the lamp stood, Crossman found dozens of footprints in the mud, but no Arihant. Had he really seen him? He felt sure there had been someone walking along, but perhaps his eyes were playing tricks in the gloaming? Lizards crawled the banks under the jaundiced light and swift bats darted in and out of the beams. Shadows jumped when he knocked the lamp with his elbow, but there were no other movements along the canal.

Jack returned to his seat, puzzled, wondering about those strange flitting shapes one experiences at the dying of the day. Perhaps the heat had got to him? It was relentless enough in the day and hardly changed step during the evening. Men shrivelled and died in these temperatures. Kidneys simply ceased functioning. Minds went mad in the hot winds. And the insects were enough to drive one insane on their own!

Shortly after this incident a woman passed him in the twilight carrying a pail and holding a child's hand. The woman looked about thirty-five and like most of the families on the Ridge, was black-eyed, haggard and worn. Lack of sleep, fear for the future and her child, being in the presence of death and destruction, perhaps the loss of a husband, father or brother, all had contributed to her state of mind and her appearance. She was wearing a sari which had at one time been bright yellow, but was now filthy. It was torn in several places, the gold trim peeling away leaving a black edge. It was impossible to tell the colour of her hair, which had obviously been dyed black at some time, but was now streaked with light and dark.

The little girl, possibly around six or seven, looked as if she had fared a little better, but then he reminded himself that children had the buffer of adults between them and disaster. They might be frightened and anxious, but there was comfort to be had in protective arms. For the adults themselves, there was no such solace. Even in the arms of loved-ones the fear did not go away.

'Ma'am,' he said, 'it's a very hot evening to be fetching heavy water. I would like to walk with you down to the canal, if you care to have me accompany you.'

Jack was still unsure of who or what he had seen down at the canal bank and he was concerned for her welfare. She, however, seemed to think he had other motives for wishing to walk with her. She shook her head and walked on. Cursing himself for his stupidity, he strode out and caught up with her, only to have her turn and stare angrily into his eyes.

'No, you don't understand,' he said, quickly. 'I didn't explain myself properly. My reasons are purely honourable, I assure you, ma'am. Earlier I saw a figure down by the water and it has worried me. I don't mean to frighten you, so if you'll just allow me to accompany you all will be well.'

Still she seemed suspicious. Perhaps she believed he had made up the story about the 'figure'. He admitted to himself it sounded rather weak, for he was not totally convinced himself.

'I am Lieutenant Jack Crossman,' he told her. 'You may ask of whom you please, you will find no one who has anything bad to say of me. No, no, that's not quite true. There are some who have reason . . . Lord, I'm making a proper hash of this, aren't I? Look, just give me your pail, you stay here and I'll go and fill it. How's that? Then you don't need to walk into the darkness with me and nothing need worry you.'

The little girl said, 'How can you carry it? With no hand?'

259

He looked down and saw that he was reaching with his left arm, the cuff of his sleeve yawning.

'Oh! You're right, young lady. Fortunately I have another one, over here,' and he took the pail with his right hand. 'I won't be long.'

Jack went down to the canal. The lamp was black with midges and mosquitoes, with the odd moth flying in. In its light he dipped the pail into the canal and scooped up water. When it was full he stood up and looked around. He could see no one. Had he been hallucinating? Perhaps there was more in this rough Indian tobacco than met the eye? Shrugging, he returned to the waiting woman with the full pail, careful not to spill any.

'Thank you, Lieutenant,' she said. 'I didn't mean to be un-mannerly, but you know . . .'

'I know,' he said, terrified she was going to say it. 'However, I'm a happily married man who loves his wife. God, you don't need to know that, do you?' A desperate change of subject. 'What's your name, little girl?'

'Sarah, and I'm not little. You said I was a young lady.' She looked at the pail. 'You are our *bhisti* now, aren't you?'

'Sarah don't be rude,' admonished the woman. She then said to Crossman, 'A *bhisti* is a water-carrier.'

'I know. I don't mind being a water-carrier. Well, where shall I deposit your pail, ladies? It's getting rather heavy.'

'Oh, heavens,' said the woman, 'it must be pulling your arm off. This way, please, Lieutenant, and thank you. I am Geraldine Stanton – Miss Geraldine Stanton. Sarah is my youngest sister. We had a house over there.' She nodded towards Delhi. 'My father was killed on the roof of our house, trying to protect us. My mother died two days ago. She had cholera but I think she died of a broken heart. I have three brothers, but thankfully they are all in England. I'm sorry, I'm chattering, aren't I?'

'You're entitled, Miss Stanton. How did you and Sarah manage to get out of Delhi? Most were killed.'

'Through the kindness of servants. Our *chowkidar* smuggled us out in native clothes. It was horrible. Horrible. How could they do this to us? We did them no harm. I hate them.'

He did not want to go into the multiple reasons, political and per-sonal, as to why a nation might turn against its foreign rulers. Also, he did not point out that she owed her life to her servants, who had probably put themselves in great danger to save her. Perhaps she knew it. In any case, she was entitled to her feelings, given that she had seen her family murdered.

'How are you bearing up? You and Sarah?'

'We're managing,' replied Geraldine, with a wry smile. 'Everyone's most kind. Mrs Blakely's looking after us. Or we're looking after her. I'm not quite sure which it is. Mrs Blakely's husband is a sergeant-major. I've never spoken to a sergeant-major's wife before. She's from Devon. Sarah finds her accent funny and she doesn't mind that. She's very kind.'

When they came into the light of more lamps, Crossman suddenly revised his estimate of this woman's age. She was probably not thirty-five. Possible she was nearer thirty. Yet, being Sarah's sister, how could that be? Such a huge gap in their ages.

'You're staring at me.'

'Oh,' he said. 'I'm sorry.'

She smiled. 'You're trying to guess my age, aren't you?'

How did they do that? he wondered. Were they all mind-readers, these females of the species. Jane had the same ability. Men, he decided, must have their thoughts written on their foreheads!

'I was nineteen last birthday,' she said, laughing at his consternation. 'I shall be twenty, soon.'

'And I'll be seven next week,' piped in Sarah, 'so you must come to my party and bring a gift.'

But Geraldine had seen Jack's expression and she was obviously mortified.

'I look much older, now, don't I?'

'No, no – I mean, it's the dirt and the lack of sleep. Not your fault. Once we get you to a safe place, where you can bathe without fear of a shot landing in your tub, and nice clean clothes, why – I'm sure you'll be the prettiest lady at the ball. Not that you're unlovely at the moment, of course, but you could do with a scrub and some nice perfume . . .'

She laughed now at his awkwardness.

'Lieutenant, I like you,' she said, seriously. 'If times were normal I should not be permitted to say that. You would think me fast and giddy, especially a married man who loves his wife.' She was teasing him now. 'And I would be shunned by my peers. But we're here, on the Ridge, and the niceties of society need not apply. Thank you for

261

your help.' She took the pail from him and handed it to a large woman with a girth that a horse would envy, 'And Mrs Blakely thanks you too, don't you, Mrs Blakely? We're very lucky to have a friend in Lieutenant Jack Crossman, aren't we?'

'I'm sure I don't know, m'darlin', for he's a hofficer and we're not s'posed to have hofficer friends. The lieutenant shou'nt be helpin' us, really. It's not his place to serve us women. He can't be carrying pails.'

'Oh, officers are good at carrying pails, Mrs Blakely,' Jack said, laughing. 'I was a champion pail-carrier back in Britain.'

'And you'll come to my party?' asked Sarah. 'Won't you, Jack?'

'Sarah!' admonished Geraldine.

'No, no – it's all right. I should be honoured, Sarah. If I'm working, of course I shall be unable to come. But if not, you can count on it. And,' he bent down and said in her ear, 'the gift will arrive whether I do or not.'

'Oh thank you, Jack.' Sarah clapped her hands.

Crossman left the women feeling a warm glow within. The encounter had cheered him enormously. It does not matter that a man has a wife he loves and intends nothing more than friendship with a lady new to his acquaintance: his ego screams with satisfaction when that young and beautiful woman finds him attractive. A man *is* a man for all that, as the poet said, and the rewards of an admiring look from a desirable woman are tremendously invigorating. He is puffed up with pride, full of himself, his vanity overwhelming his modesty, and he is content. This is not an admirable or commendable trait, but does wonders for his sense of well-being.

He went back to his bivouac again, lit his chibouque, and puffed it with great satisfaction. Later that night he was on duty. General Wilson had stipulated, quite rightly, that if you were on the Ridge you were available for any duty whatsoever. Officers made themselves available when and where they could, whatever their main work, whatever their regiment. After his tour of duty he went back to his pipe again: a comfort blanket.

Jack was still puffing away, having supped a small glass of arrack, when a cavalry officer paid him a visit.

24

Jack Crossman left Betty in the kitchen and went up to his bedroom to put on a sober set of civilian clothes, preferring to go to White's Club in mufti. It was not that he was ashamed to be in the army, but quite the reverse. The fact was, though there would be others in uniform, he had felt keenly that coachman's jibe. *Peacock*. A uniform was fine for a strutter, but not for the quiet man of taste, when gadding about the capital city.

It was a very cold evening, with a light covering of snow on the streets and Crossman took a hansom cab to St James's Street, to the oldest gentleman's club in London. He was not a member, but Major Lovelace was and wished to meet him there to finalize arrangements for India. Crossman had been to the club a few times before, his father being a member, and was familiar with its reputation as a gentleman's gambling den.

When he entered the club he was met at the doorway by Arthur's keen eyes and felt himself under scrutiny. Arthur's job was not an enviable one. He needed to spot an intruder immediately and eject him. But God forbid he should go up to an actual member of the club and request identification and proof of membership. Thus Arthur had to look for signs of underconfidence and lack of knowledge and all those other small indications that someone was uncomfortable and not in the right place.

Crossman was not a frequent visitor, was not known to Arthur by sight, but put the poor man's fears at rest by giving his name and handing young James his topcoat and hat, and asking for Major Lovelace.

263

James it was who took care of the hats and canes, though he remained only just silkily visible behind a marble pillar, but Arthur always fielded any questions regarding members.

'Lieutenant Crossman, sir,' Arthur was clearly relieved to have a name at last. 'Major Lovelace asked me to have you taken to him immediately you arrived.'

Arthur snapped his fingers and another man appeared out of regions unknown to lead Crossman through the various rooms of this one-time seventeenth-century chocolate house.

Lovelace was at a card table when Crossman entered the room. He played his hand, then made his apologies to the other players before joining Crossman sitting in a discreet corner of the room.

'Don't let me pull you away if you're on a winning streak,' said Crossman. 'What is it? *Chemin de fer?*'

'How did you guess?'

Lovelace too was in civilian clothes, but as always he looked the perfect aristocratic army officer. He was a little shorter than Crossman, but women other than Crossman's wife or mother would have said he was better looking. Blond and blue-eyed, Lovelace had just the faintest touch of cold steel in his smile. His figure was enviable from the narrow waist to the broad expanse of shoulders, where the cloth of his coat covered his muscled back without a wrinkle. Crossman liked the major for many aspects of his character, but knew him to be a ruthless man in his work. He was Crossman's immediate superior in the special duties area, the gathering of intelligence, for which Crossman had been chosen.

They shook hands and ordered drinks.

'How's the married man?' asked Lovelace.

'Very well,' answered Crossman. 'Very well, indeed. You should try it.'

Lovelace waved a hand through the air, dismissively. 'Oh, that's not for me. Too much responsibility. Besides, there're not many Jane Mulinders around. I'm not a good judge of the ladies, you know. I'd end up with a very unsuitable one, I'm sure. Someone like our mutual friend Mrs Lavinia Durham. You're a very lucky man.'

'I know it. But you know, Mrs Durham . . .'

Lovelace held up his hand. 'You're going to tell me she's very sweet underneath. But you have to admit she's a little fast. I'd spend all my time fighting every man in the club. All right, don't look at me like that – not *every* man. Anyway, we're not here to talk about women. Have you met Sergeant King yet?'

'Sergeant *Farrier* King? Yes, I wanted to see you about him. I'm not altogether happy with his approach to our work.'

Lovelace grinned. 'A bit too self-possessed for a common sergeant, eh?'

'No, no, it's not just that. He seems to think the main objective of the team is to map the interior of the subcontinent. I tried to explain to him that our primary role is to gather intelligence, but he wouldn't have it. You're right, he is a bit too arrogant for my liking. Who does the man think he is? He's only a sergeant, for heaven's sake – a blacksmith's son. Not that his father's trade has any relevance, but damn it, I am his commanding officer.'

'Only a sergeant? I seemed to remember someone who thought that being a sergeant was highly significant. Anyway, I didn't say he was arrogant, I said self-possessed. Well, he's all you've got. I think he has the makings of a fine spy. Let him think that he's in it for the mapmaking, which he *is* to a certain extent. Lead him into the water gently or he'll shy away from it, Jack. We need men like him who have a trained eye for the landscape. There'll come a time when we have to send men into unknown territories and let them fend for themselves. A soldier who can find his way in a strange country by his recognition and use of physical geography will be an asset. Colonel Hawke is very impressed with him.'

Crossman could see he was going to get nowhere by complaining about King.

'Well, I just thought I'd register my misgivings.'

'Which you've done. Now, you're all set for shipping out are you? Good.' He leaned forward. 'There's some very strange things going on in India at the moment, especially in the Bengal army. Some talk about chapatties.'

'What's a chapatty?'

'Oh, a pancake of coarse flour – unleavened bread, if you like. Watchmen and other local officials have been baking four or five and passing them on to others in the next village. It's a very peculiar affair, but it's almost like a signal. Some think it's just some sort of religious rite, but, if that's true, why has no one heard about it or seen it happen before? We've been in India a long time now and no one has heard of anything like it.'

'By no one, you mean Europeans?'

'Yes I do. Europeans, of course. It could be nothing. I mean, it does seem a little ridiculous to be concerned about natives giving each other presents of bread. I laughed when I first heard it and I'm surprised you're not laughing now. But returned officers to Britain are treating it as quite sinister.'

'Don't you think,' said Crossman, 'that they might have been out there too long? A touch of the sun? Malaria? That sort of thing?'

Lovelace relaxed a little and shrugged. 'You could be right. That's what we're supposed to find out.' He signalled a waiter who nodded and left the room. 'Here, I've brought *you* a present. Another wedding gift, if you like, but for you alone. Your wife would not appreciate it.'

'Oh, really?' Crossman said, perking up. 'Something special?'

'Indeed.'

The waiter brought a smallish parcel, which Crossman immediately unwrapped. When the brown paper was peeled back there nestled a revolver, like a bird in the folds of a soft cloth. Crossman did not take it out of its wrapping, since waving it about might have created alarm amongst the club's staff, but he admired it with great pleasure.

'A Tranter five-shot!' he said. 'Thank you, Nathan.'

'To replace the one you lost in the Crimea.'

'Yes, of course. I appreciate it, very much. With this,' Crossman waved his wooden hand, 'a revolver will have to be my main weapon. This one is perfect, with its cocking trigger as well as its firing trigger. All I need to do now is to learn to load it with my teeth.'

'You can always get someone to assist you with that and you know it.'

'No, no, I'm not being sarcastic – I really mean it – I shall learn to load it with my teeth.'

Lovelace shrugged again. 'As you wish . . .'

Crossman rewrapped the gift and then leaned over to whisper something to Nathan Lovelace.

'Do you know that man at the third card table? The one dressed in grey and with the pomaded hair? He's been staring right into my face all evening.'

Lovelace left it a little while then casually glanced round as if looking for a waiter.

He turned back to Crossman. 'Yes, I do. His name is Gilbert St James Hadrow. His father is a duke. Why would he stare at you? Do you know the family?'

'Not at all,' replied Crossman, grimly, 'but I know now why he's cutting into me like a blade. Thank you, Nathan.'

'Do I get to know the secret?'

'No, it's very personal.'

'All right then, I shan't ask. Now, about the arrangements for travel . . .'

They talked for about an hour at the end of which Crossman rose and bade the field officer good night.

'I shall see you in India then,' said Lovelace, shaking his hand, 'at a later date.'

'Yes, sir. I shall look forward to our meeting.'

'Good luck, Jack.'

'Thank you, sir.'

Crossman left the club with his parcel under his arm and went out into the night. It was even colder than when he had first set out and he shrank inside his topcoat. There was only a single four-wheeled growler outside the club, which was quickly grabbed by three older men who were leaving the club, so Crossman set out on foot.

Oh how he longed for the warmth of India. It would be a good day when the first rays of the southern sun fell on the deck of the clipper. To have Africa on his left side and the open sea ahead of him would be glorious. With these sunny thoughts in his mind he trudged through the dimly-lit capital, heading for his home in Knightsbridge.

It was only when he turned down a narrow cobbled street full of bookshops, all closed of course, that he realized he was being followed. Turning, he saw three men at the far end of the road. They stopped when they saw him turn. Another walker came into view, but passed by the end of the street, clearly nothing to do with the three who seemed to be tailing him. Crossman continued on his way, conscious that the footsteps behind him had quickened. Inside the deep right-hand pocket of his topcoat Crossman surreptitiously tore away the wrapping of Lovelace's gift.

In the next street a woman stood like a frozen shadow in a doorway. She murmured something to him as he passed, but Crossman ignored the offer. Afterwards he mentally kicked himself, thinking he could have gone into the house with her, and sorted out any misunderstandings later. Then he suddenly found himself on a broad carriageway with a large park on the opposite side of the road. He crossed quickly and ducked into the bushes on the edge of the park, waiting there for a while.

His pursuers did not appear and Crossman began to think they had given up their prey and had gone back to White's or somewhere else.

However, when he emerged from the darkness of the shrubbery, they were still there. They had pulled up some stout wooden stakes which had no doubt been supporting young trees on the periphery of the park, and were grasping them like cudgels. One of their number stepped forward and spoke.

'You know me?' asked the man.

'I've heard your name,' admitted Crossman, 'but until this evening I could not put a face to it, Hadrow.'

'I'm not going to wait on you with a blade in my hand on some misty common at six in the morning,' stated Hadrow. 'I'd rather get it over with now. I don't duel with commoners. I horsewhip them. Or thrash them with some instrument more fitting to their station.'

He smacked the club into his hand to emphasize his point.

'And you plan to do that now?'

'Beat you to a pulp, so that you keep your distance in future.'

'Rather ungentlemanly.'

Hadrow smiled. 'My friends and I are not concerned with niceties when it comes to scum. We like to enjoy our evenings at the club without looking over our shoulders to find riff-raff like you waiting to pounce. I imagine after the beating you are going to receive now that you'll stay away, Fancy Jack. I cannot for a moment think why Jane Mulinder should marry a common guttersnipe, even if she does have a faint whiff of the shop about her, but then she probably had little choice. I doubt anyone in my circle would offer for her *now*, if you get my meaning.'

Crossman almost choked with fury inside on hearing these remarks, which had been delivered with an appropriate sneer. He wanted to snarl into Hadrow's face that he was trashing the name of a far better person than he would ever be and that he was going to cut his heart out for the insult. He wanted to kill the man where he stood. Jane was his wife and someone he admired as well as loved. How *dare* this filthy braggart make such inferences! How dare he! And did it matter that her father had made most of his money through trade? But if the Crimean War had instilled one thing in Crossman it was that the man who is cool under fire is the man most likely to walk away. To lose one's temper – to be *seen* to lose one's temper – put one at an enormous disadvantage. He remained outwardly calm.

'Ah, the Fancy Jack epithet. You *do* know who I am? I was beginning to hope it was all a ghastly mistake and that you'd got the wrong man.'

'Oh I know all about you, Sergeant. Sorry, *Lieutenant*. Do you think your promotion entitles you to mix with real gentlemen?'

'As it happens, my family name is as good as your own, but I'm not going to spoil this fight by telling you what it is.'

'I know what it is. Crossman.'

'That's a pseudonym, Hadrow, but never mind.'

The smaller of Hadrow's companions stepped forward, wielding the stake in his hand. 'Come on, St James, let's get this over with.'

Crossman drew the Tranter from his pocket and pointed it directly at the approaching man.

'One step further and I'll blow your face off, you snot-nosed excuse for a gentleman.'

Crossman held the unloaded revolver steady, his arm level, not a sign of a tremble. The young man stopped and took a quick glance at his leader. Hadrow was staring at the gun, biting his lip a little in thought. Finally he shook his head at his hesitating comrade. Clearly none of the trio were armed themselves or perhaps they might have confronted him. They turned to leave without another word, but Crossman was having none of it.

'Stay just where you are,' he warned, 'or I *will* shoot.'

Hadrow turned back and stared at him.

'You couldn't kill all three of us,' he said, 'and if you only shot one, why you'd hang for murder, man, and you know it. Then where would your little wife be? A widow trying to live on a lieutenant's pension? No, you won't shoot anyone, Crossman.'

'Oh, he will if I tell him to,' said a voice from the shadows, 'and of course I shall bear witness that Lieutenant Crossman was with me the whole evening. We walked back to my rooms together, then had a few drinks. The one of you that might live, for from what I recall from our experiences in the Crimea, Fancy Jack could certainly fell two running men even in the dark, would have our word against his. That is, if he lived long enough to testify. I think Jack and I have killed enough men between us now to consider it a simple act of revenge. You gentlemen have chosen the wrong men for your enemies. We are natural killers, Fancy Jack and me.'

The speaker inhaled on his cigar which made the end glow enough to reveal his features.

'Lovelace!' Hadrow's voice quivered. 'This is none of your affair.'

There was genuine fear and alarm on the faces of the other two men, both of whom had taken a step or two back, as if divorcing themselves from Gilbert Hadrow's friendship.

'Oh, but it is. Jack Crossman and I are great friends. You see he really *is* going under an assumed name. His father is a baronet. We went to Harrow together, Jack and me. So it really is my affair too. Old school chums and all that. You understand.'

Hadrow tried not to look impressed.

'So, where does that leave us now?' he sniffed. 'If you think I'm standing here in the cold for very much longer, you're both mistaken.'

Crossman said, 'I would like personal satisfaction, if you don't mind.'

'We have no weapons,' Hadrow pointed out, tossing the cudgel into the bushes. 'At least, not appropriate ones. I carry no pistol and neither of us is wearing a sword.'

'Fists will do,' replied Crossman. 'Come on! Let's get to it, before we both freeze to death.'

Hadrow's two companions looked decidedly relieved. They had already shed their makeshift weapons and were stamping their feet and clapping their gloved hands to keep warm. Hadrow removed his topcoat and carefully folded it before handing it to one of his friends. Lovelace dutifully followed his lead and came forward and took the revolver from Crossman's hand. He also took Crossman's topcoat and draped it over his arm, before patting his comrade-in-arms on the back and standing aside.

Hadrow then came forward. He had obviously received boxing lessons, for his stance was quite professional. Indeed he jabbed Crossman in the face twice before Crossman struck him on the shoulder with a hard right. There followed a flurry of punches from Hadrow, who had clearly been taught to fell his man early in the fight, thus helping to preserve his good looks from a long and constant battering. Crossman evaded most of these punches, catching just a single one on the chin which made his eyes water.

Finally the lieutenant saw the opening he had been waiting for. He stepped forward and struck his opponent full on the bridge of the nose with a half-clenched left fist. The sound was quite astonishing to the listening ears. It was a solid *clunk* followed by the ugly noise of cracking bone. Hadrow's nose was splayed over his face and pouring claret on to the good earth of Hyde Park. Crossman followed up with a second left, which thudded into the same Hadrow feature. This time the duke's son screamed in pain. A third solid crunch laid the man out. He fell backwards like a felled tree on to the hard ground, his blood spattering the white snow.

There he lay, out cold.

'When he wakes,' said Crossman to Hadrow's companions, 'tell him to stay well out of my way in future. I promised my wife I would not blow out his brains, or run him through with a blade, but if he continues to seek me out I shall certainly do one or the other. Is that comprehended?'

Two dumb nodding heads assured him that he was understood.

The way in which Crossman was helped into his coat might have indicated the reason for his swift victory, if the other two men had been paying much attention. As it was they were too busy ministering to their unconscious friend. Lovelace slipped the Tranter back into Crossman's pocket and the pair walked off arm in arm, southwards.

'That wasn't really fair, Jack,' said Lovelace, laughing softly. 'You might have warned him.'

'That I have a fist of solid oak? Not on your life. Besides,' he rubbed his left wrist, 'that jolly well hurt my stump, I can tell you. I shall need some extra cream on it tonight.'

'If I were you, old son, I shouldn't waste a lot of time getting down to Southampton. Hadrow's father is very influential, as most of our dukes still are. If you were French of course, post revolution, you'd be a hero. But our nobles retain their power and are not to be trifled with. Gather up Gwilliams and King and take the train to lower climes.'

'What about you?'

'Oh, I'm not hanging around either. I'm due in Sheffield tomorrow. Sheffield isn't a place haunted by dukes. Good night, Jack.'

'Good night, Nathan.'

They parted on an appropriate corner.

25

'Captain Percival Deighnton,' said the officer, standing over Jack and looking down on him. 'You are Lieutenant Jack Crossman?'

The man's expression and demeanour told Jack this was not a friendly visit. He looked at the captain, trying to place him somewhere in his past. The Crimea? Possibly. Not before that. Before the Crimea, Jack had been a common private and privates in regiments of foot are creatures too low to arouse the antagonism of cavalry officers. In London then, during his short stay there? Again, possibly. White's. Had he seen this man at White's?

The officer put Jack straight. 'Gilbert St James Hadrow is a particular friend of mine.'

'Oh,' muttered Jack, wearily. 'A vigilante.'

'What did you say, sir?' barked Deighnton. 'Stand up, sir.'

Jack stared mildly up at the face above him.

'Go to hell – sir.'

'You attacked and insulted my friend,' spluttered the captain. 'It must not go unpunished. If you please . . .'

'Damn you,' cried Jack, rising now, 'you have no idea what you're talking about. This is an affair over a lady, sir. I will not discuss it further. It is private business and Hadrow must answer for it himself. I promised the lady in question I would not cause her a fuss. And I did not. That peacock you call a friend challenged *me*. Not I him. Go and bother him, *if you please*, and leave me to my thoughts and my pipe. I have no time for officers like you.' Jack was thoroughly incensed now, at having to speak of matters pertaining to his wife.

He flicked the captain's collar, 'Primped up like some prize turkey. Go away before I forget my manners.'

'You *have* forgotten your manners, sir.' The officer's hand was on the hilt of his sword. How he managed to look so immaculate in a place where the dirt crawled up one's legs Jack had no idea. 'I shall have satisfaction when this war is over, let me assure you of that. That is all I have to say, Lieutenant. Look to yourself, once we are back. I shall be there, waiting. This is no longer to do with Hadrow, this is between you and me . . .'

'I'm not fighting some pompous ass just because he feels affronted when I won't discuss my private business with him, you can be sure of that. If you feel the need to cross swords with someone, go and look for another ass like yourself. I have no quarrel with you. And I absolutely refuse to let you quarrel with me. Good God man, have you nothing better to do? Get married and start a family. Take up cards or croquet. Ride to the hounds. Anything, but leave me alone. You have far too much time on your hands, sir, if you need to fill it with trumped-up duels. Go away.'

Deighnton stared at him for a full minute before turning on his heel and marching off into the night. Jack knew he had made another enemy, but where did these people come from? They had not the sense they were born with: somewhere between childhood and manhood their strength of reasoning slipped away from them, leaving their heads empty. He was quite willing to fight Hadrow, who had wronged his wife Jane, but not at all happy about fighting this Deighnton, who had nothing to recommend him except his friendship with Hadrow. Surely Jack was not expected to fight the whole bunch of them? Hadrow, having a rich and powerful father, probably had a hundred such friends. It was too much. Just too much.

He lit his pipe again and puffed his indignant way through a whole bowl of tobacco in less than two minutes.

26

Many soldiers on the Ridge, including Jack Crossman, were becoming increasingly frustrated by General Wilson. It seemed to Jack and the others that Wilson was indecisive. Nicholson wanted to attack Delhi and so did his compatriots. The problem was that General Wilson would take the responsibility and blame for that attack, should it go wrong. So he dithered, as many would, and failed to come to a conclusion. Finally, however, the pressure became too great and he simply had to agree to an assault. Conditions on the Ridge were deteriorating by the day, his subordinates were straining at the leash, and the word was that his superiors in safer places were crying out for him to settle the business. Even Baird Smith, his chief engineer, urged him to assault the city as soon as possible.

Baird Smith drew up a plan, based on the intelligence gathered by Hodson's and Hawke's men, which of course included Crossman, King and Gwilliams. The scheme was to breach the walls of the city with batteries of artillery and the use of mines. King drew great satisfaction from the idea that it was his report which had provided the weak point of entry.

'Where else would they have got their information from?' he said excitedly to Crossman. 'We were the ones, I'm sure of it.'

The lieutenant saw no point in discouraging this thinking in his sergeant: the venture had indeed been risky and there was no reason to suppose the report was not theirs.

King, being in the engineers though not of them, helped to bring the first heavy battery into position. Many bullocks were used, and camels, to carry stores as well as drag guns. Those on the walls of the city did not allow all this work to go unpunished. They showered the working parties with canister and grape shot, causing many casualties. By the morning of the eighth of September the battery was in position.

That day the engineers had their revenge on the rebel guns situated over the gates and on the walls of the city. The Mori Bastion, which had been the source of the withering fire power during the night, was destroyed by five guns and a howitzer. Shot was poured into the Kashmir bastion, causing great damage and consternation amongst rebel gun crews.

Greatly encouraged by this, the British now went about establishing a second battery, which began to smash at the bastions and walls. Finally these guns actually breached the walls. Engineers and sappers moved steadily forward and established a third battery less than 200 yards from Delhi's Water Bastion, from behind the Old Custom House. A mortar battery was sited. Those in the city did not allow all this work to go without reprisals and many soldiers on the British side died under fire. Crossman noted that a good proportion of these were Indian troops: pioneers who had remained loyal to the British armies. When one or more of their Indian comrades were killed, they would stop work to retrieve their bodies. They would grieve over them for a few moments, then would throw themselves back into their toil.

'These people,' said Crossman to Gwilliams, 'are among the bravest soldiers I've ever seen.'

'You won't get any argument from me,' replied the corporal.

In the afternoon, King returned. He had been in the thick of it, but had survived the blizzard of iron. There was no elation in him. He seemed sick and weary of it all. The deaths had taken its toll on his spirit.

'When you're out there,' he told the other two, 'it seems as if *everyone* is going to die. Men were dropping right, left and centre, blood and limbs everywhere. Look at my uniform – gore dripping from the buttons. Not mine. Someone else's. I wanted to scream *stop* at one point. Just stop. So that we could all gather our breath and spend a moment in silent prayer, before carrying on. Of course I didn't, and nothing would have happened if I had, but the relentlessness of it all gets to the very roots of your soul and you reach the

275

point were you can't stand it another second. I'm not going out there again. I've had it. You can put me up against a wall and shoot me. I'd prefer not to go, you see, and witness that carnage any more.'

Of course, Crossman did not force his sergeant to return to the task that day, nor on the subsequent days. In any case there was little work for engineers once the guns were in place. The cannons pounded Delhi with unceasing force. Bricks and mortar had showered through the several days of the barrage, holes had appeared in the walls, the air was choked with building dust. Men and women on the Ridge could not help but derive satisfaction from the destruction. The walls were tumbling down and the rebels exposed to attack. Soon the British infantry would go into the streets of Delhi and the desperate fight for the survival of one army over the other would begin. So far it had been a war of big guns, but it was the foot soldier with his firelock who would decide who was to come away victorious.

Five columns were formed, weak in numbers – in all 3,000 soldiers not including reserves – as many men had been lost in the siting of the guns. Crossman and Gwilliams were among these few. They joined the 4th Sikhs, in the second column, under a Brigadier Jones. It was an arbitrary choice. They might have asked to go any-where, from the Guides to the Bengal Fusiliers to the Punjab Infantry. The 4th Sikhs was as good a regiment as any other if you were an outsider with no loyalty to a particular regiment. With them in the same column was the 8th Foot, a sturdy regiment. Then came the third column which included the Kumaon Battalion, under Colonel Campbell. Not the same Campbell under whom Jack had served in the Crimea, the 'thin red line' Campbell, but another. Then came the fourth and fifth columns. Brigadier Nicholson, the overall com-mander, was leading the first column.

As it happened, King was sick with dysentery and unable to join them, but whether the sergeant would have gone anyway was a moot point. Jack was glad he had not had to order his presence. Sergeant King was a small thorn in the lieutenant's side, it was true. King had gone more than willingly with the engineers, had worked heroically under intense fire, and indeed had carried out his duties impeccably. But still one could not allow one's NCO to dictate when and where he would go into battle. If one was ordered to go, one went, whether one had got out of bed that day feeling like it or not. Jack hoped King would not put him to the test in the future. The sergeant could not win such a contest. Men had tried to take on the army before now, and had *always* lost.

Weakly, from his bed, King called to Crossman as they parted, 'Look to Sajan, sir – don't let them kill him.'

'I'll do my best.'

'I have to find him,' muttered the sergeant, somewhat enigmatically. 'He's my own flesh and blood.'

Jack was somewhat puzzled by this parting sentence, but he had no time to question the sergeant further, and put it down to delirium.

Just before sunset on the evening of the assault, in that enchanting hour known as *hawa khana*, Crossman and Gwilliams had crept up to the third battery and had viewed the ground before them. This was the area over which the attack would take place. It looked very exposed. No doubt those in the city were ready with itching fingers to fire upon their attackers: they obviously knew what was coming and also knew their lives would be forfeit should they fail to prevent the storming of their fortifications.

'This is goin' to be one hell of a fight,' muttered Gwilliams. 'How many in there, you say?'

'Estimates are around forty thousand rebels, but I'm sure a few ordinary citizens might join in if it goes against us.'

'Ten to one. Pretty good odds, I'd say.'

'You don't even need to be here, Corporal. You could be in some cabin out in the backwoods of Oregon or Quebec or whatever. You're a North American.'

Gwilliams shrugged and stroked his auburn beard. 'Man gets washed up on beaches he never heard of,' he said, 'among people he never thought he'd talk with. Who knows how it happens?'

'You sure you're not running from a rope?' asked Crossman, who had long thought that Gwilliams was probably a fugitive. 'You can tell me now. You'll probably be dead in the morning.'

'Cheerful bastard, ain't you, sir? Well, I guess I'm goin' to have to stay a puzzle to you. I ain't about to reveal secrets now on account of how I usually come out of these things with a whole skin. If you think I can't go back home 'cause I'm some kind of malefactor, you could be right. Then again, it could be I'm just the roving kind, happy to find my adventures where they lay. I'm a blamed mystery to myself, let alone to my officer. Here I am, a good republican,

277

fightin' for an imperial cause. You couldn't get more contrary if you tried, now could you, sir?'

Crossman grinned at this.

He said, 'What makes you think North Americans are not imperialists? Just because you've formed your own governments? There were people there before you arrived, Gwilliams.'

'Don't get me arguing with you on politics. I've read every man from Plato to Machiavelli and I'll make mincemeat of you, sir.'

You could not help but shake your head at Gwilliams and wonder if he was some kind of throwback from Xenophon's army of Ten Thousand, who wandered Asia Minor in the days of Ancient Greece. He was flotsam and jetsam. He was driftwood. Jack had not wanted him in the beginning, Gwilliams being one of Major Lovelace's discoveries, but now he was quite glad of the man.

The pair went back to load their weapons and fill their flasks. Crossman noted with a nervous memory-reflex that ladders were being prepared. It recalled for him how he had lost his hand when storming the Redan outside Sebastopol. Both he and Gwilliams wound turbans around their heads, hoping the thick cloth might protect them from a sword stroke. Jack fitted his mechanical hand, in which he hoped to grasp a dagger. In the still air, from various corners of the Ridge, came the sound of ramrods scraping down barrels, or the testing of hammers after being oiled. Low murmurs were drifting back and forth: men leaving instructions with their friends, should they fall in the battle. Somewhere a fife was playing a lament: a Celtic tune by the sound of it, but it might well have been Old English.

To Jack's surprise and under Gwilliams' silent disapproval, the lieutenant was visited by Geraldine Stanton.

'I wanted to wish you God speed, Lieutenant,' she said, standing on the far side of the fire from him, so that they looked at each over the flames. 'May you return safely.'

'Thank you, Miss Stanton. I shall endeavour to do so . . .'

'. . . for the sake of his wife,' interrupted Gwilliams, quietly.

'I am aware the lieutenant is married, but these are unusual times, Corporal,' came the tart reply. 'One is permitted to wish a friend well – Lieutenant Crossman has shown himself to be such.'

Geraldine departed without waiting to hear any reply. Gwilliams grunted and went back to cleaning his carbine. Jack did not admonish Gwilliams. He might have done, but something held him back.

At midnight they received their orders: any man who fell was to be left where he lay; there was to be no looting; the men were to do their utmost not to harm women and children. After these instructions the British were visited by one or two churchmen, to offer prayers for the battle. Among them Jack noticed the Methodist minister Reverend Stillwell, who asked God to give his side in the war a great victory. Since the rebel priests were probably doing much the same thing, Jack thought, God and gods had a dilemma.

On September fourteenth, just before cock crow, the storming of the city of Delhi began. General Nicholson led the 60th Rifles up the glacis before the damaged walls. Seconds later Crossman and Gwilliams were sweeping forward with the second column towards the Water Bastion. Once more Jack found himself in a plague of flying locusts, which hummed and whirred around him. Soldiers were going down all along the line. On the fortifications the rebels were shrieking curses, daring the attackers to take them on. They did. Despite the fallen, they rushed forward, their own yells penetrating the shocked dawn. Both the leading columns now poured into the area between the Kashmir Gate and the church, elated by their early success. Indian and British sappers with explosives moved forward, placed their charges, blew the gate. A bugle sounded, commanders were crying, 'Charge!' and waving their swords, urging their men forward.

Through the gaps went the columns.

The enemy was thick upon the ground. Jack's sword arm went left and right, hewing a path through the screaming rebels. The faces before him were twisted into gargoyles of malice. There was fury in the expressions of his enemies and fierce hatred in the eyes of his friends. No quarter was to be given here. Too much had happened between the warring parties. Terrible deeds on both sides, which only the letting of more blood would settle.

A shot hummed by Crossman's ear. Sheathing his sword he took out his revolver, firing into the wall of men before him, but soon the firearm was empty. He stuck it in a pocket and drew his sword again. A wave of sepoys came forward, only to be beaten back by the British.

Grunts and yells as men exerted themselves at close quarter fighting. They were nose to nose now, breath to breath. Shrieks as men were wounded, some mortally. It was a heaving mass of struggling warriors, arms and legs entangled, heads butted. A great snarling knot of desperate men which moved one way and then the other, like a mindless but single living entity. Walls and buildings hemmed in the battle, contained it, held it knotted together. Then the edges began to fray and pieces broke away, as sepoys on the fringe gave up the present fight and sought refuge in the radiating streets and alleys. Some went up on the rooftops and began firing down into the writhing mass, careless of hitting friend as well as foe. Others appeared at windows only to be blown away. By now the two armies were so intermingled it was impossible to use firearms without endangering one's own. Yet the matchlocks and handguns continued to crack.

A pistol went off near Crossman's ear, deafening him. When his hearing returned the sound of clashing blades was tremendous. The first waves of frenzy gradually subsided into a determined vehemence on both sides. Crossman cut a man across the shoulder in front of him. The sepoy went down, yelling curses in his face. As he sank to the floor his victim buried his teeth into Crossman's knee and a wave of pain washed up. Crossman stabbed him in the neck with horrible ferocity. The pain abated but the biter had gone through his trousers, taken flesh, and had exposed the cartilage. Then someone took hold of the lieutenant's dagger hand and wrenched hard, trying to break the wrist. His attacker was more surprised than him when the hand came away, the straps cutting into the lieutenant's shoulder before they snapped under the fearsome tugging. Crossman sliced with his sword again, missing this time, the sepoy squeezing away through the mass triumphantly waving a metal fist holding a dagger.

A Sikh soldier went down under a sepoy's tulwar to the right of Jack. He tried to punish the aggressor, but his elbow was knocked and the blade swished over the rebel's head. Jack let out a yell of frustration. The sepoy gave him a wicked grin and melted away. Over a sea of bare and turbaned heads, Jack saw the same rebel strike a British soldier on the head, splitting his forage cap in two. Men were going down on both sides. It was impossible to gauge the numbers. The British columns could not afford to trade man for man, being outnumbered at least ten to one. Yet it seemed that for every Bengali who went down one of the assault force followed him.

'I hope they're running at the back,' Crossman muttered through gritted teeth. 'That's our only chance.'

280

'You all right, sir?'

Gwilliams was by his side.

'Yes – how about you?'

'Pricked me in the arm, but I killed him dead. I don't mind shooting a few of these bastards. I don't mind at all.'

They stood shoulder to shoulder, the pair of them, and hacked their way through the volcanic mob. They were stepping on bodies now: friend or enemy? Who knew? There was no time for fear. This was not the same as walking across a killing ground through a storm of musket balls and grapeshot. In that situation there was time to reflect, space in which to turn and run if the fear became over-whelming. Here one was hemmed in by sword-wielding fanatics, by sheer grappling numbers. Muskets, elbows, knees, heads, all dug into Crossman's ribs and back. Some men were pressed so close to their enemy that they could do nothing but stare hatred into each other's eyes, their arms pinned to their sides, their hot stinking breath going up each other's nostrils. They remained so until the pressure was relieved: then the first man up with his weapon won the right to live.

When Crossman looked back, once, he saw that the British cavalry were engaged outside the walls, charging into the mutineers that had poured from the city to attack the camp to the column's rear. Guns were blasting into mutineers who were taking their toll on the British. Men were dying on both sides, though it was still impossible to tell who was winning.

Cannons were firing grapeshot along the streets now, shredding British soldiers who chased running foe. Heavy fire came from the houses, raining on the assault force as they tried to establish them-selves in the streets. The bastions had to be taken. To reach the bastions they had to go through avenues of fire, enfilading fire, coming from the ends of streets, from the rooftops and from the windows and doorways. Gradually, however, the attackers gained control of certain streets. Units were posted at each end to protect them. The rebels began to retire behind sandbagged positions: mosques and other buildings which had been bricked up and were defended by artillery. After several hours an impasse had been reached, though it appeared the British were not in the best of positions.

Jack heard that General Nicholson had fallen, leading his troops down a street beyond the Kabul Gate. The rumour was that he had been cut down by grapeshot. The wounds were said to be fatal. He had been at the head of the 1st Fusiliers and attempting an impossible charge down a road covered by the brass cannons of the enemy, along a street where every parapet, window and rooftop bristled with enemy muskets. The charge had failed and the British lost eight officers and fifty men in the attempt.

A period of relative quiet ensued. Crossman and his comrades dug in and held the ground they had gained. They were there the whole next day, when they were ordered to smash hundreds of bottles of brandy and wine in case the British troops were tempted to drink it. Of course the beleaguered soldiers were tempted: the majority of them considered it a crying shame to destroy the liberated liquor. But under duress they followed General Wilson's orders. The streets now ran, not with blood, but with alcohol, a liquid *some* of them considered more precious than blood.

Five days later the troops were still annoyed at the destruction of their spoils, and some had refused to advance further into the city, but eventually their officers regained control. They went deeper inside. One by one the bastions began to fall. Rebels fled the city in great numbers. It was part of the British strategy. Nicholson had ensured there was an escape route over a bridge of boats for the enemy to retreat, so that the mutineers with their vast numbers were not forced to fight to the death. The general had wanted no Pyrrhic victory. The streets were still very dangerous, with gangs of mutineers still lodged in alleys and cul-de-sacs, but after another two days the city was formally in the hands of the assault forces.

The old Mughal king surrendered to Major Hodson on the promise that his life would be spared. His three grown sons were tracked to Humayun's tomb, where they were hiding, and Jack heard that Hodson had executed them without orders or instructions from his superiors, on the pretext that he was being attacked by a mob who wished to free them.

Crossman and Gwilliams relaxed. Their uniforms stiff with dried sweat, yet wet again with more sweat under the armpits, they slept with their dirt on them. They were sitting with their backs to the walls of the great palace when Sergeant King found them, snoring gently. He woke them, gave them some water, and asked them how it had been.

'Bloody,' replied Gwilliams. 'Bloody as hell.'

'Well, we beat them,' King said, defensively. 'I've been doing my share of the fighting too, on the other flank. It had to be every man in there and I'm sorry I wasn't with you two.' He looked around him. 'A lot of men have died. Over a thousand lost.'

'Just that?' said Crossman, surprised. 'I would have said more.'

'I don't think so. Those are the numbers they're giving out. Brigadier-General Nicholson's dying. I suppose you heard that. Might even be dead by now, for all I know. He was a hard man, wasn't he? But he got us our victory.'

Crossman answered this with, 'Here – but what about Lucknow and Cawnpore? There are still armies of them out there. We're not out of it yet, Sergeant.'

'No, but a victory of this size will hurt them, won't it?'

'Yes – yes it will, I suppose.'

King cleared his throat. 'Have – have you found Raktambar – or Sajan?'

'Nope,' replied Gwilliams. 'Not yet. Raktambar'll find us, when he wants to. If'n he didn't get killed in the attack. Who knows, mebbe we'll find him face down in some back street yet? As to the boy, forget him. He's lost to us. You know how many boys there are in this city? And who knows he didn't go with them mutineers, out the back door? You can kiss your sun compass goodbye, Sarge. You ain't seeing that again.'

'You think I'm worried about the bloody compass?' cried King, furiously. 'I want to find the boy. I don't give a dog's shit about the compass.'

The other two men were astonished by the ferocity of the sergeant's reply and stared at him in surprise.

King looked at them, his eyes filling with tears.

'He's my son,' he said. 'My own son.'

'Jesus Christ in heaven,' cried Gwilliams, and looked away from the weeping man.

Crossman was silent for a few minutes, then he asked in a very quiet but firm tone, 'Do you mind telling me how you know this?'

'You can see he's an Anglo-Indian,' cried the sergeant. 'Look at the colour of his skin.'

'Perhaps. I'm not so sure. But even if he is?'

'I told you I was in India at seventeen. I met a girl – an Indian girl – in that village we camped in, near the rajah's hunting lodge. We –

283

we made love. Three months later I had to march away from her. She told me she was having our baby. I – I tried to take her with me, but they wouldn't let me. I was only seventeen. I hadn't a man's authority. She didn't try to follow – at least, I don't think so.' King's expression hardened. 'That boy is mine. You can see it in him. He looks a lot like me, doesn't he?'

'Nope,' replied Gwilliams, bluntly. 'He don't.'

'He does, you damned liar. He's my boy. Anyone can see that.'

Again Crossman tried reason. 'I was the one who found the boy, waving a fan in the rajah's lodge. He was a slave. He could have come from *anywhere*, King. The chances of me walking into camp with your son, out of all the children in this vast land, are infinite. In any case, I don't think he has British blood in him. His paleness is prison pallor – he's been a punkah-wallah since he was old enough to hold a piece of string. In a dark cool bedroom, out of the glare of the sun. Sajan worked indoors his whole life, until I found him, that's why he's light skinned.'

'Crazy,' Gwilliams muttered. 'Plain crazy.'

'I am not mad,' cried King, the hotness coming to his eyes again. 'I *know* he's my son. I can feel it. Who's to say he's not?'

'Who's to say he is? Chances are he's a waif and stray from some other corner of India,' replied Gwilliams. 'This country is comin' apart at the seams with damn orphans. Your boy, if he lived that is, might be somewhere around, but who the hell knows where? In any event, Sergeant,' said Gwilliams with cruel logic, 'how'd'you know your little Indian sweetheart didn't give birth to a girl baby? Answer me that one.'

'I prefer to believe Sajan is my son,' answered King, stiffly, 'and I won't hear arguments otherwise.'

Gwilliams shrugged and Crossman thought it was time to let matters alone. If Sergeant King had decided the boy was his son, then what harm could it do? As Gwilliams had said, the baby could have been a girl. King had not been there at the birth. Or she could have lost the infant in childbirth: that happened a great deal, everywhere in world. More than likely she had been punished by her family, once they found she was pregnant, perhaps even forfeiting her life. Anything could have happened. Anything. So, if King wanted a son that much, why not let him have one. Except that Sajan was still missing and would probably remain so, making the whole argument an academic one.

In fact, they had no time to search for either Ishwar Raktambar or Sajan. The whole population of Delhi was driven out into the countryside and there were rumours that the city would be razed to the ground. Certainly, to Crossman's disgust, the local vultures had gone in and were rooting through the houses for valuables. Peasants who had nothing and wanted everything, and who could blame them? He could not find Colonel Hawke but he asked Major Lovelace whether it could be stopped.

'We have very little authority here, Jack. We're Queen's army and we're not even attached to a regiment. Things will change soon, though, it's it the wind. This uprising has sealed the fate of John Company.'

So Jack and the others had to watch as more crimes were piled on top of those already committed. Sepoys and civilians captives were tried by courts martial and most sentenced to death, with scant attention to evidence. It was a time not for justice but for revenge. You could not restrain men whose wives and children had been chopped to pieces. Bloody madness ruled in both camps, though Crossman felt those on his side should have been acting under more civilized rules.

Soon, however, regiments were reformed and on the march again, heading towards Agra to relieve that city. Brigadier Greathed left Delhi on the twenty-fourth of September and marched towards Agra with weary battle-stained troops: a remarkable achievement considering the same men had fought a huge battle and an urban street fight only a few days before.

Crossman and his men did not join the column to Agra. They had been ordered north again, back to the Punjab, the land of the five rivers. Akbar Khan had kept his promise, but some of the smaller tribes were getting restless and threatening to band together to attack Peshawar while the British and Punjabi troops were occupied in Bengal. Colonel Hawke had granted Crossman time though to search for Ishwar Raktambar, seeing that the Rajput had been a gift from a powerful maharajah.

'By the way, Lieutenant,' the colonel had said, 'well done. I hear you fought well in the battle. Your father will be proud of you.'

Jack had winced at that remark. The last thing he wanted in life was his father's approval. If his deeds warranted that, then they were wrong. Hawke's remark just about summed up the whole war for him. They were actions which his father would have relished. Putting down the native when he got too uppity. Yes, Major Kirk would have approved of that.

One evening Fancy Jack Crossman, who was feeling anything but 'fancy' after the embittered battle for Delhi, returned to the Ridge. He knew it was foolish of him but he found himself thinking of Geraldine Stanton. The pretty young woman was not his responsibility and it was dangerous to seek out someone to whom he found himself attracted. He kept telling himself he only wished to discover whether she was in good safe hands. It was a very stupid exercise in any case, for most of the non-Indian civilians had long since moved off the Ridge and were under army protection elsewhere.

Luckily, he did not find her amongst the ruins of the old cantonment, but he did see someone else camped in the shadows of a wall. The man had not noticed Jack approaching and the lieutenant walked carefully through the rubble, so as not to disturb anything and cause a noise. It had not been an hallucination that night down by the canal. It had not been a figment of a fevered brain. Here was the assassin, large as life.

Jack crept up behind Arihant and placed the muzzle of his revolver against the back of the assassin's neck.

'Do not move one inch,' Crossman warned. 'Or I *shall* shoot you in the head, do you understand?'

The man went stiff. 'I understand.'

'Place your hands, palms first, against the wall.'

Arihant did as he was told.

'Now, sir, what are you doing here?'

'Oh,' the tone was light and airy, 'I visit relatives in this unfortunate city.'

'You're lying.'

'No, no, I do not lie – I visit . . .'

Jack pressed the muzzle hard against the man's skull.

'I am going to pull the trigger.'

Jack squeezed the cocking trigger of the Tranter. The click made Arihant jump.

'No – no – please, sahib – no. This is murder.'

'Yes, your stock in trade. Don't think I won't do this. I too am an assassin by trade. A reluctant one, but nevertheless I kill those who wish to do me and mine harm, without compunction. And one more

286

body on the Ridge will count for very little. Thousands have died here, in the last few months, in the last few days. Another body will be just left to rot. Was it a man called Hadrow who sent you to kill me? Answer me.'

At that moment the worst possible thing happened. Geraldine Stanton, light shawl about her shoulders, came out of a ruined building nearby. It almost seemed as if she had been waiting for him to come and seek her out, for there was no real reason for her to be there, except that it was the last place they had met before Jack had gone into battle.

'I thought I heard your voice, Lieutenant. Goodness gracious, what are you doing? Is that man a rebel?'

The shades of evening were falling. One of those magnificent sunsets which were made to be admired was spread across the sky. God had not spared the paints, for there was not just red up there but a wonderful array of deep rich colours. Jack, however, was not concerned with beauty at this time, be it of women or skies. It was his prisoner he was interested in. Information was what he required. And he would have it, or blow a man's brains out.

'Please leave, Miss Stanton,' Crossman ordered. 'You may not like witnessing what I am about to do.'

'I have done nothing,' cried Arihant. 'I am no rebel. I am loyal to the British. This officer is crazy. Call for help, memsahib, please.'

Ignoring the Indian's words she lifted her muslim shawl to her head, to cover it from the evening gnats.

'Lieutenant . . .?'

'Go away, Miss Stanton. *Now.*'

'Shoot him – I don't care,' she replied in a bitter voice. 'Shoot all of them.'

Jack drew a deep breath. 'Miss Stanton, for the last time. This is official army business. I'm not an ordinary officer. I'm a cold-blooded killer, saboteur and spy. I am reviled by most of my fellow officers. You would do well not to speak to me again. Now you will go away and leave me to my work. I have no further interest in you whatsoever. Go.'

Her face hardened under the fading light. Jack could not afford more than a glance at her. His attention had to be on the individual under the revolver. He heard her stumbling away though, into the darkness that swept in. She did not speak again. When her footsteps were no longer in his ears Jack growled at his prisoner, 'And you will speak, sir – or die now. Who is it you have come to kill. Is it me? Tell me quickly. A name only. If you say anything else, anything at all, I will squeeze the trigger. A name, sir. Just a name. Even a grunt or a sigh will have your brains on that wall.'

'Sergeant King!'

Crossman lowered the pistol. He was a little shocked he had to admit. What he had been expecting was his own name, or Lovelace, or Colonel Hawke, or Major William Hodson, but not King's. King was a tiny pawn in the sabotage and spying service. Almost just a cover for what they did, with his obsession with surveying and map-making. This surely could not be about army business?

'You work for money.'

'Yes.'

'Who hired you to kill Sergeant King?'

'A family.'

'For what reason?'

'He made their daughter pregnant a few years ago. Her brothers killed her. When Sergeant King arrived in the village, asking for her by name, they knew he was the lover returned. They paid me to assassinate him.'

'And the child? What happened to the child?'

'I do not know, sahib. That is the whole truth.'

Jack considered the answers, which were flowing now, and felt that Arihant had no reason to lie further.

'You must have had an opportunity to kill the sergeant before now – why have you waited?'

Arihant turned and faced him in the gloom. 'There is a right time and a wrong time, sahib. I am a religious man. I take note of favour-able dates, of the phases of the moon and the position of the stars. One cannot kill a man just like that. One needs good portents, good omens.'

'Or perhaps you thought you'd wait in case the sergeant got killed in battle? Then you could collect your fee without any danger to yourself?'

Jack knew he should shoot the man under his weapon but, as always when faced with a cold-blooded murder, he felt sick to his stomach. In the heat of battle, or even in a fracas, he could take out a man as well as the next soldier. But not like this. Not without some sort of provocation. Granted, this assassin was here to murder his sergeant, but having confessed his plans he surely would not go about putting them into operation. Better to hand this creature over to the authorities and let them deal with him.

'Listen to me, Arihant. Listen very carefully. I am going to hand you over to the British army. I have no doubt you're skilful in bribing your way out of captivity, or you would be rotting in some prison cell by now, so I add this – if I see your face again, I will kill you. I will shoot you without any more recourse to talk. There will be no time for explanations. I shan't care why you're there, next time I shall simply put my gun to your head and pull the trigger. So, if they let you go, or you escape, you'd better run. Run hard and fast. Go anywhere but make sure it's out of my sight or reach. Be assured, I *will* destroy you. Understood?'

Drops of cold sweat flew from the man's face as he nodded vigorously. Jack saw that he *had* been scared. Terrified, in fact. He was right to be. He had escaped instant death by the merest shadow of a man's finer feelings. A future trial would probably condemn Arihant to death anyway, but at least Crossman would not be pulling the lever on his life.

Even now Jack knew he was being foolish, but someone had forgotten not to rip out his conscience when they sent him on special duties and made him an assassin. He marched Arihant to the nearest guard post and told them to put the man under arrest. 'He threatened to kill a British NCO,' Jack said. 'I have to leave him in your hands, but I will provide a written statement for the trial.'

The court would not need much in the way of a statement. An officer's word would be enough. Arihant's fate was sealed, unless he did manage to get away. If that happened, surely the assassin would forget any contract with this distant family and get to a place of safety without delay. This was not the way the major would have done it, but he was not Nathan Lovelace, he was Jack Crossman, and he still had a soul somewhere within him.

Much later on, while Jack was reflecting on the whole business. he realized something important: surely Arihant had been following them *before* they went into the village where King's lover had lived? He strained his memory, but much had passed since then; illnesses had warped his sense of time. Was it possible the assassin had lied and was, after all, chasing Jack Crossman? This place, this India, was full of mysteries which might never be solved.

Later that night Gwilliams came to him.

'We've found Ishwar Raktambar. They have him under guard. He's to go to the gallows tomorrow morning.'

'Execution?' said Crossman. 'Tomorrow?'

'That's what the guard said. Early. Before breakfast. Saves having to feed 'em,' Gwilliams said. 'The sergeant's speaking with the duty officer now, but he don't seem inclined to listen.'

Jack knew that Major Lovelace and Colonel Hawke had already left for Agra, so he could not count on support from higher up. Hodson knew him, but Hodson was not around either and Jack had no idea where to find him. If Crossman were to save Raktambar he would have to do it alone.

'What's the duty officer's name?'

'Captain Deighnton.'

Crossman's spirits took a plunge. 'Oh, Lord – *him*.'

'You know him, sir?'

'Unfortunately.'

Jack dressed in his uniform and followed his corporal through the darkness to the prisoners' compound. There were about fifty men in the compound, but Jack soon recognized Raktambar, taller than the others. The man was in chains behind a guarded wire fence.

'Raktambar,' he said, touching the other man on the shoulder, 'how are you?'

The Rajput's expression was naturally gloomy.

'How is a man who is to hang tomorrow to answer such a question?'

'You will not hang. I'll get you released. Just as I did before, that day out on the Punjab trail. But first I want your word that you didn't fight with the rebels, or side with them in any way, or assist them in their cause. Do I have that?'

'Yes. That night in the river, I had to get to shore. I would have drowned. Once back in the city I found a place to sleep. In the morning I thought I would try to get out, to join you again, but my heart is not in this business, sahib. I did not wish to fight my own people . . .'

'I can understand that.'

'. . . so I decided to stay. But, since I am your man, I thought I would search for the boy instead. That way I would be helping you, but not going against my people. So I scoured the city, day after day, seeking the child Sajan. I found him with one of the sergeant's men

290

– the one that ran away. I killed the man, but the boy would not come with me. He remained with the rebel sepoys and badmashes.'

'So, you left him?'

'No, I found a place nearby, and kept my eyes on him. I think I can find him, now. It is difficult to explain.'

'Right. Gwilliams, take me to the duty officer.'

The corporal walked on ahead, into the night. Crossman followed. He glanced up to see the heavens were encrusted with stars. All this death and destruction, he thought, and still they shine with such purity. All this mayhem and justice gone bad. It didn't seem right to him at this moment. A man was about to go to the gallows and the angels still sang sweetly, the stars shone brightly – and in England mothers were kissing the cheeks of their children and telling them that all was well with the world.

Outside the duty officer's hut, Sergeant King was pacing up and down. He saw his lieutenant and he shrugged.

'He won't listen,' he said, as Jack marched past him.

The lieutenant entered the hut to find Captain Deighnton sitting on the corner of a makeshift desk, with what looked like a glass of port at his lips. There was a trooper in one corner of the room, talking quietly with a sergeant. Deighnton's eyes widened when he saw who was his visitor.

'You have a prisoner in your compound,' said Crossman. 'He's one of my men. I want him back.'

Deighnton swung a booted leg on the edge of the desk.

'Really? You want him back? A condemned man.'

'I don't know what sort of court convicted him, but they would never have done so had I been called on as a witness. The man Ishwar Raktambar is a British spy. He works under me. I work under Major Lovelace, who works under Colonel Hawke. We are, in the current circumstances, part of Major Hodson's intelligence network.'

The captain looked amused and took a sip of his port.

'Hodson? The spy? He of he Plungers? Hodson's Horse. The Guides. Oh, yes, and more recently, the self-proclaimed excutioner of regents. A regicide. I suppose you know the man's in disgrace at the moment. Killed the royal princes without a by-your-leave. He'll get his come-uppance now and not before time. A thief to boot, I've heard. Fiddled the Company's books. Never did like the man. Too full of himself by half.'

291

'Notwithstanding your personal opinion of Major Hodson, the fact is he runs an intelligence network of which I – and Ishwar Raktambar – are part. Raktambar was in Delhi on my instructions. He provided valuable information to us from time to time, which helped in the assault. I would be grateful if you would release him to my jurisdiction. You cannot continue to hold a man who was working under cover for the British. Should you refuse to let him go, and he does indeed hang, I shall personally take pleasure in seeing you go down at your subsequent court martial. Have no fear, I shall spend all my efforts in bringing about an enquiry.'

Deighnton laughed out loud now. 'You think they'll court martial me after this mess?' He waved an arm in the general direction of the shattered city of Delhi. 'Why, man, you could hide the blackest of deeds amongst all the failures and mistakes that have gone on around here. No one in India will want to dig in this pile of shit, once it's all over.'

A coldness came over Jack. He knew that the captain was right. Some awful blunders had been made. Some terrible injustices were taking place. One more would only be lost in a sackful of others. Such small injustices as this would also be tossed against the pile of atrocities committed by the enemy. The massacre of the British women and children at Cawnpore; the horrors of the well; the slaughter of the families in the boats at Lucknow. When future courts of enquiry weighed all the terrible things that had occurred, on both sides of the war, this hanging would be of such insignificance it would be dismissed as just a minor error.

Lieutenant Jack Crossman stared at the grinning captain before him and made a decision. He walked forward and slapped Deighnton hard around the face. The captain fell off the edge of his desk, his glass of port dropping to the floor. Enraged, within a moment he was upright again, his hand on the hilt of his sword. The eyes of the two shocked soldiers in the room were wide and gawking at the sight of two officers seemingly in a brawl.

Jack said, 'In the absence of a glove, I had to substitute my hand. You have the choice of weapons, Deighnton.'

'You're challenging me to a duel?' spluttered the captain.

'It looks like it, doesn't it? The other day you couldn't wait to get me on the end of a sword point. Now's your chance. What's changed?'

'And how do you hope to profit by this? Will you come back here and murder these two soldiers, then spring your precious Rajput?'

The sergeant in the corner stood up. He was a burly-looking man, with fists the size of turnips.

'I have no argument with these men. You, sir, should have no interest in what happens after we duel. If I am dead, then you need not fear for your prisoner. If you are dead, what will it matter to you?'

'We can't fight now? I'm on duty, man,' roared the captain. 'Send your seconds to me, tomorrow.'

'It'll be too late then. I have to leave at first light. It has to be now. Are you afraid?'

The captain's eyes narrowed. 'Of course I'm not afraid. Of a popinjay like *you*? But there's protocol. And if I left my post for such a reason I *would* be court martialled and well you know it. And,' the captain glanced behind him at the pair in the corner, 'duelling is illegal.'

'It's your only chance. Hadrow will hear of it, you can be sure of that. I'll send him a message personally to tell him what a coward he has for a friend in Captain Percival Deighnton.'

Clearly the captain was distressed. He knew he could not go quietly behind the hut and fight a duel. There were two men in the room whose silence he could not rely on. He was one of those officers who was not well liked by the rank and file. Jack had counted on this, believing quite rightly that any friend of Hadrow would be a martinet. One thing vulnerable tyrants cannot depend on in a time of crisis is the support of those they have oppressed. These two troopers would be as happy to send him down the river as they would be to drink to the health of their mothers.

'I see you're not quite willing to ruin your career for your friend,' Crossman said, twisting the knife in the wound. 'I don't blame you. Hadrow isn't worth it. Of course, if you let my man go, I will obviously say nothing to Hadrow and the very next time that we meet I will of course be very pleased to give you satisfaction.'

Deighnton stood for a very long time, staring at Crossman. Jack could see the red marks of his fingers still burning on the cheek of the captain. Finally, the other spoke.

'You will give me satisfaction? You have insulted me, personally, now.'

'I guarantee it. You have my word. You may kill me at your convenience.'

293

'I *shall* do it, Lieutenant.'

'Oh, I expect it, Captain.'

Deighnton went to a drawer in the desk and took out a sheet of paper, pen and ink. He sat down for a few minutes and wrote in silence. When finished he blew on the page and waved it in the air, before turning it round and offering Jack the pen.

'I'm releasing the prisoner to you. He's your responsibility now. You may have to answer for this action later.'

'I shall be happy to.' Jack read the paper through and signed it.

'Sergeant?' snapped Deighnton. 'Go with the lieutenant and release the prisoner into his custody.'

'Which prisoner would that be, sir?' asked the NCO.

'The one he damn well points out to you, man.'

'Yes, sir. Right away, sir.'

Jack followed the sergeant outside. King and Gwilliams were sitting with their backs against a benign camel who had folded its legs under itself for the night. They rose to greet their officer. Soon the chains had been removed from Ishwar Raktambar and he was walking free. To say that Ishwar was relieved was an understatement. Waiting to be hanged is an experience that leaves a man limp with horror. It would be a long time before the images in the Rajput's head were driven away. It would be quite a time before the rhythms of the living returned to him. For the moment he was still caught in the meshes of a nightmare.

'How are you feeling?' asked Crossman.

'An elephant has just got off my chest.'

'I must ask you to think of the boy now.'

When dawn arrived, Raktambar led Crossman, King and Gwilliams to a small village to the west of Delhi. There, they entered a hut and found Sajan sleeping in the midst of a ragged group of Hindus. The men in the hut rose wearily at the sight of a British officer and NCOs, suspecting they were to be taken into custody. Crossman ignored them. King took Sajan by the hand and led him out of the hut. Sajan did not complain, nor even say very much, except to ask where they were going. King told him, 'To Ibhanan.'

Equipped and ready for a new expedition to beyond Peshawar, Crossman's *peloton* rode first to the area where Ibhanan and the other surveyor's men were encamped. Ibhanan was to retain the men on

294

half pay until Sergeant King sent for them. They were to look after the boy, who had promised never to run away again.

King asked Sajan. 'Where is the sun compass you took?'

'A man stole it from me.'

'You didn't sell it?'

'I would never sell it, sahib. I was keeping it for when I become a grown man. I am to be a surveyor, am I not?'

'Yet you wanted to be a rebel, too?'

Sajan hung his head. 'I am sorry.'

He was, after all, only eight years old.

King took him by the shoulders. 'You *must* not run away again. You understand. I – I will be a father to you, if you stay.'

Sajan looked up, his eyes wide with wonderment.

'You will be my father?'

'Yes, if you wish it.'

'Oh, sahib,' the boy hugged his leg and King looked around him in embarrassment. 'I am your son.'

Crossman, Raktambar, King and Gwilliams left the crew and began their journey.

Gwilliams asked King, 'You still think you're the boy's pappy?'

'I don't know,' replied King, fiercely, 'and, Corporal, I don't really care.'

'Suit yourself, Sergeant.' Gwilliams spat neatly between the ears of his horse to hit a stone in front. 'I couldn't give a damn neither.'

A majestic elephant with a howdah then passed them by and they all halted their mounts to watch it, every man amongst them wondering whether the Reverend Stillwell was behind those silk curtains.

The road to Peshawar was long. They were still living in dangerous times and had to be constantly wary. With some minor trials – minor after what they had been through in the past few weeks – they reached their destination. Crossman reported to a Major Bentley as soon as they arrived and told the major they were on their way north. The major knew who he was and offered him and his men quarters while they were in the city. The four of them stayed in Peshawar for the next three days, assessing the situation, preparing for the ride towards the border.

It was a time for relaxing and catching up with letters. Jack reread his mail from his wife, feeling a little guilty that he had almost

295

strayed from the path, but at the same time pleased with himself that it had actually come to nothing. He was slightly aggrieved, however, that in replying to one question asked by Jane, he had to report that he had not yet seen a tiger.

They are hiding from me, he wrote, *like mischievous devils.*

Raktambar gradually came back into the land of the quick.

King lay on his cot and thought about many things: some of them to do with brass instruments and coloured inks on parchment; others concerning the solemn duties of fatherhood. Sometimes his dreams combined both, and he and Sajan were wandering Nepal or Chinese Tibet as mapmakers.

Gwilliams spent his time sharpening his knife and his sword, and cleaning his carbine.

On his second day in Peshawar Crossman saw Arihant in a coffee house. He shot him dead.